BLOODVINE

BLOODVINE

A NOVEL

Aris Janigian

HEYDAY BOOKS · BERKELEY, CALIFORNIA

Fic
Janigian

Great Valley Books is an imprint of Heyday Books, created with the help of the James Irvine Foundation to showcase art and literature from and about the Great Central Valley of California.

Selected quotations appearing on pages 136–139 are drawn directly from the written and oral testimonies and arguments from the April 13–16, 1984, special hearing of the Permanent Peoples' Tribunal to determine whether the Young Turk government was guilty of genocide of the Armenian people from 1915 to 1917. The tribunal's jury included three Nobel Prize winners and ten other eminent jurists, theologians, academics, and political figures from various Western and Third World countries. The verdict was "guilty." These quotations were collected in *A Crime of Silence: The Armenian Genocide; Permanent Peoples' Tribunal,* edited by Gerard Libaridian, preface by Pierre Vidal-Naquet (London: Zed Books Ltd., 1985).

Library of Congress Cataloging-in-Publication Data

Janigian, Aris.
  Bloodvine / Aris Janigian.
    p. cm.
  ISBN 1-890771-63-5 (alk. paper)
  1. Armenian Americans--Fiction. 2. Fresno (Calif.)--Fiction. 3. Viticulture--Fiction. 4. Farm life--Fiction. 5. Brothers--Fiction. I. Title.
  PS3610.A569 B56 2003
  813'.6--dc21

                                                    2002152861

Interior Design: Rebecca LeGates
Printing and Binding: Phoenix Color, Hagerstown, MD

Orders, inquiries, and correspondence should be addressed to:
        Heyday Books
        P.O. Box 9145, Berkeley, CA 94709
        (510) 549-3564, Fax (510) 549-1889
        www.heydaybooks.com

Printed in the United States of America

10 9 8 7 6 5 4 3 2 1

To my parents—who never stood in the way.

To Albert Friedman and John Sanford—who helped me find it.

ACKNOWLEDGMENTS

Number one, my wife, In Sun. She gave me what I needed most: a full year of peace and quiet and a salubrious place to return after my daily excursions into the emotionally complicated territory of this novel. In writing this story, I needed help to recover family voices and events that had been buried for decades. Here I am indebted to my aunts Stella, Anne, Audrey, and Sue, and my uncle Luther, for their frank and sometimes painful recollections of our family history. I am grateful also for the generous and expert advice of Dave Loquaci, Jim Curtis, and the late Stan Gagarian on the cultivation practices and the agricultural climate of the 1950s, when this story takes place.

Then there are the folks at Heyday. Obviously, nobody is in the publishing shtick for the sheer love of it, but the folks at Heyday come close. It's been a delight to work with Malcolm Margolin and his staff—especially Ani, Patricia, Karen, Jeannine, and Rebecca, who believed in a book that so many others cast aside as "old-fashioned."

But for all the help from the people above, this book would not have seen print if it weren't for Mark Arax, whose determination to tell the stories of the Great Central Valley gave me faith to tell my own, whose struggle for this book was indefatigable, and who in matters of writing was my editor, in matters of representation my agent, and in matters of the heart my counselor and friend.

To those innocent persons whom this story will directly touch, what is written here may come as a shock, or disagree with the facts as they have known them. In response to this, I can only say: I am a novelist, not an investigative reporter. My interest in writing the book was never to "find out what happened," or "be true to the facts," but rather to tell a story. With that said, it is my hope that this book will help bring down the wall of silence that has divided us and made us near strangers for the better part of our lives.

BLOODVINE

PROLOGUE

THE WEEK BEFORE MY FATHER DIED, he told me a story about how his father had once seen the lost city of Atlantis while he was a sailor in the Turkish navy. They were doing maneuvers, somewhere not far off the Mediterranean coast. His father, a man "made of iron" was how my father described him, had a custom: every day he would dive from the ship and swim around it twice, even when the waters were freezing. On one such dive his eyes opened upon the ruins of a city: chariots and marble columns and statues and pots of gold undulating in the dark waters. My father told me, "He was going to go back there someday. Obviously the poor man never made it. Supposedly he made a map, except who knows where it is now." My father was only fourteen when his old man died, taking that map with him.

That was one of a number of stories my father told me that week before he died in the summer of 1989. I had just finished a doctorate in research psychology and was looking forward to a spell of deliberately doing nothing when, mid-June, he rang me up.

"How's your vacation going?"

"Hardly. More like convalescence. How are things shaping up for the grape harvest?" It was getting on that time of year.

"Well," he said, "I'm not getting any younger. I sure could use your help this season."

Nothing new. He'd fished for my help every season since I'd left Fresno eight years earlier. My instant alibi, of course, was school.

"I know I've asked you before, but I want you down here. I ain't playing this time. I need you. Seriously, son."

Seriously? "Is something wrong, Dad?"

"Think you could manage that for your old man?"

3

"Sure, Dad. You feel okay? Hope nothing is wrong."
"Naw. You know me. They don't call me 'Andy the bull' for nothin'."

My dad wasn't what you'd call reticent, but he always spared me the details. So I was surprised to find, almost the minute I got back to Fresno, that he was all geared up to talk about his past from front to back, as though he'd hailed me home for just that purpose. As we drove into the country, or sat in a coffee shop, or marched down a dusty row, he told me about his mother and father, his polio, his carefree college days way back when. Even if there was a disturbing urgency with which he needed to get these stories off his chest, I was flattered he'd decided that, for a season at least, I was going to be his best friend.

There was one story, though, that he kept to himself as usual. It was *the* story of his life. I had a few facts in hand, but whenever I'd go for more he'd make the excuse "When you're a little older." I no longer wondered if I was old enough, plus I figured that after sitting through all those other stories—most of which I'd heard before—I'd earned the right to hear that one for the first time.

"Whatever happened between you and your brother Abraham?"
"You never met him, did you?"

I had, once. I must've been seven or eight years old. We were at an Armenian wedding at the old Del Webb high-rise in downtown Fresno. Somewhere amidst the hoopla of the reception my dad said, "C'mon Baba, let's me and you go take a piss."

We'd just unzipped when a man stepped up to the stall to my right. There was a flash of recognition in my dad's face—abruptly he turned his head away. Standing there between the two men, pissing, I thought, either the man had wronged him or he'd wronged the man. Maybe my dad owed him money?

"How ya been, Andy?" the stranger said.
"Good," my dad said to the wall. "You?"
"Good."

"'I pissed up here. How far can you piss?'" By the way my dad was bending back to look, I guessed he was reading aloud what had been scribbled on the tile above his head; as adult behavior goes, kind of uncouth. My dad flushed, and I followed suit. We skipped washing our hands and made for the door.

"Who was that man, Dad?" I couldn't wait to know.

"That man? That man," he informed me, "is your uncle. My jackass brother."

His what? I had no idea he even had a brother, much less that the one he had was a jackass.

I recounted this episode and told him how confusing it was for me back then. How, in a way, it still was.

"Yeah," he said, "that don't count as a good introduction. But I figure you're right. You should know. You're plenty old enough. I'm going to tell the whole shebang. You ready for this?"

"Sure."

But was *he?*

It didn't come easy for my old man. I assumed for all the time he'd had to prepare the case, once he started he'd smoothly spread out the facts, front to back. Far from it. The way old people do, his mind would tack in one direction, then stop, then tack in an entirely other. He'd recall one damning incident and follow up with one that contradicted it. In one breath, his brother was a saint, and in another, a monster. Sad. Yes, it made me sad to see that after thirty years, nothing had been tidied up, that the events lay inside of him in pieces, a broken city still. I couldn't decide if he was trying to be fair to his brother—the man who damned him—or what. Now and again, I'd lob a hypothesis of my own his way. "I can see that," he'd say. "I'll give you that much. But it ain't the whole story." He was right. Something was missing, but what exactly? The answer would have to wait.

He wanted to get things rolling early, cash in on an early crop. Eighteen brix was the minimum sugar content for table grapes. "We'll pick at seventeen and a half. If the inspector catches us, a few lugs on the house will buy us half a point." With a refractometer, I'd measure sugar three, four times a day and give him the results: "Sixteen and a half. *Randomly* collected," I added (the proper sampling procedure). He'd limp down a row and toss a few berries in his mouth, chew and spit the mess out. "Sounds about right. I figure, though, the southeast corner is a point ahead. Soil's got energy there. Keep an eye on it. If need be we'll spot pick." After a few days of checking the sugar, I decided that my dad had already decided the wheres and whens. August 1, the day he predicted we'd start, we started, right on that southeast corner.

For me, the first day of the harvest was akin to going to the circus as a kid, except here I was supposedly part of the act. But to do what? "Just keep an eye on things," he told me. Easy enough. At dawn, a noisy organization of pickers and boxes and forklifts and tractors and trucks and packing stations assembled in the dirt yard at the top of the vineyard. Just as the sun peaked over the Sierras, the foreman whistled, and before it was anyone's business, grapes started flying off the vines. From my naïve viewpoint, the whole operation seemed to be virtually moving on its own, no sweat. The first haul of Thompsons came out of the field a little past eight. My dad examined the bunch stems and erupted, "Sons of bitches! What I figured." I ran to see what was going on. "They're milkin' the vines. Look at this!" Huh? He was in no mood to explain. He headed up a row hollering for the foreman, "PEDRO! Clippers, clippers, I don't want to see nothin' but clippers movin' out there."

Over the next hours and days, my halcyon image of the harvest faded into oblivion. The problems, they never let up, and each seemed capable of bringing the whole operation to a standstill. I can still hear my dad: *Por favor, I beg you: not twenty, not twenty-three, but twenty-six pounds to a box.* The boxes themselves were nailed together from warped wood: *Look at this twisted mess they sent me, will you?* Grapes, thrown to the bottom of the lugs, shattered from the stem: *They break my heart, these people, they really do.* The tractor stalled in the field: *Another clutch bites the dust.* Twice a day the broker whistled a different tune: *Tell me honestly now, Marty: how can a damn lug of grapes fall three dollars in one day?* Over the next week, five to five, all we did was put out fires.

We were standing beneath an old pomegranate tree, eating lunch. Even in the shade, the heat, over one hundred degrees, was clobbering. He inhaled deeply his big enterprise and said, "What do you think? I bet your dad could lecture those professors of yours on a thing or two." I didn't say it, but I felt then what I'd always felt: that it was a dead-end life, my dad's. There were no revolutions in farming; nothing but cycles, overseeing the same old problems, the same old earth, year after year. It had to be done by someone, but not by me. At least to that point, the harvest offered me little more than the occasion to be in his sweet company. I remembered how the first day out there he'd shoved a shovel into the earth and, turning it over, said, "Pretty, huh?" I liked

his fair hand with workers, how he aimed for the middle when negotiating, and his artful touch with authority. "I'll be frank with you,
Stan," he told the inspector. "I pushed the grapes half a point. You're
just doin' your job. I wouldn't blame you for red-tagging me." The
inspector was charitable that afternoon. He gave us a warning and left
the field with a lug of grapes over his shoulder.

I couldn't wait for it all to end so that we could pick up our conversation where we left off.

But we never had the chance. On Saturday, August 6, a freakish
rainstorm coursed through the valley late in the afternoon. After dining with friends that evening, my dad and I agreed to meet out on the
farm come sunrise to survey the damage. It was a thirty-minute drive
down Highway 99 out to the farm. The sky was inky with clouds.
Drops of rain pocked the dusty windshield, and outside the air was
complicated, edgy. The sun starting over the dark mountains made the
underside of the clouds blush. When I got out to the farm, it was a little past six thirty in the morning. My dad's car wasn't there. Maybe he
was rolling down a row in his old Cadillac. This, I kid you not, was his
very unorthodox method for inspecting blocks of grape. The sulphur-
dusted leaves were watermarked, the avenues of the vineyard speckled
with rain. The land, parched for over five months, quietly steamed and
exuded an ancient, ashy breath. My dad had never stood me up before.
I wondered if he'd slept through the alarm—because he had the luxury
to, because he knew I was there to fill in for him. I dragged some tarps
over the packing boxes and waited. Come eight o'clock, I left.

When I got back to my apartment, I took a quick shower. I'd just
finished up when the phone rang. It was my aunt. "Something has
happened to your dad," she told me. "Come home now, sweetheart."

As I approached my parents' house, I could see people milling
around on the front porch, relatives and friends. Seeing tears in their
eyes, I instantly knew why. He'd died, early that morning. A massive
heart attack. On my birthday, August 9, we buried him.

Back on the farm, folks who knew my dad for years, decades, came
to pay their respects and recollect stories about him. I listened with
interest, but the only story that really mattered to me at the time was
the story of him and his brother. He had left so much unsaid, and so
much, it seems, depends on the telling.

1

SPRING 1959—FOR MILES NOW, the long shadows of the vineposts leaned on the berm, and the shadows of the tall palm trees that lined the country road strobed over the bishop's eyelids. The cool air splashed gently on his face and in his ears, so that the bishop had all but fallen asleep when the priest announced, "We are near." He opened his eyes, his heart pooled with feeling, and in Armenian said, "These vineyards, they remind me of the homeland when I was a child."

"Ahhhh." The priest lifted his chin.

"But in the old country," the bishop said, "I don't remember the vines growing this way, that is, strung up like criminals on wires. No, we had bush vines and they grew everywhere wild. There was a bitter-skin grape, obsidian black. I recall ruby-color grapes that took the shape of teardrops." He clutched his index finger and said, "Yellow grapes this long, and in the summer the smell of them all baking in the sun." In Armenian he sang, "That light, that light! The Russians would come out of their dank and melancholy land, hundreds of miles they would travel just to be kissed by that light."

The bishop breathed the manured air, like a man breathes a lover's perfume, and watched crows, one by one, rise from out of a peach orchard and pepper the sky.

"Of course," the bishop said, "the vines in Armenia date back from the time of Our Lord. Just imagine, brother, the pestilence, the flood and fire, the drought and terrible earthquake they've endured. They," he said in a survivor's emotional voice, "have proven as resilient as the Armenian people themselves."

They veered up a long bumpy road parallel to a canal.

"How did it come to pass that there are so many Armenians in *this* land, Fresno?" the priest asked.

"There is a history, of course. But the answer to your question is not in a book; it is out there. Look." He traced the Sierras with a finger. "Their Mount Ararat, this. And these canals," he swept his hand over the dry one they drove across, "their Mother River, Arax. What no book will tell you is these poor, desperate people have tried to resurrect the homeland here, brother, to make natural what is alien. But what cheap copies! Our Ararat could swallow in one gulp all the mountains in America combined."

The priest nodded and slowed the car down.

"No," the bishop spoke. "Caught between two lands, what do we have? Nothing, really. We are left to beg on a bridge is all." The car stopped. "But are we here?" The bishop was sad the drive was over.

The priest checked the mailbox number against the one he had jotted down on a scrap of paper.

"Yes."

He pulled the car into the dirt yard and came to a stop in front of a dog. The bishop—a celibate city dweller—wondered aloud if this was the kind of dog likely to bite. The priest stepped out and with a hand shooed the dog away.

From the living room window, an old lady named Angel watched dust flare up at the top of the yard and then a big green car push through a tawny cloud. "Zabel," she cried out to her daughter. "They've come!" Her head wobbled as though it had come unplumbed.

"Akhh!" Zabel, who'd been cleaning from before sunrise in anticipation of the visitation, straightened her hair and rushed to the kitchen to get the coffee going.

Angel held the window frame, the way a person does when straightening a mirror, and focused on the men. The priest, tall and stooped over, reminded her of a crane, and the bishop, who bore a cane, was stout and short, like a pigeon. She watched them walk halfway to the porch, then stop to talk. About what? Maybe they already sensed between them the Evil One's presence?

Far from it; they had paused because the bishop had altogether forgotten the purpose of their call and needed his memory refreshed. The priest reminded him that a week ago they had received a petition from one Zabel Voskijian, the woman who owned this land, to exorcise her farm of spirits. Mrs. Voskijian had conveyed to the priest in detail the tragedies that befell her husband, Abraham Voskijian, in all his endeavors on that dirt. Tragedies, the woman surmised, inexplicable except that they were yoked to the Devil.

"Hmmm." The bishop nodded his head dubiously.

She spoke of how, as God-fearing people, they desired only to purify their life more fully, so that their harvest would be an offering not only to their family but also to Our Lord. With a kind of apology in his voice, the priest reminded the bishop that while en route to Los Angeles, he had agreed to stop along the way in Fresno to consult with the family about this matter.

"Be that as it may," the bishop said. "It is understood. Let us go, then."

The priest led the way to the house.

Zabel opened the door. "Welcome. I am Mrs. Voskijian." She genuflected clumsily.

The priest introduced himself and the Very Reverend Krikor Chakmachian III.

"And this is my mother, Mrs. Tutulian." With a doddering hand the old woman made the sign of the cross.

The bishop nodded and stepped inside, leading with his cane.

Zabel said, "Please sit and let me serve you some coffee."

The bishop took a seat on the couch and reached for some walnuts on the table in front of him. In his palm he admired the walnuts' butterfly shape. "What things God has given birth to." He tossed them into his mouth and dusted his hands. Then, he reached into the pocket of his frock and pulled out a red pack of cigarettes. The priest asked Angel for an ashtray, please. The old woman brought it shaking like a tambourine, and dropped it in front of the bishop.

The priest struck a match and spotted the flame beneath his superior's cigarette. Angel was impressed by the way he held the cigarette, not scissored between his fingers like a peasant or farmer, but pinched just so between his middle finger and thumb. The bishop sucked deeply and let the smoke dribble deliciously out of his mouth. This man, Angel thought, has abundant spiritual resources at his disposal.

Zabel came out with the Turkish coffee on a service platter.

"My husband is out on an errand." She handed them each a demitasse.

The bishop slurped the coffee up noisily, put the demitasse and saucer neatly back on the coffee table, and dropped his eyes to his lap, upon which his cane lay lengthwise. He stretched his fingers, regarded them, as might a woman her newly buffed nails, and said, with a kind of sigh in his voice, "Now, Mrs. Voskijian, we have made a special trip to your home. We understand you have some spiritual concerns."

"As I mentioned to the Father, we have reason to believe that this land is cursed."

"Hmmm." Through the window, the bishop examined the vineyards in question.

"We are petitioning you to exorcise it. That is, cast out the demons that have spoiled year after year the fruits of our labors."

The bishop clicked his tongue, then raised a finger and moved it after the motion of a metronome. "This is not possible," he said.

Mother and daughter exchanged looks.

"Exorcism is a very serious term that applies only to humans. There are some among our people who still hold notions—no doubt left over from our pagan past—of spirits dwelling in such things as rocks and trees. But the church is explicit here: no objects other than humans have spirits, and hence cannot be exorcised. We must be clear about that."

The old woman's teeth spontaneously clenched. Imposters!

"A *curse* on the land is a different matter. This is something the church does recognize."

"Thank God." Zabel crossed her heart.

"And for which it has made provisions. You have heard of Our Gregory of Narek, no?"

"Certainly," the women chimed.

"In his *Book of Lamentation*, he has given us a ritual—it is called the ritual of the Evil Eye—for which this purpose suffices."

"This is it!" Angel said.

"Madame Tutulian, if you will bear with us."

"In principle," the bishop proceeded, "we are here to comfort you in your distress. However, in this day and age, very few people call on the church for such matters."

"I am surprised by this too, Bishop," Zabel averred. "Perhaps our people have lost a degree of faith in the church, I don't know. These are very corrupt times. My mother herself inquired from one of our deacons if our own priest would perform this ritual, and the deacon told her it was unlikely."

"You speak of our beloved friend and brother Reverend Jambajian," the bishop said.

"I have no quarrel with our priest. He is a fine shepherd of our congregation. We are members in good standing, I assure you."

"Of course."

"My husband and I recognize that you, Very Reverend Father, have traveled a great distance to aid us, and we would humbly offer a very generous contribution to your diocese."

With a finger, the bishop bid the priest to draw closer. He whispered something in his ear.

"We are here to serve you," the bishop said. "Let us proceed. Will your husband be back soon?"

"Is it necessary that he be here?"

"No."

"Then he has asked that you start without him."

"Very well then."

Abe, who'd driven into town that morning to get some groceries, saw this gathering on his property when he turned the corner, heading up the road home. As he got closer he made out Zabel and his mother-in-law and two men dressed as priests. They *were* priests. He recognized neither of them. "Huh." Abe pulled over and parked. The tall priest clutched a vial. The other priest was working a cross this way and that and reading aloud from a book held close to his chest. "What the…?" He tiptoed over.

"He is cleansing the land of evil spirits," his wife whispered.

Evil spirits? Abe bowed his head and crossed his arms over his stomach.

"Shhh," she said, as though Abe's puzzlement was audible.

The bishop reached for the vial. He traced the sign of the cross in the air and poured holy water on the ground.

2

WINTER 1956—THE DAYS HAD GROWN LEAN and as the sun came over the Sierras, the earth below glowed in its rosy light. Abe Voskijian sat on his porch with a cup of coffee, looking numbly over his vineyard. The vines lined up behind the endposts like so many crucifixes, and the rows were carpets of brown brittle leaves. The valley floor was sedate, the harvest behind it faded, but still there were marks on the land, and marks on the men who worked the land. For two months—August and September—legions of tractors, bins, trailers and boots pounded the earth. In the breathtaking heat, ochre silt roiled and rose and hovered in the air like a specter.

Abe rested the cup on the arm of the chair and loosened a clinker of snot from his nose. No sooner had he flicked it over the railing than his thoughts drifted back to a dream he'd had the night before about a fellow soldier, Les Sardo, L.S. In this dream, Abe sat next to Sardo on a bench, each man cleaning his rifle. Done, Abe admired the sure feel of it in his hands, the way its lean body lay cradled in his arms. Sardo, though, kept cleaning, running a towel down the rifle shaft over and over again, as though it were an heirloom. When Sardo (who in real life perished on the second front) was finished, he turned the rifle around, stared down the long barren barrel, and said with a chuckle, "I'm just like my old man." That's when Abe woke, wondering about his own father, who died when Abe was just nine years old. He wondered if he bore a likeness to him.

Abe's wife, Zabel, whom he sometimes called "Babydoll" or "Mama" or just "Ma," was annoyed that he was out there "having a good time" while she was in the house taking care of, all on her own, two kids who'd risen from bed with colds.

"ABRAHAM!"

But he was so worked up by these feelings about his dead dad he hardly heard her.

"ABRAHAM!" She sounded like a woman whose options had run out, not just begun. Her frustration was automatically everyone else's. Teddy, at eight the eldest kid, sat cross-legged on the carpet with his hands over his ears while viewing Saturday morning TV.

"ABRAHAM!!"

All of them endured her hysteria as if it were her birthright.

A hundred and sixty miles or so west, well out of earshot of the hollering, Abraham's half-brother Andy watched sprinklers beat over a field from the bleachers of a football stadium. He checked the time, buttoned his jacket, and balled his fists into his pockets against the chilly ocean air. The season was over, and so was his life in football, he'd decided, even though he'd been happy coaching, happier during that time than he'd ever been in his life. He climbed down the bleachers and took in the field, the empty luxuriousness of that trimmed green expanse, already nostalgic for the game, for those sixty minutes when one is no longer part of the order of machines but the physical participant of an animal past. Now, he was headed back to the farm, home. After seven years on the field—four as a player and three as a coach—he'd be permanently exiled to the stands.

Driving away from campus, he couldn't help feeling that his college days had been a long detour that brought him straight back to where he had started, as though there was only one course available all along. He could feel the land tugging at him. Was he returning because he felt obligated, and if so, to whom? His brother Abe? Himself? Or maybe he was running *to* home, away from school, from Cassandra, away from "the situation."

Rocky was his best friend. Cassandra was Rocky's girl, or rather, had been. When they got news of Rocky's death, he consoled her the whole night. Rocky had committed suicide in some pup tent, in the middle of the night. Not a Korean in sight. A bullet, from the barrel of his own gun, straight through the head. Suicide. They turned the cruel word around in their mouths. Rocky had been like his brother, more so than his real brother. Neither of them could believe it, both of them felt betrayed. How could he? Cassandra's tears rolled warmly down Andy's neck. They were grieved, confused and ashamed. They met regularly and exchanged letters Rocky had written. Suicide. She heaved and shuddered against his body. Her body was fragile, and in her anguish, vaguely erotic. In a way Rocky had betrayed them both.

And Andy had betrayed Rocky in return. What else would you call it? In the back seat of Andy's car, no less. "I love you," he told her. Perhaps from their brokenness they were trying to make something whole. Whatever it was, Andy continued to be amazed at how short-lived was their passion. After that first night, they had turned from each other in shame, disgust. Either way, the damage was already done. "The turkey," as his friend Tommy Kay put it, "was already cookin' in the oven."

She got the abortion at some doctor's office in L.A. He could still see the old foxed maps that hung on the waiting room walls, the primitive blotches made by rain on the ceiling. A few dated magazines lay on an end table next to a dusty bowl of hard candy, an ashtray into which he crushed one cigarette after another, listening to cars swish by outside. How the pain had thickened time. And when Cassandra walked out, dazed, her dress unzipped an inch at her hip, he knew right then he would never forget the blankness of her face, a kind of shock. "Here," he said, gave her his arm and opened the door. Andy remembered them stepping into rain that came down in curtains, and how the big city's sounds rushed past them, and how his life seemed to have stopped moving by comparison.

Surfacing from the wave of memories, he realized he'd reached Kettleman City, the halfway mark on his drive back home, where he usually stopped for fuel. Andy pulled off the road and rolled his '50 Chevy up to the gas station, a shack with a single pump up front. Save for a few autistic oil rigs, all around him there was dirt, nothing but. Andy always marked this spot as the beginning of the great San Joaquin Valley, in all of its raw, brutal possibility. He stepped out of the car into swirling dust.

The gasman opened the door of the shack, secured his hat and moved Andy's way.

"Can I help ya?"

"Couple of bucks' worth, thanks."

"Check yer oil?"

"Thank you, no."

The man sunk the nozzle into the tank and regarded Andy's letter-man's jacket that was hung up in the back.

"Play fer Cal Poly, huh?"

Andy had pumped gas there a hundred times before, but still the attendant didn't recognize him.

"Coached." Andy wondered if such vast vacant spaces toy with men's memories.

"Yeah," the guy said. "Damn near beat Fresno State. Always root for yuh. Mainly, I like what ya call yer underdog."

That fit Andy's profile of a recluse.

"Underdog's right. Can you believe this was all a lake once?" Andy asked, letting the emptiness out there fill his eyes.

"Yep. Yer lookin' at the bottom of a lake is what ya is."

"What makes the soil so rich."

"That right."

"Hard to fathom. Get to feel 'bout this small." From between two fingers Andy squeezed out all but a seed of space. "When you consider your own life against this earth's."

The gasman grunted. They both watched the numbers fly by.

"Lookie there." He pointed his chin at the hull of a charred car across the road. "Last year someone's come out here and set the thing on fire. Like a bale of hay. People's sense of decency loses them out heres."

"Sense of decency loses folks in other places, too," Andy said.

"The ways I see it, people reckon just 'cause there ain't no eyes around that they can stop lookin' at themselves. But there's the eyes of God."

"Two buck'll be 'nough," Andy said.

The attendant withdrew the nozzle, slung the hose around and hung it up. Andy pulled a dollar and change out of his pocket, counted two dollars out, handed it to the man.

Andy wondered what kind of religion a man without a church to attend might be part of.

It was a little over an hour more to Fresno on Highway 41. The first crops he hit were alfalfa and cotton. But as he drove deeper into the heart of the state, crossed into Kings County, then Fresno County, winter-stripped vineyards and fruit trees (apricots, peaches, nectarines, and plums) began to appear, and walnut orchards came into view, with their generous dark rows speckled green with grasslings, still wet from rain.

His destination was Biola, the town where he was born and raised, a small farming community fifteen minutes east by country roads from the center of Fresno.

He had gone to Central High School, where he was captain of the football team and homecoming king. He was phenomenally strong for a man who stood a mere five foot six inches tall. He'd had polio when he was a kid, and from years of working crutches he'd developed a broad, granite-hard torso. The left leg, the good one, was sturdy, pumped up like a Clydesdale's from its singular charge of carrying nearly the entire weight of his upper body. Though the bad leg was two inches shorter than the good one, he'd somehow managed to attenuate his limp to the point that he sometimes fooled you into believing he didn't have one. He had fine white teeth and a cherubic face. His almond-hued eyes were alert and they fixed on things so as to embrace them more completely, only rarely to calculate them out to his advantage. Children and animals were naturally drawn to him. Sometimes, though, you'd get the sense that he was toying with you and that behind his generous smile sat a locker-room trickster. He'd give you the shirt off his own back, even if it wasn't his. He didn't like saying "no" or even "enough."

Especially when it came to drinking. In college he once downed twenty-three beers in a contest that ran all night. The rumor goes he shot two rounds of pool and won one before he blacked out. As is the case with many men, he became an exaggeration of himself when drunk, to the good fortune of the guy sitting next to him. He was like an off-duty Santa Claus from the way he bought rounds of drinks and doled out cash like there was no bottom to his pockets. He would promise to solve everyone's problems within a matter of days. Only rarely, when it dawned on him that his kindness was being taken advantage of, would he turn violent.

Teddy, his nephew, had waited for Uncle Andy all day. Every three minutes he'd jump up and scream, "He's here!"

"Enough, Teddy," Zabel said.

"Uncle Andy's comin' for goods this time, though, huh?"

Teddy relished the idea that his uncle, "the big coach," was going to be his roommate for good. He was so proud he started running around the furniture with a football tucked under his arm.

"Quit it, *vie, vie,* quit it." It was driving Zabel crazy.

"*Vie, vie,*" Teddy chanted. "*Viiiiiiiiiiiiiiiiiie.*"

"Akhh."

"He's here!" Teddy bolted out the door.

Zabel saw Andy's Chevy roll into the yard. Teddy danced in front of the car, daring his uncle to run him over.

"TEDDYY!" She grabbed Nancy by the arm and rushed out the door to save her eldest son.

By the time Zabel got out there, Teddy was on all fours on the hood, staring Uncle Andy down through the window the way a tiger does through bars at the zoo.

"Relax, Zab," Andy said, stepping out of the car.

Zabel thought, Who is he to tell me to relax? but said amiably, "Relax?"

"Hop on, Teddy."

Andy offered his back for a saddle. Teddy jumped on and rode him for a spell like a rodeo star. "Yeehah, Yeeeeeehah."

"You don't know what evil he got into this week," Zabel complained.

"Awright, kid." Andy reached back and broke the lock Teddy's arms had around his neck.

Teddy dismounted and kind of growled. Andy put a finger up. Teddy went to break it.

"'Member, Teddy, fingers are fer pickin' your nose."

Teddy bubbled up with laughter.

"He's driving my head crazy, Andy."

3

AFTER ANDY SHOWERED AND CHANGED, he went outside on the porch with a beer. Supper, a pot of stuffed eggplants, bell peppers and squash simmering in stewed tomatoes, was on the stove. The sun was backing out from the vineyards, leaving behind smears of rusty light in the rows on the side of the barn. Holding a glass of whiskey, Abe stepped outside, stood.

"Take some weight off," Andy told Abe.

"Huh?"

"Relax."

Abe pulled up a chair and sat on the edge as if he might soon have to leave.

"What you so agitated for?"

"Things around here got to get fixed, that's all."

"What's the particulars need fixin'? What's your hands all shakin' for? What the hell's a matter?"

"I don't know."

Andy had been back as often as he could for the last seven stinkin' years. Whatever needed fixing had been fixed by Andy. But what use was making the obvious obvious?

Abe said, "You'll see someday. That's all, that's all I can say."

"I've seen plenty already. Don't worry about it. Hey, Abe, something's been buggin' me. I just checked on my old stuff from the garage. Someone's just chucked it into a bunch of boxes."

"Somethin' missing?"

"Just sloppy-like, like it was goin' to the trash eventually."

"Hey!" Abe threw up his hands. "That's Babydoll's territory. Anyway, you was gone so long it was occurin' to some you was never comin' back."

"What are you talkin' about? Who's this?"

"Look," Abe said. "Someday you'll have a wife and kids and pressure of your own, then you'll get the picture."

"Whoa." Where did that come from? Pressure?

Abe stood up.

Andy said, "You mean moneywise. Where you goin'?"

"Moneywise and otherwise. Sometimes I think I'm going to crack, I swear."

"Don't worry about it, Abe."

Abe sat back down.

"It's like I'm getting buried." Abe ran his hands over his face as though it were covered with goo.

"I don't see a soul goin' hungry 'round here. You?"

"Even that goddamn mother-in-law's on my ass."

"What's she babblin' about now? She still got them worms crawlin' around in her?"

"Days, I swear, wished I was back in the army. Facin' death isn't all that bad as people might figure. At least your job is but one: killin'. Everything else, it's done for you. No, there's a lot worse other things than war."

Andy thought, War in your own home?

"Why don't you take a break? Drive the kids and Zabel up to the mountains for a few days. I'll hold down the fort."

"You'll be getting hooked up soon," Abe told him. "We don't have the spread to support two families. Fifty acres ain't enough, that all."

"We've been through this before. We build together, Abe. We branch out. There's our future. We've talked about this before, haven't we? Haven't we talked about it?"

"All I'm saying is we have to be up front about this situation here. We have to start seeing things for the way they are, not the ways we wished they was."

"I didn't see no complaints when I was living away from here. Everybody seemed pretty happy about me plowing my share of the field then. Now that I'm back, I hear it. Little weird to me."

"I'm just saying."

Andy said, "Let's start looking for another piece of dirt, then."

"You got someplace already in mind?"

"Let's take a look at this desert deal. We'll see what Benjamin's got to say about it."

"Just so that you know our situation here, now that you're home for good and all."

The light had all but drained from the yard, and the air was getting fuzzy with tule fog.

Andy said, "Let's see what we're looking at and take the next step. Main thing, brother, we don't mess with what we have. This here is our base. I got some plans, brother."

"You better hell have. We didn't send you off to school for four years to learn how to make donuts."

In Andy's estimation, nobody had put him through school but himself. There was good reason he'd waited until he was nearly twenty-two years old before he went to college. For three years after high school, he'd labored like a jackass and blinkered himself from any pleasure, saving every red cent. He had picked up odd jobs in the off-season, stayed home on the weekends, wore the same pair of overalls. And while in school, there had never been a semester when he didn't have a part-time job. He did all of this so he wouldn't burden the family. Over the years, Abe and Zabel had made similar comments, and he'd let it pass with a shrug. Now he questioned the wisdom of having done so; left unchecked for eight years, their fantasies had fossilized into facts.

"We?" Andy asked.

"Hell yes, 'we'," Abe came back. "If we didn't send you to school, who did—your fairy fucking godmother?"

4

"YOU SEE WHAT THEY HAVE DONE TO ME?" Angel asked the empty room.

Her whole body shook abstractly, as though what should have been firing in one direction inside of her was firing in a thousand directions at once.

She struck a match and tried to steady it over her pipe.

"Akhh," she cried, and puffed furiously until smoke scrolled up from the bowl. With a sigh of relief, "It is no way to live," she said. *"Mer Christos!"*

She had taken up the pipe when she saw how the neighbor sedated his bees with smoke. If smoke worked on bees, so might it work to sedate the eels that kept slinking up her throat. For fear of quickening them she resorted to sipping water from milk bottles, or letting ice cubes melt innocuously in her mouth. Cold colors also retarded the eels, so for nearly a month she wore the same blue dress, pocked with food that she ground into mush and slowly fed herself. All orifices were possible entryways of evil. Just the other day she saw one turn mockingly at the bottom of the toilet bowl, eliciting great agony in her over her own depth, so that she was this close to suturing each opening shut with a sewing needle and thread. Oh how she yearned to flatten her body, turn into a pure and sanctified surface with no inside, nowhere to hide. To look at her wretched thinness, the way her skin hung on her bones like rags, you'd think she was well on her way there. But there were two depths—her body and her mind—and the second proliferated like locoweed in an abandoned field.

Zabel and Abe had just pulled onto the long drive heading up to Angel's house. They motored parallel to the vines, if they could even be called vines anymore. Already skeletonizers were sucking the life out of three-acre plot that surrounded the house. Patches of leaves were blanched and brittle as crepe paper.

"I'm sorry Babydoll, but this here is a shame," Abe said.

"How many times do you have to say it? That's the way she wants it. Enough then!"

They drove on.

The dust surged out from under the car and marbled the air. From where Angel sat, it appeared that a malevolent spirit (perhaps the same one corrupting her vines?) was kicking up some dust.

"Who is it?" she asked. The pipe bowl bobbed in her hand as though she were estimating its weight.

The car materialized from out of the atoms of dust, rolled up to the shrubs and stopped. Everything seemed full of mischief, winking at her.

Zabel stepped out of the car.

"*Oor es?*"

Why the hell is she asking where we are? Abe thought. We're right here. Jesus. She's gonna drive me crazy.

"*Oor es, oor es?*" the old woman repeated.

The woman's gonna make me lose my mind.

Zabel touched her. "Here, Mama, I'm here. Let me look." She took her mother's hand, stroked it. Abe stepped inside to make some Turkish coffee.

"This life, it is black. Everywhere," the old lady said, "is in the Satan's grip."

"Where?"

"Where? What do you mean, where? Here!" She clamped a fist against her stomach. "Here," she said. "In places where the eye cannot reach."

Zabel saw her mother as an omen, an appointment not yet met, a center not yet reached.

"About that boy, the lame one, I've had these dreams."

"I am so upset about him being back, Mama."

"What? Does he think these things—chopping limbs, pouring water—happen all by themselves?" Her voice was accusatory, punitive. She reminded her daughter, "All you have is that farm."

"Things will change, Mama."

Abe swung the wooden frame door open. He was holding a service tray with three demitasses steaming with Turkish coffee, mud colored and mud thick. "Let's drink a coffee." He put the tray on the cement pedestal and served them, then himself. He sat in a metal-back chair, took out a cigarette, tapped it on his thigh and studied the sky. A wind was coming in from the west, carrying with it clouds that looked like tattered rags. He slurped the coffee up. In these two women's company he felt thin, reedy, as though if they dared blow on him he'd whistle. But by the same token, with these two he felt queerly protected. The way they ground down between them even the most refractory surface to the slickest possible stone, virtually looking-glass smooth, required a talent, a genius, he had to admit.

The old woman threw her head back and yelped, "Akhh!" A deep gurgle, a dog's snarl, sounded from her stomach.

"Does it hurt?" her daughter asked. "It's gas."

"What gas?! Does gas come this way out of your ear?" And with a finger she showed how the eel sinuously moved.

Abraham turned his cup upside down on the saucer. The gritty viscous residue began to cut an occult figure in the hollow.

"Look," the old woman noted. "Look how he smells."

It hit him, a sour, air-curdling stench. He held his breath and waited for it to pass.

"Would you read the cup?" he asked Angel.

"Give it."

She held the cup as though she were warming her hands. Abe and Zabel leaned forward in their chairs.

"What is it?" her daughter asked.

The old woman let her eyes drop ever deeper into the cup. "I don't know. Wait," she urged them.

From a distance one might have mistaken the cup for something over which she was huddled in pity, a crippled bird.

"Look."

She marked a spot with her eyes.

"Through a mountain, water runs. The water tears the mountain in two. Both sides of the mountain are dry, the water does not feed the land, no fruit, nothing green." She turned the cup a little more in her hands. "The water is running to something else. To the bottom. Something waits there to drink. It takes the shape of a man, but on all fours it walks. A tail follows behind, and his ears are the ears of a beast. Ah, here we understand a little more."

With a finger she held shut her lips, to keep from speaking before she was certain.

"It is very old." She traced a long line with her hand through space. "Older than even the earth. There is nothing older," she said. "Look!" A ribbon of coffee had dripped over the lip and snaked to the base where it split at the collar's groove. She rotated the cup in her hand, showing that it had run the circumference. They watched her turn it, back and forth. They watched with the minds of children. They watched a model of the future.

5

THE NEXT WEEK, ABE AND ANDY HEADED SOUTH to Pasadena to talk to their sister Catherine's husband, Benjamin, about putting together a deal in the Imperial desert. If he'd give them a loan they'd pay him better than a bank would in interest, plus a part of the action once things got off the ground.

Benjamin, a cautious businessman, told them flat out that the desert was risky business.

Andy said, "They've been saying it for years. But I'll be damned if folks aren't growing all sort of crops out there. The market is dry those months. Think of what produce will draw."

"I don't know, Andy. If it were such a good idea why aren't more people doing it?"

"Because they're not farmers, that's why. They're a bunch of suits who don't know the first thing."

"Say we did lose some of our crop," Abraham added. "The land is so cheap, the water's damn near free. We'd have to be totally wiped out to lose a penny."

"The most we'd lose, Ben, is our time and energy. I'm willing to take that risk. Since when haven't I worked my ass off to get nowhere?"

They nodded their heads, "Since when haven't we all."

"I just think you boys should grab up a little more land where you are, close to home. That way you can manage it better."

"I see your concern, Ben. But one of us will manage the Fresno piece and the other will be down south. First we'll go in with tomatoes. If we make a few shekels, we'll expand. Nobody's talking about throwing our lives down there," Andy explained.

Benjamin picked up a pencil, made a couple of columns on a writing pad and said, "Well, gentlemen, what do you have on your own?"

"We figure it'll take us ten thousand to get set up. We're sitting on five. Ain't that right, Abe?"

"About, yeah."

Benjamin took it down like an attorney.

"And your estimate of the crop?"

"The first year, if the market is, say, three bucks a box, we'll make some change. That's a very low market..."

"Hold on. And boxes, how many do you estimate per acre. And..."

Ten minutes later they'd calculated the bottom line: two bucks a box to break even.

"Sounds right. Anything above that is gravy," Andy said. "But I wouldn't be surprised if the market goes six, seven. We really don't know."

"Let me think about it."

"We appreciate it, Ben."

"God bless you two. It's good to see brothers working like this."

"Well, this is only the start."

Benjamin turned to Andy. "Your old man had such ideas."

"But *our* dad," Andy emphasized, "didn't have a brother to work with, Ben. There's our advantage. There's two of us where there was only one of him. Ain't that right, Abe?"

Benjamin made a call to an associate of his who had once mentioned a parcel of land that he was willing to rent cheap. When he called, it was still available. Rather than fronting his own money, he would set up a partnership with the brothers. Benjamin would rent the dirt, and the brothers would cultivate and farm it. They'd split the profits in half.

The fifty-acre parcel was in the southeastern part of California in a place called Perris, not far from the Mojave Desert. Fifty miles northwest of Perris on Highway 10, citrus groves thrived in the city of Upland, and in Claremont, where some colleges were. And a little east of there, in Cucamonga, there were a fair number of plantings in Italian varietal that supplied grapes for a few local wineries. But as you went farther out, the plantings thinned, and for miles on end there were long open plains, spare of human life, reminiscent of the nearby desert.

They drove past a well beside the plot of land. Cheap water. With enough of it any piece of dirt could be made into a producing farm.

"Well, whatcha think?"

Andy saw the land as a sort of natural underdog, full of potential and starved of attention. He reached for a shovel out of the back of the truck, placed blade to ground, shoved a foot down and sliced into the earth and turned it over, crouched down to look at it, smell it. He took some in his hand and shook it like dice.

"A natural for row crops."

"Sure the hell wouldn't want to be planting walnuts here."

"I think we can take it places."

"I think so too."

"Let's walk it."

They moved over the earth. Dust kicked up from under their feet, the sweat gathered on their brows.

"Badgers." Andy pointed at a gouge in the earth. "Rabbits too, probably. Nothing that a shotgun couldn't handle."

Andy unzipped his pants. The piss drilled a hole in the earth and pocked his dusty boots.

"The thing is, we'll get a jump on every market," Andy said. "Everything'll come in a month earlier down here."

"Tomatoes."

"We'll start there. But eventually cukes, bells, cauli."

"Fifty acres is a good start."

Andy thumped his pecker, zipped up his pants and said, "It's our future, brother. We have to diversify."

"Too damn many raisins. How many raisins can people eat?"

"Lettuce'll grow down here like some kind of weed. What's your wife's attitude?" Guessing the answer, Andy looked out into the distance, said what until then had gone unsaid. "So I suppose it's me who'll have to come down here."

"I don't see no other way. I can't pick up the family and leave like that."

"We'll work it out."

There was a shack at the far corner of the field.

"Equipment shack," Abe nominated it.

Andy tugged the door open. Slivers of sun came through the wood siding, and a rhomboid of light wobbled at his feet from a square of sheet metal blown loose from the roof. He heard something flutter and, from reflex, ducked. A sparrow panicked in the corner and vanished through a hole. A bowl of twigs balanced on the corner rafter. Boarders, Andy thought. He walked slowly forward. Two dusty whiskey bottles, one cracked in half, were strewn on the dirt floor.

"What do you think?" Abe asked, coming through the door.

The light behind him hid his face and eyes.

"I've slept in worse."

"Babydoll will set you up."

"That's no problem."

Behind him on the wall was a single cupboard, the size of a medicine cabinet. Abe opened it. A water glass and a pair of bifocals. Abe picked the glasses up, amazed at the thickness of the lens. What blind bastard, he thought, had to wear these?

"I'll be damned."

Andy was regarding a mattress that lay next to a woodstove squatting in the far corner. Abe came up next to Andy.

"Bullets," Abe said.

Andy flipped the mattress over quickly and took half a step back.

"Look at this."

They both looked at it.

"Someone got shot here," Andy said, poking it with a toe.

"Who knows how long ago," Abe said.

They examined it in silence.

It made Abe's stomach swerve. He could see the bodies of so many of his fellow soldiers lying there, the wide-open eyes, the haunting stare of astonishment, as though death, however near, always came as a surprise.

Abraham roamed the room with his eyes. "Let's get out of here." Something was crabbing up his back.

"Spooky," Andy said.

When Abraham told his wife about it the next day, her response was, "He maybe deserved it."

Abraham wondered if she was right, and imagined for the first time the particulars of the scene. Was the dead man young or old? The murderer? Did he owe the man money? Rape his wife? Or was it just some drunken criminal on the run who he'd naïvely given a spot to bed down for the night? Without his bifocals, did he see the man lift the gun from his bag, holster, boot, or was he snoring, dreaming of paradise when the bullets sizzled through his body? Did he go quickly? Or did he go slowly in diminishing throes, as though racked with voltage? It was true, he thought, some men did deserve to die. Some men one was obliged to kill.

Zabel said, "What does Andy think?"

He told her they both thought it was spooky.

"The land. The land!"

"It's a good deal."

"Mother says it's very hot there."

Since when had his mother-in-law been that far south? Abe wondered.

He said, "Heat's no problem."

"What will it cost us?"

"Haven't figured that one out yet."

"You haven't figured it out!"

"We got money, Ma."

"From where? I don't want you to put the only thing we have in our hands at risk."

"It's not a risk. We've got it figured. You're the one who's been talking about splittin' things up from here."

"That's not the way I thought."

"Then what way? What other way is there?"

6

IN THE MIDDLE OF MAY, ANDY HEADED SOUTH in his two-ton truck, pulling a tractor and till behind him on a wide lowboy, with other riggings, an array of manual tools, and a fold-out cot in the truck bed. A shotgun lay on the passenger seat.

It was late in the afternoon when he arrived. With road-weary eyes, he scanned the land and breathed deeply the mild brittle air, which over the next few months would become a kind of kin.

He unhitched the equipment near the shack and unloaded the tools from the back. Then he lugged the "haunted" mattress outside, doused it with diesel and ignited it with a match. He watched until the mattress was smothered in flames. Then he cleared out the rest of the shack. The bifocals and water glass he stuck in a burlap bag, tied a knot at one end and set it in the corner, out of reverence for their owner. He cleaned out the old wood-burning stove. He'd use the shack for storage and a place to nap or escape the sun for a spell. He folded out the small army cot close to the stove.

A few miles down the road from the acreage sat a squat cinderblock structure, the Agua Motel. The front doors all faced the road, and the back windows afforded a lonely view of brush. It was a cheap place to bed for truckers en route to L.A. Two double-axle trucks were parked in the oversized lot when Andy drove up.

Andy dusted his jeans off and stepped into the office. A baseball game was playing on a radio. To his left, an older gentleman was snoring with one finger moving up and down like he might've been chiding a child in his dream. Nobody was behind the desk or anywhere around. He couldn't tell if the man was a boarder or the manager of the place. His street shoes and long socks were more suited to office work than not. Andy tapped the bell on the counter. The man woke with a jerk, lifted himself up at the elbow and ambled behind the desk without greeting Andy, as though his official role had to be postponed until he got into the right position.

Andy said hello.

The man squinted like he might have been missing his glasses. Andy imagined that once a person lost something of importance in such an out-of-the-way place, he'd just have to make do for a while.

"Like a room for a few weeks."

"Weeks?" He shook his head, either astounded by the request or making plain that he couldn't grant it.

"I'm planting some tomatoes down the road. Suppose I'm looking to be a sort of lodger."

"There's no issue there. Just nobody cared to stay that spell before. Fred Ladel."

Andy introduced himself in return.

Fred reached beneath the counter and pulled out a form. He said, "It's five bucks a night. Just fill in this piece of paper here."

Fred cocked his head and watched him fill out the form.

The light was getting tired outside, turning the color of pewter.

"Two bits a day extra for sheets and towels."

"Whatever it is."

"That'll be five twenty-five then, due every day. We don't keep tabs here."

Andy turned the paper around. Fred looked it over.

"Tomatoes you said?"

"Yes sir, tomatoes."

"Didn't know they grew nothin' but brush out here."

Fred reached for a neat stack of towels and bedding, set the key on top of it and handed the bundle to Andy over the counter.

"Number's six. Can't miss it," he said, and added, "No phones."

"I was just gonna ask you 'bout that."

"But there's one right outside your room there. It rings plenty loud when it does, which ain't but once in a blue moon."

"'Preciate it."

"That your rig there?"

"Yes sir, it is."

"I keep an eye on things out here. Don't want no trouble."

"I'll be too tired to give you any."

"So it's the room just down the ways a bit."

"Thank you, Fred."

"Night."

"Night to you."

A gust of axle grease and sweat and cheap wine hit him when he threw open the door. He flicked on the light. A bulb dangled from the ceiling in the center of the cinderblock room. It was like the desert itself had reached inside the space. It possessed the silence of the body at the brink of limbo. The mattress was wide and sunken in the middle, as if it had once borne the bulk of a sumo wrestler. To the bed's left, without so much as a Gideon Bible on it, was a nightstand. Home.

He made his bed, took a shower and just lay down, thinking he might go down the road for a sandwich in a while. But once in the bed, he stepped into sleep swiftly, deeply, as though he were stepping into snow. Outside, the wind grew chaotic, and strange images—fusions of animal, mineral, and man, black doves, whirlwinds of words—occupied him all night. So disturbed was his sleep, it appeared he might've been wrestling for his life. He woke in the middle of the night, alarmed that Teddy's bed was not across from his own where it should have been. A few seconds of excruciating confusion passed before he recollected where he was. He moaned and fell back to sleep.

On the tractor the next morning, Andy sensed for the first time the delicate temperament of the region. He was used to rain and occasionally hail at this time of year, but not such thumping wind. He looked back over his shoulder. A huge plume of dust rose from behind the till. He reached the end of the first pull, lifted the till, turned the tractor around and headed back in. The land started to exude a rich mineral smell.

By the time he was halfway done, he could no longer feel his body. The vibrating machine put him in a kind of hypnotic, time-collapsing trance, so that he sat acutely exposed to himself and his memories. He traveled back to the old water tower he had used as his summer sleeping quarters when he was in high school. A couple of times he had invited girls up there, out of earshot and eyesight of Abe and Zabel in the main house below. One night the smell of smoke woke him from a dream. Strange shadows, amoebas of light quivered on the ceiling, and there was an orange hue to the sky outside. He lunged out of bed.

The side of the house was on fire. The air heaved, growled. He went to the other window. Lava-hot smoke hit his lungs and shoved him back against the wall. Great living twists of flames came up the crosswise beams. A single flame lapped up from between the floorboards. He opened the door, crouched and jumped. For a split second there was this terrible weightless feeling, an eclipse of everything real, and when he hit the ground, a powerful splintering slam. He lay on the dirt wondering if he was dead, or rather how somebody who had fallen two stories might theoretically survive. When he opened his eyes, the head of the water tower was aflame, and he saw a baroque column of smoke, darker than the dark itself, move the moon. His last thought before he passed out was, It's going to fall on me.

In time he healed. After all, he was young and fit, except of course for that foot. But questions from a different sort of injury remained. They claimed the house had caught on fire first. At first they couldn't find Teddy and they panicked. But Andy knew that Teddy, barely a year old, slept right next to them. They said they grabbed Teddy and hurried out of the house. Then Zabel remembered their cash can in the back of the freezer, *a lot of money we had saved.* She sent Abe back in to get it. Empty-handed, he wended his way out, sick with smoke. Only then did they realize the water tower had caught fire too. They found Andy on the ground just minutes later, that's true, and rushed him to the hospital first thing, not bothering to save anything else. *What else could he want?*

But why was their attention on the dough in the house, not Andy? If they'd gone in to fetch their child, or even a dog, okay. But money is what they were after? Fucking money. Wouldn't a loved one first look to see if everyone is safe and sound? By the time they turned their attention to Andy, he might've been barbequed up there. What was money next to a family member, any human life?

The longer he sat on the tractor thinking about it, the more he wondered why he hadn't realized before how terrible their response was. Money was important, true. Especially in those days, especially for Zabel. She was petrified of losing what little she had, just as she'd lost her father to the Turks. But were the Turks an excuse or the cause? Andy dared to wonder. Seemed every damn wrong could be blamed, or at least explained, by that terrible turning point in his people's history. Hagopian was a murderer. So? Wasn't he mad with rage over what the Turks did to his mother?

Garabedian the bookie: What is left to a man but cunning? Nehar is stingy: When you see your father trolling the desert floor for locusts to feed his children, then you can tell me what this word "miser" means!

But how did the genocide account for his own saintly mother, or Anoush Paloutzian, that old gal in Selma who saved every penny she had and gave it away on her deathbed to orphans in need? Or the retired one-eyed priest, Kevork, who spent his summers carting lugs of grapes from door to door from his five-acre plot for all the elderly who hadn't the means to get about. *Free Apple For World,* a sign read in Armenian off Madera Avenue heading into Kerman, posted by a man who remembered how his own mother had savored them so much that her last delirious words, spoken through her last wafer-thin breath before she was swept up in the desert dust, were, "Let's have an apple."

Was the issue a person's past or a person's character? Andy had known people happy to be rich in charity while in poor in every other way. Seemed, in any case, that the whole world turned on how deeply a man could love in spite of his past, his fate. That much was settled; but there was something else that Andy had surmised over the years: only a greater love could absorb a lesser love, the way a deep dish could take the contents of a shallow one, but not the other way around. So those with the most love lived in an oddly lonely world. A great lover hungered, hungered for something to reflect his love back to him, and the whole of humanity—past and present and future—was a great jewel from which the love of God eventually came sprinkling back to God. This is why God needed to create humankind—to satisfy a hunger. And evil was the opposite, a bottomless pool of pitch, or better, a reflectionless surface that only consumed. That was the secret of black.

Andy hadn't survived anything like the genocide, but neither had his life been a cakewalk. His parents were dead before he was old enough to drive. He'd spent half his youth in the Shriners' hospital in San Francisco—three hours and a million miles from home. He couldn't even recall how many surgeries he'd had to "correct" his polio. There was a time when he'd reckoned he'd be in the hospital for the rest of his life.

The Polio Wing, they called it. But in no way did it resemble anything that might up and fly. Thick concrete walls, he recalled. The cold circulation of nurses and doctors in and out of the rooms. And he remembered the echoes, the sick dribble of sounds, the voices that came to him from up the long corridor, wrung of meaning. There had been three beds in his room, the foot of each against the long window. He could no longer remember the names of the kids who had slept next to him, what they had looked like. What he did remember was the way the window had framed the world out there, how the grassy field had glittered with dew and, farther in the distance, how long gray eucalyptus trees had swayed so freely.

Visitors were not allowed. But every day, women could be seen shuffling over the grass up to the long row of windows behind which lay the children. Willa, his oldest sister, who lived in San Francisco, was determined not to leave her baby brother there alone. Each day she would walk two miles to the hospital and stand outside his window. Frequently, a gray chilling rain would drift in. From inside, as the window gradually blurred, as if it were melting the entire world beyond it, Andy could barely make out the black arc of the umbrella beneath which the smeared figure of Willa stood. In spite of Willa, it was in the hospital bed that Andy first remembered having to choose between bitterness that bent the spirit backward—a magical revenge against the world out there—or kindness, whose aim was to save that world from the same pain he knew.

A coyote loped across the field. By the angle of the sun he figured it was a little after noon, a good time to break for lunch.

At the diner, smoke hovered over the tables where truckers sat with their hands around cups of coffee. He slid into a booth and picked up a menu. A fat waitress chugged toward him breathing heavily. He ordered a roast beef sandwich au jus on a roll, french fries and a beer. The waitress scribbled it all down, filed the menu away beneath her arm, and abrupty left. Her brusqueness made him feel lonely, so much so that he lost the mood to eat. He stroked the side of his water glass while he waited. He ate half of his lunch, then paid the bill. When he stepped outside again he felt like a stranger, a stranger in a land where everyone was a stranger. Only the colossal sun up there was at home.

7

AFTER ANDY HAD WORKED UP THE SOIL and dug the furrows, he set the stakes out in bundles of five down the rows. Then he walked down those rows and, with a single whack of the mallet, drove the yard-high stakes into the dirt, allowing about a pace between them. He liked his stakes as upright as a marine. If a stake didn't go in straight, he'd pull it out and mallet it in again. At the end of each row he'd stop, drop to his haunches, and line his eye up on the row of stakes. He made demands on himself more suited to a furniture maker than a farmer. By the end of the first day he'd staked a quarter of the plot. He sat on a pail looking at his day's work still holding the mallet. His overalls were glued to his thighs and he could feel sweat beetle down the crack of his ass. He looked at his watch—it was three o'clock. A few hours of light remained in the day. He could set up a few more stakes. But he liked to pace himself—he'd get sloppy if he was tired. On the other hand, what else was a man to do?

He hadn't read in a while; maybe he'd pick up a book at the drugstore in town. A girly magazine while he was at it. He thought of some old Armenian story he once heard where a guy was so churned up he fucked some gopher hole. Andy stood, turned the bucket over and chucked his hammer into it. His fingers were fixed in the letter C and they ached when he tried to straighten them. He now remembered it wasn't because the guy was so churned up that he fucked the hole. It was deeper, some pagan thing; the belief that a man's seed impregnated the earth. He moved to a nozzle next to the standpipe, turned it on and dropped to his knees and let the water run over his hands, good and cool. He caught the water in his mouth, took a few enormous gulps and rinsed his face and ran wet fingers through his dusty hair. Slowly, he lifted himself off his knees and looked around. Did he have the energy, really, to pick up a girl? He felt a touch of exhaustion just thinking of all the drinking and sweet-talking and slow dancing, the general mickey-mousing around he'd have to go through before he hit any pay dirt. There was a whorehouse down the road from Perris that he might track down. He hadn't been to a whorehouse before and he thought he might give it a whirl. Left all alone the way he was in that desolation, he felt he'd the right to do or think whatever the hell came to mind.

Fred was hosing down the walkway when Andy drove up.

"How ya doin', Fred?" he asked, stepping out of the truck.

Fred squinted, as if he was trying to find Andy in the dark.

"Keepin' the deck scrubbed, is all," Fred said.

"Where's Road 23, about?"

"Road 23?" Fred answered blankly. You'd think the road dead-ended at a whorehouse.

"That's all right," Andy said, and turned toward his room.

"Hurt your leg?"

"I had polio when I was a kid, Fred."

"Didn't notice it before. Great-aunt of mine was in one of those iron lungs," Fred shared.

"Plenty of people were. I thank God I didn't get it worse."

"I'll say. I couldn't think of anything sorrier than to be cooped up in one of those things," Fred said. "I suppose I'd just as well pick up and die."

Andy thought he'd give that Road 23 another shot. Maybe it was his suspicion of himself that made him suspicious of Fred.

"I heard some guy was farming tomatoes down Road 23. Where might that be, Fred?"

Fred gave him directions there.

That evening Andy would've given anything to have been born outside the church. One minute he'd grow hard and the next minute he'd go limp. Decide either way, Andy, he told himself. You can't just sit in this chair all night waffling, it's this in-between stuff that'll kill you. He'd already showered and put on some clean duds, so he told himself it was a waste not to check it out. If it doesn't suit you, you can turn back. Who knows what these whores will look like? Could be a bunch of fat pigs in greasy lingerie. That'll stop you dead in your tracks.

When he saw a neon sign blinking in the distance, his teeth started chattering. A few shabby pickups and a semi sat off to the side of the brick building. He drove past and rolled a full mile down the road before he hung a U-turn. He let the car crawl back. Seeing those grungy cars in the blue neon light that sputtered *Gentleman's Bar* emptied his stomach. Now he wished he hadn't come. But he'd driven a good thirty minutes, so that alone committed him to at least go in and check it out. He parked behind the semi, shook himself like a boxer stepping into the ring, and hopped out of the truck.

There weren't any whores around that he could see, at least none parading around in their nightgowns the way he'd imagined they would in a whorehouse. There was a jukebox going, guys standing at the bar, each with a girl perched on a stool next to him. He liked the low-key atmosphere of the place. Only it smelled the way he'd imagined a brothel might smell. The air was all gooey with cotton candy perfume. As he ambled to the bar, he watched the bartender nod to someone in the shadows. Andy asked him for a scotch and water, if he would be so kind. Without a word, the barkeep shoved the drink at him, as close to a snarl as a gesture like that can get. The drink looked thin, the glass water-spotted, and where there should've been three ice cubes there was but one floating alone at the top. Andy sipped his drink, reached into his pocket and put a five-note down. He'd hoped to get kinder reception, to settle his nerves and to at least enjoy a drink if the other thing didn't work out. But how high can your expectations be of a barkeep who works at a whorehouse day in and day out? Andy wondered if one of his fringe benefits was a poke at a girl every now and then. Or maybe, Andy thought, one of these girls is his, or maybe he's the pimp—which would mean all of the girls were his.

How, in fact, does this place work? thought Andy. Not to be crude or anything, but do you take the girl they send you, regardless of whether you like her looks? If you don't like her, do you tell her, or does she leave after a while and a madam asks you what you thought?

A girl came out from behind a curtain at the far end of the bar, slinging her hair over her shoulders. She was a skinny little waif in a blue polka-dot dress. This girl looked like she could be someone's kid sister.

She sat next to him, closed the slit of her dress, modest-like. She turned on her stool to face him, her knees pinched together, her hands folded neatly on top of them. With her head cocked to the side, it was like she was going to ask him to buy her an ice cream cone. Andy was on the verge of laughing.

"Name's Ruthy." She floated a hand onto his shoulder with a near-weightless touch. Could have been a feather that landed there.

Andy smiled. "Ruthy," he said.

Ruthy smiled. "What's yer name?"

"Andy."

"Would you buy me a drink, Andy?"

"Sure I will."

Ruthy got the bartender's attention. He came over, working a toothpick in his mouth this way and that.

"Give me a gin and tonic."

The bartender poured her the drink, took a dollar from Andy's change in front of him. Ruthy scowled when the bartender turned around. Must be some politics going on between the two, Andy thought. A kind of politics that he didn't care to know about.

"Thank you, Randy," she said.

"Andy," he said. "Anytime, Ruthy."

Ruthy sipped her drink daintily.

"You think I'm pretty, Andy?"

Andy was beginning to think she was. She had big blue eyes, brown hair—thick and straight as a horse's—parted to the side. And though there was something boyish about her body, her movements were graceful, like a ballerina's. A closer look revealed that she was hardly a girl. Little lines materialized around her face when she smiled; her skin was kind of tired, but not dead, or not yet anyway.

"Yeah," Andy said. "I do think you're pretty."

"You got some smile."

"Do I?"

"I bet you're a gentleman, too."

Andy wondered, In a whorehouse is that a good or bad thing?

"Well, thank you."

She stroked Andy's arm as if he was her boyfriend.

"You're a natural, Andy."

Andy was amazed how much information this girl could pick up in so little time. He imagined prostitutes had to calculate things swiftly.

"Where you from, Ruthy?"

"Barstow."

"Just down the road, then."

"A stone's throw."

He wanted to ask her how she had become a whore. He wanted to ask her how long she'd been doin' it. How old was she, and had she any other plans? Her parents, what kind of people were they? Did they know what she was doing? Were they even alive to wonder? But most of all he wanted to ask her if she had a boyfriend. Somehow, the thought of her having a boyfriend mattered. He didn't like the idea of laying another guy's girl. What right had he to ask her any of these questions anyway?

"Mood Indigo," one of Andy's favorite songs, came on the jukebox.

"Would you like to dance, Ruthy?"

Ruthy nodded her head yes.

He took her by the hand and led her out to a pool of parquet. He slid one arm around her waist and cupped her hand with his. She draped an arm over his shoulder. Ruthy was not a very good dancer, but was open to every suggestion he made. He could feel the muscles move at the small of her back, the tautness of her stomach. She smelled like baby powder. Andy chuckled at himself, the way he was turning this into a date. He was sorry to think that somewhere along in this masquerade he was going to have to flip his mask off. Probably when she asked him would it be a head job or did he want to go the whole way?

"What you laughing about?" she asked.

"Myself."

They danced some more. He didn't care that she couldn't dance very well—it felt good to have a woman in his hands. Made him realize just how much he'd missed it.

"You're one of these serious kind of guys," she said, as though cataloging him.

"I am? Sure I am." He wanted her to know that he wasn't just some other john. "I am serious."

When the song ended, Andy could all but feel something inside of her drop dead. Andy wanted to dance another one. But Ruthy was distracted. She stood there like she was waiting to be told what to do next, like it wasn't obvious anymore that they were on a dance floor. He thought to ask her what was the matter. Then Andy noticed a couple of guys with cowboy hats who had walked in and were taking a spot at the bar. Maybe she figured her chance of making money was better with these cowboys. Maybe she'd done it with one of them before. Both of them at once.

Andy thanked her. She shrugged her shoulders as if it were no big shake. She hung back a couple of paces as they walked back to the bar, then veered over toward the cowboys.

The cavalier way they leaned back with their elbows against the counter made Andy guess that he was out of his league. He was happy that his drink, thin as it was, was waiting there for him. He polished it off in one giant gulp and asked the bartender for another. From the corner of his eye he could see that for the cowboys she'd put on a sassy hand-on-hip pose. With a toe she kept tracing little circles on the floor. Now and then she'd throw back her head and chortle. Then she pointed her chin at Andy. He yanked his eyes away. The cowboys lengthened their necks to see who she was talking about.

Next thing he knew, Ruthy was standing beside him.

A part of him hoped she'd pull up a stool.

"Have a seat, sweetheart."

She sat on the edge, like she might have to go at any second.

"So, Andy? What do you want to do? I'm sure you didn't come here just for a dance and a drink."

He was amazed at how flatly she'd put it.

Andy searched his heart and mind.

"Well, what I'd like is to have a few more drinks with you."

"That's sweet. But I'm a working girl."

"I understand that."

"And I've got work to do."

"Go right ahead, Ruthy."

"You sure?"

Andy reached into his pocket and pulled out a five-dollar bill.

"Here." He tucked the bill in her hand. "Thank you for the dance."

"Thank you." She put the bill in the pocket of her dress without missing a beat. "Come back now." She took his hand and stroked it sweetly.

"I will."

It was a long ride home. The money he'd dropped was nothing next to the loneliness he felt. He searched for the source of his loneliness. It wasn't because he was physically alone; it wasn't because he was out in the middle of nowhere without so much as a memory of a kiss to take with him to bed. No. It had to do with the way Ruthy had recoiled when he'd said that he was serious. It had to do with his need for women to see the thoughtful man that he was, and his disappointment when they didn't seem to get it. What the hell were you figuring to begin with, Andy? he wondered. This was like giving a photograph to a blind man and getting upset that he didn't appreciate it. Even after he told you he was blind, even after you saw that he lived among the blind, in a blind world. This, Andy thought, is no fault of anyone but you. You've got no excuse.

He looked up from his thoughts and saw two amber amulets glow in the dark in front of him. He felt an impact, then his car stumbled. He pulled over to the side of the road, trembling. What the fuck? The right headlight of his truck was out. He looked around. On the shoulder of the road, twenty yards or so away, he spotted it lying in the acute light of the moon: a coyote. A big powerful coyote. From the way the animal kept jerking its head up, Andy decided it was still alive but it was going nowhere. He'd always thought a coyote was like an uncurbed dog, but up close now he noticed that its big ears and close-set almond eyes and the great slope of its snout all seem shaped for living in the wild. He could hear it sigh deeply, defeatedly when it lay its head back down.

Andy walked back to the truck and felt around for a crowbar in the bed. He couldn't just let it rot away like that. He stood over the coyote, watched its bulky chest heave, and in the cold he could see its breath. He got down on one knee and stroked it. He didn't know how hard a coyote's skull might be. He noticed how calm he was, how true the metal felt in his hand when he placed the neck of the bar on the coyote's head and lifted it and dropped it, like a priest anoints one with a cross. He raised the crowbar and with all his might, with all the raw power of that immense torso, slammed it down. He could feel the bone crush, as though chunks of it had shot through the metal all the way up his arm.

He tossed the crowbar in the back of the truck. On the road again, he wondered if there was some logic to how the evening had turned out. No, he told the coyote, there's no logic to it. There's no logic to anything. One thing follows the next and we string it together to get it to make sense.

Andy worked long days. He decided that any attempt at human intimacy in such a place was bound to fail miserably. So he fell into the kind
of mindless rhythm of work that prisoners know well. By the end of the
month, the field was ready to irrigate. Andy filled the standpipe, laid the
elbow-shaped pipes in front of the rows, opened an alfalfa valve and let
the water drain down the ditch. Slowly, like a bathtub, the ditch filled.
When the water level crept up higher than the field, he got on his knees
and started piping the water out. He took the siphon pipe, submerged
one end in the cool ditch water, popped the other end with a hand to get
suction and flipped it over the bank, where it drained off into the furrows. Water inched up the row like a thermometer heating up, turning
the earth dark chocolate. Andy crabbed from one row to the next, his
knees caking up with mud. He recalled how, as a child, he'd scooped up
a handful of the stuff and tasted it, one time smearing his body with
mud, head to toe, and marching out of the fields to see what his mother
would think. She hadn't been impressed. "Stand there," she'd said,
"before your father sees you," and had blasted him with the hose.

Andy stood up and checked the ditch. He estimated that the water
pressure would allow him maybe fifteen rows, but you could never take
your eye off it entirely: if the ditch water got too low, it'd break the
flow, or if it got too high, it'd break the bank.

Abe was scheduled to arrive that afternoon to help with the irrigation
and go over some finances that Zabel had been badgering him about.
But he never even made it out of bed. He woke in the morning with the
room spinning. He'd never felt anything like that before and believed he
was lethally ill. They called Roxie Shishmanian over straight away. In
Armenian she diagnosed him with turning illness and told him to drop
warm olive oil in his ears four times a day until it went away. They asked
her how long that might take. In impeccable Armenian, she said that
how it comes and when it goes are equally unknown. Zabel noted he'd
had unusually strong gas the night before. Could something he ate have
brought it on? "Some think," Roxie said, "very hot peppers like the
Mexicans eat will do it. Rightly, though, Armenians have no such
food." True, she'd known gas to do stranger things than this, but a blow
to the head is more likely the cause. Now Abe recalled he'd experienced

something similar when he'd cracked his noggin against a rock while swimming in a canal as a kid. But the dizziness then had lasted only a matter of minutes. The thing he had now was going on five hours.

Nothing, Abe swore to Zabel, even sitting in the trenches of war, had made him feel so helpless. It was as though he had ten pairs of eyes, each with its own point of view, that began to contend with each other when he moved. If he should fail to recover within a week he would surely kill himself. With his eyes locked on the ceiling, he asked her, "What am I going to do? Andy is expecting me this afternoon."

"Don't worry about him. He takes care of himself." She said it as if there were something criminal about it.

"But the man hasn't seen us for weeks."

"And have we seen him?"

"But he's been there by himself, Ma."

"I will call him in a few hours. Now let me get you something to eat."

Abe reflexively shook his head no. "Vakhh!" He'd set things in motion again.

"I'll bring something small."

"I will vomit."

"Maybe later then."

Perhaps if something in his head had been kicked loose another kick might fix it.

"Zabel," he said, "get a board from the barn and hit my head with it."

"Have you lost your senses?" Zabel said.

"I beg you."

"In Christ's name," Zabel quickly crossed her heart, "I will not."

Exhausted, Abe shut his eyes. The inside of his head was seesawing.

"I will warm the olive oil."

Lying still, he began to envision his head as a pool of water on which the world rested like a ball. The less movement there was in the water, the less the ball would spin.

By noon Andy had irrigated half of the field. The water flowed quietly down the furrows. Andy sat against the shed in the shade with his lunch. A wind swaggered over the land and cooled his body down. He pulled his boot off, rolled down the sock, shook it loose of dirt and draped it over his lap. He traced a finger over the scars that resembled strips of dried glue, rips in a lady's stockings. He recalled how, when he was a kid, he'd slather the entire foot with mud, honey, or wax, or put it in a wooden vice, or clamp clothespins to his toes, as though that foot was a kind of voodoo doll. As he massaged the bad foot he wondered what he had meant to achieve through those rituals. Were they his way of punishing the foot, or his way of befriending it? A truck threw up dust on the access road. It didn't sound like Abe's truck. When the dust cleared, he saw it was an old Dodge, not Abe's Ford, rolling up. Andy stuck his boot on in a hurry, neverminding the sock. The truck pulled up parallel to the shack and stopped.

The man cut the engine. "Howdy," he said through his window.

"Howdy to you."

"Looks like yer puttin' in tumaytuhs here." The man flicked his chin at the land.

"Yes sir, I am."

"I passed by here a couple of times and saw it from the road. Just though I'd see who was farmin'."

"I'm Andy Demerjian."

"What's that?"

"Andy Demerjian's my name."

"I'm Jules Ahearn. I farm 'round these parts myself."

"Pleased to meet you, Jules."

"If you don't mind me asking, them trellises are awful tall, ain't they? Plus, yer a little early on them tumaytuhs."

"I don't know, am I?"

"I don't farm 'em myself. But Clyde Boyd does, and so does Rocky Moss. Both of 'em are tumaytuh farmers. Maybe you use some special method, though."

"Nothing special, Jules. Just farming like I always farm."

"'Round here, do ya?"

"'Round Fresno."

"Fresno."

"Yes, sir."

"Well, son," he said with a chuckle, "this here's no Fresno by a long shot. Weather's got a different sort of constitution out heres."

"I've noticed that," Andy said, looking up at the sky. "What do you farm, Jules?"

"Cukes."

"They grow nice out here, huh?"

"I've been lucky. Last season, though, half the patch didn't size."

Andy shook his head sympathetically.

"Farmin's one of those kind of things, though. One year to the next."

"I've seen it myself."

"Five years back I got cukes where the insides was all seeds."

"Can't beat the dirt, though," Andy said, scooping up a handful. "I even like the smell of it."

"Minerals there, that's for sure. Hungry 'nough, dogs'll flat out eat it."

Andy agitated the dirt around in his hand until it sifted away.

"Have a chat with them two boys Moss and Boyd."

"I plan to do that."

"Seeing the winds and all, I just never done seen anybody plant so early and up so high. But they're year-to-year too. Maybe you got a trick up yer sleeve."

Andy thought, What the heck is he talking about? "I appreciate it," he said. "Where do I find these guys?"

He gave Andy directions. Andy nodded his head.

"What'd yuh say yer name was again?"

"Andy. Andy Demerjian."

"What kinda name is it, Demerjian?"

"Armenian."

The man shook his head. "Never heard it. But I'm just a damn Okie, so my opinion don't mean hay."

"Thanks for comin' by," Andy said.

"Anytime."

Andy watched Jules' truck wobble back up the road and wondered what he meant by weather, winds. He could've planted one month earlier or later, but how could that matter much? True, maybe he might have gotten color a little earlier if he'd planted in April. Maybe I should look into this, he thought. He took a slab of jerky out of the sack and chewed on it absently. Then again, people are used to doing things a certain way out of habit and they get spooked when someone comes along and does it different. Still, he'd like to meet Boyd and Moss. In the future, if things go well, he might get one or the other of these locals to farm the place for a fee.

When Andy got back to the hotel late that afternoon, Fred came out to relay that some lady had phoned for him. His first thought was that Abe had been in an accident. He called Zabel immediately.

"What is it?" he asked Zabel. "Abe okay?"

"It's nothing. But he can't come."

"What happened?"

"He woke up this morning sick in his head. Something in his ear so that he gets dizzy."

"No kidding."

"He can't stand up without falling down. He's no good to anybody right now."

"That's too bad."

"We don't know when he's going to get better. I don't know how I'm going to get anything done around here."

"Can he talk?"

"He can't get out of bed."

"That bad, huh?"

"What? You think I make these things up?"

"Tell him not to worry. I'll manage on my own till he feels better."

"How is the crop coming?"

"Pretty good, pretty good."

"I hope so. We have a lot of money invested down there."

"Don't worry, Zabel. Your dirt's not going anywhere."

"What do you mean?"

"It was a joke."

"You've gotten a big mouth lately."

"Anyway, have Abe call me when he feels better."

She hung up.

He went to his room, lay on the bed and smoked. One cigarette, then another, and another. What is it this Zabel wants from me? Here I am in nowhere land, in this cheap, dingy motel, shouldering this entire deal on my own, and she acts like I owe her something still, or I'm going to cheat her out of whatever. Jesus.

48

Andy needed a drink.

"There a quiet bar around these parts where a fella could get a beer?" he asked Fred.

Fred recommended the only place there was to recommend, a trucker's bar about five miles into Perris proper.

Sure enough, there were four double-axles lined up parallel on a dirt lot across the road. Andy didn't much like truckers; he didn't care for the way they smelled, and he didn't care for the way they behaved. All that sweat and heat and grease and solitude played on the mind. A man who lives that sort of life is quick to pick a fight, almost like he has to mark something beside the road.

When he walked in he saw a few guys perched on stools at the bar, watching a ball game. A dead jukebox sat on the other side of the room. He walked across the floor beneath a dusty glitter ball.

The bartender came up to him with his hands across his chest and nodded once.

"Beer," Andy said.

The bartender nodded once again. With one eye on the TV, he pulled the beer out of an icy tub and held it. Andy wanted that beer something terrible. Just then, someone hit a ball deep to left. The bartender set the beer on the counter and watched the runners round the bases. Sitting there all sweaty, the beer looked awful thirsty itself. A couple of guys slapped each other's backs. "Son of a bitch," the bartender said.

"That's ten bucks, Ike," a guy cackled.

The bartender shook his head, reached into a register and delivered on the bet. Two more guys were digging into their pockets.

"Who won?" Andy asked.

"Indies," the bartender said.

"How's that beer comin', barkeep?"

He slid it in front of Andy, then squared up on Andy's eyes like he was trying to place him.

"You a farmer?" Ike could tell from the dust in his hair.

"Yeah. Tomatoes. Just down the road. You get many farmers in here?" Andy asked.

"Now and then a few." The bartender tossed a paper doily in front of him. "There was some boy that was farming back here five, six years ago," he said. "For a second I thought you was him."

"What was his name?"

"Don't recall. But more than a couple would curse it if they heard it again."

"What happened?"

"Owed a lot of folks money."

"Gambling?"

"Thief. This was three or four years back. This guy, let's call him Joe, come in here from out of nowhere and planted himself some tomatoes. Claimed to want to do big things out here, claimed the fifty or so acres he was cultivatin' was his own and that he planned to expand. The few farmers been workin' out here for a spell welcomed his company. Hell, his companionship. More the merrier. Helped build up the market or something. I don't know what."

"That's true enough. The more farmers you got concentrated in one spot, the better it goes for everybody."

"So Joe plants these tomatoes. The way the story goes, looked like he knew what he was doing, too. Regular farmer. Tomatoes come in, pretty as debutantes. But around harvest time, Joe's dough runs dry. That's not unheard of in the farming racket, I hear."

"It happens. Get so ahead of yourself trying to cultivate a crop that the money gets thin by pickin' time."

"Okay. So you know, you've been in the business long enough."

"Since I was a kid."

"Where you from?"

"Fresno area."

"Fresno. The heartland. Name's Ike."

"Andy."

The bartender pointed to his bottle and asked, "Another one?"

"It's empty, ain't it?"

He smiled, tossed the empty under the bar, pulled a fresh one out of the tub, popped it open and set it in front of Andy.

"So, where were we?"

"This guy Joe is comin' up on the harvest."

"And he doesn't have the dough. So, he takes in Boyd and Moss, two local boys been farming around here for years, on paper as partners. I don't know how much money passed hands, but enough to harvest. I don't know how much that would be."

"Depends on the acreage."

"I think we're talking fifty acres."

"Plenty of money, then."

"Whatever it was, he took it. Next thing ya know, this Joe goes to round up some Mexicans near the border for labor. A few days pass, and no sign of him. A week."

"Don't tell me."

"Word is he got him a pretty little señorita. After that, it was adios. Last anybody saw of him."

"Jesus. He took off and left them on the vines? I can't believe it."

"His partners, they couldn't either. Didn't believe it. Till it was too late."

"Are you going to tell me they didn't take them off themselves?"

"For that, I blame Boyd and Moss. They claim they were too busy with their own harvest, but if you ask me, the insult was so outrageous they refused to see it. Blind to the truth. Eventually they got to him. By then, though, most of it was good for makin' salsa in the field only. By the time it reached the market, mush."

"That's a sad story."

"All went to slop for pigs."

"I'll be damned."

"Naw, there's somethin' about farmin' that breeds a different kind of people, 'specially out here. Out here, risk-takers one and all. That includes you."

8

SOMETIMES LIKE BATS, WEREWOLVES, Angel would stay up all night. Suddenly, at midnight, her telephone call would jar awake a friend, relative, someone she'd once met at church.

"Hallo," she'd say, "this is Madame Tutulian. It is late at night, and still, they possess me. What do they want? I wonder, are they over there tonight too?"

Naturally they wondered who she was talking about.

"Who?" she'd answer. "All of them. That's who."

Her interlocutors would try to dispel her fears, and when they hung up they'd matter-of-factly observe, "She's mad," as though madness were a kind of trait, like stinginess or saintliness. In fact, madness was not uncommon in those days—after what the Turks had done, some Armenians claimed that every member of the race was afflicted with some measure of it. Lunatics, along with half-wits, the sexually bewildered, the ones found groping a horse or violating a lamb, men who lived with their mothers their entire lives, or deranged spinsters with whiskers, were indulged with the stoicism and patience usually reserved for poets, children and bad weather.

On this afternoon, what Angel needed to talk about was the heat. The temperature had reached a hundred degrees and had stayed put for three weeks now, like it might never turn back. From a distance the air looked like water running down a pane of glass. A shrill cicada-like sound was needling her ears. Worse, her limbs were ballooning up with blood, and her fingertips and toes tingled as though they had become points of contact for an electrical current. The palms of her hands were moist and red, and they reminded her of plum meat. She wondered what this signaled. Was she turning into a sort of jam? For a second, she considered slathering her skin with melted wax to preserve herself. She began to search for candles and then, sighting the phone, decided to summon her daughter instead.

"My soul?" Her voice was desperate.

"Hah, Ma."

"Akhh, Zabel! My child. You must come."

"What is it?"

"My hands and feet," she told her daughter. "They are red and they buzz. They look like the meat of plums."

"It's the heat, Ma."

"In such a way, in the old country, jam was made. But these things they never did to people. Are they starting to do this to people now too?"

"Nobody is doing nothing, Ma. It's nothing. Drink some cold mint tea."

"In the mouth of the Turk I shit."

"It's the heat, Mother, the heat! My hands feel the same sometimes."

"To you too! *Christos!* Both of us!"

"Later I will come and see you."

"Without you, how will I rest?"

"This afternoon."

Angel went out on the patio and sat. At the bottom of the steps, a cloud of gnats pulsed over a shriveled sickle of watermelon rind. At the base of the tree, flies feasted on the pus-like ooze of rotten apricots. The white leaves of the grapevines were in the sun eerie and translucent. The sun in the center of the sky, it blared, by God, it seemed to have lost its mind. Around her eyes, sweat began to pool and a harsh pickling-juice odor leaked from beneath the folds of her skirt.

Her aunt Araxie used to stuff barrels with cabbage, celery, green tomatoes and carrots. Pickling juice. Her aunt Araxie buried them in a hole before the first snow. In the spring her aunt cracked the barrels open. Angel could taste the briny juice when she crunched into a celery stick. In a barrel beneath the earth she could smell the strong juice. Her breath more shallow by the second. Beneath the earth. Among her tormentors:

things that flap in the wind

the toilet's cover at Ani Nalbandian's

the shriveled foot
the clay pot on Eva's porch
the double-pronged gardening tool that Hasbed uses
the cracked hose in the back
the clock that went tick tock
the teakettle crouched on a burner at Garabed's kitchen
the springs in the bed in the barn
the bowl of Manoog's hat
the dogs across the road

Two hours later her daughter found her asleep, her palms penitently turned up, her head limp on her chest, a withered *pieta*. Zabel stood by the old woman for a while, listening to her spastic snoring.

"Ma?"

The woman rolled her head.

"Mama?"

She opened her eyes and looked at Zabel emptily.

"Come, let's go inside."

"Akhh."

Zabel put the old woman in the big red chair and lifted her bloated feet onto the otttoman.

"Let's drink some cold *tahn*."

"Ah." Angel rested her head back with a sigh.

Zabel cut the cucumber in long quarters, then briskly chopped down the shaft. She spooned some yogurt into two tall glasses, added the cucumbers, filled the glass with water, stirred it with a spoon and dropped in a few ice cubes. When Zabel returned with the *tahn,* her mother was regarding a photo of her late husband on a lamp stand next to her chair. On her knees, Zabel took her mother's hand in her own. It was moist and smooth as a bar of soap. She longed for the days when her mother would stroke her head with those hands.

The old woman sighed and brought the glass trembling to her lips. She took a slurp and sighed again. The thin milk dribbled down the side of her mouth. Her head shook as though she were mightily disagreeing with something. Zabel picked up the photo.

"Papa was such a handsome man," she said.

"And how he loved our Lord," Angel said. "Every night he would read from the Psalms. When the Turks ate him, it was honey in their rotten throats."

"I wish my Abe was such a man."

"If he was alive, he would teach Abe, instead of you having to teach him."

Then, out of nowhere, the old woman's thoughts shifted. She asked where the children were.

Zabel told her they were with her friend Lucy.

Angel did not like Lucy. She had just recently decided it.

"Her eye," she told Zabel. "It is bad."

She broke the news to Zabel without hesitation, as though Lucy were a maid or a hairdresser, not Zabel's childhood friend.

"No. Do you think so?" She put the photo back on the table.

"I tell you, my daughter, your children—keep your eye pinned on them."

"I never thought…Lucy?"

"When someone is close to you, it fogs your eyes of who they truly are." She passed a hand back and forth over her own eyes like a mesmerer testing the depth of a trance. "She has no children of her own, no?"

"She doesn't. But what would she do to my own?"

"Against you she'll turn them." She made a flipping gesture with her hand.

"Lucy? My Lucy?"

"It is certain that it will happen. Akhh."

The old woman flinched from some pain in her hip.

"Wooooo," a tremulous breath escaped her, as though she were whistling without success. The woman fell back into wide-eyed silence.

Not Lucy, Zabel thought. The air was at a nauseating standstill outside and in. Zabel went to open a window. When she looked back, the old woman seemed to have stopped breathing; her chest no longer moved. For a panic-stricken second Zabel imagined her mother was dead.

"Ma?" she asked.

"Hah," the old woman revived. Zabel asked her if she was ready to go to bed. The woman shook her head no. A couple of dogs commenced barking from across the road.

"They begin," the old woman said. "The black dogs of Satan."

"I must go," Zabel said.

"Yes, get the children."

As she drove up to Lucy's, Zabel could see a hazy white light fibrillating in the front room. From the window, Zabel made out the figures of her two boys on the carpet watching television. Where is my girl? She opened the door and flicked on the light. The boys looked up and adjusted their eyes. Nancy was curled up on the couch, sleeping with her head on Lucy's lap. On the armrest next to Lucy was a half-darned sock.

"Shhh," Lucy said, so as to not disturb the girl.

"Let's go," Zabel said.

"Your mother? Sit. How is she?"

"Fine," she answered and scooped her daughter up in her arms.

"Let's have some coffee," Lucy said and fluffed her hair up with her fingers.

"I don't want any. We have to get home."

"Sit a second. I have some good *baklava*."

Teddy stumbled toward his mother.

"No."

"I fell asleep myself," Lucy said.

Zabel said nothing else.

In bed that evening, Zabel asked Abe what he thought of Lucy. He wondered if she was speaking of the woman who she bought her eggplants from in Selma.

"Lucy Papazian?"

"No."

"Our Lucy?"

"Yes."

"What are you saying?" he asked. "Is she sick?"

"Why hasn't she married?"

"Married? Why many women haven't been married. Poor girl, lost her man in the war."

"Many women lost their men in the war."

"She was a beautiful girl. You remember how she wept?"

"Who hasn't wept?"

"Dikran was his name, wasn't it? I don't know why."

"Yes. Dikran."

"You almost lost me in the war."

"How frightened I was."

"What would you have done if I had died? Married another man?"

"A woman needs children."

"Maybe her love for her man was too great?"

Zabel wagged her head, dubious of the romantic he'd suddenly become, and said, "This is why you are crazy."

"I have to sleep now."

"I keep asking myself why."

"Ask her instead."

Lucy's parents had died in the genocide, but not before they bore a girl revered for her beauty. With green eyes and blond hair, she seemed, stepping off of the train in Fresno with the aunt who would later adopt her, a creation the gods had conjured. Not a month had passed before she met Dikran (named after an ancient king of Armenia), a tall sad-eyed schoolteacher with a big scroll moustache who recited the great Armenian poets, Sayat Nova and Siamento, by heart and made people weep at their words. One summer evening at the river's edge, she heard him read a poem by Charents and fell in love.

In the afternoons, one could see them strolling arm in arm down Kearney Boulevard toward the park where, under the shade of a tree, they would feed each other slices of apples and pears and cheese. No one had ever seen the teacher smile that way before. Six months later he was called off to war. And a year after that he was killed. He left behind only a stack of letters, written in prose so eloquent and exact that they were a kind of poetry themselves, conveying the other tragedy he'd known, that such a tender soul should ever have had to endure something as crude as war at all.

After his death, Lucy quietly retreated inside of herself. Many men approached her but she respectfully turned each away and instead lived with her aunt and kept a clean house and simple garden, toiling during the day in the packing sheds. She kept Dikran's letters in a bundle beneath her bed. On weekends she and Zabel would go to Armenian picnics together and play card games on a blanket on the grass or go hand in hand in step with each other during a dance. Zabel took pride that she was with such a beautiful girl and coveted their intimacy, as if she were a kind of suitor herself. Zabel never introduced Lucy to a man, even after she married Abe.

Only once did Lucy come close to crossing the threshold. Harry Arsen was one of the wealthiest Armenians in Fresno, and handsome as well. Everyone knew that his eye was fixed on Lucy. His only fault, if it was one at all, was that, at forty-five, he was twenty years her senior and a widower twice. Tragically, his first wife had succumbed to pneumonia barely a year after they were married, and his second passed away while giving birth to their only child, a lovely daughter. None of this seemed to bother Lucy, who felt that his age and travails had only made him more knowing and gentle-natured. An older man was perhaps what she'd been waiting for all along. Zabel was against the relationship from the start.

"Will you ever hold his heart? Haven't two other women possessed it more deeply?" or "Can a child who was nursed by another woman be your own?" or "A woman lives through her daughter. Even if he desired you, his daughter would never let it be," or "You know how unfaithful older men can be. They want younger women for play-things, that's all. Wait for another man, Lucy. Money isn't everything."

"He could be a peasant and it wouldn't matter, Zabel."

"I know, I know. But, surely there are other men in the world. Don't sell yourself so short! Oh, Lucy, do what you want, but don't be naïve."

As fate had it, Lucy's aunt had a stroke. Zabel told her, "Don't worry about this Harry for now, Lucy. If he really wants you, he'll wait. What you are doing for your aunt is what the Lord wants. This good woman saved you from an orphanage; you have no other choice but to be by her side." Three years passed before the aunt died. By then Harry had taken another woman, and Lucy had learned the nun's secret of giving to oneself by giving to others. Zabel became like a sister, and Lucy loved Zabel's children no less than she would have loved her own. And Lucy had been a godsend during the worst time in Zabel's life so far, when Zabel got cancer. Lucy was the first one by her side and the last to leave.

Thus, Zabel's mother had said something that made no sense. At one level Zabel understood this perfectly, but at another level deeper still, she doubted herself. She wondered if this doubt had been there all along and her mother had only brought it to the surface. "A cold eye," her mother had said of Lucy. And wasn't there something to it? There had always been something holier-than-thou about her.

9

FROM OUT OF NOWHERE, in the spring of 1955, the cancer popped up like toadstools on an immaculately kept lawn. Abe noticed it first, in the dark, beneath the blankets, but it had been so long since he'd last touched Zabel's breasts—after three children what was there to touch?—he couldn't remember if maybe it had always been there and he'd just forgotten. Watching Zabel fumble with a bra the next morning, he brought it up.

"I felt something beneath your breast. Last night."

"What?" She took off her bra and felt herself with a hand.

"The other one," Abe said.

Zabel probed that one. She furled her brow.

Abe asked, "What is it, Ma?"

"It's something."

"What something?"

"I don't know."

"Was it there?"

"I didn't notice it before."

"But it could've been there."

"It could have."

Abe scrutinized his own chest, digging beneath the muscle with his fingers. He could feel nothing of the sort he'd felt on Zabel.

"It's hard," she said. "And it moves."

"Maybe something popped loose," Abe conjectured. "Does it hurt?"

Zabel turned to face the dresser mirror, her back to Abe, who was sitting on the edge of a bed, still holding a sock that he planned to put on. Zabel alternated between probing and looking in the mirror at what she was probing.

Her reflection seemed to turn her body into someone else's body. Her thin neck protruded from her pinched-forward shoulders. The collarbone jutted out from either side of a cavity at the base of her throat. On the two hollowed-out bags of flesh, brown aureoles were set with a twist, and on those smudges of flesh the large nipples stood oddly pert and gnarled—the crushed butt of a cigarette. At the bottom of her stomach, covered with a thick dust of hair, flesh gathered in pleats.

"I suppose," Zabel said, "I should see the doctor."

"Maybe if you massage it for a while you will loosen it up and it will dissolve."

"No. We will go see the doctor."

"Should I call Roxie Shishmanian?"

"An American doctor."

Abe nodded his head.

They went to the American doctor. He felt her breast, took x-rays of it. He sat them down in his office and showed them on the x-ray where it was located. It was the size of an acorn, barely enough, Abe thought, to cause alarm. Still, two days later, they shoved her into surgery. Abe waited in the hospital, kneading the word *mastectomy* over and over in his brain. They would have to check the lymph nodes to see if it had spread. Before Zabel went in for surgery, Angel took the eye off from around her neck and swung it over Zabel's chest to ward off evil spirits. The hospital's air was spiked with the smell of rubbing alcohol, and the white lights fell uniformly over everything. The linoleum floor was so glossy that Angel could see her reflection in it when she stooped to test its cleanliness with a finger.

Andy came down from school to be with Abe during the surgery. In the waiting room, they paced around each other like dimwits and smoked one cigarette after another until smoke filled the room like fog. Angel sat in a chair and muttered words beneath her breath. Except for Lucy, nobody outside of the family knew about it. Thank God they had Lucy. Who else would have taken care of the kids? Zabel's face, raked over by fear, kept flashing in Abe's head. He'd never known Zabel to be speechless before; her fear had stunned her. He took her hand before the surgery and was moved by how warm and frail it felt, how defenseless she was, how much she looked like a little girl in her pale green hospital gown. Abe kept asking himself what he had done to bring this upon her. For what sin of his was she being punished? He made one and another pact with God. He vowed to be faithful in heart as well as in deed. He went so far as to vow never to argue with her again.

The surgeon, whom the American doctor had recommended, came into the waiting room three hours later. He told them that he had removed it and that within a couple of days they would know whether it had spread.

Abe felt he should ask him a question or two. But all he could do was nod his head. Angel wanted the doctor to sit for a spell, and perhaps they could all discuss it over a Turkish coffee. She asked Andy to pass this invitation on to the doctor. Andy told her that this was America, and in America doctors have things to do besides sit and have coffee.

"For now she's okay though, huh, Doctor?" Andy asked.

The doctor said that what he had told them was all that he could tell them.

Angel switched her head back and forth between the doctor and Abe, begging for an interpretation.

Andy told her in Armenian that Zabel was fine.

Angel looked at Andy suspiciously.

Angel asked in Armenian, "What about her tit?"

Abe was wondering about that too.

Andy asked about the tit.

The surgeon told them that when he'd gone inside of her, he'd found that he had to remove it entirely.

Inside of Abe, the shock was like someone broke a stick. He pictured Zabel without a breast. He remembered having a dream like that once.

Andy told Angel exactly what the doctor had told him.

The old woman didn't get it. "She has no tits?" she asked.

"She has one," Andy clarified.

"Akhh!" the woman wailed, and began swaying from side to side in her chair as though she were trying to bust loose of ropes. The doctor left the room.

"Her tit, her tit," she lamented, holding her hand out as though she were holding it up.

A nurse came in and told them that Zabel was in the recovery room. They should be able see her in a few hours.

"What did she say?" Angel asked.

They told her. This calmed the woman down. She told Abe to ask the nurse where the breast was. She looked at the nurse and smiled, as if getting the information required a degree of charm.

Abe cringed.

Andy said, "It's no more," and wiped his hands, the way Armenians did to show nothing was left.

"Where did they put it?!"

The nurse observed this exchange patiently.

"Thank you," Andy told her.

"She'll be falling in and out of sleep for the first few hours."

"Thank you."

"If you need anything, just let me know."

"We appreciate it. All of us do."

Zabel's torso was all wrapped up in bandages. Dye, the color of healthy shit, stained the fringes of the bandages and bled out onto her skin. Her face was drawn and yellow under the lamp, and a wet, amphibious smell rose up off her. Tubes trailed from her arms to upside-down bottles.

"Zabel," Abe called. Zabel moaned.

"Akhh!" her mother cried. "My child, what have they done to you?"

Her mother's voice seemed to come from a great distance. Her eyes were full of exhaustion. She struggled to open them.

"How do you feel?" Abe asked her. "Does it hurt?"

She lowered her eyes to the bandages on her chest and raised a hand to indicate something about them, then dropped it as though it had skipped her mind.

"Would you like some water?" Abe asked.

She lifted her eyes to the man at the foot of the bed. Andy thought that there wasn't much difference between the way that she usually looked at him and the way she looked at him now. He smiled.

There was a knock at the door. Lucy shuffled in with one child in her arm and the other two hanging onto her skirt.

"*Vie, vie,* my soul!"

She passed Nancy over to Abe and took Zabel's hand.

Now that Lucy was there, Andy figured this was a good time to take a break.

He stepped out without announcing it and went down to the cafeteria, where he took a stool at the counter. The pudding looked good on the glass shelf behind the counter. He asked the waitress, who was a nun, if she had tapioca, and she said they were all out. "I'll take some chocolate pudding, if you would," he told her, "and a cup of coffee."

He didn't realize how happy he was to get out of the hospital room until he took a spoonful of that smooth pudding. The whole scene up there gave him the creeps. He was suffocating in that room. Except for maybe Lucy, there wasn't a clear head among them.

Sure, what Zabel had was bad, really bad. He wasn't discounting that. But it was as though these people were waiting for an illness just to give them an excuse. You'd think that by the way they acted, nobody before had ever had such a sickness—like it had been invented just for them. There was something sick inside of her sickness, maybe even sicker than the sickness itself, and there was no knife that could reach it, no pill, no flood of radiation that could contain it.

Unexpectedly, the pudding and coffee wiped him out. When he stepped into the elevator, his fatigue was suddenly awesome. I need one of these beds myself, he thought. Then, what the hell, he went and found one in an unused room a few doors down from where Zabel lay. He let his mind exhale, relax. He let himself drift outside of that room, outside of that hospital, outside of that life altogether. He let it drift back to college, to the beach and the ocean and its quiet, muscular waves. His heart became reverential whenever he thought about how deep and vast was the ocean's character. In college, whenever he was overwhelmed with work, he'd drive down to the beach and park his car and listen and look out onto the ocean. He hated nothing more than the small chatter of the world, and imagining a big oceanic force mercilessly swallowing up the whole chattering world relieved him. In fact, it kind of pleased him. Maybe what was going on in that hospital room, he thought, had to do with the opposite of that bigness. Maybe what disappointed him was that everywhere he turned these days, all he saw was smallness.

For the first two weeks after she got home, Zabel lay in bed like a corpse. Except she could complain. Some old medicine lady told her that in the old country when people got sick the way she did, they would eat almonds. Her mother confirmed this. Abe went and got her a potato sack full of them and set it beside their bed. Every now and then she'd reach into the sack for almonds, place them in her mouth, and chew on them as slowly as though she were chewing taffy. For ten days she couldn't shit. Nobody thought to put two and two together and tell her to stay off the nuts. She said she was going to explode from the buildup. The pressure was so intense that she was afraid the stitches up above would burst. Lucy gave her an enema as Zabel lay curled up on the bathroom floor. *"Jesus Christos,"* Zabel whimpered. It dribbled out, black and hard, in small licorice balls.

In her presence, no one talked about the missing tit. Not even Angel. As though the tit weren't missing at all. They worked so hard to avoid talking about the missing tit that, in a way, the tit was all they talked about.

It seemed inconceivable in the eyes of some mothers from church that a woman who had borne three children should be stricken with such a disease. Others, mostly spinsters, believed just the opposite: the tit that was used to being full was more susceptible to such disease when empty, the way rust collects on the inside of a drained pipe. For the men, the thought of a woman without a breast, if they dared think about it at all, filled them with a combination of revulsion and pity.

Lucy moved into their house, more or less. She made meals and kept the house clean and tended to Zabel and Abe as best she could. Nancy, who was only a year old, was virtually grafted to her hip. As was his habit whenever faced with great difficulties, Abe took to tinkering with his stepfather's Model T, which he'd been restoring since he'd come back from the war. The car was located in the back of the barn, where it was dark, and even when he threw open the doors it was no light in which to handle small automotive parts. Still, Abe liked to work on it in such a dim and lonely niche, away from the eyes of others who no doubt would judge his project as a bit of tomfoolery if they saw just how much energy he'd expended, and to what end? In fact, according to Andy, it was the impossibility of finishing the project that attracted Abe to it in the first place. Every so often Abe would wander into Zabel's room, his shirt smudged with grease, and ask her if she needed anything. Zabel would rattle off her complaints. Abe would nod his head and walk away, intending to address each and every particular. But no sooner did he try to recall what her complaints were than he forgot them.

Over and over again, he told Lucy, "Zabel wanted me to do something, but I can't remember what."

"Don't worry, go back to your car, Abe. I'll take care of it, you poor soul."

Zabel wouldn't speak of taking the big bandage off. In Zabel's mind, as long as the big bandage was attached, so might be the tit. She also kept it on lest anyone think she'd healed before she had, which—as long as the threat of its reappearance loomed over her—might be never. Because Zabel refused to change it, the bandage was spotted and stained like an infant's bib. Lucy pleaded with her.

"Just close your eyes, Zabel, and I will do it."

Zabel agreed, but no one—not Abe, not the children, no one—should visit her until she strapped the bandage back in place. Zabel trembled and whimpered as Lucy unpeeled the bandage and re-dressed the wound.

After two weeks the pain began to subside significantly. Her consciousness of the missing tit began to crop up. She didn't know which she dreaded more—the pain or what it made transparent in its absence. She thought she'd let her hand get familiar with it first. She reached up under her blouse, under the bandage, and pressed her fingers on the flesh next to one of the small gauze bandages, which were taped over the stitches. She felt nothing. She stroked a finger over the area, the way a person befriends a cat.

From the bathroom where he was shaving, Abe heard Zabel shriek. He dropped the razor and ran into the bedroom. She was crying hysterically.

"What is it? Does it hurt?" he asked.

"No," she said, but her face was full of fear. She caught her breath and said, "When I touch here," she pointed a trembling finger at her missing tit, "it's over here that I feel." She indicated her belly.

"How can that be?" Abe thought she was losing her mind.

"Akhh, Akhh!" Zabel cried.

"I'll go get Roxie," he said.

Abe rushed out the door.

Zabel sat up in bed, trembling. She unbuttoned her blouse and slipped it off her shoulders. Once again she felt the area with her fingers. The sensation again referred to her belly. It was as though her body had been disassembled and put back together hastily. She could feel the immensity of her loss. And though she shook from fear, she wanted to see it all now. She peeled back the tape. The swatch of gauze flapped open.

From the far side of the barn, the two boys—the little girl was with Lucy—heard the cry and looked up from some snails they had sprinkled with salt. Young as they were, they understood from the deep warbling sound of the sobbing that grief, not pain, was the root. They knew that their mother had to be left alone. On the ground in front of them, the snails bubbled and spit.

Months later, back at school, Andy would wonder about Zabel's suffering, the nature of suffering itself, the way that Zabel was already using her cancer to master those around her. Ever since Zabel left the hospital, everyone had jumped to their feet to meet her smallest requests, even when these requests had no bearing on her illness, no correlation to her pain. He remembered Abe saying to him, "Zab can't take no pressure no more. All of us, we gotta make sure she don't get taxed. Whatever she says, just let it be." And Zabel seemed to be saying, "Do this, do that, *or else!*" *Or else* what? The answer, to Andy, was obvious. *Or else* the cancer would return. It was like Zabel meant the family to understand, "My suffering could've been any of yours!" or worse, "I suffered so that you wouldn't have to!"

From there on out it was like the family owed her a debt. "Poor Zabel," he'd heard over and over again, but the fact was that the subtraction of the tit had added to her might. Debt. It was an invisible force equal to any batallion, and as long as there was the chance that her cancer might return, the family was left holding a note that could never be fully settled. In some ways, Andy thought, Zabel has been waiting for this cancer her entire life.

10

ANDY HAD BEEN IN THE DESERT OF PERRIS for two months now, and not once had Abe made it down as planned. First Abe couldn't go on account of that spinning sickness. Then the kids got sick, the barn needed repairs and Zabel's mother had to see the doctor. One thing after another. Andy would have made peace with working the Perris patch alone if only Abe and Zabel hadn't been hassling him to help with the raisin harvest too. As if all that weren't insult enough, Zabel called him once a week, wanting to know where their dough was going, down to the last nickel.

"We're right on budget," he told her.

"Budget? Since when do we have a budget?"

"Talk to your husband about it, Zabel. He'll fill you in."

"Where are you going to sell the tomatoes?" Zabel asked.

"I got a broker down here. Relax."

"Don't tell *me* to relax. You relax. Broker?"

"The guy who sells the fruit."

"How much does this so-called broker make?"

"A dime a box."

"Ten cents?!"

This kind of thing. Back and forth. It got to be that Andy felt like a hired hand, a kind of farm manager.

The tomatoes, though, they were coming in nice, heavy in number, and plump. They were so pretty, Andy was loath to leave them behind.

He told Abe, "Let's get the grapes down early so I can get back down to harvest these tomatoes."

"Don't want to get 'em down too early or they'll fry. How early?"

"Once the sugar is there. That's all."

67

Abe said, "Remember, *this* harvest is our bread and butter."

"You remember too, *this* harvest is our future."

Abe grunted.

"All I want is a little breathing room, Abe. As it is, I'm gonna be scrambling back and forth."

"Like I've got breathing room?"

"I don't know what you got. Anyway, Abe, turn the water off and work up the ground. That'll kick the sugar up a point more."

Abe said, "I'll give Gabe a call. We got our regular Filipinos."

"Weather?"

"Clear as a bell."

Abe worked the soil up the next day. He hooked the discs up to the big John Deere and dragged them down the rows to loosen up the dirt that had caked up and gotten crusty. Since the episode with his ear, he'd been shy of being on the tractor. He was afraid that whatever mechanism got jarred loose might get jarred loose again. Sitting on one of these things, he thought, could be dangerous to a man's health. He could feel his balls vibrate and wondered if, after so many years driving a tractor, they hadn't gotten thrown off balance too. Not that he needed them in his present situation, married to Zabel. In that way the question was moot, especially since Zabel's surgery. But if, say, the opportunity to get laid were there, would he have the means to take advantage of it? The answer wasn't obvious anymore.

Fifteen years ago he would have in a lick. In a lick, hah, fucking in a lick. His thoughts strayed back to his stays in Paris, to evenings on leave from assignment, when he had ambled down her winding yellow streets, drunk. He remembered the first time, sitting on a wooden bench overlooking the Seine with a whore whose name he couldn't remember but that started with an S—Sylvie, or Sonia, or was it Lucinda? Whether he had trembled from the cold or his nervousness he didn't know, but he remembered the cold flow of the river down below and the warm puff of air beneath her wool skirt as he fumbled his hand to the wiry hair and coil of flesh like a rooster's neck. She took him by the hand up the steps that were rank with the smell of magnolias, steps that whinnied beneath his feet like a horse, and then there was a draft of pink light from the bottom of her door, and he remembered how his teeth had chattered when she stuck the key in the door and pushed it open. And although he was muscular and fit then, proud of the body that the army had shaped, he was surprised at how puny, awkward and uncharted he felt navigating the nameless routes of her body. Then a lance of light from the street lamp outside cut across her face, and he saw a glint of pain in her raw, brown eyes, and suddenly something took hold, sparked in him a cold animality not unlike that which he'd known in the throes of combat. He exploded inside of her after barely a second, then lay on her bed in a sort of ecstatic shock that dissolved into anxiety in short order. He stumbled out of her bed and searched for his pants on the ground, for his shoes, as if he were look-ing for some escape hatch in a smoke-filled room.

"Fume toi?" she asked, and struck a match.

He was surprised at how mundane her chalky body looked, lying there on the bed. He was glad when she blew the match out, he was thankful for the dark again, he wished it were even darker, so that she might disappear altogether.

He tossed a few balled-up bills on the bed.

"Merci," she said then. "Come again."

To his surprise, he did come again, and—who can help saying it— again, and again, and again. How many times had he slept with Lucinda, Sylvie, Sonia…what the fuck's the name matter anyways? he now wondered. What he remembered was that he'd felt like he couldn't get enough. At times he had been thankful for the war because it had brought to the surface this hunger in him, so much so that he was sad-dened by the thought of being called back home. Maybe he had already known that this first chance might also be his last to mess around.

Zabel had come into his life just before he left. She had plans for them, and the fact that she had plans, had direction, made their mar-riage a matter of fate more than choice. He'd never had that same fire for Zabel, he'd never been able to work up that crazy appetite for sex with her. Truth was, ever since they'd been married he'd gotten more pleasure from the memory of sex than from sex itself. He left the hunger behind somewhere in the streets of Paris, but not before he'd gotten his fair share. Now nobody could ever say he hadn't fucked around. He'd fucked around plenty, brother. He never grew fond of Lucinda the way so many of the other GIs did with their whores, he didn't once take her out to dinner, nor did he buy her a trinket when he left. No, his goal was to get his money's worth until it hardly became worth it to her anymore.

He had started on the big block, and by late afternoon he'd ploughed through fifty rows. Enough for the day. Zabel had scheduled a six o'clock appointment for her mother with Doctor Tahan in town. The old lady was having trouble with her breathing again and Zabel insisted she see a real doctor.

Strange, because lately Abe was having some breathing problems of his own—a constriction in his chest, a shortness of breath like he was suffocating, so that he had to stop whatever it was he was doing and lie down or else he was going to face-down faint. It was as if something was boxing him in. Maybe all that smoking was catching up with him. Age too. He couldn't understand how that damn stepfather of his had stayed healthy as a horse all those years. All that rage should've killed him off before he was thirty. But no, it was like his rage was the source of his strength.

He pulled the tractor into the yard and shut it down. With the machine beneath him dead, he sat there for a spell. There was a good strong breeze, and in the slanting orange light the dogs napped tranquilly under the elm. They looked so comfy that for a moment he wished he were a dog. The old mutt took him in for a second, then lay his head back and sighed deeply, luxuriously. Seriously, he thought, these dogs have one hell of a life. As he stepped down off the tractor and slowly passed under the tree, his desire to be a dog struck him as no joke. "That's how fed up I am," he said to himself, but he had no idea why he felt that way, why he said it. He was this close to claiming a patch of grass alongside those mutts when all of a sudden he was brought to a standstill by a commotion of leaves up above. He looked up. The leaves on the tree were alive, all achatter. Like they were talking to him. Huh? He wondered what they wanted him to hear. The voices got louder and louder, enormous, until he found himself stuck, as though sound had become material and required some effort to pass through. He reached for a rake that was leaning against the tree. More leaves fell and the few at his feet rushed off as though they were in a hurry to get somewhere, to leave this place behind.

Zabel had screamed at him from the kitchen window not once but three times now. He needed to shower before they went to the doctor's. "What is the man doing out there?" she asked herself out loud. "ABE, ABE!" And what's with that rake? It's like all of a sudden he's forgotten what to do with it. The orange sunlight saturated his body. He's getting old, she thought. This is what old men do. "ABE! ABE!"

Teddy was wondering what all the shouting was about.

"Akhh, Teddy! Bring your father," she told him. "What is he doing out there?"

Teddy didn't know where "out there" was, much less what he was doing out there.

"Where?" he asked.

"With the dogs," she sneered.

When Teddy turned the corner of the house into the long copper light, he saw his father standing beneath the tree. His eyes looked closed. Teddy wondered, Do people sleep standing up? As he moved closer, he saw his father's eyelids flutter. This made him freeze. Then Abe opened his eyes and gestured for Teddy to approach. His son walked up to him not knowing what to expect, kind of scared. Abe turned Teddy around, so that he stood facing the gilt light with him, and put his hand on his boy's chest. Teddy could feel his father's hand tremble. He felt a kind of madness in the air.

"Wait," his father said.

For what? Who are we waiting for? Teddy thought. Everybody's here.

11

MAYBE THE FACT THAT ZABEL and Abe's first child, Teddy, was born premature gave him license for excess that would have otherwise never been tolerated. Until Teddy was five, his mother protected him from any possible peril, however remote. The devotion he received from Zabel was unusual, even for Armenian mothers. She held him by her side and claimed to have gone without sleep for an entire year, so assiduous was her watch over him. She breast-fed him until he was three years old. Each step he took in development—however normal, like cooing or crawling or mumbling "da da"—occasioned a cake. A simple wobble across the room was introduced with the kind of histrionics usually reserved for circus acrobats.

"Watch him, watch him," she would demand of any audience when he started to walk. "Bravo, my soul! Bravo."

Nobody could have guessed by looking at the sickly baby Teddy was that by the age of five he'd grow to be a fanatical little suzerain who ran the household into an emotional shambles. He derived satisfaction from watching an adult's face freeze from horror or wither in exasperation. Witness Teddy sitting naked in the middle of the road. Teddy using his own poop to make mud pies. He didn't play with toys so much as toy with people.

When Andy could come home on the weekends, Zabel's first complaint was about that kid.

"Akhh, Andy!" Zabel cried. "You don't know how he worried us this week. Teddy almost buried himself alive. What things we have to go through while you're at school!" she said, insinuating that his being at school was the cause of these problems.

"Buried himself. Teddy?"

Teddy lowered his head in shame.

"He dug a hole and covered himself with the dirt."

"I can't believe it. Teddy, what were you trying to do in that hole?"

"Hide."

"I can see that. But that's a waste of what, Teddy?"

Teddy tugged on Andy's shirt so that they could get on with the day.

"We're not goin' nowhere, Teddy, till we get this issue here settled. Now, what's being wasted when you bury yourself in a hole and stuff like that?"

"'Sential power."

"That's right. That kind of motion is a waste of your essential power. You see, Teddy, it's like I keep reminding you. There's two ways to use your essential power. You can build things up, like the great ballplayers do. Who are some of those great ballplayers, Teddy?"

"Ty Cobb?"

"That's one. How about another?"

"Babe Ruth."

"That's right. And the other thing you can do with your essential power, which is what you did when you dug that hole, is tear things down. Can we see eye to eye there, Teddy?"

Teddy shrugged his shoulders.

"Well, there's no question about it, Teddy. Now the other thing is, when was this?"

"Two days ago," Abe said.

"Well, two days ago was two days ago."

"But we couldn't find him for three hours."

"Two days ago is in the past. One thing about the past is when it's past, there's no use talking about it anymore. Isn't that right, Teddy?"

Teddy nodded his head.

Abe and Zabel looked at each other, confused.

Teddy would follow him around like a puppy the entire weekend. Side by side they'd work, Andy chatting with Teddy the whole time and telling him there was no way he could get the truck fixed without Teddy's help, or that the tractor wouldn't run without the energy Teddy provided by sitting there next to him. If Teddy looked like he meant to throw a pancake across the table at his sister, Andy would remind him that Teddy's essential powers would be wasted by such behavior.

"It's a shame, Teddy, because we have a hell of a lot of work to do."

Teddy looked at the pancake in his grubby little hand, visibly weighing whether it was worth it. Zabel started to grab his arm, and Andy raised his voice to stop her.

"It's up to you, Teddy."

Teddy's eyes narrowed and his face screwed up.

"Let's go, Teddy. We got building up to do."

Zabel was suspicious. "What is he telling that child?"

"Hardly matters, Ma. Howevers you turn it, it works."

"What do you mean, it works? Wash your mouth out!"

"It's a fact. My brother's got a way with that kid."

"I don't like him hearing these things—essential power. What kind of talk is that?"

"It's just a way for him to get the kid to think twice about what he's about to do. That's the way I see it, if you're up to reasoning."

"There's nothing in the Bible about essential power."

"I suppose you're right there."

She shook a finger in the air and said, "No, this is the language of something else."

Abe knew where Zabel was going with this line of thinking.

"Maybe he picked it up in school. Maybe he got some reverse psychology or something going."

"You notice that the child goes mad after Andy leaves."

Abe shook his head in confusion.

Zabel said, "Maybe he's teaching Teddy things when he's here. You see how he treats me in front of him. Tells me to keep my mouth shut! Who is he, anyway?"

"What are you saying? That Andy shouldn't come down on weekends to help with the farm?"

"I don't know."

"Are you nuts? What do you mean, you don't know? Don't stir the kettle, Zabel. The kid's already driving three hundred miles a week to get here and go back. Give him any reason to quit and he'll run with it."

"He's on vacation at this so-called school. What are you talking about?"

"All I'm saying is there's no way I can do without him right now, so don't agitate the situation."

"How about the way he agitates my child?"

"You take care of it, Zabel, just don't say a word of it to Andy."

Zabel began to take the children over to her mother's on the weekend. If he was naughty at home, Teddy became a diablo when he was away. He especially relished tinkering with his grandmother's mind. When the old lady slept in the afternoon, he'd enlist the help of his sister in going *"ooooOOooo,"* the sound of spooks, just outside the window of her room. More than a few times Angel found earthworms churning at the bottom of a glass of *tahn*. Since spirits already surrounded Angel, she was hard put to isolate Teddy from the others.

Andy kind of missed Teddy.

"Where's the kids?" he asked Abe.

"She decided to get them out of our hair for the weekend so we could get more done around here."

"That's crazy, Abe. They don't get in the way of nothin'."

"That's not how she sees it."

"I don't know, Abe, it doesn't add up. Why don't she at least bring 'em back here to sleep?"

"She figures her mother doesn't get enough of them, I guess."

Andy stopped his work on the tractor to try to figure it out.

"Let's not talk about it."

"I'm just saying."

"Whatever Zabel wants."

"She's the chief."

"You got to get it—these aren't your kids."

"I'm their uncle."

"Sometimes Zabel wonders what you are."

Andy was confused. He always imagined everybody agreed that he was a good influence on the kids.

Andy said, "To be frank with you, Abe, I think Zabel's too tied up with them kids, especially Teddy. It's okay when he was a baby and all. But he's getting to a point where he needs men around."

"Men?" Abe laughed darkly.

The air went flat for a spell.

"Fuck men."

Where the hell did that come from? Andy wondered. It sent a chill up his arms. Abe said it how some men would say "Fuck women" after they'd had a few drinks. Fuck men? How can a person say that about his own kind?

Abe was a little surprised to have uttered it himself. The conversation triggered for Abe a memory. Catherine, his younger sister, was graduating from high school. The family, all nine of them, were ready to go to the ceremony, when all of a sudden Yervant—Andy's father and Abe's stepfather, a man who liked to put on the drama—claimed he was too sick to move, that he had a ferocious headache. In bed he tossed and turned. "Leave me alone," he cried, "or else *you are going to kill me!*" Finally their mother, Calipse, after much pleading, convinced Yervant to get up and drive them there. The whole way and into the ceremony he kept on about how they were going to kill him. Never mind that this was Catherine's day. The girls were crying and Calipse was trying to settle everyone down.

They got through it the way folks do a funeral. Afterwards, they went home to a spread of homemade ice cream and chocolate cake Calipse had prepared that morning. Abe and his sister Betty got in a little scuffle about the piece of cake they were handed—his was bigger than hers, vice versa, kid stuff. Out of nowhere, Yervant erupts and stomps out of the room. The family goes blank from fear. From down the hallway, Abe can hear Yervant threatening to smash Abe's skull in. Abe bolts out the door. When he looks back, his stepdad is coming after him with a baseball bat. On bareback, Abe shoots off on Manoug, their horse.

Men? His first father went off and got killed when he was a child. His second father nearly killed him.

It was only a matter of time before Teddy caught on that he was being kept away from Andy on purpose. After that, his tricks went from subtle to blatant, until they were as obvious as if a torturer were screwing bolts into your knees. Their weekend visits to Angel's house ended when Teddy, with a stick, carried a dead rattlesnake through the field and set it at his grandmother's feet as a kind of pagan offering.

"He makes my heart jump," she told Zabel.

Teddy glowered at her from across the room.

"Enough then," Zabel announced. "Let's go. Give your grandmother a hug," she told the kids.

12

ANDY GOT TO FRESNO ON AUGUST 7. The place was in a shambles, big and small equipment out of order, as though disposable, abandoned where it was last used. Abe, he was nervous, distracted, focused on stupid details instead of the big picture in front of him.

"What's goin' on here, Abe?"

"Seen that fat crowbar anywheres?"

No, Abe wasn't himself. Then again, it'd been such a long time since Abe was Abe that Andy was starting to think that maybe he never was. How long do you have to wait for a man to come around before admitting that he never might?

These were questions Andy hadn't the time to answer, really. Only ask. The crop was coming on strong. They called their crew boss, Gabe, and together planned to start the next day.

Just before sunrise, three scrapyard cars pulled up perpendicular to the vines.

"They're here," Andy said. From out of the dust, pickers stumbled out of cars wearing baseball caps, long-sleeve shirts and dungarees caked with dirt.

"Shabby lookin' outfit," Abe said. "*Braceros*. I don't see Gabe's van."

"Let's get out there."

When they reached the corner, the pickers were sharpening their knives, getting ready to go in. Abe didn't want anyone to start before his crew boss was recognized and the chain of authority, starting with Abe, was in order. Abe said, "Where the hell is Gabe?" to an older picker who sat squat beside the standpipe. *"No sé,"* he said, and just kept working his knife in little circles on a rectangular palm-size stone.

"Buenos dias." Gabe walked up from behind them.

"Didn't see your van, Gabe."

"Cheby more better."

They all three regarded the car, then turned to business.

"Since we're all standin' here," Andy said, "might as well start on this end, Gabe."

"Okay, *Patrón*."

"And I don't want any bullshit out there, Gabe," Abe said. "This crew doesn't look like what you'd call hand-picked."

"No look good, *pero* pick good."

The crew boss whistled.

In the anemic light they paired up, two men to a row, one on each side of the vine. They each dropped to a knee and inched down the dim quarter-mile corridor. Abe could hear the workers chatter, he could hear the rush of leaves, the snap of canes, he watched the whole vine shake and saw bunches come flopping out from beneath the canopy. Gradually the terraced row started brimming with grapes. Though he'd gone through the same routine, the same age-old method of harvesting since he was a boy, what was going on out there suddenly struck him as strange.

At nine the foreman whistled. It was lunchtime. From out of the row they came, blowing snot from their noses. They grabbed their sack lunches from the cars and peeled off to shady spots. Abe told his brother that he felt like he was kind of losing control of the crews, the only way of putting how he felt.

"Or just losing control, period. What's gotten into you, Abe?" Andy asked.

Abe nudged his hat up an inch, wiped his brow with a bandanna. "Nothin'. Just..." He made a vague gesture with his hands.

For a full hour after lunch the pickers lugged forward, fighting against the fatigue that came at them in waves. By eleven the sun glowered overhead, the pickers were shellacked with sweat, and everyone was getting a little punchy from the heat. A tractor rolled by, pulling a trailer piled high with trays, a little faster than necessary.

"YOU GODDAMN SPICKS, SLOW THE FUCK DOWN!!!" Abe shouted.

The driver's response seemed to be the casual cloud of dust that wafted over them in the tractor's wake. Which pissed Abe off even more.

"Settle down, Abe," Andy said.

"What?!" Abe said it the way an old man, hard of hearing and all torn up by bitterness, might say it. "They're leaving all sort of grapes on the vines. Look at 'em! They're dancing too fast."

"Maybe you're dancing a little *slower* than usual, Abe. But let's me and you take a peek."

Andy started up a half-picked row. He pushed aside the canes and poked his head up under the canopy.

"Clean."

Abe had his own head beneath a canopy two vines down.

"Hows about this?!"

Abe was pointing to a bunch stuck between the canes at the crown.

Andy laughed. "Jesus, Abe, you'd need tweezers to get to them. No crew working by the tray is gonna get that. You can't expect that."

"The hells."

Andy grabbed Abe by the arm.

"Abe. Leave the boys be." Andy's voice was calm, strong.

Abe grumbled.

"I'll handle things out here. Go check that sifter. You need to be around equipment now, not men." Andy released his arm, patted Abe on the back. "Go on, Abe."

Abe put his hands behind his head, like he was catching his breath, and shuffled off to the barn.

If Andy hadn't been so dead tired at the end of the day, he might've had a chat with his brother. They had a lot of land to look after, and this was no time for Abe to lose his head. What was obvious was that Abe didn't like handling the vineyard on his own and he needed Andy around to lighten his load mentally as well as physically. Not that Andy could blame him. It'd drive anybody, Jesus H. Christ himself, loony to be left with Zabel and her mother. On the one hand, Andy pitied his brother, but on the other hand, Abe had brought it all upon himself. Wasn't Abe the one who said the farm wouldn't support two families? Still, they could have expanded closer to home. That way Andy could be two places at once without it tearing him to pieces.

"Abe," Andy said the next morning. "I slept on it last night, and I figure we need to reevaluate this situation down south."

Zabel listened over her shoulder from the stove where she'd just nudged some sliced *soujouk* sausage off a cutting board into a cast-iron pan.

"It's takin' an awful lot out of me, that's for sure," Abe said.

"What kind of crop you think I'm farmin' down south, Abe? The kind that grows on its own? I've been busting my balls down there."

"Clean your mouth out," Zabel hissed. She beat the eggs in a bowl and poured it over the *soujouk*. The eggs bubbled up in the *soujouk*'s paprika grease.

"Pardon my French."

"Why you insistin' it?" Abe asked.

"I'm not insistin' nothin'. When we're done here, done down south, we'll bring everything back to headquarters and see where we go from there. This is the decision I've come to. In the meantime, everybody relax, and if need be, I'll take care of both of these harvests on my own."

With a spatula, Zabel slapped helpings onto their plates. The men dug into the food without another word. When Andy was finished, Zabel said, "When did you get so important that you could all by yourself make these decisions?"

"When nobody else can make it for himself. That's when."

A quirky smile mounted on Abe's face, like he was relieved to see Andy taking control of the situation, like he was some fatherless kid watching his older brother put his insufferable mother in her place.

The Mexicans pulled up into the yard.

"Looks like the boys are here."

Abe popped out of his chair. "All right," he said, "then that's settled. Let's get us to work."

Abe got in under the vines with his clippers, side by side with the pickers whom he'd cursed for no reason the day before. His transformation was so swift that Andy stood in awe of his own powers of persuasion. Maybe that little confrontation at the breakfast table, he thought, was just what the doctor ordered. Today, though, it was Andy who had the disposition to curse.

"Gabe," he called. The crew boss came out from the row. "Let's us two walk this row."

Gabe followed Andy in.

"What do you think about these trays, Gabriel?"

Gabe stooped down, picked a bunch up by the stem, twirled it in his fingers, and laid it gently down again, with two hands, the way a person puts a baby to bed.

"Linda."

"Damn rights they're pretty. But I'm not askin' your opinion of my daughter, Gabriel."

Andy hated to come out and say the obvious. He wanted every situation to be a kind of learning experience. He'd rather make the evidence clear, then let the crew boss come to a summation of his own.

Gabe stomped some dirt from his boots as if he was making to stroll out of the field.

"What do you think of the spacing here, Gabe?" This was piecework. If the trays were too closely set, the workers would use this as an excuse to spread the grapes on more trays than were needed per vine. More trays equaled more money for the pickers.

"What you mean, *Patrón*?"

"This is your regular ten-ton year, ain't it?"

"Looks to me. Ten, eleven ton."

"Then why you spacin' em like twenty ton to an acre out there?"

"Ooohhh."

"'Ooohhh' is right, Gabe. What do you think, I just got off the banana boat?"

"Nooooo."

"How much I pay you?"

"The way your brother say, five cent."

"That's decent money for piecework, ain't it?"

"The way you say."

"Good price, huh?"

"Sí."

"Well, we're going to have to renegotiate if this keeps up."

"Nooooo." Gabe shook his head aggressively.

"Then tell the swampers to allow a couple of feet between the trays, not a couple of inches."

"I tell 'em."

"Thank you, Gabriel."

It wasn't a bad idea to get in there with the crews, to keep them in line by example, but Abe was going overboard. One set of eyes, Andy's, wasn't enough to keep track of the mess of pickers they had out there.

From a distance, Andy watched Abe shove a canopy open, hold it there with a shoulder, crouch into position, cradle a bunch in one hand and with the other clip it from the stem, and before the bunch even hit the tray, damn near repeat it again. Without ever taking his eye off the vine, he'd clean it in what seemed a matter of seconds with that certain deftness, not just speed, that a man who picks his own grapes has over even the most experienced worker.

When Andy reached his brother, he shucked the hat off his head and tossed it to him.

"Here. You're going to fry that egg of yours." The heat was ungodly, excessive. "We're lookin' at three figures today," Andy said.

Abe threw his arm over his shoulder and slapped something on the back of his neck.

"Okay, Abe. Guess I'll go check on the crew across the road. Figure we need to keep an eye on things."

"Good enough."

"Guess you got these boys covered."

Abe looked down the row and nodded. The dirt was weighed down with grapes, already beginning to soften under the countless kilowatts of light.

They finished just past noon on the fourth day. Damn near five hundred tons of grapes lay in mounds on the terrace. The air around the vineyard was thick, syrupy with baking raisins. This accomplishment, which might otherwise have warranted a hearty meal and a few shots of whiskey, barely went acknowledged. Andy had to hit the road for another harvest ten hours away.

"Why don't you stay a couple of days?" Abe said.

"Naw. Better get going."

Though he'd been patient with his brother, somewhere along the line some resentment had seeped in. Now that the harvest was over, he could feel it. As taxing as the tomato harvest was looking, part of him couldn't wait to get out to the desert again.

"Nothin's gonna run away down there," Abe said.

Maybe I'm the one who is running away, Andy thought. From Zab, Abe, the farm. That's bad, Andy thought. When a man has an urge to flee his own land, something's wrong.

"Take care of the home front, Abe. I'll see you, God willing, in a few weeks."

The last hour's stretch of road was starting to blur, Andy was so beat. When he got back to the motel, he unloaded his bags in the room and sat on the edge of the bed, too exhausted to sleep. He decided to drive to Ike's and have a drink or two.

A great big silver moon lay a luminous silt over everything. There wasn't a single car in front of the bar when he drove up, no trucks across the road, nothing. The sign on the roof, it was missing. Had Ike closed the place down? He tugged on the door, half expecting it wouldn't open. Ike was sitting at the bar watching TV. Andy wondered whether Ike had been robbed, or maybe he'd lost his license.

Ike poured him a beer and set it in front of him just as he sat down.

"What's up, Ike? Things sure are dead around here."

"Always that way after the Santa Anas. How'd you make out?"

"Well, we laid 'em down. Now we'll wait and see."

The two men were talking about two different things.

"Lot worse than last year. Damn near threw this building on its butt," Ike said.

"What are we talking about here, Ike?"

"Santa Anas, what else?"

"What's the Santa Anas, Ike?"

Ike looked at Andy like he was the poor bastard who was the last to know his wife had cheated on him.

"Wind."

"Wind?"

"Andy, where you been?"

"Fresno."

"Came through here five days ago something vicious. Knocked out electricity. Tore everything apart."

"Don't fuck with me, Ike."

"I wish I was, partner."

Andy thought of the tomatoes. Ike was thinking the same thing.

"Probably them tomatoes of yours, too."

"Everywhere?"

"Like I said."

Back in the car, Andy could see himself shaking. He tried to calm himself. Had to be Ike was exaggerating. Andy couldn't fathom what such a wind might do to tomatoes, couldn't get a picture in his mind. What kind of winds was Ike talking about? A hurricane would've had to reel through here to do the damage he'd claimed. A fucking twister. He began to see signs of tumult he hadn't noticed on the drive to the bar. Tumbleweeds were climbing over each other against walls of buildings. He noticed sand clumped in the gutters, sand spread across the road. In spots, he heard his tires pick up loosened gravel.

Then he remembered the conversation he'd had with Jules. The words "trellises" and "weather" boomed in his heart. Here he was, thinking how clever he had been to jump ahead of the market. Shit! He drove up the back side of the acreage. By the light of the moon, he started to make things out. Harvesting buckets littered the entire yard. He cut the engine, got out of the truck full of fear, as if some rabid dog were near. Stakes were strewn over the silvery stretch of dirt. Everything was nightmarishly on the ground, almost buried with dirt. He dropped to his knees and picked up a vine in his hand. Sand shed off it in sheets. He could tell from its weight that tomatoes were still attached. He picked a tomato. It was wet. The skin broken. He threw it aside. He heard it plop somewhere in the dark. He stood up and started limping up the row. Beneath his boots he could feel tomatoes squish. "SON OF A BITCH!" he screamed at the moon that glowed lavishly overhead. He screamed it again, this time to whatever was beyond the moon, to whatever cruel being was behind it. What would Zabel say, what would Zabel do? He could see her pulling her hair out from its roots, and his brother's face go dumb. "Abe, it wasn't my fault!" He could hear Zabel: "Akhh, akhh! Akhh! Akhh!"

Andy hadn't the energy nor the will to make it back to the motel. He didn't want to sleep in a bed that night, the motel's or another. He felt as though he didn't deserve to sleep in a bed at all anymore. He was so tired he was nauseated. He lay down in the cab, curled up the way children do, and fell instantly asleep. He slogged around in muddy dreams.

Twice during the night he woke with the hope that, just maybe, what had happened out there had simply been a bad dream.

In the morning, the land was something to behold. Andy was less pained than astonished by what it had undergone. It reminded him of the Bible, of Moses and all those plagues. It looked like a tractor had first gone berserk down the rows, and after that the acreage had been crop dusted over and over and over again. Walking over it, he kept shaking his head and repeating to himself, What a shame. He could smell the tomatoes fermenting in the fields. He could hear flies sizzling. Tomatoes were barely visible under the mounds of ashy dirt. Other tomatoes were clumped together, getting shelter from each other. Tomatoes were all over, busted open, bleeding, naked and veined and exposed to the sun and flies that had now come to feast on them in droves. He almost wanted a camera to document it so that some day his kids could see what their father had lived through, what kind of fiasco he'd survived down south. He thought about getting some Mexicans in there to pick up what they could for slop for the pigs. But it didn't take a banker to calculate that with the cost of labor, he'd barely break even. A few stakes somehow managed to stay bravely upright. He went and fetched a dozen buckets and started to pick what tomatoes he could off the vines.

Andy picked all morning. Never mind what he was going to do with them. It was something that he had to do, even if it was no more effective than panning for gold. He took extra care with what he did find, brushing it clean and shining it up against his shirt. He filled the buckets and set them next to the shack. When he'd filled them all, he sat, studying the tomatoes' ruby color, shapeliness. He picked out the prettiest ones and lined them up on a wooden board, sliced them into quarters with a pocketknife and proceeded to make lunch of them. The tomatoes were good and sweet, which made the situation all the more bitter. He munched and laughed. Fuck, he thought, these tomatoes taste good. FUCKING EXCELLENT TOMATOES! He pitied them, himself. He sobbed dryly. Over his shoulder he slung a big fat tomato. It landed with a "wank" on the shack's tin roof. He stood, assumed the position of a pitcher. "Fuck you," he hollered and hurled the tomato at the shack "blam." Again. And again "blam, blam"— juice was going everywhere. The side of the shack was all tomato juice and seeds. He emptied three buckets of tomatoes that way, until he was exhausted, until he couldn't see straight through the tears any-more. The senselessness of spending a better part of the day picking the very tomatoes he was throwing away hit him like a joke. Same as that guy—what was his name?—who can never get the rock up to the top of the hill, whose whole life was spent trying to get it up there. Just like him.

Andy pulled into the drive near midnight. Not expecting him, Abe heard the dogs bark and a truck roll up the drive, and he came outside in his pajamas and slippers toting a shotgun. Better that gun than Zabel at his side, Andy thought, and stepped out of the cab. Abe was getting his eyes adjusted and didn't recognize Andy's truck until he heard his voice.

"What the hell?" he asked. "What are you doing here? What, did ya get in an accident?"

"Kinda."

"What?"

"Bad news, Abe. Let's pour us a drink," Andy said and stepped into the yellow porch light.

"What drink? What happened?"

"Tomatoes got blown to the ground. That's what. There's nothing left."

"Blown to the ground?" All he could think of was a bomb.

Andy explained it. Then they got themselves a drink. On the porch they could hear the crickets chirp in the grass. They held the *raki* in their hands absently, as though someone else was planning to come around and drink it. Andy told him how the crop looked, that the patch was torn up no less than if a horde of Mongols had run through it. Abe took it in without saying a word. He could tell by the compo-sure in Andy's voice that he wasn't exaggerating.

Andy shook his head and said, "It's like there's a curse on us, Abe."

Abe got up from his chair. He felt heavy, impotent against the malevolent forces that had visited them, his entire being a sort of debt that could never be paid off.

"Don't tell Zabel that," Abe said. "She already believes there is."

Zabel or no Zabel, what was done was done. The way good farmers do, they blinkered themselves and clopped along. The question now was what they were going to do next, how they were going to finance the upcoming crop. There was no question that they were going to have to get a loan since their bank account was down around five thousand bucks. It was Andy who brought up the idea of Abe's looking into GI loans. Had to be some government program to get GIs back on their feet. Abe looked into it. He found there were loans available with hardly any interest attached—four percent. Too good to be true. Only one hitch, though.

"Since the dirt is in both of our names, I can only get a partial loan," Abe said.

"How much we talkin'?"

"They'll lend forty percent of the value of the land."

"I figure, to be on the safe side, the dirt's worth eighty G's."

"So we're looking at thirty thousand or so."

"So, half of thirty thousand."

"Sounds like."

"That won't do."

"Might. Just. But at four percent, I'd love to get my hands on another fifteen."

"Too bad."

"I went to Saroyan in town the other day."

"The attorney Saroyan?" Andy asked.

"He had an idea. He says that you can sign your half over to me. We get the loan, then let a year or so pass."

"We farm the land in your name?"

"After a couple of years I sign it back to you."

"Ain't there some danger there?"

"Saroyan says no."

"Why didn't you tell me you were meeting with him?"

"I was in town and stopped by is all."

"We'd be up shit creek if the feds found out." Andy shoved a rock with his shoe. "I don't want no trouble with the government, Abe. That's some sort of fraud. Say they look into it. Say they found out. Then what?"

"Like I told you, I asked Saroyan about that angle, too."

"And?"

"And he says it's no problem."

"How the hell does he know that?"

"He's an attorney."

Andy chuckled sarcastically.

"That ain't good enough, not by a long shot, Abe."

"You entertainin' some better idea?"

"I'd just like to flesh this thing out more."

"We might even get enough dough to develop another piece. I was thinking of that twenty acres in Kingsburg."

"Let's take it one step at a time. I want to study this thing carefully."

"We can pay them yearly or in a lump sum at the end of three years."

"Sounds like a bargain. But still."

"We're scheduled to see Saroyan at the end of the week. Ask him whatever else you want then."

That Friday they met with Saroyan at his office in town. After the introductions were made, they sat down.

"So tell me," Andy asked, "you related to this writer Saroyan?"

"Distant cousins or something."

"I hear he's a big shot these days."

"All he talks about are Armenians, old-time Armenian things that only an *odar* would be interested in. What the hell do I need to hear about Armenians? I've got them barking in my ear every day."

"Andy wants to ask you some questions, Harry."

"He'd be careless if he didn't. I've reviewed what Abe's given me," he said, putting a hand on an envelope in front of him.

"I appreciate that, Harry. The problem is that since Abe's a GI and I'm not, and since the land is in both our names, he can only get a loan on half of it. Do we agree on that?"

"That's the way the government has set it up," Harry said.

"And half the money, which would be in the neighborhood of fifteen thousand bucks, isn't enough. Not enough, anyways, to pay our debts and keep our stomachs full while we're farming."

Abe said, "Problem is—and we've looked into this too—if we turn to the banks we'd hardly get maybe that much. And the interest would bury us."

"That's your decision," Saroyan said.

"So," Andy said. "Assuming we do take this GI loan, I'd like to discuss our options."

"Your options," Harry said, "are two."

"Go ahead, Harry."

"Like I told Abe before, you can sign your half over to him in what they call a quit-claim. It's a simple piece of paper that requires only your signature. Once it's recorded, by all rights your brother would be the sole owner of the farm."

"Then I wouldn't be on paper, no trace of my name anywhere."

"That's correct."

"Just like Abe said," Andy said. "Now my question is, can the government then look back, say, and question this so-called quick claim? You see where I'm headed."

"Quit-claim. I suppose they can," Saroyan said. "I suppose it's not the first time it's been done."

"Then it would look suspicious."

"The feds aren't jackasses, but neither do they have the time or manpower to turn over every rock."

"What would the feds do if they found out?"

"It would be difficult to prove any wrongdoing, since a quit-claim is recognized by law. So it's highly unlikely, if it's possible at all, that they could prosecute you for fraud. But the government has the right to review title, review your books at any time, and to call in the loan if there is any impropriety. Remember, the land is the government's once you sign that loan agreement. If they thought something suspicious was going on, they just might call in the loan."

"Which would leave us where?"

"It could be bad, depending on the timing."

"You mean if we dumped the money into the land and were, say, a few months short of the harvest. If they called the loan, say, in April."

"That's right."

"In that case, we might have to sell the crop on the vine."

"Whatever it would take. If they call the loan and you don't belly up, they'd foreclose on the property. Mind you, technically Abe's the one at risk here."

Abe nodded his head.

"Where he's at risk, so am I. Everything we have is both of ours."

"I'm just giving you the facts."

"That's all we want. Now," Andy said, "how about once we're back on our feet?"

"As long as it's in Abe's name, as long as things stay the way they are, you can renew the loan. Once you've decided you don't need the loan, you pay the government what you owe them. Then Abe brings you back on the title. That's just a matter of signing a few papers."

Andy nodded his head.

"But as your counselor, I want to stress two things again," Saroyan said. "First is, once this land is in Abe's name, though you are brothers, the law will recognize Abe as legally responsible for any debt or suit. That's the way it will hold up in court if things go sour. Second is, Andy, you legally will have no rights to the land. If Abe should sell the land and run off to Jamaica, you wouldn't have a claim to even a bucket of it."

They all chuckled.

"This goes for the house too?" Andy said.

"Everything except the equipment."

Later that afternoon Andy said, "Sounds okay, Abe."

"A steal. Thanks to you."

"Yeah. Listen, one thing, let's us sign a paper between us."

"Paper?"

"Yeah, just something between us. You know, that says the way it really is."

"Like our word isn't good enough to each other?"

Andy expected that answer.

"I'll write it up, Abe."

"Go ahead. But I don't see no point."

Although he believed he had the facts firmly in hand, when Andy went to convey them on paper, they fled all of a sudden. The words protested the exercise—balked, scoffed, sneered—and sentences that seemed sound one second, the next second slinked away.

I, Antranik Demerjian, do hereby release my half-interest in the land.

We, Antranik Demerjian and Abraham Voskijian, brothers, half-brothers

~~do hereby agree to the following.~~ *Antranik Demerjian will release half his interest in 7778 Shaw Avenue, Biola, California, to Abraham Voskijian.*

As a college graduate, Andy had always felt more or less in command of what he wrote, but getting the words to do what he needed this time around was comparable to an inmate trying to rally prison guards for a raid.

~~The land is released because we need a loan. The land, though released, is still~~ *The reason that the land was released was in order to secure a GI loan under Abraham Voskijian's name. ~~Half the interest in the land is still Antranik Demerjian's in fact,~~ Though Abraham Voskijian holds title to the land, half of the interest is still Antranik Demerjian's, as is half of the debt assumed in farming the land. Both Antranik Demerjian and Abraham Voskijian bear witness to this truth by their signatures below.*

What should've taken half an hour took half a day. But when it was all said and done, what he was finally left holding felt less like something an attorney might've drafted than the work of a member of the junior high school debate team, and he had to admit that a picture flashed in his head of an adult looking over this so-called agreement one day and chuckling at the seriousness with which it was executed.

Abe wasn't joking when he told Andy that Zabel thought there was a curse on the land. What Abe did not know was that Zabel was convinced that the curse came through Andy, and that it had traveled in his blood for two generations, starting with his grandfather Jonig, who the family claimed had been killed by the Turks.

Jonig was a powerfully built man with an even more powerful reputation as an attorney and orator throughout the area of Bursa, located forty miles or so southeast of Istanbul. On one summer evening in 1895, Jonig walked across the village to attend a meeting of intellectuals who had convened to discuss the worsening situation among Armenians in the district. The family was expecting him home that night. But he didn't return. The next morning there was a knock at the door. When Yervant opened it, hoping to find there his father, or someone bearing news about him, he instead discovered at the doorstep a burlap sack, draining blood. Inside of it was the hacked-up body of his father. As a man of authority, Jonig had been among the first to be singled out, along with other intellectuals and poets and writers, for slaughter by the Turks. This was the way Yervant, Jonig's son, reported it to his family, and this is the only story that Andy knew.

But there was another version. It was Andy's aunt Asniv who told Zabel that Jonig had held the title of *Agha* in Turkey. Orators, poets, statesmen were *Aghas*. But so were some local taxmen—Turks and their Armenian cohorts who took a slice of the taxes they gathered for themselves. Though publicly revered, these local sellouts were privately despised. What type of *Agha* was Jonig?

Angel knew a woman who had migrated from Jonig's hometown who provided an important clue: Jonig's widow, who trailed the horse-drawn hearse, had flung dirt at and cursed the Armenians gathered along the cemetery road. Angel had concluded that Jonig, Andy's grandfather, had been seized by his own people, butchered not by Turks but by Armenians exacting revenge. What else could explain the tragedies that had later befallen his son Yervant? A curse hung upon his very name because of his father's betrayal of his own people, try as he did to expunge the curse by changing his name from Chooljian to Demerjian when he came to America. No, Zabel thought, it is as the Lord had said, for their father's sins four generations must pay. Hadn't all of Yervant's projects turned to ashes, hadn't the very foundation upon which he'd built his future turned to shifting sand? The curse was on Andy as well. Witness his withered leg. By some terrible turn of events, her husband was yoked to the carrier of this curse. And as long as they were linked to him, Andy's fate was their fate, his curse was hers.

They went ahead with the quit-claim and decided that all the money would go in Abe and Zabel's account and, of course, Andy would get whatever he needed, whenever he needed it. When they collected the harvest money, Abe would pay off the loan and split whatever was left with Andy. As long as the loan obligation was regularly met—there should be no reason for the government's involvement thereafter. The brothers also signed the handwritten agreement Andy had drafted. Fresh start, they agreed. Now, let's get on with it.

13

WITH HIS EAR PRESSED AGAINST THE BEDROOM DOOR, over his mother's sobbing, Abe, barely nine years old, made out the story this way. His father, Sarkis, had run out of gas on a country road with a friend. They were making toward the nearest gas station on foot. A truck, brimming with grapes, driven by a driver still drunk from the night before, blew a tire, veered off the road and killed him and Baron Megerdichian, his boyhood friend.

A fuller account might have added this: when the truck lost control, the tanks flipped over, casting a green sludge of Muscat into the vine-yards and twenty yards down the road. It lay in mounds, steaming in that hundred-degree heat. The driver crawled out of the cab and studied the lost crop, wondering what next? A neighbor who'd been harvesting his own ran over to help.

"Did ya kill 'em?" he asked frantically, looking around for the bodies.

"Kill what?"

"Them two men."

"Two men where?"

"Jesus."

The neighbor dashed back to fetch a shovel and a rake. Ten minutes they raked and shoveled, knee-deep in the sticky, muddy juice, the amber-green berries clinging to their clothes like slugs. The neighbor's boy, who'd gone to take a shit some twenty yards down a row, spotted Megerdichian. His body lay heaped against a vine in the shade of the canopy. At first he'd figured it was a Filipino napping. One down, one to go.

They found Sarkis' leg first, snapped off his hip and pointing off to the side so he looked like a ballet dancer holding a position. They lugged him out by the arms and lay him in the shade of a tree. His eyes were wide open, and his body was smeared and jammed, wherever there was an opening, with grapes. Yes, so some claimed, even up there. They swung him onto a vineyard trailer and rushed down an avenue toward the nearest barn. Underneath a tree, a woman washed him down with a hose, plucked the berries from his mouth with a finger and, after making the sign of the cross over his corpse, drew his eyes shut. Now, she said, if one of the men would put his leg back in place, his wife could see him without shame. It was a death so gruesome that many thought it had the overtones of a curse.

Abe, the oldest child and only son, became the putative head of his household. Men and women he barely knew, all dressed in black, agreed in public without his consent that he was *the* man now. His aunt whispered in his ear that he had no time to waste crying about his father anymore, since the family depended upon him. If he wanted to honor his father, he would pick up where the man had unfortunately left off. He didn't know which petrified him more, his father's absence or this new responsibility. No time to waste. Those words turned over and over in his head.

He had never known that time *could* be wasted, he had never thought that time, like other things—a carton of milk, a jar of jam— ran out. His father's time had run out, that's what dying meant. Now *he* was told not to waste time. You're next in line, they seemed to be saying, and your time has begun. Being an adult meant there was nobody between you and death. Being an adult meant your clock had started. He crawled into the closet and hid. Maybe if they couldn't find him he could avoid the clock entirely. He felt cheated, he wanted someone between himself and death. He was too young to not waste time. He hated his father for putting him in this situation. He wanted his father back so that everything could go back to normal. He wondered if he was somehow the cause of all of this. He prayed to God, promising to never sin again, if only God would bring his father back.

Little Abe protested; Willa, the eldest, could take care of the family much better. We will all do it, his mother, Calipse, told him. We will all take care of each other. But who will provide for us? the girls asked. They slept by their mother's side, on quilts on the floor. When their mother hid her face and cried, they drew straws to decide in what order they would be orphaned. Calipse was brave, although her heart quaked whenever she thought of having to support these five children on her own. And who was there to guide Abe at the precise age when he needed his father the most? Who would teach him how to be a man?

Thank God, Sarkis had taken out a life insurance policy valued at fifteen thousand dollars. To probate the estate, Calipse hired an attorney, Mr. Weathers. It was at this attorney's office that she first set eyes on Yervant, but not before Yervant had set eyes upon her. Yervant was sitting cross-legged in the reception room, counting his beads, when he heard a woman say, in broken Armenian-English from down the hall, "Tank you, Meester Veders." Watching her close a door behind her, he regarded the fair skin of her arms, her full, plump figure. Her worried eyes were green, striking. She wore no wedding ring. Yervant rose. Polite but not overly so, he opened the door for her. She nodded, absorbing for a second his brown eyes, their directness, their composure, and his jowl, powerful and square. In Armenian he said good day. Her reply caught in her throat, she flushed. It had been so long since anyone had looked at her that way that she'd forgotten it was possible. She nodded and stepped outside. Her husband had been dead for six months, and for the first time she admitted to herself that she was a single woman again, that she might be the object of some man's desire.

Yervant doffed his hat upon entering Weathers' office. He wore a suit and cut a natty, dignified figure, as though there had been a time when all he wore were hats and suits. Weathers understood he was in the presence of someone, even if this *someone* was an Armenian farmer.

Yervant took a seat, hung his hat on a knee, and got straight to the point, as he'd heard that attorneys charge by the hour. In his broken English, he told Weathers that he had relatives he wanted to bring over, and that he'd come to a professional for this matter in order to hasten the process, and because neither he nor anyone else he knew could write in English.

"You understand it is not easy, Mr. Demerjian. The government does not take kindly to foreigners these days, especially as these are hard times for this country."

Yervant waved the insinuation away with a hand and asked him how much money it would take. Weathers said it would be somewhere around three, four hundred dollars per person, and that he would need a retainer—money in advance of his services—in order to begin.

Yervant reached into his pocket, pulled out a cylinder of dough, and rested it on the desk like a pile of poker chips. Weathers took information. Who were the people? (His cousins, Manoog and Esahag, his sister Asniv, and her three children, Aram, Mariam and Harry). Where they presently lived, their trade and other details. He told Yervant that he would get back to him soon, that there was the matter of sponsorship that must be addressed.

"Now, that would be, in good faith sir, four hundred dollars up front."

Yervant licked a finger and counted it out in denominations of twenty. Weathers tapped his finger for every bill that hit the desk.

"One thing." Yervant held the money as though there was some link between it and what he was about to say next. "The lady. She come before me."

The attorney told him the sad details.

Yervant listened studiously. When Weathers was done, Yervant leaned forward in his seat, handed him the cash and asked Weathers whether he knew of the plight of the Armenian people.

"Of course, Mr. Demerjian. We grew up hearing 'Remember the starving Armenians.' Our parents would remind us of your people whenever we refused to eat the food put in front of us."

"Hah," he grunted. "We come to this country, America. Why? Turk." He flicked a finger across his throat. "You understand this?"

As though it were a command, not a question, Weathers straightened up in his seat, cleared his throat and said, "Yes. Many Armenians have flooded into the valley over the past few years. You are agricultural people, I believe."

Yervant shook a finger no. "We are education people. I have five tongue." He declared them all: Armenian, Turkish, Greek, French, Bulgarian, and English. "Don't take us Armenian for Everyman Joe Farmer. My father, like you, lawyer."

"I have several farmers for clients, Mr. Demerjian."

"Someday, in this Fresno, Armenian will shake the ground," he flexed his arms. "I swear you."

It was spoken like a threat. What kind of man is this who's sitting in whose office? It'll be a cold day in hell, Weathers thought, before some foreigner, *especially* an Armenian, gets the better of him or his kind. Weathers tapped the pen on the desk to indicate that the clock was running.

"Okay," Yervant said. "But I talk about this lady. Very sad. She come America and this happen her husband. *Pacht chooneh*."

Weathers narrowed his eyes.

"*Pacht.* American say 'fate.' She has a bad fate."

"Indeed she does, sir."

"This reason, I will marry her."

Weathers was shocked. Immigrants; he'd dealt with them daily, he'd observed the curious concatenations of their brains, their naïve ambitions, their abrupt shifts in mood, their reckless way of advancing into the future, against all common sense and natural odds. But he'd rarely seen such an irreverent fellow as this Yervant. Weathers cleared his nose and throat and said, "Well then."

Yervant stood, hat in hand, and told Weathers that he expected the money earned by the sweat of his brow to be used well, and that he would return in two weeks to make sure it was.

"We will do our best," Weathers said.

Yervant raised a finger and held it before the attorney's nose. "Here bring my family. This best."

The very next Sunday, Calipse was on her knees, waiting for the sacrament, when she noticed a man come to kneel beside her. When she recognized it was Yervant, she quickly dropped her eyes. Perhaps Calipse feared that her face would betray the fact that she'd made inquiries about him since their chance meeting in Weathers' office. Of the several friends she queried, three knew something about him. Each opined that he had a reputation for enchanting women, even though he was not an especially handsome man. They agreed that he dressed well, was a dazzling dancer, and that he spoke *makoor*, clean Armenian. In describing him, the women had also used the word *zoravor*, strong, which in the context of the conversation meant less physical strength than a force of mind and will. All in all, in his bearing he possessed the aspect of a dignitary, or the son of a dignitary. But a shadowy rumor of something unmentionably terrible shrouded him, something linked to his past, above and beyond the terribleness of the massacres.

With their shoulders almost touching, from the corner of her eye Calipse weighed his praying hands. They were made for physical labor, but not consumed by it, she thought. His hands were as much suited to holding a book as a shovel. For a second, she wondered what she would feel should they hold her.

Her musings were interrupted by the priest. She bowed her head, laid one open hand on top of the other and accepted the body of Christ. She sipped from the chalice of blood, crossed herself and, with her children a step ahead of her, rose. As they walked back to their seats, she wondered if he was behind her. Then, at the small of her back she felt a hand guiding her into her row. A current of emotion moved through her. She turned her head and smiled. Expecting it, Yervant returned the smile and continued up the aisle. Later, outside on the steps of the church, their courtship began.

Nearly three months from the day they first met, Yervant married Calipse, just as he had predicted. After the death of her husband, she found she wanted, more than anything else, someone who could protect her and care for her children, and perhaps someday even adopt them. She believed that if he gave her nothing else, this protection he would give her. The kids didn't know what to think. Would Yervant relieve them by shouldering the family's burden, or would he further disrupt their lives?

This was his second family. That his own life was saved, even as his first family's was lost, never ceased to haunt him. Yervant, as a young man, had been married but two years when he began to investigate *Agha* Jonig's murder. He parsed rumor from speculation, speculation from fact, until he had surmised the identity of those who had signed his father's death warrant. He began quietly studying these men's schedules and means of travels, the paths they took to and from their work, their coffee houses, their whorehouses and mistresses' flats. All along, he was accompanied by his only accomplice, the wounded ten-year-old boy inside of him to whom Yervant had vowed in revenge to spill tenfold the blood that had been spilled in his father's death.

Over a period of a year, he slit the throats of three Turkish officials in the city of Bursa. Shortly after the third victim was found dead, his carcass crammed into a barrel used for making cheese, his head nearly severed from the neck, Yervant was fingered as the assassin and forced on a moment's notice to flee, leaving his family behind so that if he were caught they might not be hanged alongside him. That was the last time he would see his first wife, daughter and son, who shortly there-after were herded into the desert with a million others to die in response to the Armenian Question.

Torturously, and full of rage and sorrow, he had made his way to Bulgaria. There, outside of a bar, he stabbed to death a Turk who had insulted him. For the price of a gold trinket, he was smuggled aboard a cargo ship that was headed for America.

He worked in the coal mines of Kentucky, daily his nature turning akin to the mineral he was excavating. For six years he'd worked tire-lessly, saving every cent until he had earned enough to move out west to Fresno.

Many people, upon chugging into the valley on their long train ride from the east coast, thought that what they'd fallen into was a hoax, or worse, a sort of ambush. As they crossed over the Sierras, there was nothing but flat land, barren as a desert below. If there was water in that bleak place it was nowhere evident. They might as well have come searching for oil or gold. What, besides weeds, could possibly grow in this godforsaken place? they must have asked themselves. When finally the conductor hailed "Fresno," men and women and children remained sitting in their seats, balked at getting off. They probably looked like mourners coming to attend a wake as they stepped off the platform into the stupefying heat or layers of fog, drifting in front of them like the bedsheets of the dead.

Still, they carried with them recipes for prosperity. They knew how to dry grapes and plums, they had in their pockets the seeds for a cucumber that they would name "Armenian." They would introduce the country to melons—Persians with orange meat and filigreed skin; casabas, which looked like yellow pumpkins and whose white juicy meat was sherbet sweet.

If it had been a white nation that slaughtered them, and not the dark-eyed Turks, whose reputation for carnage preceded them even to the backwaters of Fresno, the Armenians would have been run out of town. Instead, these people who resembled Jews were harassed, glanced upon as something mongrel, barred from stores and from purchasing prime plots of land. To the Volga Germans and Swedes, these Armenians, Christian or not, spoke in a tongue and wrote in an alphabet that had no correlation to their own. All in all, these large, dark-eyed foreigners, with their shamelessly hung noses, were suspect, and the attitude that their reputed starvation was somehow deserved was not uncommon.

Even if you could not spot them by their looks, since some Armenians were as white or whiter than the whites themselves—it was easy enough to do by inspecting the spelling or sound of their last names. Hence, they clipped or changed or finessed their names to sound American: Clingirian became Clinger, Casparian became Caspar, Chalkayan was neatly shorn to Chalk. More radically, some became Peters who were previously Bedrosian, or Coffee, whose father was a Dikranian. Others found it easiest to drop the "ian" in the pronunciation of their names to *odars* at social functions or in passing: Mr. Jelladian began to introduce himself as Mr. Jelladan. These same persons might leave it that way in writing if the document they were signing was not binding. Others changed their names to other Armenian names, perhaps to leave their past behind. In Fresno, at the age of forty, Yervant Chooljian would become Yervant Demerjian.

His marriage to Calipse was a financial boon. They took the insurance money and bought fifty acres of vineyards in Biola with a barn and a three-bedroom house out front. For the first time in his life, Yervant owned the dirt that he worked. When his clan arrived, it would be evident how he had prospered.

"There is land everywhere," he wrote them. "Air sharp and clean and water jumping up from wells. Emerald grapes hang from the vines. The mountains are powerful. They are not Ararat, but that no longer is ours either, is it? If you throw a seed down in the fall, it will surely flower in the spring. Armenians are growing in number here like the trees themselves. Everywhere there is possibility."

If Yervant had inherited five children, then Calipse and her five children would soon inherit a motley assembly of relatives.

Yervant's nephew Aram Arax, named after the Mother River in Armenia, arrived first. The family watched their new cousin, eighteen years old, step off the train sporting a beret and speaking not Armenian, but French! Abe had never seen such a queer person before. No sooner had he hit the platform than he announced his intent to enroll at the University of California at Berkeley, demanding Yervant take him there *tout de suite*. Yervant hauled him instead to a potato-picking job in a place called Weedpatch, south of Bakersfield. He told Aram, in no uncertain terms, that his first duty was to help him raise enough money to bring the balance of his family to America, that he would not rest a single day until Aram's mother—Yervant's sister Asniv—and her two other children, supped with them again.

So Asniv came next, and with her Mariam and Harry, her two other children. Now with his only sister and her family close at hand, Yervant worked on getting his two cousins, the twin bachelors Manoog and Esahag, over from France. Those two showed up a year later.

Each day, Yervant would drive them to work in his car. All of these relatives were from the city, accustomed to their morning coffee and paper. They were members of the church choir in Istanbul, used to a nightlife of music and dance and poetry recitals and orations. All of this changed when they started their life in the valley as fieldhands. They moved steadily apace with the crops: apricots, peaches, nectarines, and plums. With other Armenians, they packed table grapes in the fields, pitched watermelons and cantaloupes onto trailers, on their knees dug potatoes and onions out of the dirt.

Four, five nights a week the living room turned into a kind of men's club, thick with smoke and drinking and music. Abe and the other kids would watch from a crack between the hallway door and jamb as these strangers took over their house. Their mother conveyed coffee and *raki,* cheese and bread and *soujouk,* back and forth from the kitchen, as though she were a maid. They overheard conversations.

"What it is about the Armenian that makes him so naïvely embrace the man who will later stab him?"

"Because. It is our nature to trust."

"What nature?" Aram blamed the church that taught them to turn the other cheek. It seemed like the priests had slowly lulled them to sleep. A smarter people would have seen the writing on the wall.

"Weren't there pogroms in 1894, '95, '96, in 1909?! Wasn't the entire history of Armenia—spotted with blood as it was—evidence enough to keep a man awake?"

"It is because our people are divided in two."

"True, true."

"If we stood as one, things would have been different."

The men recalled life amongst the Kurds and Turks, stunned still that their own neighbors, men to whom they had loaned tools, women their wives had drunk coffee with, should turn so suddenly savage. Those stout, tufa-stone churches, some red as pomegranates, those hand-carved *khatchkars,* ancient stone baptismal bowls, and vines— akhh, what fruit they bore—planted before even the Lord was born, all of it theirs no more. It was as though the land had been snatched out from under Ararat itself, with one ruthless jerk.

Asniv and her children rented a bungalow down the road from Yervant and his family, and the twins, Manoog and Esahag moved to the north side of Kerman, four miles away. Any money the relatives earned went in a kitty over which Yervant ruled. Yervant made all the important decisions, and for the first year or so they deferred to him always. He doled out the cash liberally, yes, but always as though it were a gift. Things began to fray between him and the other men when they first saw him strut into their house with a brand-new suit on. Then, a little later, we drove up in a natty Model T Ford. When they began to grumble, Yervant reminded them that they would have nothing, they would *be* nothing, if it weren't for him! Yervant had a harder and harder time getting them out of bed to work. "What opportunity do we have?" they'd ask. "We toil in the heat all day long only to hand over to Yervant our money, what, so that he can spend it on his fancy cars?!"

Asniv defended her brother and told them to shut their mouths. If Yervant, who had labored alone to save enough money to bring them to America, wanted ten new suits, that was his right! Already she felt they were all disappointments, especially her sons. Nobody gets rich in America working all day in the fields, they would holler. This is the land of opportunities!

So, at the age of twenty, Harry left the family and started panhandling his way across America. Before long, his hand was in other folks' pans. It started with petty crimes—shoplifting—which eventually led to bigger stuff—burglary, larceny, theft, check forging, fraud. His aliases grew as steadily as his rap sheet. It wasn't long before Asniv received news that he was wanted for killing a cop and that he was among the ten most wanted by the FBI. The shame he brought on the family was insufferable. Eventually he was nabbed by the feds and would have been sentenced to death if his attorney hadn't shrewdly calculated the following defense: Harry's regrettable behavior was the result of unfathomable atrocities he'd been exposed to from birth. The wretch had seen his entire family, except his mother, brother and sister, wiped out by the Turks, and in these crimes was acting out a pathetically aimed revenge. Instead of the electric chair, Harry got life behind bars at San Quentin.

To Harry's brother, Aram, humans were one way or another all imprisoned, slaves to a capitalist system that would in the near future, come hell or high water, topple. In the meantime, there were those who worked and those who, like himself, worked on behalf of those who worked. Aram's dream was to stroll in the shadows of ivy-covered buildings, down walkways strewn with leaves, reading Bakunin, Lenin, and Marx. Instead, in Fresno he was stranded among men whose politics were neanderthal, men who thought bourgeoisie was a type of French pastry! He took to writing revolutionary poetry beneath peach trees and lecturing to anyone who cared to hear of the evil state of the imperialist world.

Manoog and Esahag were no better. Their goal, though, was to become cigar-smoking capitalists overnight. After a couple of years working other folks' dirt, they wanted a slice of their own. They begged Yervant for a loan. He gave them half the money they needed toward a down payment, and from God knows where else they got the other half. They bought themselves forty acres of Thompson grapes, which they summarily yanked out of the ground. In its place they planted soybeans. Yes, soybeans. It was the crop of the future, Manoog predicted.

Although he played the safe practical man, Yervant's ventures were no less perilous. He rented a hundred-acre patch of dirt and grew watermelons, a crop that had never been planted in more than twenty acres at a shot and was mostly for an immigrant market. If the potential white customers could only get past the embarrassment of having to spit out those terrible black seeds, in two or three years, watermelons, he claimed, would be as common as apples. From the back of a truck he sold these watermelons and peddled them to grocers in the area. Before long, he secured for himself the title of Watermelon King, a name he bore with pride even if for three years in a row half the crop rotted in the fields, not even worth the cost of labor to pick it.

Once again with the mind of targeting the *odar* market, Yervant started bleaching raisins. Perhaps, he thought, white people might take better to a raisin that was closer to their own color. He produced an amber morsel that glowed in the sun, but his customers couldn't come to terms with the sulphurous trace it left on the tongue, nor, perhaps, the ten cents a pound more than they would pay for regular raisins. The market for bleached raisins crashed before it even got off the ground.

Year after year Yervant lost money, parlaying profits from his raisin crop into these more esoteric ventures. Everyone, including him, kept thinking that one day he would hit pay dirt. He is a man ahead of his time, many people would admit, but what of it if every time you see him he's going broke.

Along with his relatives, he had in his stepchildren a ready-made work-force. Before the cock crowed, they were up milking cows, pruning vines, irrigating rows, laying grapes down, working whatever patch of dirt he'd rented. When they came home from school it was more of the same.

Within three years, the children would have to make room for two more siblings. The baby girl, named Betty, came first. A year later Andy was born. Yervant coddled his baby boy, named after his massacred son. And the rest of the family equally adored him. The girls debated who loved him most, who would get to hold him or feed him or rock him to sleep. Andy, that little roly-poly boy, was just what the family needed to bind them together; they all owned an equal share of him, he was everybody's baby. Maybe the children understood, too, that the only way to get a portion of their stepfather's love was through their baby brother.

Yervant was not big, standing straight and stiff as a pitchfork at five foot eight, but his fierceness, his implacable will, seemed to override his size, to virtually contest it. His lean face, stern jowl, and dark eyes animated by some unknown, diabolical force—altogether a countenance chiseled clean of any nonsense—was enough to make even a prize-fighter think twice. One story goes that, frustrated with a horse that wouldn't stand still for a shoeing, he whacked it in the head with his fist and knocked it flat out. Men twice his size, twice as rich, tiptoed around him. There was no turning Yervant back once he got going, so that losing a fight against him was less an issue than having to kill him to win. Once, a Filipino who'd likely drunk too much the evening before excused himself from work on the grounds that it had grown too hot to work. Yervant told him to stay. The Filipino told him to not be a cheap Armenian, put out a hand, and asked for half a day's pay. Yervant stomped out of the field, swung the door open and went for a gun in a drawer.

His wife thought he'd spotted a badger or maybe a snake.

"What are you going to shoot?" Calipse asked.

"A Filipino."

"A what?" his sister Asniv asked. "What did he do?"

"I'll teach that bastard," he seethed.

He marched out the door. Seeing he was serious, the women jumped at him. All three of them tumbled to the bottom of the steps. The children had gathered a few feet away in a little pack, dumbfounded and afraid. Abe had always wondered what people meant by a dog foaming at the mouth. Now, observing his stepfather, he knew.

Abe sprinted back into the field and told the Filipino, who thought Yervant had gone to fetch his wages, that his father had a gun and that he could shoot and that he'd killed a man before. The Filipino shuddered and ran. When Yervant finally got out from under the women, he was ranting and swinging the gun around swearing in Turkish that he was going to shoot the Filipino and then shit in his face. For three hours he searched for the culprit, to no avail.

As was his custom, to cool down he went and lay lengthwise in a ditch, as though hoping to find there a measure of the serenity of the dead. As it neared nightfall, ditch or no, Calipse readied him his *raki*.

"Abe," she said, "take your father his drink." She handed him a tray.

Your father, he thought.

"Out to the ditch."

Abe walked out the door praying. He could feel his body jump from fear. The girls watched from the window. Just a trace of light was left in the sky, ash gray. The jiggers of *raki* jiggled on the tray. He stepped up to the ditch a wreck, ready to have the life mauled out of him. He cocked an ear and listened for any sound, cursing, snoring, just breathing. He heard nothing. Sometimes, in fits of rage or despair, his stepfather would throw dirt over himself too. Abe wondered if, by a stroke of luck, this time he might have buried himself alive. When he peeked into the ditch, he saw Yervant lying with his hands folded over his chest. It was too dark down there to decide whether his eyes were open or closed.

"Papa?"

But even as he said it, Abe was thinking of his real father, how he'd never seen the man drink, must less drunk, and how overwhelming, compared to his real father, to any man Abe had ever known, this Yervant was.

A startled grunt.

"Your *raki* is here."

He sat up. Abe lowered the tray to him. Yervant drank one after another and without a word climbed out of the ditch and went to bed.

On the weekends after work, Yervant would fraternize with his fellow émigrés at the Azbarez club in town. It was there, between games of pinochle, that he met Leo Stamboulian, who said he knew of a man who had a copy of the Black Book. Yervant had wanted to read the Black Book for years, ever since his aunt had told him that his own father had once read it. Perhaps he felt that somewhere deep in the Black Book he would find his father again.

What was in the Black Book? Those who hadn't read it knew only this: whoever mastered its contents saw through things as though they were sheets of glass, could make himself invisible at will, in an instant could transport himself to distant places, and could tamper with people's minds or set fire to things with his eyes. But in reading it, men had also gone berserk or turned into idiots or wandered into the hills like lost sheep. After studying just a few chapters, Levon Koroyan— one of the great *oud* players of his time—was said to have pitched his beloved instrument into a river, sold all of his worldly possessions and lived in a cave crouched beneath Ararat for the rest of his life.

"You've seen the Black Book, Leo?"

"With my own eyes. But read it, no. Old man Krikor who owns the coyote has it."

"Krikor of Caruthers. The coyote man."

"The very one. The book is old."

"What is his commerce with that coyote, anyway?"

"No one knows. He lives alone with it is all."

"Is the coyote his dog?"

"After a fashion, yes."

"Does it come when he calls?"

"It comes when it pleases."

"Does it protect his land?"

"From what little I've seen, it is shy."

"But about the Black Book."

"Yes, about it."

"Tell him I, Yervant Demerjian, have asked to read it."

"I have already. He wanted to know the kind of man that you are."

"I understand. Tell him my father, a great orator in Van, knew the Black Book by heart!"

Stamboulian handed it over to him the next week. Yervant told his wife that he should not be disturbed for three days as he was studying something very deep. His wife watched him enter the barn, without even a bedroll to sleep on, this book tucked under his arm.

It was mid-winter and it was cold. The air was clouded like when lemon juice is poured into water. She had known her husband to do crazy things before, but nothing close to this. By the middle of the second day, she began to fear he'd made good on his regular threats to kill himself. She sent Abe to find out what he was doing in there, not to come back until he was sure Yervant wasn't dead. The boy crept out of the house, plodding through the fog as though through a minefield.

As he climbed up the ladder to the loft, he prayed he'd find Yervant dead down below. How many times Yervant had beaten him he could no longer recall, but suffice it to say that not a moment passed when he wasn't conscious of Yervant's presence, even in his dreams. Abe was so afraid of making the wrong move, of setting off the bomb, that the only moves he really made anymore were imaginary. Up against the far wall, Yervant sat on a stool used for milking cows. He seemed to be studying a book. For a desk, he was using a bale. Yervant had a hand shoved in front of him, as when a man signals for a car to stop or slow down. Ten minutes or so later, Yervant closed the book and slapped his hand on top of it, the way a pastor makes adamant a point from the Bible. Then he stood and began jumping up and down, running in place.

His mother had been waiting, pacing back and forth across the kitchen floor. Abe told her that Yervant was not dead. Far from it, he was quite energetic. He recounted everything he saw.

The children imagined feeding him like a caged animal through a small door they'd make within the barn door. When friends asked them where their father was, they would tell him he'd gone away, or even that he had died. But to the children's chagrin, he emerged the very next day. Calipse came out on the patio with a steaming, heaping plate of stuffed eggplant and a large towel draped over her shoulder. He walked right past her with a shovel in his hand and headed into the vineyards.

Yervant could see the Black Book leading him down increasingly narrow passages to a room that, should he enter, he would never be able to leave, a world, really, parallel to his own, a world infinitely transparent and infinitely deep at once. And he knew if he were to ever step into that world, he could never live as he'd lived before. He'd be of flesh but without hunger, have eyes but lack desire. In exchange for the mind of God, he'd forfeit the comfort, the pleasure of earthly illusions.

It was at that point, only a third of the way through the Black Book, that he decided he could no longer go on. When he threw open the barn doors and stepped into the fog, he felt at first unbearably insubstantial, as though he were made of fog himself. In the white mist he saw spirits flicker before his eyes. He heard a voice tell him to pick up a shovel and dig.

Dig he did. He started turning that furrow and kept at it until, five hours later, he had finished the row. The kids wondered if what he'd learned from that book was some foreign farming practice. Then he dragged his shovel to a weedy patch of open ground. By the end of the second day, word had spread beyond the family that Yervant was digging some hole. His wife and sister agreed to tell everyone, including the children, that Yervant was making a well. But those who knew him better, and knew also that no man in his right mind would dig a well in the dead of winter, guessed that Yervant was preparing his own grave—that after he'd dug six feet down he'd do himself in. The children kept waiting to see water shoot up from the bottom, and they wondered if there was any chance that he might drown when it did. At night in the bitter cold, Calipse kept vigil, bundled in blankets in a chair at the edge of the dirt perimeter that had formed around the hole. Calipse listened to the monotonous digging, *cshh, cshh, cshh, cshh,* that was simultaneously a source of torment and a sign that he was still alive.

On the morning of the fourth day she woke to an absence of digging sounds. Panicked, she looked down into the hole. He was gone. By her guess he'd dug ten to fifteen feet deep, so naturally she wondered how he had gotten out. The sun was coming over the Sierras clean and bright, and crushed diamond frost glittered on the ground. Footprints on the frost. She followed them as far as the front porch.

From the top of the hall she could hear her husband snoring. She quietly opened the door. He looked like a creature dredged up from the bottom of a lagoon. Mud, a half-inch thick, was caked on his trousers, his shirt, his head. Calipse gently mopped his face and arms with a warm towel, though nothing short of scrubbing him down with a wire brush would get to the deepest layers of dirt.

The whole day he slept. The children were told that they should not disturb their father, who was recovering from the work he'd begun on the well, for any reason. His snoring was emphatic, intense, a kind of animal language. The next morning he woke with a shout, as though he'd startled himself awake, or was startled that he was awake at all. Calipse was there by his side, and with her eyes, she took his in.

"Yervant?" she whispered, as though she wasn't sure herself anymore.

"Ah, Calipse."

"Akhh, Yervant." She embraced him.

"I was going to tell you something."

"What is it?"

"It died in my thoughts."

"It doesn't matter."

"Ah, I remember now."

"What?"

"My father, he was a very great man."

"Yes, he was."

"Very great," he said. "Very."

14

CARAVANS OF CLOUDS DRIFTED IN from the west. Big and bruised they came in, one behind another, their movement slow and steady, a kind of elephantine ballet. For ten hours the rain came down hard, then stopped. The eastern horizon looked like a charcoal band whose thick gray dust had been smeared with an upward stroke of the thumb. The rest of the sky roiled as though with smoke, huge gaping holes in flux.

The canopy of vineyards was toasted brown on top, and long canes draped to the earth in tangles. The bark of the fruit trees was black with rain, the avenues between the trees a stretch of orange leaves. The cotton too had been harvested. Tarps were hung over gray-white bales, stacked and tied in front of an expanse of black twigs to which beads of cotton still clung, looking desolate like the aftermath of a conflagration. Flocks of crows wheeled in the air over them and descended in stages in the fields, picking at worms. Bituminous barns looked deserted and failing in the cold. Crows perched on their gables, on telephone wires, on every pole, fence and railing, their presence constant, like an element of the air itself. The sun came through sporadically and only for a short while. The leaves, the trees and brush and grass, glinted in that silvery light as though they hadn't been rained upon but instead were sweating.

Inside the house, a fire was crackling. The children sat around playing cards, and the adults were putting on their Sunday best. They were going to Andy and Abe's sister Martha's house for Thanksgiving dinner. Zabel marched down the hall and pushed open Andy's door. Andy was in front of the dresser mirror straightening his tie. She asked his image in the mirror if he was ready to go. "We are going to be late," she said. Andy was never late, anywhere. He told her to give him five minutes and would she please shut the door. She turned around and left with a puff of disgust. He sprinkled some Vitalis on his hands, worked it into his hair and dragged a comb through until it was slick as a crow's wing. What energy such disgust as Zabel's took. He wondered where the hell she got all that spare energy. He cleared his nose into a tissue. No, Andy admitted, sick as it is, what with the amount of energy it took, Zabel's all-around and unending disgust amounted to a kind of achievement. You've got to give her that.

At Martha's the appetizers—what Armenians call *maza*—had been placed on the table. There were *yalanchi* dolmas, rice cooked in a broth of tomatoes and onions and parsley, then spooned onto the middle of a young grape leaf, rolled and folded into a package the shape of a thick finger, cooked again, cooled and stacked on a plate, and garnished with lemon slices and parsley. There were *basturma,* thin diaphanous strips of cured spicy beef layered on a plate in the arrangement of a sunflower; there were rounds of eggplant baked with onions and garlic and tomatoes; and *hommus* taking the shape of its oval dish with a consistency similar to paste, sprinkled over with paprika and guttered with olive oil. What else? Sliced *soujouk,* a kind of Armenian sausage that made the body reek of garlic. *Taboule* salad made of bulgur and minced parsley and tomatoes and green onions over which fresh lemon was squeezed. On a table in the corner there was pumpkin pie and cherry pie and pecan pie, all fresh, still warm in the middle, and there were persimmon cookies and *baklava,* pastry made of paper-thin leaves of dough with a middle layer of chopped walnuts mixed with cinnamon and sugar, baked golden, and cut into diamond-shaped pieces with syrup drizzled over them. There was a sweet *soujouk* in the shape of an intestine next to a knife on a wooden cutting board. Persimmons were ripening on the windowsill above the sink, and the kitchen smelled of paprika and cinnamon and garlic and parsley and onions skewered between cubes of lamb stacked on a platter on the sink. Sizzling vermicelli was browning in butter for pilaf at the bottom of a big pot that sat squat on the stove when Andy walked in.

"Hey, hey, smells good," Andy said, a smile beaming on his face.

Martha turned around and smiled and lifted her arms up.

"Happy Thanksgiving," she sang.

She wiped her hands on her apron and took his face in the heels of her palms and kissed him.

Abe was next. She gave him a kiss on the cheek and then bent over and kissed the kids, who were lugging on their hips a small sack of walnuts each. Zabel had a big jar of *tourshee* cradled in one arm. She set it on the kitchen counter and looked around as though she were puzzled by the surroundings.

"Zabel's famous *tourshee*," Martha said, admiring the variety of pickled vegetables crowded in the jar. Zabel put on a smile and said she hoped Martha liked it, since she only got around to making half a batch this year.

In the backyard, Martha's husband, Kirk, was getting the fire going in the hollow of a rectangular brick shish kebob pit with slotted iron railings where the long skewers could be fitted and turned. From the window, Andy saw him out there all alone and went to keep him company.

"Brother-in-law," Andy said and put out a hand.

He tossed a stump on the fire, smacked his palms free of dirt.

"Brother-in-law," Kirk said. He shook Andy's hand. "What do you think?" Kirk looked up at the sky.

"I figure it'll hold off most of today."

"Thank God we built this canopy," he said.

Andy picked up a stump and put it on the fire. When it met the flames it popped and crackled and spit.

"Good wood," Andy said.

Andy heard another car pull up in the driveway.

"Tell you what, Kirk. Go on in and say hello and I'll watch the fire."

"You sure?"

"No sweat."

"I'll pick up the meat on the way back out," Kirk said.

Wherever Andy was, he liked to have a job. He was most comfortable with his family, but even there, he felt a little out of place and alone. The vine stumps were gnarled and shedding their outer bark in curled ribbons. He wondered how old the vines were. He pushed them around with a fat iron rod. The heat shoved him back a step. He stared at the flames that put him in a kind of trance. He thrust the rod into the center of the fire and moved it around like he was fencing. Sparks swarmed up and died in the air. For shish kebob you need a good hot fire. The stumps on the bottom started to glow orange. He thought of fire, how it could burn you to a cinder, how it could serve you.

Hearing the back door open, Andy looked over his shoulder and saw Betty was taking short steps toward him across the rain-slicked cement. He regretted that he wouldn't have some more time to himself with the fire.

"It's not *too* cold," she said. "How are you, brother?" She pecked him on the cheek.

"Fine, sweetheart."

"I'm a little worried about you," she admitted.

"What for? Hell, don't worry about me," he said, putting his eyes on her stomach, which was all plump with baby.

"Oh," she said. "I feel fine. What going on with the farm?"

Andy was hoping nobody would bring the topic up. He didn't want to have to deal with it on Thanksgiving day. By now everyone knew about the fiasco down south, that he and Abe were in some sort of trouble.

"Betty, I don't want to talk about it."

"Something about a loan? Abe said something about a loan."

There was no way he was going to avoid it.

"Yeah, we got one from the government."

"Did you do what I told you yet?"

Nearly a year ago she had sat him down and told him he had to draw up some papers, some contract that would squarely divide the land in half. Andy didn't like anyone butting into his and Abe's business. Especially his youngest sister.

"Who do I have to protect myself from, my own brother?"

"Your brother, no. But your brother isn't alone."

Betty was suspicious of Zabel because of an episode a few months before. There were a few odds and ends leftover from her parents, and they'd sat around Abe and Zabel's house for years, collecting dust. Betty decided she'd grown partial to a quilt and a few other items hand-sewn by her mother. On the patio one Sunday, she casually mentioned to Zabel that she wouldn't mind having them. Zabel swung out of her chair and ran the length of the field like a jackrabbit. A few minutes later, Abe marched into the house and declared everything in the house his wife's.

Betty didn't have to remind Andy that it was that incident that prompted her concern.

"We're fine, Betty. Look, I'm not stupid. You think I haven't thought about this? How are we supposed to split up the equipment? How do you split up the house, the barn? It's not so easy. In the long run it's less of a headache if we farm together. This way we've got more leverage over situations too. I remember what our old man told me. You can get one person to break, simple; but it takes a helluva lot more effort to break two. No, Betty. We work as a team or we go down as a team."

"You're not in any trouble, are you?"

"Hell, no. We're expanding."

"You're going to buy some more land."

"Probably rent for the time being."

"But you're going to start your own family soon. You're going to need your own place."

"When that time comes, we'll tackle that problem. One thing at a time."

"You can't live in that house forever. Not with Zabel and the kids and all. It won't work. Believe me. Just think about what I said, Andy."

"Okay," he had said. "I'll think about it."

He poked at the fire some more as he recalled that conversation.

"Naw, Betty," he said, "I didn't. I didn't do what you said. Anyway, good thing I didn't or we maybe wouldn't have got this loan."

He was relieved when Kirk walked up with the meat.

"We ready to turn 'em?" Andy asked.

They had all gathered around the table. Andy, Abe and Zabel and the three kids. From San Francisco, their sister Willa, the oldest but youngest of heart, had driven down with her husband Art, who owned a small liquor store and kept a ring of keys clipped to his belt, and their two children, Dot and Babs. The latter played the classical piano. From Modesto, with a superior air came their sister Connie, whose boisterous voice made grown men wither. Her husband, Victor, ran a trucking outfit and had a nose as big as a lobster's tail, and eyes that were red and watery all the time. With them were their two, Linda and Chucky. Patty, Betty's girl, was beside her mother, and another, two months away, was kicking up a storm inside of Betty's womb. Seerop, her husband, a spectacular dancer with deep brown eyes who earned his living as a carpenter in town, stood beside her. Martha was at one end of the table and Kirk the other. In the middle of the table, standing with the reverence of an altar boy next to her husband, Benjamin, who was about to pray, was the fourth sister, blue-eyed Catherine. They'd made the trip up the evening before from Pasadena with their three kids, whom Catherine was now quieting down. The conversations petered out in spurts, shhhh, shhh, and then a lull. Benjamin cleared his throat and began.

"Let's pray." All heads now bowed. "Dear Heavenly Father, we come here today to give you thanks for the many blessings you've bestowed upon this family. Lord, when our people came to this country we had nothing, only the terrible memories of the past. In this God-loving country, you have made it possible for us to prosper. The food on this table is a reminder of the day when our people had no food, the security in this land is a reminder of the time when we had no such thing. Most of all, Lord, thank you for the love that the members of this family have one for the other. Keep us safe in your hands, keep all those who cannot be with us today safe. Lord, bless our president and this great country. Amen."

Everyone said amen. Martha sang, "Help yourselves."

Hands flew across the table, steaming platters were passed and plates were filled high with pilaf and shish kebob and cuts of the fat and juicy turkey and yams and cranberries and thick *peda* bread with toasted sesame seeds on top. All the *maza* had been transferred to the long table too. The windows behind them steamed up, except in blotches where the two dogs kept shoving their noses. Conversation was general above the clatter and tinkling of silverware. Everyone was asking everyone else how things were going, and everyone was saying things were just fine and would they please pass this or that. Abe was chewing at the gizzards of the bird, and Andy was tearing away at a wing slobbered with gravy, trying to forget the conversation with Betty, when Kirk stood up with a wineglass extended in front of him. Martha chimed her own glass repeatedly with a fork until all heads had turned toward her husband.

"Now," he said, and elevated his voice. "I consider myself a lucky man to be in this family…"

"Ohh now."

"No, wait a minute. I'm serious," Kirk said.

"Go ahead, brother-in-law!" Seerop said.

"It's your table after all, Kirk," Catherine said.

"The table is all of ours," Kirk said. Mellowness came over everyone.

"Well, I've got my beautiful wife." Martha put her hands on her heart. "All of the sisters have fine husbands. Abe has Zabel. So, who I want to make this toast for is our brother Andy."

Andy looked up from his food, cleaned his fingers of gravy.

"Andy," Kirk continued, "we don't have to remind you that you're not married yet..."

The company burst out in laughter.

"What is he saying?" Zabel whispered to Abe, as though she were too old to hear, or too young to understand.

"He's toasting Andy," Abe said.

"We also don't have to remind you," Kirk went on, "that you're a fine brother and brother-in-law. A well-educated man, good-lookin', and of a good Christian family."

"Fresno's full of nice Armenian girls," Martha put in. "I don't know what's wrong with him." Several others nodded in agreement.

"Anyway. The day comes when a man needs a wife and kids, he needs these things to settle him down and make him happy in a way he couldn't be alone."

Kirk winked at Andy. Another round of laughter.

"May this blessing be yours next, Andy."

In a broken chorus, "May it," they sang and toasted.

Andy smiled wide and thanked Kirk, and Kirk said that what he said was the truth, and Andy reckoned he was right.

When dinner was done, one by one they lugged themselves out of their seats as though from a mud bath. Andy flopped on a couch in the den; he'd eaten so much he was out of breath. Some of the older kids were on the floor next to the log fire, haggling over a shoe, a hat, a dog, a car, a thimble and who would be the banker for Monopoly. Next to him, Kirk and Benjamin had pulled chairs up to a coffee table, where they were setting up discs on a backgammon board. Catherine and Abe and Betty and Seerop all sat around a fold-out table, sorting through cards for pinochle.

Margie Simmons was Andy's girl for two years in college. And before her there were plenty of others. Maybe that was the problem, Andy thought. Best idea is a guy gets married early before he has the chance to snoop around beneath too many skirts. That'll spoil you, plus if you wait around too long you get to seeing the way a woman can play tricks with a man's head. But what about Margie? He couldn't even remember the names of half the women he'd been with, but Margie's face kept appearing to him in the shower, in bed, in dreams. She treated him like a prince. He had his chance there, and he let it pass. Why? He made all sorts of excuses at the time, but the truth was she wasn't Armenian. He had it in his mind to marry an Armenian girl the whole time, so this blue-eyed leggy *odar* took him by surprise. In the end the prospect of mixing blood, of watering down the milk of his people, had felt like a betrayal. But he stayed with her, even as the chance of marrying her closed in on zero. When they broke up, he felt guilty about having dragged it on. He hated to hurt women, but short of marrying them, could he avoid it? They all wanted to marry him. Shit, with the war and all, he'd been nearly proposed to half a dozen times. Was he as good a catch as these girls thought? Yes and no. They saw one side of him, the side he let them see: the gentleman, the opener of doors, the flipper of bills, the faithful, forever-wise boyfriend who listened to them deep into the evening talk about their dreams. He knew how to treat women. In that regard, he'd taught his friends a thing or two.

"Turkish coffee?" Martha was bent over with a tray of steaming demitasses.

He took it with two hands off the platter and thanked her and said he was so full he was going to bust.

She laughed. "Good."

He slurped the black stuff up. Turkish coffee, the only thing the Turks ever gave us that was worth a shit, his father once told him bitterly. He could remember how it felt with Margie, a blanket wrapped around them as they watched the full moon tinsel the water. The ease of her head on his shoulder, the quiet of her closed eyes, and the innocence of her knees bending in toward his. Watching the children play, he had a visceral yearning to see his own child among them. He wondered what it would have been like if he had kept that child, if Cassandra hadn't wanted an abortion. Sometimes he would follow Teddy's warm deep breathing in the middle of the night as though it were the breathing of his own. With the thought that he would never have children, never find that Armenian wife, a cavity opened up inside of him. He wondered if that fire was still going outside. He wanted to be out in the cold, alone, close to something warm.

Back home that evening, he felt more left out than ever. The clouds had cleared and it was bitingly cold. Andy put on a coat and went and sat on the patio with a glass of whiskey.

"What is he doing out there?" Zabel asked Abe.

"Looks like he's drinking some whiskey."

"He's drinking too much these days. Is he crazy?"

Abe turned his head and looked. Andy was in the rocking chair. Smoke burst out of his mouth from the cold, as though inside of him fire smoldered. Now and then Andy shook his head, like he was recollecting something, something disturbing. Abe wondered what Andy had learned in school that would make him so pensive. He wasn't like that when he was younger, before he left for college.

"Leave him be," he told Zabel.

"So that I have to take care of him when he catches a cold?"

Abe threw up his hands.

Zabel exchanged places with Abe at the window. She pressed her palm to the glass, then quickly crossed her arms in front of her and shivered.

"Let him stay out there, then," she said to Abe, who was passing down the hall. She thought, What's he have to complain about? She thought, What right does he have to stay in my home any longer, anyway? If Andy wants to, let him stay out there forever, for good.

15

PRUNING TIME. The winter fog lay even and low, and Andy entered the vineyard as if it were a sanctuary. It was unbelievably tranquil in there, the dank earth giving a little beneath his boots. With double-bladed shears, he snapped at the canes. Within minutes, they lay in tangles behind him in the middle of the row. A bluebird jumped out of a vine and vanished into the white. Andy stopped to see a nest cradled between the canes. Two beautiful eggs, oval and blue, lay in a delicate basket of twigs. He remembered crushing similar eggs cruelly beneath his boots when he was a kid and proceeded past them with a pang of shame.

Abe was on the other end of the vineyard. Though the loan had lifted them out of the financial rut that the tomato crop had put them in, there was a vague tension between them. Andy thought that Zabel and Abe still blamed him for what had happened down south, strange as it might sound. Andy hoped that once this harvest was over and they'd put a few bucks into their pockets and paid down the loan, Abe would be able to see straight again.

Half the farmers he knew had one time or another gone mad over a crop loss two years in a row. Ten years later they'd still be moaning. They might be sporting a brand new truck, they might have quadrupled their acreage, but to hear them tell it they were always in debt and barely squeaking by. It was as though they'd never recover, like every day a plague was on its way. Total crop loss will make the healthiest man sick in the head, Andy thought.

Not that Abe was all there to begin with. Lately, though, things were worse than usual. Andy noticed that Abe's eyes were jumpy from nerves, and that when he talked it was as though he expected the devil himself to pop up from behind and go boo. No, Andy thought, that damn war screwed with my brother's brain. What with Zabel and that crazy bitch of a mother-in-law, Abe's chances were zero. While mulling these thoughts over in his head, Andy had come to a standstill. In his hands, the pruning shears bobbed like a divining rod. He shook his head, as though to wake himself from a dream. He could see his breath leave him in bursts. He could feel the heat beneath his shirt. He pruned on. This must be, he thought, how men survive on a field of war. Surrounded by a thick fog of ignorance, moving forward, cutting men down one after another without even knowing whether their sacrifice would profit them. Such men, he thought, have to be governed by more than the outcomes of their efforts, they must be governed by the simple fact that there is work to be done to keep the world going, as though they were part of nature's machinery itself, with as much choice in the matter as has the sun or the moon. What say do the vines have in the course of things? Trained, fed and tended to, they must bear fruit. Andy's hands were red and cold. Like ice. He could barely feel them anymore. He had powerful, muscular shoulders, trained to prune. He lifted the shears, and he used these muscles to cut the canes down. The raw power of his torso was a comfort; at least he could count on the precise and wholesome action of his physical body. A whistle cut through the fog, sounding as though it came from a great distance. It was his brother calling. But he didn't care to break for lunch just then, he didn't care if there were a billion acres to prune, he didn't care if the row never ended.

Before he stepped out the door, Andy knew he would get drunk that night, not fall-down drunk but drunk enough to make whatever matters not matter anymore. He hadn't gotten loose in a while, and frankly, he felt less a man as a result. He wanted that first drink so bad, just thinking about it was getting him happy.

He pulled on to Chateau Fresno and started south toward town. The full moon was so icy clear and crisp white that it throbbed in the sky. Andy rolled the window down and his eyes started to tear from the cold, and for a second he wondered whether he was tearing from an approaching memory. Perhaps it was creeping up from behind him, like a pair of headlights in your rearview mirror. Or maybe these tears had no meaning at all, maybe they were waiting for a meaning to be given to them. Could be a memory, could be the wind or a fleck of dust in his eye.

The bar, The Egg and I, was slow and cozy. The barkeep, Sammy-boy Boyajian, was Armenian, and the bar had a jukebox stuffed with jazz; Stan Kenton, the Bird, canaries like Sarah Vaughn, Billie Holiday.

"Well, Andy-boy," Sammy said. "Haven't seen you in a while."

"Been workin' hard, Sammy."

"Scotch?"

"A double."

Andy watched as Sammy poured the drink over some ice, nice and high, threw a napkin in front of him and set the drink on top of it.

He noticed Sammy-boy was edgy.

"Looks like something's bugging you, Sammy."

"Naw. I just had to throw someone out before you came."

"So early in the evening."

"I'll tell you, Andy. Every now and then you get a whiff of what these fucking *odars* really think of us."

"Some guy say something about you being Armenian?"

"Same shit. Made some remark about how we're taking over this town, how you can't turn anywhere these days without running into an Armenian."

Andy took a sip of his drink. Shook his head.

"Volga?"

"Looked like it. Him and a friend of his. Tried to make it into some sort of joke. But I had his number. Showed him where the door was. Gary Shapazian was sittin' right there. He saw it all. You know Gary," he said, pointing his chin down the bar.

"Shapazian?" In Armenian the name meant "the spoiled one's son."

"Farms fruit trees out in Reedley."

He waved Shapazian over. Gary brought his drink with him. Sammy introduced them to each other.

"Wasn't that something, Gary?" Sammy chuckled nervously.

Gary shook his head. Sammy-boy and Andy shook their heads in response.

"Naw," Gary said, stewing over it still, "if it was left to them, they'd haul the whole lot of us out of here in gondola bins. I don't care what they say. Like we are all a bunch of niggers."

He straightened a crook in his neck. "These *odars* are just another type of Turk. Just the other day, who was it…Vince Chopchakian, out in Kingsburg, he was telling me about his kid who plays ball down there, you know, Little League."

"Kingsburg. All Swedes," Sammy said. "They care for an Armenian as much as they care for a jackrabbit in a lettuce patch."

"So Vince tells me his kid's coach refuses to play him. That the kid had earned some playing time. Okay. So, he taps the coach on the shoulder after one of the games and real polite-like asks him, 'Hey Coach, how 'bout givin' the kid a swing at the ball now and then?' You know what this coach's answer is? 'What do Armenians got doing playing baseball, anyhow?' Like all we're good for is selling rugs. Can you believe that shit?"

Andy could see the evening turning into some sort of nationalist rally. He'd never been the target of bigotry himself, though he'd heard enough similar anecdotes to know that the situation they were pointing to was real. Still, he couldn't help thinking that these Armenians who complained must be doing something to bring such animosity their way. Of course, this was nothing he could say out loud. Must have been something about his body language that was communicating it though, because just then Gary asked him, "How about you, Andy? Ever know anything like this?"

"Can't say I have, to be square with you. But I'm no less sorry for that kid of Vince's. That's a damn shame. That coach deserves a lickin'."

"When'd your folks come over?"

"My folks? After the genocide. What else?"

"I guarantee you they knew it. 'No Armenians allowed on premises,' these *odars* here wrote on their shop windows. That's how bad it was then."

"Worse than that," Sammy said. "In the title instructions of real property, there were stipulations that the land couldn't be sold to Armenians. Ever."

"I live in one such house," Gary said.

Andy shook his head, showing he was sorry it happened.

"Well, thank God we own the stores now," Sammy said. "Let them try and throw us out of our own places."

Andy had finished his drink.

"Another double, Andy?"

"Please."

Andy slid the glass toward him. Sammy dropped a few cubes of ice in it and poured the scotch generously over them.

The wind had picked up outside. Through the window Andy could see the tattered leaves of some tropical trees thrash around.

Gary asked Andy, "You belong to the Triple-X?"

This was an Armenian social group that most men of his generation belonged to.

"Naw."

"Bet you've been to a few of their dances, anyway," Sammy said, seeing that the conversation was heading in an argumentative direction.

"Oh, those I've been to."

"Down at the Rainbow Ballroom?"

"Why don't you come to one of our meetings someday?"

A couple of people had walked in. Sammy went to help them.

"Be honest with you, Gary, I don't find much use in it. Those kind of organizations aren't for me, that's all."

"What kind of people are they for then?"

"Guess you'll have to answer that for yourself."

Gary asked him what kind of Armenian was he?

Andy quietly nursed his drink. The alcohol had put him in an I-don't-give-a-shit mood. The narrowness of these Armenians struck him as sort of comical; he thought, Maybe the whole culture has small-man's complex.

"The kind, I guess, that don't care for the Triple-X."

"You're not one of these Reds, are you?" Gary asked.

Andy wasn't a Communist, but if he should say straight out what he thought of the shenanigans that had gone on in Washington, he would've been targeted as one in a lick. The way that McCarthy and his pack of jackals had fed on innocent citizens was the worse sort of abuse of power he could imagine.

Andy said, "I think the basic working stiff hasn't gotten his due. I think there's probably plenty of folks would want to see him work for free if they could get away with it. No," Andy said, "I'm not a Red and I'm not a member of the Triple-X. But I'll tell you, I respect the right of people to do and think what the hell they please. I don't want any suit telling me what I can and can't say. If things've come to that, maybe this system needs some shaking up."

"It was this system that let your father and my father into this country."

"That's true enough. No argument there. But just because something is true doesn't mean it can't be improved. It's true the rain these last few days has given us water, but that don't mean we don't need ditch water, do it?"

"Water's one thing, betraying your country is another. These people are sellout artists, these Reds want the downfall of this country."

"I never talked to one of these people personally, so I wouldn't know what they're after. Have you, Gary?"

"What's there to talk about? They're Communists. I think we should deport 'em all. All of them. Let them go back to Mother Russia where they belong. They stink."

"Well, I suppose every man has his opinion about it. And I suppose these Communists you know so well have theirs. That's the point. Let every man have his say."

"If they came and took your land, I guarantee you wouldn't be talking that way."

"I don't have to wait for them to take my land away. Be truthful with you, Gary, the way things are shapin' up, the banks will do that before the Reds have a chance."

Drunk, Andy cut the lights and rolled into the yard. For a minute or so he just sat in the car, listening. The giant junipers on the side of the road nodded in the wind like a bunch of Muslims praying. He felt how miserly was the whole human world next to the exuberance of the wind. He wondered if there would ever be a world where people would give themselves up like this wind, a human hurricane that would leave standing in its wake only the most robust, the fittest. He wanted to be part of that wind, that world—a world where men would look you straight in the eye, where acts of kindness came from the overflow of life, where there was no distance between what a man said and what he was.

He noticed a patch of yellow light on the barn door at the back of the house. It was damn near one o'clock in the morning. Abe and Zabel must still be up, he thought. Then he noticed Abe's car was gone.

Abe was shuffling down the hallway when he opened the door.

"What's up?" He closed the door quietly behind him. "Where's your car?"

Abe could smell the scotch on Andy's breath.

"Old lady's sick or something. Wind," Abe said. "Zabel took the car. Alone."

There was some kind accusation in Abe's voice. "So?" Andy said.

"Someone had to watch the kids."

Andy asked, "What? She wanted you to drive her?"

"You expect her to drive alone in this wind?"

Was there some threat that the wind was going to blow the car off the road? What was the issue?

"Well, go ahead." A snigger in his voice. "Take my truck. I'm home now. Go ahead."

Abe looked at his watch.

"When did she leave?" Andy asked, forcing back a chuckle.

"Couple of hours ago."

"You expect me to be back at eleven o'clock? What am I, some schoolboy?"

"Where did you go tonight?"

"I had a drink."

"You had a *few* drinks."

"This conversation's over." Andy handed Abe his keys.

"With whose money?"

"Mine. Who else's?"

"So you think."

"Am I on an allowance now? It's that what it's come to?"

"You're drinking too much."

"Just enough."

"Your college days are over. Better get that straight in your head."

"I can see this isn't working out, Abe. I don't deserve this kind of harassment."

"You don't know what harassment is."

"I can't help it if your old lady is leaning on you. Just tell her to stay out of my life."

"It's not just her anymore."

Andy brushed by Abe and start limping to his room.

"Don't wake the kids," Abe said.

Just looking at all the mayhem outside got Angel so jittery that she reckoned her intestines might shake right out of her bottom. Her joints, they creaked when she moved, and it took everything in her power to crawl up out of bed and call Zabel. She grabbed a cleaver from the kitchen and sat back in her velvet chair like a butcher's homicidal wife, waiting. A violent gust broke a limb loose from the sycamore and pitched it on her porch steps and sent it clattering against her windowpane. The white limb scraped against the glass and wailed the sound of a cat in heat, and now and again lurched at her. From fear her hand shook, as a chef's does when working a salt canister. When she saw a halo of light bob up the drive, she thanked God, put her cleaver down, crossed her heart and slowly approached the door. Zabel trembled too, from fear of the wind or from rage toward Andy, or perhaps a volatile mixture of the two. When she took her first step up the porch, Angel flung the door open, poked her head barely past the jamb and pointed at the limb against the window with her chin. Zabel froze. Was a cat burglar hiding in the shrubs? Where was Abe now?

"What is it?" Zabel whispered.

In Armenian she said, "The tree."

Zabel understood she meant the limb. She heaved it over the railing.

"Was it only that?" she asked, stepping inside.

"Watch your mouth! You don't know how naughty it was."

There was only a single lamp on in the corner.

"Why are you in the dark?" Zabel asked her as she felt for the light switch on the wall.

"So that their eyes couldn't catch me."

The light was like melted butter on the ceiling.

"Sit," Zabel beseeched her. "I'll make some mint tea."

A gust of sweet curdled air hit Zabel when she stepped into the kitchen. When she flipped on the light, her stomach jumped. The kitchen

counters were piled with food and the sink was brimming with a putre-
fying, almond-colored pool that had spilled over onto the floor. She felt
dizzy and leaned back against the refrigerator. She saw a pile of tomatoes
shift, and adjusted her eyes. Bands of ants swarmed over everything. At
spots they were so thickly clumped they seemed to be a vegetable themselves. She turned around and swung the refrigerator door open. The old
woman had taken all the fresh food out of the refrigerator to make room
for cans! My poor mother, she thought. She reached for a tin of green
beans. What was she thinking? The wind must have knocked the electricity out, Zabel thought. That's what happened! Poor soul!

She closed the door, held her breath, and tiptoed through the puddles over to the sink. Her mother had emptied her refrigerator into the
sink. Who knows how long she's been alone without electricity. She felt
damned for leaving her mother alone for the last four days. She could
hear her mother's words: *What you do to your mother your children will
someday do to you.* Zabel could see the day when Abe was dead and the
children had gone away, she could see herself living alone drifting into
oblivion, alone in a world seething with ants. My Lord, sweet Jesus,
please forgive me, please, the Lord of our forefathers, the Lord of our
church, my sweet Jesus, look past my sins.

For a good half hour Andy stood in front of the window absently
studying the violent energy of the wind outside. Now and then he'd
chuckle bitterly at the wind, at himself, his fate, who knows what?

"Uncle Andy?" Teddy said.

"It's me, Teddy," Andy said.

"Is everything all right?"

"Everything's all right, kid. Go back to sleep."

He slipped into bed, fully dressed. I'll tell you what, Abe, he said to
himself. Why don't I just leave the whole place to you and Zabel so that
all of us can get a decent night's sleep. No, Andy thought, the answer's
easy. Just pack up and leave and let them have it. Is any of this worth
your peace of mind? Nothing is worth a man's peace of mind. The
whole world is crawling over each other just to get to a little crumb of

bread. Some people are so desperate they'd kill for that crumb of bread. Do you want to be like these people? There is a place outside of all that noise. What the hell did Jesus need? How about those rag heads—what did they call themselves—the Sufis? Remember Buddha?

He got himself up to make it to church the next morning along with the rest of the family. Abe and Zabel were in sour moods—nobody had to ask why. For Andy's part, he was a little hungover but generous-hearted and, painful as it was, ready to put the evening behind him. On the road there, Andy asked Zabel how her mother was doing. Zabel grunted. Andy was amazed how a woman who was on her way to church could harbor such hostility. Andy thought people shouldn't even be allowed in church if they intended to tote the same dirty laundry out that they took in. What's the use of a church then?

By the time they drove up, he was a little sorry he hadn't decided to stay home. He could've had his own private church service on the front porch. They shuffled into the church, twenty minutes into the two-hour Mass. The air was already congested with incense that smelled like burning leaves. Andy let the family go ahead of him down the aisle and when they'd seated themselves, he stepped into a pew behind them. The black-hooded priests with long black beards and jet-black eyes were circling beneath the tall apse like grounded ravens, violently jerking the censers as they went. Andy recalled how, when he was a boy, he'd pray to God, above all else, for his own safety, because he was afraid that at any second one of those censers would break loose of its chains and slay him. The priest was somewhere between a proclamation and a song—"Our God, the most heavenly..."—and then the voices of the choir rose in response: "AAAAAAMEN."

He watched the smoky incense drift and marble the air and become corporeal in the yawning cylinders of light that came through the clouds, down through the pale blue dome overhead. An ancient woman whose foxed skin hung down in pleats was kneeled next to him, her bony hands knit together on the pew and beating as though between them she were struggling to crack open a walnut. Our church is sixteen hundred years old, his father had told him. And it seemed that these old folks had been there from the start, as though they were ageless, born old, as though old age were not a feature of them but rather the thing from which they were shaped.

Andy watched the priest's fist shake on the staff as he told a story of the building of the church of Lake Sevan. This church was built by a King in the year A.D. 590 for his daughter, the princess Nairi. It took many years to build, as it was erected on an island in the middle of the great Lake Sevan, where the most delicious fish in the world could be found. "Once," he said, "you could go to the church and feel protected by the water that surrounded you, you could be in a spirit of perfect contemplation. But now," he said, "the lake has receded. The church overlooks what is left of the lake on a stony hill. This," he said, "is how it feels to be an Armenian. God has seemingly withdrawn from our people, the way the water withdrew from the lake. One is then vulnerable to evil from all sides. But that church, like our people, still stands. So must we stand in the midst of persecution. As our forefather stood firm in their faith, so must we. Amen."

Andy stepped in line for the sacrament, behind men in fraying gray suits, behind old women all draped in black, their eyes lowered behind black shawls bound around their heads, their hands crossed in front of them, inching forward with all the somberness of a funeral procession—which in a way, Andy thought, is what the sacrament is. When he reached the altar, he dropped to his knees. The priest tapped the wafer on his tongue, whispering, "This is our Lord's flesh." Cradled in a cloth, the chalice was tipped to the lips of those waiting with necks stretched—lambs themselves ready for the slaughter. He saw a grizzled old woman lean against the railing and wail *"Mer Christos, mer Christos,"* and he knew—as did everyone else—that she was reliving for a moment the horror of the genocide.

After the *"Hyer Mer"* was sung, they filed outside the church. Children ran up and down the steps or clung to their mothers' skirts, their big black eyes earnest, alert. Zabel and Abe and the kids weren't around. They'd probably gone for *chorag* and coffee at the reception hall around the corner. Andy lit a cigarette. The air was clean and cold and the clouds were smeared in the sky like spilled milk. He was a little lightheaded from the whiskeys the night before, and puffing deep on the cigarette didn't help. He dropped the cigarette and crushed it out with his foot and wondered whether Abe wasn't right, whether he was drinking too much these days. The priest had now made his way outside and was shaking hands. Andy caught his eye, and they each took a step toward each other.

"Antranik."

"Father Jambajian," Andy said. "How are you?"

"Thank God, very well."

Andy wanted to know whether those fish in Lake Sevan were a kind of trout or bass or what. The priest pondered this question. Then someone caught the priest's attention and he scuttled off, leaving Andy's question dangling. When Andy turned around to see who was so important, he wasn't surprised that it was one of the largest donors to the church—that little shit Karnig Samuelian. Andy could swear the priest kissed this Samuelian's ass, and he wondered whether the priest knew that the loot Samuelian had pledged for the new church was all dirty, that this Samuelian got rich by buying grapes on the vine and then shorting the farmer. It was all done on a handshake. He would prey on farmers who were short on cash, giving them half their money up front and promising them the moon once the market price was set. But when that time came around, he had a million excuses why the crop he'd bought wasn't up to par, why the farmer would have to make do with what he gave him. Without fail (surprise!), the market was lower than anyone had expected. According to Samuelian, he was always losing money, but then how the hell could he afford that fucking Jaguar and the minks scowling from over his wife's shoulders? Andy shook his head in disgust and went down the steps. Disgust with the farmers too, who didn't have the balls to pursue it in court. All they did was bitch and moan. And Samuelian knew that's all they'd do. Because, though he was a crook, he was still Armenian, and it was a shame to bring one of your own people into a court of law. Never again, they'd say. But with his own eyes, Andy had seen Samuelian swindle the same farmers over and over again.

No, Andy thought, money will make a bad man good. It'll turn a slob handsome. And his witch of a wife, voila, a debutante. It made his stomach churn. Inside the reception hall, Zabel and Abe were discussing something with Dr. Sivas, chomping on *chorag*. Sivas was another of the big donors, but unlike Samuelian, he was a quiet man who always seemed overworked. He treated dozens of old Armenians who couldn't afford healthcare otherwise, for free. Sivas was nodding his head at some point Zabel was making with a finger lifted in the air, when Andy stepped up. Zabel was putting her two cents in about the new church.

"Baron Andy," Sivas said.

"Doctor Sivas."

In spite of the fact that Sivas was a decent guy, and obviously educated, Andy couldn't help thinking that he too was getting bamboozled. There was no need for a new church. The only reason they were building one was because they were competing with the other Armenian churches in town.

"What do you think, Andy?" Sivas asked. "Should we pattern the church after Etchmiadzin, or something else? After today's service, your sister-in-law thinks Sevan."

"I'd appreciate if first someone could tell me why we need a new church. Then I might be able to give you an educated answer."

Zabel looked at him as though he'd cursed.

"Doesn't God deserve to be honored?" Zabel asked.

"I think he's honored plenty right here."

"But this church is old," Sivas said. "The children have no place to go. Without heating in the winters it's too cold for the older members."

"I understand," Andy said. "But does this congregation lack for the elderly? Have they stopped coming because it is cold? Look around you. And the children, they've sat in their parents' laps for years. They don't need no separate place to go."

Abe said, "Look at it, though, Andy. It's getting to be a barn. The place is falling down."

"Nothing a paint job and a few strong backs couldn't cure."

"Shame on you!" Zabel said.

"Look, I don't mean to take the place of the Father here, but whatever happens in a church happens inside of us. We could congregate in a ditch for all God cares."

"A ditch!" Zabel jumped at him. "Would God want to be praised in a ditch? Should my children," she said, clutching her son Greg, "worship our Lord in a ditch?"

"But Andy, if our forefathers thought that way," Sivas said, "would we ever have the likes of Etchmiadzin, or Keghart?"

"With all due respect, Dr. Sivas, we already have our Etchmiadzin our Keghart in this very church. I'm going to get some coffee."

16

THE SUMMER DAY WAS WIDE AND BRIGHT beside the river on the southern end of Kingsburg. From a dirt lot where cars were parked, families had weaved their way down—with sacks full of peaches and apricots and figs, and lawn chairs, backgammon boards and blankets— to the bank of the slow-moving Kings River. Already elders had secured seats at the periphery of an outdoor patio with a broad roof and cement floor where the players unpacked their precious instruments: the *dumbag,* the *kanoon,* the clarinet, the fat-bellied *oud.* Mothers waded with their children in the shallows as the men, bent over card tables set up in the shade of ash and elm trees, played pinochle or ferocious rounds of backgammon. At the brick barbeque, cubes of lamb, skewered between onion and pepper and tomato, were stacked on big platters. Three men wearing aprons were already drinking beer to cool themselves down from the flashing white heat of the coals over which the meat sizzled and blistered, emitting delicious gusts that drifted over the grass, down to the river where Kareen stood ankle-deep with her flower print skirt tied just above her knees, her hands gently skimming the water as though she were befriending it.

"She's nice," Andy's sister Martha said. "Very pretty."

Andy had already concluded that the Armenian women from Alexandria, Egypt, possessed a different species of beauty than other Armenian women; feminine and refined and fair, something of the Mediterranean breeze in their hair. Andy knew Kareen's sister Alice and Alice's husband, Arsen, who worked at the gas station just outside of town that Andy frequented. One day Arsen pulled a snapshot of his wife from out of his wallet and showed Andy. Andy asked him if his wife had a sister. A few days later Arsen showed him a picture of a woman in a beige dress, maybe twenty, leaning against a rock at the beach. She had a thin waist, full breasts, and a face that was pretty in a classical way.

At noon, the music began. A man led, hankie in hand, nodding and then throwing his head back, and one by one men and women and children jumped out of their seats and joined hands as the man cracked the hankie and the dancers whipped forward in a human chain. The *oud,* each note plucked from the gut, the shaking tambourine, the dum-dum—dumdumdum—of the dumbag, the clarinet, a dancing wasp, and the silver pinging of the kanoon, all together they conversed ecstatically, rising and dropping with the dancers, man and music all one piece.

Alice got Reverend Jambajian involved, asking his opinion of this man, Andy, his money. Of course, the priest told them that Andy's farm was so vast the eye could not see the end of it. More, he was from a good family, though sadly he had nearly reared himself, since his father had died when he was fourteen, and two years later his mother had died of a stroke, poor woman, before they understood about such things as high blood pressure. The entire family was clean and proper and the two brothers worked the farm together. What their arrangement was he could not say. He is very educated, a graduate of college, athletic, and the limp, it's nothing to worry about, he had polio as a child like so many others, but it had only made him more of a man. A man with a strong heart and generous to a fault. You can be sure that he will stand close to his own family as he stands close to the Lord. He is the proper age to be married. Financially secure and of a solid character. I tell you, my daughter, your sister would be lucky. He is one of the best catches in town. Let them see each other and see if they care for what they see, they agreed.

Kareen stepped out of the river, picked up her shoes and walked over to a blanket draped on the grass. Andy watched her smooth the blanket with a hand, sit down and dry her feet with a towel. By the fluency of her gestures alone, he could tell that this was no farm girl. She tilted her head back and let the sun caress her face, as though she were trying to re-create in her mind the Mediterranean's luxurious atmosphere. She seemed to have lived her entire life amid finery. He wondered if she was conscious of her beauty, if she could feel the eyes of men climbing over her as she rose and sauntered across the grass and slipped past those seated at the perimeter onto the dance floor. She was lovely, he thought, the kind of woman whose beauty would fade slowly, if ever.

With her eyes half-hidden, she had taken him in as well. Her impression? A man with an open smile, knowing and calming brown eyes, broad and confident shoulders.

If she hadn't been out there, Andy would not have joined in the dance that afternoon. Perhaps because he was afraid that dancing would draw attention to his bad leg, he better enjoyed sitting with those too old to dance, instead dancing along in his imagination. He cut in two persons down from her, and when, after a couple of songs, those two left, he was hand in hand with her. He felt his heart rise as the music began again. She looked at him, tossed her head back and laughed girlishly, as though they shared a secret. Then a woman came across the floor and with a wink took Kareen's hand out of his. Kareen and this woman danced fluently together, familiar with each other's steps. This, Andy thought, must be either her mother or her aunt.

It was her mother. The story of her life is a book in itself. If it weren't for the fact that she was young and pretty, Valentine Keadjian might never have escaped the genocide. In 1914, the Turkish officials had started the systematic murder of those people who occupied that land for nearly three thousand years. News of pogroms spreading like a plague in the countryside reached the citizens of Dikranagerd, where Valentine and her family lived. She was only fifteen years old, both of her parents were dead, and she lived with her maternal aunt and uncle. In her town, the Turks had already confiscated all their weapons. But her village had no knowledge that most of their able-bodied men, drafted into the army, were already dead—sent weaponless into ambushes. Such was the fate that one of Valentine's brothers had already met, and the other, Hagop, had barely escaped.

One evening in the early spring of 1915, she saw on a ridge to the east a swarm of lights. Soon, the earth thundered with soldiers on horses coming down the foothills. Through the window, in the sawing light of the torches, Valentine searched for her two brothers among these soldiers. She could see long swords glint on the saddles. She heard whip cracks and gunshots, and then there was a call for all Armenians to come out of their houses. Her aunt quickly dropped to her knees and prayed. Her uncle took her by her arm, and together they stepped out into the cold. Valentine saw Turks slide in and out of the dusty darkness. A command was given: pack only what you can carry under one arm. If that should be an infant, then pack nothing at all. In the morning they would be deported. The air suddenly seethed with protest, the barks of dogs. Then, out of a flurry of horses, Valentine watched a woman, handcuffed with a long rope, dragged into a circle of Turks. She saw her spit at the horseman who had the other end of the rope tied to his saddle and hiss that they had killed her husband already. "Look how you have left me!" she wailed, and lifted up her dress like a whore gone mad. Her bald and bloated stomach was smeared with orange torchlight. Valentine understood she was with child. From between the shifting horses, she saw a Turk draw a long sword from his scabbard, nudge his horse forward, and with a flick slit open the woman's womb. The woman gazed for a second at the curdling zipper of flesh in disbelief, and collapsed into a pool of water and blood. Shrieks of horror. The horses sidled and stamped. Two elderly women began beating at the horses with their fists, others fell to the ground and began beating at their own chests. The minds of more than a few young mothers instantly snapped. Once the violence was set in motion, the morning could not wait, as though violence itself had a sort of momentum and urgency to compound itself.

Although the Turks had guns, this was no substitute for the scintillating immediacy of a sword. Babies were pitched on them, then set on a pyre in the middle of the village to roast like squabs.

Armenians were called dogs by the ones whom they called friend.

And Turks said, *Anyone had been mistreated it was the Turks, no one else*

They sat him in a chair and tied his legs. Then they cut up his little three-year-old son on his knees and stuffed bits of the boy's flesh into his mouth and made him eat it.

The figures are most likely exaggerated

Women and children and old men who were too old or young or feeble to fight were shoved into the church and the church was set aflame.

I saw piles of Armenians in the fields. I saw two ravines filled with the corpses of Armenians.

One of the soldiers, an elderly Turk with a long moustache, slit open her stomach and warmed his feet in it.

Casualties of war

Infants were taken out to sea in little boats. At some distance out they were stabbed to death, put in sacks, and thrown into the sea. A few days later some of their little bodies were washed up on the shore of Trebizond.

Since there was no genocide, Turks cannot accept responsibility for something that did not happen

When the Turks started to push them out of their homes, they raped women and then pinned them with big nails, still living, to the front door.

From one town to another, from one steppe to the next, men had their hands tied behind their backs and were rolled down cliffs. Women were standing below and they slashed at those who had rolled down with knives until they were dead.

Corpses of violated women, lying about naked in heaps on the railway embankment at Tell-Abiad and Ras-el-Ain. Many of them had had clubs pushed up their anuses.

Unless they are forced, Turks are the world's most tolerant people toward those of other religions

Because of their violations, all these girls later showed symptoms of mental derangement. A girl had been raped so many times by Turkish soldiers in one night that she had completely lost her reason.

All Armenian villages in the Samsun area and in Unieh have been Islamisized.

It is very certain that the Armenians did not originate in Anatolia, nor did they live there for three to four thousand years, as claimed

In the concentration camps: people hungrily eat both raw and cooked locusts, grass roots, even stray dogs and dead animals.

Dying people were also killed and eaten. These events took place roughly between April and July of 1916.

A purposely created myth that serves political and territorial ends

Women were disemboweled by the Turks who were looking for coins they might have hidden in their bellies.

Some of the more beautiful girls were made to marry Turks; in one instance, a strikingly pretty twelve-year-old girl was forced to marry a seventy-year-old *pasha*.

Great care was taken to make certain that the Armenians were treated carefully and compassionately as they were deported

Children cried themselves to death, men threw themselves to their deaths on the rocks while some threw their own children into wells and leapt into the Euphrates. How long could they expect to eke out a miserable existence with nothing to eat but grass and the few grains of corn they could find in the horses' dung?

Out of the some 700,000 Armenians who were transported in this way, until early 1917, certainly some lives were lost

The people deported from Samsun were headed for Urfa. Clearly no Christian Armenian reached that destination. According to news from the interior, the deported populations of whole towns disappeared.

How many Armenians did die? It is impossible to determine the number exactly, since no complete death records of statistics were kept during those years

A group of Armenian girls were told to strip, climb up a tree and sing the Lord's Prayer. One by one, the Turks picked them off with bullets, like birds.

The heat was intense and there was no water, so women resorted to drinking the urine of the horses.

The Armenians comprised a very small minority of the population in the territories being claimed in their name

The name Armenia was dropped from all Turkish documents and maps. The Turkish government changed the names of towns, villages and hamlets. Today in Turkish-occupied Armenia there are no Armenians, except for dissimulated ones of uncertain number.

Armenian territorial demands appear to be even more senseless considering that currently there are no Armenians living in eastern Anatolia

Armenian monuments, some dating back to the fifth century, were marked for destruction. Churches provided convenient targets for artillery practice during maneuvers of the Turkish army.

The finely cut stones used on the facades of Armenian churches made perfect prefabricated building materials used in construction of village dwellings.

A purposely created myth

Armenian churches were converted into mosques, prisons, granaries, stables.

Exaggerated figures

In the entire plain of Mush all the way to Bingol no trace of Armenian churches remain.

It never happened

Armenian identity was neutralized by effacing Armenian inscriptions on monuments.

Reattribution of a building to Turkish architecture, usually medieval Seljuk Turkish, was common. The most famous examples are the tenth-century churches of Kars and Aght'amar, which ironically were built before the Seljuk Turks existed.

No such massacre took place at this or any other time

It is understood that Rauf Bey had already arranged the disappearance of documentary material implicating himself and Enver Pasha.

This is the truth behind the false claims distorting historical facts by ill-devised mottoes such as "the first genocide of the twentieth century"

I am confident that the whole history of the human race contains no such horrible episode as this.

And the Americans said, *had Turkification and Moslemization not been accelerated there [in Anatolia] by the use of force, there certainly would not today exist a Turkish Republic...*

The blackest page in modern history

...a Republic owing its strength and stability in no small measure to the homogeneity of its population, a state which is now a valued associate of the United States

The great massacres and persecutions of the past seem almost insignificant when compared to the sufferings of the Armenian race in 1915.

And *It never happened.*

By daybreak the rich earth was soaked with blood. A kind of rust-colored vein wended through the middle of Valentine's village. Women lay limp and butchered over *khatchkars* (stone crosses), others lay crushed beneath them. In the hills they lay littered, shot dead in their tracks. Only the young and beautiful girls were spared. About three dozen girls squatted and shivered against a stone wall. Blood was caked in their pubic hair, blood mottled the insides of their thighs, and they sat at the edge of the midden that was once their village, holding shawls to their noses to keep out the stench rising from the smoldering churches inside of which bodies still broiled.

Valentine had not been found until very late that night and would have been raped upon sight except that by the time they collared her, the Turks all but had spent themselves. She was a wildly exotic, green-eyed beauty, and, perhaps knowing she would be raped, her aunt in hysteria told her to flee, find a gutted animal and hide inside its carcass. Rather, she had climbed up a tree and hid on the roof of their house. Sometime during the night, with her ear pressed to the roof, she heard Turks bust in on her family and drag them off screaming. *Mer Christos, mer Christos.*

A Turkish official who had just come on the scene dragged her out from the trembling pack of girls and rode off with her on his horse.

The Turk had a minor position in the *pasha* government in Istanbul. He'd been ordered to deliver a sealed document to the *vali* of Dikranagerd settling the ambiguous issue of the fate of Armenians who had converted to Islam. The document instructed that they too should be killed, adding that any Turk who harbored an Armenian—Moslem or no—should be hanged in front of his home. He had traveled to Van by train and advanced from there on horse. He knew there was the Armenian Question and that it entailed the deportation of some Armenians, the rounding up of revolutionaries whose sympathies lay with the Russians, but beyond that he had little knowledge of what was happening in the eastern prelates.

By the time he reached Dikranagerd, his education was complete. He'd passed Armenians piled into ditches, he'd passed a pumpkin field of severed Armenian heads, he'd passed infants who sucked still on the tits of dead mothers, he'd passed tide after tide of famished eyes. There was a sort of auction going on when he clopped into the village late that morning. He pushed his way through a herd of Kurds who were haggling over the price of a girl. Already half of the girls there had been sold for a few coins, or a head of cattle, or two sheep. Alarmed, he bought a girl to save her life.

Valentine did not know what to expect, but she was thankful that at least this Turk was young and handsome. She'd already seen half a dozen girls dragged off by men who were old enough to be their fathers. They made their way back to Istanbul, the Turk saying hardly a word.

For months the Turk never so much as laid a hand on Valentine. It is said that each evening he would get down on his knees and plead forgiveness for what his people were doing to hers. It is said that he washed her feet with his tears.

Nearly two years passed before her surviving brother, Hagop, was able to locate his sister. He sent a message to her that he had secured means of smuggling her by boat across the Mediterranean to safety in Alexandria. The time and contacts were given in detail, and she was told to follow the instructions precisely. What he didn't know was that she and the Turk had fallen in love, and that she had given birth to a boy, now a year old. Torn between her husband and her people, one evening she bundled this child up and boarded the boat to cross the Mediterranean. What should have been a two-day crossing turned into six, so terrible were the waves. Hardly could they eat, and hardly could they sleep. Fresh water grew short. People took to drinking water from the sea. On the fifth day, her baby, whom she had held to her bosom throughout the passage, stopped breathing. If it hadn't been for the captain and six other passengers who had to restrain her physically, she would have thrown herself overboard with the child, so deep was her anguish.

In Alexandria she lived with Hagop. For two months she holed up in a room and refused to be consoled. Her wailing was so ceaseless and fierce that some thought the poor girl would never recover her senses. Lost was a brother, her sister-in-law, nieces and nephews, and now a child and husband, her homeland and home too. Each morning she would rise and feel her heart capsize inside of her.

Slowly, however, her pain dissipated and she began to feel the air and sun on her face again. Many Armenians had escaped to Alexandria with stories of atrocities of their own to tell. She understood, even at the age of eighteen, that as terrible as her lot was, there were others who had it even worse. Perhaps even more terrifying than what she had been through was the blackness of her future. After five months, her choice seemed to be between two absolutes: learning how to forget, or forever being weighed down by her past.

At the open market one evening, she felt a hand on her shoulder. She thought it was a mugger and swung around, ready to scratch his eyes out. Standing before her was her Turk. For six months he had been searching for her. His love for her had not diminished, he told her. More than anything he wanted to see his child again. She knew that if their child had still been alive she might have left with him, but with her child's death had died her commitment to the Turk—but perhaps not her love. Nothing could bridge the great chasm between their peoples, nothing could drown out the roar of the massacred below. She told him what had happened to their son, then said, "Leave me now, and never make contact with me again."

Because she'd been married to a Turk, she became a sort of pariah to the families in Alexandria, whose eligible sons nonetheless pined for her as she strolled on the beach in the afternoons. Three years would pass before she would marry Aristages, a firm-handed, well-to-do businessman who was serious and very Protestant and twenty-five years her senior. The match was from the beginning hopeless, because Valentine had become a voluptuary, with only one unassailable belief surviving her travails: the hour is here to live and live fully. She was known in Alexandria as a *kefgee*—a lover of parties—a nomination, according to Aristages' canon, that a married woman—any woman—should be ashamed of. But nothing Aristages could do, no citing of scripture, no admonishment, no threat could break her carefree spirit. So he got her pregnant. And at the age of twenty-one, Valentine had a child. It was not that one, but the last of the four children Valentine would eventually bear that Andy was now courting.

17

A FEW WEEKS AFTER THE PICNIC, Zabel dropped the kids off after church and went shopping for her mother. Angel was at her usual post on the porch, smoking her pipe, when Zabel drove up. Zabel grabbed a couple of bags, bulging with groceries. from the backseat and hauled them in her arms up the steps. She kissed Angel on the head and carried the clove and cinnamon scent of her mother's hair with her into the kitchen. Her mother had once explained that all the sins of a woman could be traced to the strands of her hair. It is a sign of blessedness when the hair of an elderly woman smells sweet. Just as Mary's hair smelled when with it she dried Jesus' feet. She unloaded the goods into the refrigerator and cupboards and then made some Turkish coffee.

Zabel placed the platter on the cement pedestal and with two hands offered her mother a demitasse. The old woman set the pipe on the armrest, took the coffee on her lap and sighed deeply. The two women slurped up the coffee and looked out at the pale blue day.

"I'm tired the way a tree is after a great wind."

"Why?"

"Last night he came," her mother said.

"Who?"

The old woman poked the pipe in her mouth and reached inside the pocket of her dress and fumbled for a matchstick. In one motion, she struck the match expertly against the chair and put it sizzling up to the bowl of her pipe, sucked and tossed the match, still burning, on the ground. Zabel snuffed it out with her shoe. After a few puffs, the old woman's nerves settled.

"To look into the face of truth, what suffering we must pass through," her mother told her.

"What truth?" Zabel asked.

"Last night he came. Against my window, fluttering. I asked the dark, 'Who is it?' Then my eyes, they turned heavy as a sack of coins. And his wings, they brushed against my chest." Angel winced.

"What kind of spirit was this, Mother?"

Her mother's face showed a cynical wisdom. "Don't be mistaken, only our Jesus is perfectly clean." She made the sign of the cross upon her chest. "In the name of the Lord, one must command them to do as they were assigned, not as they wish. Here," she said, and cocked a thumb beneath her earlobe, "he grabbed my ear."

"What did you hear?"

The old woman coughed up smoke. From out of her mouth, a slug of phlegm hurled and stuck to the arm of her chair. Zabel rubbed her mother's back to stop the coughing. She could feel the old lady's bones getting thrown. The woman cleared her throat and moved her mouth free of some gummy film. This bout of coughing seemed to have changed the route of the old woman's mind. Her eyes wandered aimlessly over the vineyard, as though Zabel were no longer there.

"Mama?"

"Hah?"

Her eyes were red and veined and watery like melon meat. She tried to re-light her pipe, which had gone out in her coughing fit. Zabel watched the matches swing over the bowl. When the tobacco glowed orange, she told her mother, "You should have heard what he said in church the other day."

"The one who limps?"

"He said there is no need to build a new church."

"Animal."

"He said that we should congregate in a ditch."

"Filthy."

"When he was young, he was a good boy. Everything you told him, he did. Not one word came back from him. Not a word. NOT A WORD! But since he came back from college he is an animal."

"Who knows what he grew into there? What kind of evil he brushed up against," Angel said.

"And now I hear he likes some girl from Egypt. Like some big shot! Like he's some Casanova! God only knows how much money he is going to spend on her."

"He spends our money?"

"What else?"

"With the family you have to nurse?! Satan!"

"My Abe says nothing."

"Abe, between two currents of blood, is caught." Angel raised a hand up to halt the conversation. "Now it returns to my head," she said. "This spirit, this angel, what he said."

"What, Mama?"

"I hesitate to tell you," her mother said.

"Why?"

"You must be sure nothing comes between you and your husband. God has bound you together as one vine."

"But did this spirit see a wedge between us?"

"No." Her mother shook a finger. "He said that blood runs under your land. He said that your land is watered by blood."

"Our land?" Zabel asked. "What does such a vision point to?"

"There will be a sign. The one who limps will carry it. Keep your eye pinned on him."

"What kind of sign?"

Her mother's head bobbed.

"You will know it when you see it," she said.

18

ON THEIR FIRST DATE Andy brought Kareen home half an hour past her ten o'clock curfew, cause enough for Valentine to beat her daughter into the bedroom with a slipper and to continue railing and swinging the same slipper at Andy until he was half a mile down the road. She wasn't going to let just any man have his way with her daughter. If he had been a younger suitor it would have scared him away. But at the age of thirty, Andy knew that this sort of high drama was typical and expected of mothers from the old country, and that Valentine was driving home a point—with a slipper or a shoe or a broom—that her daughter was pure.

He didn't know how close another man had come to Kareen. He knew that she would welcome his hand only after he'd asked her for hers. Twice now, he'd felt an urge to protect her, though from what he did not know. He could already tell she was the type of woman who, though not without means to defend herself, would prefer a man do so, to preserve her delicateness in his eyes.

From his bed, Teddy watched his uncle Andy get ready for his date. In his boxer shorts, Andy was looping a tie around his neck in front of the mirror. This gave Teddy a chance to study Andy's legs. One was sturdy and hairy and the muscles bulged like a horse's whenever he shifted around. Except for a few straggly hairs, the bad leg was bald, and tapered to the semblance of a baseball bat. A few times Teddy had wished he could touch Andy's leg, and sometimes he would walk or run with a limp just to see how it felt. If his mother saw him, she'd chide him and swear that if he limped like that, one day his leg would shrivel up. Sometimes Teddy limped without even knowing it, and he wondered if this meant that Uncle Andy was his best friend. Andy sat on the edge of the bed and put on his trousers. He stood, sucked his gut in and tugged on his belt.

Abe and Zabel were just starting in on dinner when Zabel brought up the subject of Kareen.

"So who is this Egyptian girl?" she asked Abe. "He's getting serious."

"Some gal Arsen Bakalian hooked him up with."

"Arsen Bakalian?"

"You know, he pumps gas down in Selma, married to that girl, Alice."

"She's straight off the boat."

"More or less, I suppose."

"I don't trust 'em."

"What's there not to trust? One time or 'nother we all came off the boat."

"Not like these newcomers. No, they have only one thing on their mind."

"Well, it's his life. Whatever he wants to do."

"His life! What do you mean, his life?!"

Abe pressed a piece of *kheyma* in a cradle of *lavosh* bread, then took a pinch of chopped onion and parsley and sprinkled it all over the raw meat. He could feel sweat gathering on his brow, his body agitated, as if ants were swarming over him.

"Damn hot today," Abe said. He looked around to see if all the windows were open. They were.

"They come here with nothing, and the only thing they have on their minds is the money in your pocket, that's what!" exclaimed Zabel.

Abe was working to get the meat down his throat.

"I know their ways." She got up from the table to get some more bread.

Abe let out a puff of air, as if he'd been holding the damn thing in, and dropped his fists onto the table in front of him. He could feel himself shake, and something stabbed him in the stomach, hard.

Just then, Andy stepped into the kitchen. Abe and Zabel both looked at him as though he'd just caught them stealing something of his. It was obvious they weren't going to tell him to have a nice date or anything like that, and he didn't want to ruin the start of his evening by getting mixed up with whatever had made Abe pale-faced, so he headed out the door without a word.

Valentine came to the door puffing on a cigarette. She told Andy to come in out of the cold. If he would make himself at home, everyone would be with him in a minute. She said she was cooking and that she hoped he'd brought his appetite with him. Andy took a seat on the couch. In front of him, in the old Armenian style, sectioned mounds of walnuts and raisins and dried apricots were on a leaf-shaped platter. The living room was dimly lit and warm and filled with the scent of mint. Andy had planned on taking Kareen out, but to turn down a meal made by his girlfriend's mother was out of the question. What the hell, he thought, and tossed a couple of walnuts into his mouth. Valentine came out of the kitchen, drying her hands on her apron. "Now," she said, and sat down across from him on a stuffed velvet chair.

"Where's Kareen?" he asked politely, careful not to give the mother the impression that her own company wouldn't suffice.

"Ahhhh," she said, "you want to know where *Kareen* is? You like?" she asked.

"Your daughter?"

"No, my hair."

"She's a nice girl," he said in Armenian.

"How do you fill your pockets?" she asked in Armenian.

Andy was certain Kareen had told her he was a farmer. What he did for a living was the first thing she'd have wanted to know.

"I have vineyards," he said.

"Wineyards." She wagged her head approvingly, impressed.

"Yes, me and my brother."

"Dat's good," she said.

"I didn't realize," Andy said, "what eyes you have, Mrs. Keadjian."

Her face relaxed into a smile. She told him that in her day she had dazzled men with them. "But many, many year," and with a hand she brushed time behind her.

"Your daughters are beautiful," he said, nodding at a picture on the coffee table of all three, "but none has your green eyes."

She asked him who he was courting, her daughter or her.

Andy chuckled. "For the time being," he said, "both."

Pruning back his charm, she asked, "Your leg? Every time I see you, you limp."

"Polio," he said. Valentine didn't comprehend. She shook her head and took a drag on her cigarette.

He couldn't think of what they called it in Armenian, except for the generic word *topal*, meaning lame.

She asked him if it was in his blood.

"No," he said and suppressed a cackle. Next thing, he thought, she's going to check my teeth.

Now, how did he farm with such a leg?

Mincing no words, "I do it," he said.

She was glad he'd answered forcefully, as a man should whenever asked about his capacity for work.

"Good," she said.

Kareen popped her head into the room.

"What are you doing, girl?" her mother asked. "Getting ready for your wedding?"

"Akhh, Mama." She blushed. "What are you telling him?"

"We are just passing some words between us," she said.

"One moment and I'll be there," Kareen told Andy, pinning her hair up. The smell of hairspray feathered Andy's nose.

"Take your time. I guess we're eating here."

Valentine got up and said she would prepare the table. Andy asked her if he could help, and she said no, that he should rest, for his work as a farmer was likely exhausting enough.

From the kitchen Valentine told Andy that in the old country they'd had vines dating from the time of our Lord that gave up grapes each the size of a plum. She said she was amazed that America, with all its machines and things, could not make a grape that way. "When you would bite into one of these grapes," she said, "it would fill up your mouth with sweetness. Where it would take a bunch of grapes to satisfy you in America, in the old country a few berries would do."

Kareen came out wearing a plaid wool skirt and a soft pink sweater with buttons that emulated pearls. It seemed impossible, but since he'd last seen her she'd grown even more lovely. With each outfit she seemed to transform into yet another variation on perfection. She sat across from him, crossed her legs and folded her hands on her knees artfully.

"Your mother and I were talking grapes." He winked and whispered to Kareen, "You look beautiful."

She pursed her lips, widened her eyes and daintily raised her chin, as though she were judging her features in a mirror.

"Mrs. Keadjian," Andy announced in Armenian, "next season I will bring you the finest grapes in the valley."

"And now," Valentine said, "come. You will eat one of the finest meals in the valley."

They stood up. Andy extended a hand—a ripple of ripe lemons and soap as Kareen passed into the kitchen. Andy pulled a chair out for Kareen, tucked her in and walked to the other side of the table so that Valentine could sit between them.

A mound of pilaf was steaming on the table and alongside it a salad of tomatoes, cucumbers and red onions. Behind him the margins of the windows were clouding up. Over his nerves, Andy could feel his appetite open. Valentine stepped up to the table with a steel pot and set it on the linoleum table and lifted off the lid. Okra! Okra. The only food in God's creation that made him gag. She scooped a harrowing helping of it onto his plate. He dreaded everything about it. As he studied its fuzzy skin, its gooey, seedy meat and uncircumcised shape, his stomach started to rebel. A mound of slugs wouldn't have been any worse. To not eat it would be a terrible offense, he thought, a virtually damning offense. Kareen ladled some pilaf next to the okra.

"Do you have bread?" Andy asked. He wondered if they could hear his voice tremble.

"Dear one, of course," Valentine said and reached back to grab a basket full of flatbread.

Eat it, Andy, he told himself. This is what being a man is all about. He quickly shoved a forkful into his mouth. He tore off a chunk of *peda* bread and chewed on it.

"What is it? Don't you like?" Kareen asked.

Andy swallowed, "Very good."

Valentine smiled and told him to help himself to as much as he liked.

Andy nodded his head thanks.

After several helpings of pilaf, which he used to camouflage the okra, he finished what was on his plate. It was as though they'd been torturing him, holding his head underwater. He sat back and caught his breath.

"Eat," Valentine said.

"I'm fine."

"For a man that is so hefty, you eat the way birds eat," Valentine remarked.

"I savored each bite." Andy warmly patted his stomach.

Kareen got up to clear the plates.

"I'm afraid it closed your appetite," Valentine said.

Andy protested.

"Do you like *kufte?*" Valentine asked.

"That is my favorite. I like okra, but *kufte,* I love."

"Next time I will feed you *kufte.*"

Over the sound of running water, Andy could hear Kareen bubble up with laughter. Andy looked at Valentine. She smiled broadly. Was this all some cruel joke?

"You don't like it," Valentine said and burst into laughter.

"Akhh, Andy," Kareen said and wiped the table down with a wet towel.

She looked into Andy's eyes. She took them in the way a mother takes in the eyes of her child. She gently cupped his face in her hand and said, "He's a very good-hearted boy, Mother." Then she burst out in laughter herself.

Valentine, nodding her head, agreed.

"Yes," Kareen said, "next time make him some *kufte,* Mother."

Andy lowered his eyes and wiped his mouth with a napkin. Then he started laughing along with them. He laughed at his embarrassment, at the okra, he laughed for joy—because she thought well of him, because she had touched him.

"You know, Abe," Zabel said, "the land, this house, now that it is in your name, it is the way it should have been all along."

"How's that, Mama?"

"Let's look at it, sweetheart." She put down her rolling pin, pushed a strand of hair away from her face.

"You lost your father when you were very young, God rest his soul. Your mother had five children to raise on her own. But with what money? She had no money. Only the seven thousand dollars from the life insurance. Then that street dog Yervant came along. We can't know what things he told her. What lies. All we know is that he was an evil man, that, once married to your mother, he beat her children and treated them like farm animals. Like common dirt. He never loved you."

Abe nodded. Up to this point, she had said it just as it was.

"Except he was different with his own children, Betty and Andy. Wasn't he?"

"Of course."

"All of his love went to them, all of his support. Your brother was treated like a *pasha.*"

"I think everybody pitied him for his leg."

"His leg, yes, his leg. How long must we hear about it? Haven't every one of us had to suffer? Didn't you have to suffer the death of your father? And how about my mama? She lost her husband in the massacres, and I," she crossed her heart, "a father. Wouldn't you have taken polio over losing your father?"

Abe had never thought about it that way.

"Of course you would have. And another thing you forget, Abe. Andy, because of that leg, did not have to go to war like you. I don't care what they say, that leg of his was a gift. Instead he got a college education. And what did you get? No, if not for that leg, he might have been killed, like so many other young Armenian men. Your poor mother, then, married this dog Yervant. But why would he marry her? What man would marry a woman with five children?"

"He married her for something."

"No," she said, "not for something. For only one thing: money."

Abe stamped out the figure of his palm on the flour.

"Don't do that," she said. "And with that money he bought this land and rode around in fancy cars and wore fancy suits while he worked the family like animals."

"You forget one thing, Zabel. It was my mother who willed the land to us. Both of us. And the girls got basically nothing."

"What are you talking about? The girls have husbands to support them. They are all married and they are all doing just fine."

"Thank God," Abe reminded Zabel.

"But what was your mother to do? Andy also was her blood. We can only thank God that Yervant died before her. If that cursed dog had survived her, you might have had nothing. He would have given it all to his little *pasha.*"

"Maybe he would have."

"It is certain he would have. What I'm saying is right, Abe. God has had his hand upon us: the land is now in your name and it is as it was supposed to be. This is your father's land, he bought this land with his blood. With his blood. With his life!"

Even more than talking about money, all that talk about his step-father got Abe very emotional. He stood up from the table as though he had somewhere to go.

"Such things," Zabel said, "are very hard to hear. But if I don't say it, who then?"

Abe sat down again.

"Andy is young and healthy and he is educated. You have no reason to pity him."

"Okay, Ma. Enough already."

"You don't want to hear the truth."

"I said, Zabel…"

Zabel clapped her hands free of flour and swung out of the chair.

He felt as though he'd been clobbered.

The lights were off in the house when Andy drove up. Everybody must be asleep, he thought. In the half-dark, he could see Abe's head over the back of his chair. Had he fallen asleep there?

Abe felt like armies were lining up on either side of him, and if he didn't choose one side or the other, he'd be caught in the cross fire or get trampled under their advance. What he really wanted to do was climb up a tree and blindfold himself and stick plugs in his fucking ears. Or maybe hang himself from such a tree. But there was no tree in sight. So what he did, for the time being, was sit in his smoking chair and make a tree of himself. When Andy walked in two hours later, Abe was still sitting in that chair. He could turn neither right nor left, for fear of quickening some evil genius in his head. Andy wondered whether he should wake him. Abe was pretty sure it was Andy who had come through the door. But say it wasn't, say it was a burglar, a murderer? Even then Abe wasn't sure he had the where-withal to turn around and look, much less defend himself. Andy thought how nice it would be if he and his brother could just crack open a couple of beers and shoot the bull about his date, that crazy okra scene. Hell, whatever.

Andy was getting serious about Kareen. But since Abe had hardly asked about her—forget about Zabel—he couldn't say whether Abe even knew Kareen's name. The couple of times she'd come up in conversation, they'd both referred to Kareen as "she" or "her" or "that girl." Outside of talk about business, they were mute, as if they'd sworn to a code of silence in regard to anything having to do with their hearts. Here we live in the same house, Andy thought, work together, break bread together and yet where it really counts, we have nothing to do with each other. Andy was lonely for his brother, especially when he thought of how it used to be. Abe bought him a wagon, his first bike, had taught him how to fish and how to fight! Was Andy at fault? Half-brother or whole brother, Abe was his only brother.

Sitting in the chair, Abe was amazed at the sandbag density, the sandbag weight of his body.

"Abe," Andy whispered.

Abe, Abe thought. My name is Abe. Abe must be me. He heard himself say "Andy," but no "Andy" came out of his mouth.

He must be asleep, Andy guessed.

Someone might as well have sliced Abe's tongue out.

Better get him to bed, Andy thought.

Paralyzed people, this is kinda how they must feel, thought Abe.

Andy flipped the switch. The light—it was sharp, hurt. He walked around the couch and stepped up to Abe, ready to wake him. "What's up?" Andy chuckled nervously.

Abe slowly shook his head.

"You all right, Abe? You sick?"

Abe mumbled something.

Jesus Christ, Andy thought.

Abe didn't actually feel pain. What he did feel was all the awesome annihilating potential of pain from outside and from within. In a way, the kind of pain that's worse than the real thing.

That night, Andy had a dream. He had gotten into farming wheat. Alone. He was walking through the middle of a golden field that stretched out farther than the eye could see. The wheat was ready for harvest, and he felt proud and relieved that on his first try he'd grown such wonderful wheat. There was a black man sitting on a harvester, and this black man tipped his hat to Andy as he passed. This field was surrounded by water. Andy could see boats sailing out there. On one of these boats was Kareen, and he was asking her what she thought of his wheat. She embraced him and told him that she thought it would make fine-smelling bread. Out of an oven she took a loaf of her own, and told him that though her bread was good to eat, she was certain that Andy's would be better, since her mother had told her that Andy's bread was made of gold. Gold, Andy laughed, and ran a hand through Kareen's hair. He could smell a queer odor all around. He paid no mind to it, turned and nodded to the black man. The black man started up the harvester. The machine cut the wheat down so that it piled up behind, and Andy wondered how they were going to get the wheat off the ground, and then he remembered wheat that was stacked by hand fetched more at the market than wheat that was stacked mechanically. He had been watching the harvesting from a hill and now walked down to the edge of the field where a threshing machine was going. Already, kernels of wheat were mounded in bins. He shoved a hand deep into the bin and scooped some wheat up. Some kernels had split, and out of them oozed a substance that looked like mud. Andy raised the open kernels to his nose and sniffed. It smelled like shit. It was shit! When he looked in back of him the entire field was a pile of shit! The smell of shit filled the air. And then he remembered that his father had told him all wheat smells like shit before it is harvested, but only those who recognize the smell, who pay attention to the smell, can stop the wheat from actually turning into shit by applying a special fertilizer imported from Armenia.

Absurd. Still, Andy woke the next morning anxious to see Kareen, feeling he had some explaining to do to her, but about what? The dream? He didn't know. Anyhow, he'd have to wait because the vines needed dusting. It was a wet spring, and a few farmers around their parts had already caught traces of mildew in the crop. The shoots were eight to ten inches in length already, and as far as Andy was concerned, they'd already put the sulphuring off too long.

When to sulphur was a bone of contention between the brothers, since Andy's philosophy was that you had to sulphur as often as possible—with every new growth of the shoot—to keep mildew from ever becoming a problem. Abe saw it the other way around: you don't dust, you don't disturb the vines, yourself or your pocketbook until you see mildew cropping up in the field. The whole issue, as Andy had told Abe until his jaw waxed stiff, was that Abe didn't properly understand what sulphur did. Abe had the old-fashioned notion that sulphur burned the mildew off the leaf, where Andy knew for a fact that sulphur's main purpose was to create a sort of barrier between the leaf and the spores. That when the spores landed on the leaf, what they settled in was that sulphur dust—a very hostile camping ground. So if they did it Abe's way, once the mildew took root, dusting couldn't get rid of it; it would only, at most, keep it from spreading. Which, the way the season was shaping up, wasn't going to be good enough.

"I've got a degree in Ag, Abe. Remember?"

"If you say so," Abe said.

Abe had been a farmer since birth, and no amount of schooling, he told Andy, could match that. Andy's last words were, "This is flirting with disaster." Abe waved the statement away with a hand and told Andy to quit exaggerating. But the situation pointed to a deeper division between them. Andy looked to short any possible blowup, preferring to take precautions. Abe, Andy thought, liked to play with fire. He pushed a situation to the edge so as to be able to heroically save it at the last moment, so that he could puff himself up and say, "Look what I did" afterwards. Andy couldn't decide whether this was the characteristic of a man who trusted his own power or didn't trust it enough. And again, how would you square that with the way Abe kowtowed in the presence of his wife?

They hooked up the Gustafson to the tractor and shoveled the sulphur into the barrel. Andy tied a bandanna around his face to keep from gagging on the rotten-egg taste of the sulphur dust. Abe claimed to fancy the smell. But then again, Andy thought, Abe loved, more than normal, the smell of his own farts. Andy watched Abe pull the tractor and rig into the vineyards. Out from the exhaust pipes the yellow chalk flew, throwing out the canopy like a skirt. Andy lit a smoke and watched the air start to turn sallow. He'd have to scrub himself down with steel wool if he planned on seeing Kareen later that afternoon, he thought, and then he wondered what Kareen, all cosmopolitan and refined, made of being with a farmer. For the first time he asked himself, Would she take to me if I were poor, if instead of my owning the land, I worked for someone who owned it? The tractor was out of sight behind a big canary-colored cloud. Andy limped into the vineyard.

To save some sulphur, Abe cut the fan just before he hit the avenue, letting the dust drift over the end of the rows. He turned the tractor around in the avenue and pulled back in with the Gustafson sliding in neatly behind him. The great debate that was raging in Abe's head the night before had shaken down to this one absolute: there was no way the two of them could work the land together for much longer. And if it came to a question of Andy or Abe, it was Andy who was going to have to go. What with the kids and Zabel, there was no other way. But the timing was bad. Worse than bad.

Abe was coming to the end of a row, and he could see Andy standing there with his arms folded over his chest. Andy looked cross, as though he'd been reading Abe's mind. A fight was one thing he didn't want to get into with Andy. Abe cut the fan and pulled out onto the avenue and let the tractor idle. Andy was pointing at the Gustafson, and then Andy slid a finger across his throat. Abe cut the engine. The tractor burped and died.

Abe stepped off the tractor and looked down the row. What's he talking about? Looked fine. *Little* heavier on the right side, but nothing to shout about.

"I fixed that drive," Abe said before Andy had a chance.

"Drive's not the problem. Looks to me," Andy said, flipping a finger at a stitch of yellow dust deposited up the row, "the left exhaust pipe is cracked." Andy walked to the back of the rig and got on his knees. "Blowing through this hole," Andy said.

Abe walked over and had a look. "Probably just busted. Let's weld it."

"You need glasses or something, Abe?"

"What?"

"I thought you said you'd given the rigs a go-over. Look at this thing."

It was plain as day that the pipe was rusted, on the verge of crumbling apart.

Abe grunted and said, "I don't know how that happened."

Andy went to the other side, to check the left pipe. That one was about to give too. Abe stood with his hands behind his back, like the situation deserved some studying. He grunted again.

"Abe, first of all," Andy trailed off and shook his head.

"What?"

"Well, first of all, you cut the sulphur short of the ends. Between me and you, it's not worth the few pennies you save."

"You and me got different strategies."

"But according to your own strategy, Abe, with these busted pipes you're losing ten times what you save shorting the ends."

Abe tossed up his hands, as if it was out of his control.

Andy said, "These exhaust pipes are gone, pure and simple."

Abe didn't care for how Andy was speaking to him. Even though he knew Andy was right, he didn't care for it.

"Abe, I don't know why we're even arguing about this." Andy said. "I don't see this as something to argue about."

"I don't either," Abe said and pulled the bandanna down off his face. Andy couldn't remember the last time he'd seen such a face—something between a smirk and a taunt—on Abe. It was the sort of look a weakling might give you just before he pulled the booby-trap rope.

"Anyways," Andy said, "let's see if we've got a couple lying around."

"It'll hold," Abe said.

"What, you got something else better to do?"

"Maybe I do."

"Like what?"

"That's my business."

"This is *our* business."

"Today it's yours," Abe said and walked off just like that.

First Andy had to replace the exhaust pipes, then he had to dust what crop he could—maybe fifteen acres—by himself. Abe was nowhere to be found. He had taken off in his car with Zabel and the kids. By the end of the day, Andy was so exhausted that even the picture of Kareen that he'd held in his head all day had faded. What worried Andy, more than any other craziness Abe had displayed, was his brother's not working. Until this point, no matter what, when it came to cultivating the land Abe had put all grievances aside. Hell, even when there wasn't work, Abe would dig up something to do. It's one thing to bitch and moan, but another thing to wipe your hands of your chores. This signaled some serious problem. This was a form of madness.

19

VALENTINE AND KAREEN LIVED ON BALCH STREET in Armenian Town, a two-square-mile area bounded by Ventura Avenue to the north and Butler to the south, M Street to the west and Cedar to the east. Saroyan grew up there and attended Emerson Elementary, where he began his peculiar championing of Armenians. The homes were small two-bedroom bungalows with cement porches set behind neatly trimmed lawns with hedges of rosebushes and oleanders. Sycamores and carob trees lined streets wide enough to use as makeshift baseball fields during summer or after school. In the early evening, old men, too old to work but too young to die, strolled down these streets thumbing their worry beads—the abacus of the soul—and paused to watch boys shoot marbles or toss jacks in the dirt alleyways.

In the heart of Valentine's backyard was a small rose garden. Off to the side of this garden was an apricot tree, and under the leaves of this tree a wrought-iron table and three wooden folding chairs. Kareen came down the stone path in a white dress balancing a tray in her hands and with a gingham tablecloth draped over her shoulder. She set the tray on a chair and over the table she draped the cloth and on the cloth she placed a plate of string cheese and *chorag* and a bowl of olives and a bowl of homemade apricot jam. She lifted a spoon from her dress pocket and poked it into the jam and sat down. Roses perfumed the air. In the soft sunlight, Kareen could hear bees humming.

She tried to imagine what it was like to drive a tractor, to shovel earth, to be under the sun all day, the general strength it took to be a farmer. She could not say why her feelings had grown for this farmer, how she had become so quickly accustomed to, even drawn to, his smell of sweat and earth. Kareen felt very feminine and protected around Andy, as though she herself were a kind of garden. Yet if she'd written down a list of all she wanted in a man, Andy would hardly fit the bill. He was not tall and dashing, he was not a doctor or lawyer. He was charming, yes, but not refined. She was not swept off her feet the way she had expected to be. Still, she had chosen him, even if from a place inside of herself that she could not locate. Her mother had always told her that when she met the right man she would know it. But did that knowledge come from her head or her heart? Or from someplace else entirely?

Valentine heard Andy's truck pull up to the curb in front of their house, and she straightaway started the coffee boiling. This Andy was starting to grow on her too, limp and all. As he walked up to the back-yard, the coffee hit him like the aroma of freshly plowed earth. From behind the picket fence and through the fruit trees and the tangle of rosebushes, Andy could see Kareen. The neckline of her white dress had the shape of a spoon, her shoulders were creamy in the ebbing light. She had a hand on her cheek and seemed to be daydreaming. He hesitated to open the gate lest he disturb a dream about him, lest he disturb his dream of her. Valentine watched the Turkish coffee mush-room in the copper pot. She took it off the flame, added four teaspoons of sugar and put it on the flame again. She hadn't seen Andy pass by the kitchen window and wondered what he was up to. Then she heard a whistle and the scratch of the wooden gate against the dirt and the latch clink as it closed.

Kareen instinctively threw her shoulders back into an elegant pose. Valentine poured the coffee into three demitasses. Kareen met Andy on the porch and told him they were waiting for him and extended a hand. He put his hand in hers and let her lead him into the back of the garden, to the apricot tree.

It was approaching five o'clock before they all three were seated beneath the tree. A breeze bumped the leaves of the trees. Now and then the roses agreed. Andy noted that the weather was perfect this time of year. They slurped their coffees and nodded and Valentine told him that spring was her favorite season. "Look at the roses," she said, admiring them. Andy told her that indeed her roses were beautiful. "What things God has made for us," Kareen said. "Soon it will be time," Valentine announced, "to pick grape leaves. You must pick the leaves when they are still tender. The secret is you must still be able to see the sun through the leaves."

Andy was eager to invite them both out to his farm. His sister-in-law and her friends picked this time of year too; he was sure Valentine and Kareen would be welcome.

"Speaking of your sister-in-law," Valentine said. "Do you know this Lucy Torozian, Andy?"

"Yes, of course."

"She is a friend of your sister-in-law. Kareen, you've never seen such a beautiful Armenian girl as this Lucy. Akhh," she raised her eyebrows, "What she must have been when she was young!" Valentine let her head swoon. "Eyes round and green as the berry of a Muscat. Like this," she said, and formed a circle of her forefinger and thumb. "And a heart," she said, tossing all that aside with a hand, "like gold, like gold."

"I want to meet her, Mother," Kareen said.

"If you do not, it will be a tragedy."

"Lucy is an old friend of Zabel's," Andy said. "You met at church?"

"No, we sit with coffee together at Roxie Shishmanian's. Just down the street."

Andy nodded. "Yes, Lucy is a gem."

"But there is a something else, recently, no?"

"I haven't heard. Is Lucy sick?"

"Her body, no. But her heart…"

"Yes," Andy said, "it is well known she lost her man some years ago in the war."

"This I did not know," Valentine said.

"Yes, he was a poet."

"What he was does not matter, only that she was in love with him."

"You don't think well of poets, Valentine?" Andy said over a smile.

"This girl," she said, pointing to Kareen, "when she was young she would lock herself in the bathroom like a mouse and read poetry."

"Lock herself up?"

"She wasn't even twelve years old!"

"My mother wouldn't allow it," Kareen explained.

"Poetry, especially at that age, it makes the soul grow dim and weak. Women already have too much poetry in their hearts. To give them more is unhealthy."

"I see," Andy said.

"No, poetry is for men. Old men."

Kareen's laughter was a song.

"In my village," Valentine said, "we had many poets. They would make up these poems and read them and people would gather and listen. I went to hear these poets read too. But I could not understand a word they said. Maybe I am too young to understand, I told myself. After all, all the older people seemed to think this poet was important. When I asked my uncle or aunt what the poet meant, they would begin to speak and then go silent. When I pushed them to tell me, they said, 'Go away, girl.' What kind of words are these, I thought, that make people shut up. Can such a thing be good? Then I will tell you what happened. There was a wedding celebration. Everybody was dancing and drinking and music was playing and food was being served. Many of the people from the village were there, including the poet Karnig. Karnig the Poet, they called him. There was a dance going on, and outside of the circle I saw this Karnig standing. Maybe, I thought, I can understand a little bit about the nature of poets by watching him dance. So I waited and waited and waited for him to join the circle. Everyone—except, of course, some very old men—was dancing. Even the priest was dancing! Only these old men and Karnig were watching. When I got close to the poet, I saw that he had a very sour look on his face, like a child who felt cheated. Being a child myself, I knew the look well. I came to the conclusion then that poets are sour-faced men who feel cheated. They are good for the old because these people too have been cheated: cheated of their youth, cheated by the many terrible turnings of life."

"How about love poems, Valentine?"

"If a man loves a woman, let it show in how he treats her. That is the mark of a man. Many fancy words add nothing."

Andy noted that Kareen was nodding her head.

"If you push me I will tell you that we Armenians have too many poets and not enough men." Valentine paused, then added, "But everyone to their own. What is wrong for one person is right for another.

Maybe if Lucy fell in love with the poet there were things other than his poetry to love. Only she can say."

"Of course," Andy said.

"But this is not the cause of her heartache."

"Yes. Her heartache. What of it?"

"She says that after years of being friends, your sister-in-law, what's her name?"

"Zabel."

"This Zabel refuses to talk to her. On this account, the poor girl is crushed."

"Tsk." Andy shook his head.

"One day Zabel came to pick up her children and she hasn't talked to her since. They've been friends from very far back."

"This doesn't surprise me, Valentine."

"What kind of woman is this Zabel?"

"A different kind," he said.

"But a woman who doesn't have the heart to tell her best friend why she is upset with her?"

"I can't, by my life, think of a reason. Lucy was an aunt to the kids."

"She misses them deeply. Like they were her own."

"I'm sure the kids miss Lucy too."

"I'm wondering," Valentine said, "if someone could not find out what happened? Where is the cause of Zabel's anger?"

"I will try to ask her, Valentine."

"God will bless you."

Kareen, who had quietly followed the exchange, asked, "How is it that people can turn so cold overnight?"

"I've seen it all my life, daughter, and still I ask the same question."

"What do you think, Andy?" Kareen asked.

Valentine turned the handle of the demitasse away from her. Kareen set her demitasse back down on the saucer perched on her knee. They waited for his reply. Somehow they had concluded that his words had gravity. What had he done to earn this respect?

"This coldness is the sign, no doubt, of a very troubled heart," Andy said.

Mother and daughter nodded.

Andy chose his words carefully. "I've noticed that when a grape turns to rot, it seems to do so suddenly. One day you pass a bunch and there is no trace of it. The next day the entire vine is in its grip. If left alone, it will grow and consume the whole vineyard. But after years of farming, I learned that the ground for the breeding of rot is in the making a long time, sometimes from spores left over from the season before. So maybe, Kareen, things don't happen so suddenly."

Valentine nodded her head aggressively.

"In this way, the seed for a cold heart has always been there," he went on. "Perhaps people failed to notice, or perhaps they were afraid to notice. No, people do not change, they only show their faces more clearly."

"Akhh," Valentine exclaimed, "he speaks well."

"A good-hearted boy will grow up to be an even better-hearted man. A black-hearted girl will grow up to be a woman with an even blacker heart."

Valentine stood up.

"You said it well," she said. "Listen to him, sweetheart, he sees things with a clear eye."

Valentine started putting the empty plates onto the tray. When she had stacked up everything nice and tidy, she made for the kitchen. Kareen was silent. Maybe, Andy thought, this is not what she wanted to hear? Maybe, at the age of twenty-three, she saw things in a different way. Andy wondered if he hadn't put it too strongly. The sun had lowered past the trees, past the pitch of the roof, and they both took in the golden residue of light on the horizon that flocked with gilt the edges of the leaves and trees.

Kareen let her eyes drift to the ground. She brushed a crumb off her lap. "How do I know," she said, "which kind of man you are?"

Andy studied Kareen's face. Was this a question about his character, his honor, his sincerity? Was it her way of telling him that her own heart was at stake in the answer?

"I cannot convince you, Kareen, of my character. In the end, as your mother said, only how I treat you will matter. I know only this: every man is a good man in his own eyes. But how he stands in the eyes of a woman is something else. Some women might look at me and see a mere farmer. Others might see a man who owns land. Other women might look past all that. I can only tell you this, that I have hidden nothing from you. When I smile when I see you, I have joy in my heart. When I open a door for you, it is because I cherish you."

Kareen's expression mounted into a smile.

How little women need to be assured that their hearts are secure, Andy thought as he drove home that day. I have hidden nothing, he had said. But this was a lie.

Orange and lemon groves were planted on either side of Highway 180 leading to Pine Flat Reservoir. Dirt roads cut in across private land down to the banks of the Kings River. Andy had fetched trout out of that river as a youth, and the water that flowed from that river irrigated the valley land. They drove in as far as the road would take them and went the rest of the way by foot. Andy was toting a wicker picnic basket, and Kareen a blanket under her arm. On a patch of grass between the trees, Kareen unfolded the blanket, lifted and swung it open with a jerk and let it alight over the grass. She kept her sweater draped loosely over her shoulder, even underneath the drum of that July sun as she stepped gingerly up to the riverbank. The river moved so smoothly that it seemed not to move at all. Now and then, a tree branch or piece of brush meandered, as though by its own volition, down the water's satin surface. The birds chirped in the oaks and the mosquitoes hissed in the bank's tall grass. The cool wind swept the smell of wet wood and algae up under her nose. Kareen watched a few leaves turn in an eddy, and lifted her eyes up-river, where the water snagged against a boulder.

Andy reached into the basket for a beer. He cracked the can open, guzzled the beer down and tried to breath deeply and evenly.

"How beautiful it is," she said. They could feel the river's pulse vaguely, like the pulse of blood in their veins. How beautiful you are, Andy thought, as he watched her spread the lunch out on the blanket: flat bread, string cheese, *basturma*, Greek olives, tomato wedges and shafts of peeled cucumbers.

"Do you like America?" Andy asked.

"I do, but I miss the beach, the sea and its cool breeze." She folded the bread over the string cheese and handed it to him.

"Thank you, sweetheart. One day I will take you to our ocean. It is only two hours away."

"I miss my sister too."

"Nairi?"

"Yes. Do you know the story about how my sister Alice met Arsen?" she asked.

"I've heard *his* side of the story," he said.

"My mother would go every day to the immigration office in Alexandria and stand in line for hours trying to get us to America. Every day she would come home and we would ask her if we were going to America. 'Have faith,' she would say, 'have faith.' Then one day, we got a letter from America telling us that a young Armenian man, Arsen, was coming from America and was supposed to meet Alice to see if they would be suited for marriage. On the day that he was supposed to arrive, Alice took me and Nairi aside and said, 'Look, you go to the ship and see what this Arsen looks like. If he is ugly, run back and tell me and I will hide.'"

They laughed together.

"I wonder if Arsen has heard this?" he asked.

"Maybe he doesn't know." She fed herself a shaft of cucumber sprinkled with salt.

"I'll be sure to tell him."

"Tell him, what can it hurt? He's married now. Do you need anything?" she asked Andy.

"No, sweetheart, everything is perfect."

"So," she continued with relish, "on the day Arsen was supposed to come, many girls and a few boys stood waiting against the railing where the ships came in. When we asked them why they were there, they said that a young man—this was Arsen—was coming from America. The word had gotten out. 'What are we going to do?' we asked each other. If this Arsen was handsome, we had to let all the other girls know that he was our sister's suitor. If one of these girls got him before Alice had the chance, she would kill us. But if he was ugly, we had to keep our mouths shut. I tell you sincerely, we were very confused about what to do. We knew only that he would be wearing a sailor's outfit. We kept our eyes glued on the ship as it came into port. When Arsen walked off, Nairi and I—our hearts jumped. This man was so handsome our breath was taken. By God I swear, two or three girls fainted."

Andy found this hilarious. "Fainted?"

"Yes, many girls fainted back then."

"Were you going to faint, Kareen?"

"No, I told Nairi that I wanted him. I told Nairi to tell Alice that he was ugly so that I could have him."

"You did?"

"But Nairi told me I was too young to be married, and that before I could be married Alice had to marry, and then Nairi herself. So we ran back home with the news. 'Alice,' we said, 'he is not just handsome, he is beautiful.'"

"He *is* one handsome fella," Andy said. "And a helluva nice guy on top of it. Your sister is lucky."

She went on to tell Andy that Alice had written to them every week after immigrating. She had written about Fresno's heat and the cold winter fog and how flat and waterless it was compared to Alexandria.

"But I could not believe it," Kareen said, "because whenever I thought of America I saw in my mind paradise."

"It's true," Andy said. "This is hardly Alexandria."

"But it is beautiful in its own way. The mountains and rivers and lakes. The fruit that grows on the trees. The blossoms in the spring. But Alice could see none of this because she was looking at the world, looking at Fresno through a fog of loneliness. When you are lonely, no place in the world is beautiful enough. Those were difficult years for Alice. She was alone. We were like this," she said and knitted her fingers together. "Now Nairi is the only one left in Alexandria. How I miss my Nairi. Every day I think about her. Every day."

In her hands, Kareen caught chips of broken light that came through the trees.

"We will bring her here," Andy said.

"It is so difficult. She is married and has two children now. Where will her husband, Asbed, work? They will not let him in without someone putting on paper that they will sponsor him in his work."

"I know," Andy said. "But still, we will bring them here."

Andy lifted a cigarette out of his pocket, poked it in his mouth and lit it. She is still a girl, he thought. He took her hand and smiled nervously.

"Sweetheart," he said, and flicked the cigarette away. "The other day I told you that I would never hide anything from you."

"Yes," she said. "I remember. And I believed you."

"I told you the truth. Except for one thing."

Kareen searched his eyes.

"You know I have a limp, but you've never seen my leg."

Kareen shook her head. There was a serious look on his face. "I want to show you."

As he rolled up his pant leg, Kareen could see that Andy's hands were trembling. She wanted to ease his hands, the look on his face. She knew that it would not matter to her in the way that he thought it might. Her only question was how much more she would love him after she'd seen it. She noted the infantile calf floating in the boot even before he tugged it off. Then he pulled the sock off. Her first thought was not how ugly it was, but of how he had endured it all these years.

"Does it hurt?" she asked.

"Yes, it does. Almost always."

She studied it more closely now, the way a sculptor does a hunk of marble. As a pedicurist in Egypt, she'd seen many feet, but she had never seen anything like this. The tangled toes sloped toward the big toe for support, and the nails were broken bits of shells swallowed up by the surrounding flesh. The ankle bone had been shaved down to a nub. Scars crisscrossed the foot.

"You need a good pedicure," she said. "Tomorrow I'll give you one."

He looked at her. Was she insulting him? His heart sank. Then she slid her hand beneath his foot. His insides jumped. He could feel his whole body flush. The last person to touch it had been his mother. Kareen turned his foot gently to the left, to the right. He watched her study whorls of calluses and corns. She was gauging how long that foot would have to be soaked in soapy water. She estimated the pressure on the nerves. She was thinking of the layers of skin that would have to be razored away, pumiced smooth.

Her hands were warm water. His whole life he had imagined what this moment might be like. But he had never imagined this. Kareen, he thought, will be my wife.

Zabel had been working out the numbers in her head. If Abe was going to buy Andy out, they needed cash, more than they had. The harvest was three months off. And depending on the yield and the market price, that would give them, tops, ten thousand dollars. There was no way they could do it in a single year. Andy would have to be paid off in installments over a period of three, four years. Besides that, they'd be forced to renew the loan. It was a blessing that the interest was next to nothing. In a strange way, thank God Abe had gone to war. If he hadn't, they would have been buried with debt—they might've had to sell the land. As the Lord said, all things work for the good for those who love Him. Gradually, Abe would have to be let in on her plans. For the time being they needed Andy's help with the harvest. We will settle matters in October, Zabel thought.

20

IT WAS SEVEN O'CLOCK IN THE MORNING and the sun was flickering in the sky. With Kareen up front, and Alice and Valentine in the backseat of the car, Andy felt like a big brother or, perhaps, a father to these women. He reached for Kareen's hand. It seemed to have been waiting for his all along. It warmed his heart to know that they trusted him, and he could tell that Kareen was proud of him in a way that he would never, ever betray. Andy had expected to be anxious about introducing the two families, but all of his insecurities were overshadowed by the sureness of his love. Still, his heart yearned for all of them to get along. He wanted one big family, not two divided. In the mirror, he watched the women soak up the land with their eyes. The spring air was buoyant. The canopy was luxuriant with diaphanous lime-green leaves, and beneath the canopy, baby berries—the size and hue of young peas—clung to the bunch stems. All around the valley, Armenian women—grandmothers, mothers, and daughters—were out in aprons harvesting these leaves for *dolma* and *sarma,* which they would use right away or preserve for the winter in fat Kerr jars.

"Do you like it?" he asked.

Valentine remarked that the air in the country was sweet and clean. With a hand she brushed some up under her nose. Alice took a deep breath of the air and nodded her head. Andy was flattered by their regard for the land, the air, as though he himself had shaped them both.

"This is it," he said. He slowed the car down so that passing the farm would take some time. "On this side too," he said, pointing to the ten acres across the road. They switched their eyes all together.

"You can pick as many leaves as you want, Valentine," Andy said.

Valentine wagged her head at the charmer that he was.

Kareen could see the house cropping up over the tops of the vines. As Andy pulled up the dirt drive, she noted the tractors and other farm equipment at rest near the barn. Andy slowed the car down to keep from kicking up dust, crawled up to the big oak and cut the engine.

The women stepped out of the car, each with a wide-brimmed hat in her hand, an apron tucked under her arm. It was a perfect day for picking leaves. A breeze now and then ruffled the air. Kareen took a stroll around the yard with her eyes. A couple of dogs were asleep on the porch steps. She asked Andy in Armenian if they bit.

"They are farm dogs," her mother said, as though that answered the question.

Andy told her not to worry, the one was so old he could barely chew his food and the other was safe as a lamb.

Zabel had been standing behind the window. Watching the women surveying the yard, the land, she automatically calculated what a bundle of grape leaves might be worth, what, when the day was done, they might owe her.

"Abe," she called, "your in-laws are here."

Abe was at the kitchen table, reading the morning paper. He picked up his coffee cup, walked into the living room and stood next to Zabel, who had her arms crossed upon her chest. All at once he took in the scene: two women, one young and one old, standing beneath the oak tree, their dresses the same pale white color. Behind the car was another woman, a girl really, with chestnut hair and a strong back exposed between the parentheses of her white dress. It was as if the yard had been transformed by their presence, as though his yard with those three there wasn't his yard any longer, as though his own brother was something different too. Kareen stepped out from behind the car, her hourglass shape suddenly in full view. Abe felt a quiver in his abdomen, close enough to his groin to have caused him confusion if he'd cared to reflect upon it. The other girl—just as pretty as Kareen, with her head now resting on the shoulder of the older woman—must be Kareen's sister, the one married to Arsen. None of them looked Armenian. He told Zabel.

"What do you mean?" Zabel asked. "They look very Armenian. Look at the nose on the mother."

But the women were all turned away from them. Abe couldn't make out her face. He wondered how Zabel could.

Zabel said, "They look like newcomers, that's for sure."

Arm in arm, the two girls began strolling up to the patio, two paces behind Andy and their mother. Zabel jumped from where she was, meaning to catch them before they got to the front porch. In one motion she swung the front door open, stepped out and closed it—like someone harboring a fugitive. The little group halted at the porch, actually dropped back half a step, perplexed, intent on being courteous at any cost. Abe opened the door, shook his head vaguely and stepped behind Zabel.

"Welcome," he said and showed an open palm.

Andy introduced Valentine first, then Alice, and then, placing an arm around her waist, Kareen. "My brother, Abe," he said, "and his wife, Zabel."

Zabel said good day in Armenian and nodded her head.

They all said good day. The moment was so awkward, Andy jumped ten steps ahead.

"Well. Maybe we should let the ladies pick before the sun gets too hot."

Zabel was supposed to join them, so he had thought, so he had told the women. But the way she stood made Andy think otherwise.

Valentine was thinking the same thing. "Will you join us, Madame Voskijian?"

"I have a few things to do inside," she said. "In a little bit, perhaps."

The two girls nodded their heads, as though they perfectly understood.

Andy figured the tenderest leaves were on the ten-acre block on the other side of the road. Still, he asked Zabel where she might pick, hoping to at least get her involved in the planning so that the ladies wouldn't feel totally left on their own. Zabel crunched her shoulders as though she had no opinion about it.

The whole introduction was going down like sour milk.

"Well," Andy said, as upbeat as possible, "let's just start on the small block and see if the leaves look good there."

Valentine told Zabel that she most certainly hoped she would join them later. With three children, was it—Zabel nodded her head, yes—she must be very busy.

Zabel nodded her head again.

The women smiled. Andy extended a hand up the yard and said, "Then let's go."

The women each put on an apron and then tied the ends to the shoulder straps to make a little pouch for the leaves. Kareen felt hurt by the introduction. They must not have liked me, she thought. Andy was ashamed. He went over and gave Kareen a peck on the cheek. Kareen forced a smile, lifted a few hairpins out of the apron's pocket, poked them in her mouth and, with a few quick twists, fixed her hair up in a bun. She fixed a long-brimmed hat on top of her head and stepped into the vineyard. He watched them swiftly clip off the leaves at the stems with their forefingers and thumbs, then drop them into the baskets in their laps. He lit a cigarette and stood there for a bit, admiring the agile genius of their hands. Especially Valentine's. Her leaves were piling up faster than both of her daughters' put together.

"Are the leaves good?" Andy asked.

Valentine told him they were sweet and tender.

"Just like him," Kareen said.

All three women giggled. Andy blushed. "Back to business," he said. "You're going to need a sack to dump them in."

"Yes," Valentine said. "This we forgot. If you would be kind enough to find us one."

"There is no problem there. Pick as much as you want," Andy said.

Sweet and tender, Andy thought. Yes, it's true. My heart is sweet and tender for you, my love. And for your mother and your sister, too. Anyone close to you is close to me. It doesn't matter, he thought, what Zabel and Abe think. Don't worry. It doesn't matter anymore. He was beyond the point of caring what anyone but Kareen thought. With these words, spoken to himself, Andy could feel his emotion for her magically bloom. The old dog, whose name in Armenian was *Shoon* (Dog), spotted Andy crossing the road, jerked himself up to his feet and loped toward him. He stopped in front of Andy and lowered his head, his tail flopping drowsily behind him. Andy patted him on the head and told him that he was a good old dog.

Andy could see Zabel pass by the kitchen window and wondered where the kids were. By the angle of the sun, he estimated it was getting near nine o'clock. Maybe, it being a Saturday, they were sleeping in. Over near the barn, Abe was changing a tractor tire. Andy wasn't in a mood to talk, even though he knew that Abe had tried his best to pull off a welcome.

Abe told him he was having a hell of a time getting the nut loose.

Andy paused a second and shook his head sympathetically, then passed into the barn to fetch a few burlap sacks.

Five minutes later, Abe was still trying his damnedest to get the lug off. When Andy stepped up to the problem, he saw Abe's hands were shaking all out of proportion with the job. Abe looked up at Andy and handed the tools over to him like some kid admitting he'd gotten in over his head. Maybe, Andy thought, this was Abe's way of apologizing. Andy tightened up the wrench and jumped down on it hard with his arms. Huh? He gave it another try. "Son of a bitch." He studied the lug this way and that, as though something more complicated was going on, and picked up the mallet. He tapped the head of the mallet on the end of the wrench a couple of times, then whacked it hard. The lug snapped over.

Andy handed the tools back over to Abe and told him—to break the ice—that that was one tough nut to crack.

"How they doin'?" Abe asked.

"Pretty good."

"Have them take what they want, now."

"That's kind of you."

"I didn't mean it that way."

"These days, it's hard to know what you mean."

Abe wiped sweat from his brow.

"You think," Andy said, "maybe we can make these ladies a cup of coffee a little later?"

Abe took a deep and shaky breath that came out a sigh. Andy wasn't about to feel sorry for him.

"Think maybe you can talk your wife into that chore?"

The wrench bobbed in Abe's hand. Andy had the queer feeling that Abe might just then jump up and whack him over the head with it. Not out of anger, but out of frustration, out of wanting to get rid of the cause of his frustration. The steel wrench glinted in the sun…

He stands up with fire in his eyes, and then, suddenly, you see the wrench rise. You duck instinctively—and feel the metal blow over the top of your head. You let go an uppercut and catch his chin. He staggers back seven, eight feet. The wrench dangles in his hand. He calls you a fuck and comes at you once again—in one motion you reach for the hoe and swing it. The hoe catches him in the temple, the two prongs stick in his head. He screams

"Zabel!" and collapses. You hear something behind you and turn around at the ready. Zabel is coming at you with a knife. You pick up the tire iron. She waves the knife wildly in the air, screaming that you have killed her husband. You bring the iron down on her arm first, snapping it in two. The knife drops to the ground. You jam the iron into her stomach, then wheel it around and down on her fucking head. You should never have fucked with me, you bitch. Look what you've done, look at the mess you've made!

Jesus Christ! The image erupted so suddenly, viscerally, he was afraid of himself. He glanced at Abe, grabbed the burlap sacks off the ground and hurried off. Halfway across the yard he stopped...

In back of you, you hear a moan. It's Abe, coming to. Apparently, you didn't catch him in the temple with the prongs. You smacked him, yes, but with the flat side of the hoe. He sits up and puts a hand to his head. From a deep gash he's bleeding, badly. "Let's get you to a hospital, Abe." Zabel lies on the ground, stiff, wearing a halo of blood. "She's dead, Abe," you say. "She came at me with a knife." On his hands and knees Abe crawls over to her. "Ohh fuck!" he screams. He starts shaking, crying. "She's gone, Abe." "It's my fault," he says. "It's my fault!"

A buzz. With a hand, Andy swiped a fly away from his ear. He wondered how the hell he'd gone from one extreme to the other like that. One minute he was basking in his love for Kareen and the next he was imagining his brother trying to murder him. Twisted. He couldn't even say how long he'd been gone, long enough anyway for the women to have picked through twenty or so vines. He whistled to get their attention and hurried up the row. Kareen was already fat with leaves. She greeted him with a smile, sweat glistening on her brow. "Thank you," she said. As Andy held the sack open, she made a funnel out of her apron and poured the harvest in. She stooped to pick up a few leaves that had tumbled to the ground and asked, "How is your sister-in-law? Will she join us?"

"Maybe later," he said, knowing full well that there would be no later. He reached for the leaves in her hand, but she closed her fist on them. "Don't worry," he assured her.

"Perhaps we could sit down for some coffee later."

"If not today, tomorrow," he said.

"If not then," she said, "the day after tomorrow."

21

EARLY AUGUST. It was going on 110 degrees for two weeks and there was no relief in sight. In the pale blue sky, the sun was an inexhaustible source of heat. It seemed to have pummeled even the air into submission. Only rarely a weak breeze hobbled by. In town, men sat on their porches for hours on end and sipped cold water or iced tea, hardly saying a word, now and then puffing from exhaustion. In their underwear, children hosed each other down on the dry, wheat-colored grass. They cooked eggs on the sidewalks, set aflare ants, beetles and worms beneath the pinpoint heat of a magnifying glass. The rich white folk were up at the lakes, waterskiing. The poorer kids made do with inner tubes pulled by bikes or motor scooters in canals. Every year, a few little ones drowned, their bodies snagged somewhere upstream, found bobbing facedown in the water that surged through their dark glistening hair.

Out in the field, Filipinos and Mexicans and Armenians and Italians perspired side by side, their communication reduced to the bare minimum—water, money, pick, here, there, finished—as though words were a kind of volatile substance, a bomb that could go off if handled too often or without the right skill. Fights were general, gunshots and curses exploded out of nowhere. Now and again, there was a murder. Over what? In the heat it didn't take much, a mere quibble—say, an unmarked tray or the true weight of a gondola.

The brothers were in the field, checking sugar. Andy opened the canopy with a hand. The grapes were heavy, succulent, a secret prize on the vine. He plucked a berry from the top, from the middle, from the bottom of several bunches and squeezed so that the juice squirted out from the bottom of his fist into a mason jar that he held with the other hand. He flicked his hand free of the pulp and skin, swiveled the glass to mix the juice up and took a swig to measure the sugar.

"I'd guess two weeks. What do you figure, Abe?" Andy asked, holding out the jar for him.

Abe slurped some up too.

"Maybe sooner if the sun lets up a little."

They both looked up at the sun, searching for a hint. Irrigation was an issue.

"They'll need a drink, anyways."

"A quick one."

They appreciated the grapes, heavy and pregnant beneath the canopy. They admired the crop the way parents admire the well-developed muscles of eldest sons. Andy picked a bunch off the vine, brought it to eye level and turned it by the stem. With one hand, Abe cupped it in his hand like a tit and pinched a few bottom berries between his fingers till they burst. He tasted the juice on his fingers.

"No water berry here," Abe said.

"Maybe we'll have a little on the far side. Otherwise," he said as he tossed the bunch aside, "looks pretty clean."

"As a nun's crack."

"I did sniff a little rot cropping up on the far end."

"We always got that problem."

"Water gathered down there worse than usual this year. This winter I'm going to take care of that."

Up until now they hadn't mentioned the tonnage. It was considered bad luck to talk about a crop's yield, along the lines of counting your chickens before they've hatched.

"Tonnage's there too, Abe." Andy couldn't help himself.

"Never can tell. That's the thing."

"What's old man Peters think?"

"I don't know, I saw Donny Mosesian the other day and he's banking on twelve to the acre."

"Maybe down that way."

"We got better dirt here by a long shot."

"I thought he's got sandy loam."

"Alkali."

"Huh."

Abe winkled a booger out of his nose with his pinky. "Didn't Donny Mosesian have a falling out with that Ralph, his brother?" he asked, rolling the booger into a ball.

"Yeah. Ralph. He was a gambling fool, high roller."

"Played the horses up and down the state."

"He was a good ol' boy, from what I remember, though," Andy said. "First person to buy you a drink. Give you the shirt off his back."

"Ended up in court, didn't they?"

"Brothers. Damnedest thing. Listen, Abe."

"What's that?"

"I'm getting serious about Kareen."

Abe swiped something from his eye.

"Hoppers," he said.

"Well, if that's all the worry we got, we should count our blessings."

"I hate fuckin' dealin' with hoppers," Abe said.

"*Braceros* do too."

"Fuck the Mexicans. The fruit trees are light this year—in two, three weeks, they'll be squirtin' to get work."

"Anyways…" Andy said.

"So you're looking to get married, huh?"

"I'm thinking about it."

"She's a good gal," Abe said. "Pretty enough."

"I'm glad you think so, Abe."

"It's your choice. What I think's got nothing to do with it. So, when you figuring on asking her?"

"After the harvest."

"Got to keep our heads on straight for another month or so."

"Of course."

"Don't need anything sidetrackin' us right now."

"Wouldn't think of it. Keep it between us, though, would you, Abe?"

"I'll let you tell Zabel on your own calendar."

"Thank you, brother."

Abe buried the shovel in the dirt.

"Well, let's give her a drink."

"Every other row?"

"Sounds about right."

"Sundown or sunrise?"

"Let's wait till tomorrow."

"Fine. I'm walking in a little. Check the rot on the far end."

Abe nodded his head and went out of the row the other way.

Every fifth or sixth vine, Andy spotted hoppers—grains of rice that could jump, and that sounded on the leaves like pellets of rain. They seemed to have popped up overnight. Seemed. He wondered if, had his mind been trained on the vines and not on Kareen, he might've detected them earlier. It was too late to spray for them. He was sort of disappointed with himself. Hoppers were a nuisance, even if they weren't a threat to the grapes.

Unfortunately, he couldn't count on Abe to spot them. These days Abe couldn't spot his own asshole. He'd been spending more time working on that damn Model T than on his livelihood. Talk about sidetracked, he thought. Abe's words started throbbing in his head: *sidetracked,* he heard. *Pretty enough.* Pretty enough for what? Comparing Kareen to Zabel was like comparing roses to crabgrass. Sorry, but there *was* no comparison.

Andy had reached the end of the row. He sniffed the air for traces of rot and shoved the canes aside. There was a *shooosh* of leaves, like when taffeta is gathered up. He held a bunch in his hand and lifted it to peek at the underside. Sure enough, here and there was rot, some berries pocked, like the skin of old men. He pulled out his knife, swiped a bunch clean of its stem, pried the bunch open with his fingers and caught a gust of rot. With another watering, things are going to get worse, he thought. He checked a few vines behind it to see how far the rot had crept. Third vine in was clean. Andy estimated a couple of weeks before the situation took another turn. It was a race between these three: sugar, heat and rot. They needed God to speed up the first, put the breaks on the second and altogether curb the third. Assuming the labor was there, they could lay down the grapes in ten days, two weeks.

Andy scrutinized the sky. There were no clouds in sight, which, ironically, worried him. He would have preferred to have a few clouds stagger in now and then, parceled out, as it were. He was afraid they might be gathering up for a blitzkrieg somewhere in the distance.

He wondered if Abe would tell Zabel about his plans to marry. It dawned on him that asking Abe to keep the matter between them was a kind of test of Abe's loyalty to him. What did it matter if Zabel found out? A part of him wanted to stay clear of the house in order to avoid discovering that Abe had betrayed his wishes. We play these stupid games, Andy thought. We put a person to the test and then we shy away from getting the results. Better we don't test people at all. Better we just get on with the business of living and not worry about how one or another person is going to line up behind us.

The clothes on Zabel's laundry line took less than an hour to dry in the sun. They came off stiff and runneled and hot. First Zabel undid the all the pins, then she lifted the clothes off the line and dropped them into her wicker basket. Andy passed by her and asked if he could help. She waved him off. She didn't want him to get the idea that helping her in this late stage of the game would in any way lighten the burden. To emphasize her labor, she grunted and groaned audibly. Her face was moist with sweat. Sweat blotted her red dress like ink. She puffed strands of hair away from her face. The fabric was glued flat at the patch of flesh where once there was a tit.

The next morning, Andy and Abe were up early to irrigate. All night they had tossed and turned in air that still throbbed with heat from the day before. It was so hot that the only sign it was still night was the dark. Andy and Abe stepped into the yard as though into a dry sauna, both of them surly.

Abe's first words of the day were about the heat. "It's going to be a son of a bitch again."

"This farmer's life is no life," Andy said.

The moon hung in the sky thin as a shaving of skin. The tractor turned over drowsily, again and again, *uhh, uhh, uhh, uhh,* and coughed until globs of black smoke rose from the exhaust pipe and stained the sky, which was now blood red from the breaking sun. They drove slowly athwart the ditch, distributing two pipes to each row from those piled on the trailer.

The usual spread—*chorag,* cheese, *basturma* and eggs—was ready on the kitchen table when they went in for breakfast. They washed their hands, poured themselves coffee and sat down opposite each other with all the seriousness of card sharks. Zabel kept a plastic cover over the table and during the summer, when everyone was all sweaty, it was like eating on a surface smeared with glue.

"Think we could do without this plastic thing for a couple of months?" Abe asked.

"What's wrong?" she asked.

He demonstrated how his finger clung to it, like tack cloth.

"It's sticky is what it is," he said, and tore into a piece of sausage like he'd been holding a grudge against it.

"I'll take it off then," Zabel said.

"I'd appreciate it."

"I said I'll take it off."

"I believed you the first time."

Andy dispatched what was on his plate in short order, leaned back to catch his breath, then promptly lit a cigarette, as though all along all he had ever wanted was that cigarette, as though eating the food was a hoop he had to jump through to get it. Abe was running just behind him. When he was done, he dropped the flatware on his plate, like he too had crossed some finish line.

"Well," Andy said.

"Well," Abe said, wiping off his hands on a napkin.

"The sun's not going to break for breakfast."

"Enough then. Let's go."

Outside, the sky had turned a dusty blue.

"I figure we can finish by noon," Abe said, hoping to beat the afternoon heat.

"Whenever we do."

They worked energetically, twisting and turning on the berm, Abe on one side of the vineyard, Andy on the other. By eleven o'clock they had covered the long block. The water spilled down the rows, absorbed slowly and steadily by the loam. They walked perpendicular to the rows to check the flows. A few pipes were stopped up so they banged them loose of mud and rocks and set them up again.

When they were done for certain, they stood in front of their vineyard for a few minutes, listening attentively to the gush of water as though it were a kind of sermon. Andy felt clearheaded and calm standing there next to his brother. He knew that if only they could keep their focus on the task at hand, then nothing would ever come between them. It was only when Abe stepped back from the land that the problems began.

Abe said, "Well?"

"Let's look at it and see where we're at this afternoon."

Abe nodded his head. They listened to the water some more. They listened as if they bore some likeness to it.

For the next ten days they watched the vines carefully. They watched the sugar, the rot. The hoppers were out of their control. Talk now opened up about a market for greens—grapes used for wine and concentrate—what in the industry is called "juice." Word had it that the wineries were short and a few brokers were out signing contracts. Andy liked the idea of bypassing raisins and going juice.

Andy sniffed around to see what the neighbors figured. All of them wanted to stick with raisins. But to Andy, it didn't make sense. The numbers were right there in front of them. Look, he said, and drew it all with a finger in the dirt. They watched the numbers go up, nodded their heads and threw up their hands—*no contest*—then erased the calculation with a boot, as though it were bad luck to leave it there in plain view. Raisins they knew. Raisins, their bread and butter.

Down at Mel's coffee shop, where local farmers convened in the afternoon to drink iced tea, the consensus was the same. Only the big farmers were signing up.

In Zabel's kitchen, Andy said, "You see, Abe, the heavy hitters—Hiyama, Coelho, even Chamichian—they're all going green." He could see Zabel making faces from over at the kitchen table, where she was rolling grape leaves.

Abe raised an eyebrow. "Chamichian's going green?"

"I'm telling you."

"I don't know," Abe said. "Chamichian, huh?"

"What's there to know? The figures are plain."

"We never done any business with these people."

"What are they going to do, run off with the grapes?"

"Or the money."

"If that was the case, why the hell would the savviest farmers in town sign the earliest?"

"All right, call them out here. What's that suit's name?"

"Jameson."

"Some Okie?"

"What's it matter he's an Okie?"

"Matters plenty."

"Like you've never been taken for a ride by an Armenian."

The next day this Jameson rolled up the dirt drive in a spiffy green Hudson Hornet. He was a big fat man who puffed when he walked. Abe looked him up and down as though he'd come to court his daughter. With a physique like that, it was clear he'd never really worked any earth.

They sat down, all three, on the front porch, and Jameson placed his briefcase to the side of his chair.

"I understand you folks might want to sign."

"Not just yet," Abe said.

"We have a few questions," Andy said.

"Now," Abe asked, "how does this deal work?"

Jameson explained to them that he was a broker charged by the wineries and concentrate operators to purchase grapes by the ton. The grapes would be picked at around twenty-one sugar and delivered in tanks to specified locations around the valley to be crushed. Within thirty days, Abe and Andy would get paid. That was it.

"Who's the money coming from, you or the winery?"

"Directly from the buyer."

"What do you get for it?" Abe didn't like the thought of anyone getting a cut of the action.

"Of course," Andy interjected. "Everybody's got to make a living. The important thing, Mr. Jameson, is that the price is there."

Zabel came out with three tall glasses of lemonade. Jameson sucked his belly in, made a vague gesture to stand. "Thank ya," he said politely as can be. Jameson cupped the glass of lemonade in his tubby hands on his lap, like a kid. Andy was a little tubby himself. For that reason, maybe, he trusted tubby people.

"We were at the money part," Abe said.

Jameson told them they'd get seventy dollars a ton, plus two dollars a ton hauling allowance.

"On your word," Abe said.

"No, no," he said. "This is all in writing."

"Writing?"

"Do you have that writing on you, sir?" Andy asked.

Jameson opened his briefcase.

"Let's us look at it," Abe said.

"Here you are." Jameson handed the contract to Andy.

Jameson took a big gulp of lemonade, set the glass gingerly down on the armrest and puckered his lips. Abe noticed that Jameson's nails shone in the sun. They looked polished, and Abe started to wonder all sort of things about Jameson, even as far-fetched as whether he was a fruit. Sequins of sweat were pinned on Jameson's brow. He wiped it with a sleeve and repositioned himself in the seat.

Abe had never done farming business other than on a handshake. He didn't like being locked into anything, but on the other hand, he *did* like the idea of the wineries being locked in.

Andy passed it over to him. Abe made to scrutinize it, then abruptly said, "We need an afternoon to what you call review this piece of paper."

"That's up to you," Jameson said, "but I've got five other farmers to see today."

"We'll take our chances," Andy said. "If you stop by tomorrow, say, noontime, we'll have a decision for you."

Jameson rose from his seat, puffing.

"Thank you for coming," Andy said.

"Pleasure."

The brothers shook hands with the man and walked him back to his car. Zabel came out as soon as Jameson drove off.

"What is happening?" she asked.

Abe explained it to her.

"Are you going to do it?"

"Yeah," Andy said, "we're going to do it."

"Then you did it. Abe?" Zabel's voice was getting hectic with alarm.

"We're going to," Abe said, "but we don't want to let him know that, not just yet."

Andy said, "At that price, hell yes we're going to do it. We'd need our heads examined if we didn't."

The next day they signed up: a one-year contract with a seventy-two-dollars-a-ton minimum, including hauling; impossible to beat. Abe was reinvigorated by the negotiation. He put some extra work into the forklift and reconditioned a few gondolas that had all but gone to pot in the back of the barn. The farmers in the neighborhood kept an eye on their every move, like they were up to some skullduggery. Andy made a deal with old man Sivas down the road to do the trucking for near nothing, which meant they'd pick up a few pennies on the hauling allowance.

In the meantime, the crop was coming along. The bunch rot had stayed put, even after the last irrigation. The berries were still sizing up, plump and firm and tight skinned. Only the vine hoppers were getting out of hand. Sugar, Andy estimated, was creeping up one point a week. Everyone talked about a bumper crop that could affect the price of raisins either way, depending on the demand.

Then, in mid-August, the table grape market started to sag. And the next week, the packing houses came out with a price for raisins: fifty bucks a ton, ten dollars lower than the year before.

Plenty of farmers started kicking themselves for not getting on board with the wineries. The brothers' neighbors—Freddy Souza, Vince Takahashi—trundled into the yard like whipped dogs, asking for the name of that broker. Andy put a call in on their behalf. Jameson told them the contracts were filled, but maybe next year. Andy passed the news on. "Damnedest year," he told them.

The guys going raisins—what was their option—started terracing. Jameson had only come by once since the contract was signed. The brothers started to fidget; they needed to know whether to give the grapes another shot of water—to keep them fresh. Also, if the sugar wasn't already there, it was pretty damn close. Andy put a call in to Jameson. Jameson said he'd been by the farm and had noticed a little slip-skin on the small block. Shit, Andy thought to himself, part of the reason a guy goes juice is so he doesn't have to worry about shit like slip-skin in the first place. In so many words, he conveyed this to Jameson. Jameson agreed with his point, which made Andy wonder why he'd brought it up at all.

"What do you say on the sugar?" Andy asked.

"Sugar's getting there," said Jameson.

"Should we give 'em a quick drink?" Andy asked. "We don't want them to start backing out on us. Could lose some weight if they do."

Jameson said he'd let him know on the irrigation. Also, he'd try to pin the winery down on a pick. Andy said he'd sure appreciate that. No disrespect, but given this was the first time they'd done business together, he'd like a schedule he could count on.

Andy relayed the details of the conversation to Abe.

"I swear to God," Abe said.

"The thing is, if we give them water now, even with this weather, we won't be able to get in there for six, seven days, the rows'll be so wet."

"That'll put us at September fourth."

A twitch started up in Abe's right eye.

"Don't panic now, Abe."

Andy flipped through the contract to see if there was any mention of a cutoff date for picking.

"You call that son of a bitch and tell him if he doesn't give us a date, I'll tear this fucking contract up."

Zabel rushed in and asked what was the matter.

"Everything's fine, Zabel," Abe said.

"No cutoff date. But, let's just look at this thing, Abe. Say worse comes to worst, we get to the fourth and haven't heard a thing from this Jameson. There's no reason we can't right away terrace and shove some Filipinos out here to lay 'em down. We'll be ten days behind everyone else. The weather looks clean; I don't see any reason this situation should cause us any consternation at this point."

"We wait any longer than that and we're looking at shatter."

"Looks like we got to watch for shatter even going juice this year."

Zabel's head was switching back and forth between Abe and Andy.

"I'm gonna drive by Chamichian's and see what's going on with him."

"You do that."

Chamichian lived up to his name, which translated to "son of the raisin man." He farmed close to four hundred acres of Thompson seedless down around Hanford. Andy always considered him a good source of information, not only on account of his being a successful farmer, but because he was something of a philosopher to boot. Aram Arax, who was a diehard Communist and never spoke a kind word about anyone who wasn't in the party, considered Chamichian a gentleman scholar. So when Andy had heard that Chamichian was going green, it had given him confidence to jump on the same wagon.

Chamichian was overseeing some tractor repairs when Andy drove up. Andy doffed his hat and approached with a hand raised. Chamichian knew Andy from church, but that was the extent of it.

"Baron Chamichian," Andy said.

"Antranik. What is your business out here today?" He put out a hand. Andy shook it firmly.

"Just was in the area and thought I'd stop by and see how things were going."

"Right now we've got a tractor that Luis here is trying to give another life to. So how are things going for you and your brother?"

"Well, we're trying something different this year. Going green. How about you?"

"Well, I let a few ton go that way. Looked like a good year to diversify."

"That's what we figured."

"We'll see, though."

"How's that?"

"Wineries have a reputation for shorting farmers. Lot of Muscat has gone to Gallo, the Italian Swiss, from this area for years, and its no secret that more than a fair share of farmers have walked away sorely disappointed. Now they're looking for Thompson growers."

"Yea, I heard that. What kind of wine can a Thompson make?"

"Not much of one. Except when you're short, you're short. Just about anything that's got juice will do the trick. Truth is, with the way this raisin market's shaping up, I'll probably be sorry I didn't sign up more for juice."

"How much did you sign?"

He pointed his finger over Andy's head. "That hundred down there."

"With this Jameson fella?"

"No. No, this guy's name is Roberts. Troy Roberts."

"You heard anything about this Jameson?"

"Not one way or the other. Has he been giving you the run-around?"

"Nah, we're just a little bothered that we don't have a pick date."

"We're scheduled next week."

"Next week?" Andy tried to sound casual.

"Sugar's there. I taste twenty-one, twenty-two."

"We've got near about the same."

"We're always a point ahead of Fresno."

"Maybe twenty, then."

"What winery yours heading to?"

"Gallo."

"We're contracted there as well. Maybe they got you on a different program?" Chamichian asked.

"Could be."

The mechanic slipped out from beneath the tractor, stood and slapped his pants free of dirt.

"What's it look like, Luis?"

"I tink dis one pinish, boss."

"Well, Andy."

"Thanks for your time."

"It's nothing. Good luck. Let me know how things go."

"Will do."

When Andy got back, he saw Abe messing around with the irrigation pipes.

"What's up?" he asked, rolling the truck to a stop where Abe stood.

"That guy called. Jameson. Says we won't pick till about the eighth, ninth. Says shovin' some water on 'em wouldn't be a bad idea."

"Okay."

"What'd the Raisin Man have to say?"

"Nothin'. He's scheduled, though."

"Well, now we are too, looks like. What'd he get for his?"

"I wouldn't ask him something like that, Abe. What, you crazy?"

"Why, did he get more?"

"I'll tell you, Abe, you're starting to think like your wife. It's getting to be that saying nothing automatically amounts to hiding something."

"Anyways," Abe said, "I figured we'd hop into this block this afternoon."

"Let me park this jalopy."

Andy and Abe waited for their day to pick. Everything was ready to roll: tractors, the gondolas that were hitched to them, trucks. On September 7, they got a call from Jameson. He told them that Gallo had decided to push the crush off a week more. Sorry, but they were looking at the thirteenth.

"That's strange," Andy said. "So, Gallo's not crushing Thompson yet?"

"That's right, Andy," Jameson said.

"Well, I got news for you, he is crushing Thompson."

"He's crushing Thompson?"

"You know that as well as I do."

"Not to my knowledge."

"Well, Gallo's crushing Chamichian's. We didn't just drop off the banana boat, Jameson."

"In your area?"

"That I can't say. But in Hanford he is."

"Hanford's a different story."

"By a point, maybe."

Jameson didn't reply.

"You told us twenty-one sugar, no?"

"Whatever sugar they need."

"What sugar do they need now?"

"Twenty-three."

"I didn't know Gallo's making pancake syrup these days."

"There's nothing to worry about. The grapes are beautiful. They're holding up just fine."

"We're concerned they stay that way."

"Let me talk to Gallo," Jameson said.

"I'd appreciate it."

They hung up.

"That cocksucker." Abe's face was all screwed up.

"Hold onto your hat, Abe. Let's give him a few hours."

"I'll tell you what," Abe said. "If that son of a bitch doesn't give us a pick date by this afternoon, I'll stuff his fucking contract back up his ass where it came from!" A vein on his forehead bulged.

"Don't give yourself a stroke, Abe. There's no reason to panic."

"I know what Gallo's up to. He bought more than he could chew. This crop's fatter than he figured. His tanks, they're flooded, and now he's hemmin' and hawin'. He's done it before. What's next he's going to do is show up five or six days from now and claim the grapes aren't up to speed."

"They're clean as a whistle, except for a spot or two."

"All he needs. From that he'll claim the whole damn field's gone to shit."

"Remember we're on contract, Abe."

"What? He's got every judge from here to Bakersfield in his back pocket. Get your head out of your ass."

"Works the other way too, Abe. If we pull out, Gallo can come after us for breaking the contract."

"Bullshit! What? Are we supposed to wait till they turn to raisins on the vine?"

"Everybody's got their point of view. Gallo will have his. And the judge, like you say."

"Goddamn dago can kiss my ass."

"Look. Everything you say is possible, Abe. But the other possibility is that Jameson and Gallo are shootin' straight with us. That what you're doing is exaggerating the situation, getting riled up as usual."

"As usual?"

"That's right."

"Maybe I've got the right to get riled."

"How's that, Abe?"

"In case you don't remember, this land is in my name!"

"What's that got to do with anything?"

"It's got plenty to do with it. It's my ass that's on the line if our bills don't get paid. Fertilizer, water, gypsum, sulphur."

"I signed on those accounts too, Abe."

"It's me they'll squeeze. Not you. On paper you ain't got nothin'."

"On paper. Paper my ass! If they take from you, Abe, they're taking from me. What the hell is wrong with your head!"

Abe didn't say anything.

"You surprise me, Abe."

"Forget I said it. Let's just figure this thing out."

"Maybe you need to see a shrink."

"I said forget it."

Andy shook his head in disgust. "All right, Abe. Let's just lay low. See what kind of plan of attack this Jameson's got formulated."

Jameson telephoned a couple of hours later and told them that Gallo was sticking to their pick date. He told them to keep the water off in case Gallo changed his mind and wanted to go in a little sooner.

"I say we hang in there, Abe. But I'm not the only one here."

"You sure the hell ain't."

"We've established that. Now, what do you want?"

"Lay 'em down."

"I guessed you'd say that."

"We never should've walked into this shit. We'll terrace tomorrow. That's the end of the story."

"We're not doing nothin' till we get a release from Gallo. Let's do it right."

"You do whatever. I'm going in tomorrow. Fuck Gallo. Who the fuck does he think he is?"

"Gallo's Gallo. That's who he is."

Abe snickered. He seemed to enjoy the thought of a showdown with the biggest handler of juice in the county.

"I'll talk to Jameson and tell him the situation. Real polite."

Andy called Jameson and told him that the way he and Abe saw it, the grapes were hanging on the vine longer than they had expected. He told him he was afraid it was going to start stressing the vines and that they were in no position to lose any tonnage from dehydration.

"We're small-time farmers, Mr. Jameson." Andy hated admitting it, even when it served his cause. He said, "This here is our livelihood, our bread and butter."

"Well," Jameson said, "I might be able to pick up the tonnage somewhere else. But it's late in the season. Let me make a few calls."

"We'd like out, sir, in any case."

"There is the matter of my commission too," Jameson said. "That's *my* bread and butter."

"I understand that."

"We're talking in the vicinity of seven, eight hundred dollars."

"If that's what it is, we'll make sure you're taken care of. We're fair people."

"I like you, Andy. For you, I'll do it."

"I'd appreciate it. Maybe next year we'll take a look at another juice program. We've just got a lot on our plate right now. It's a touch-and-go year. I'm sure you've had your share."

"I understand."

"Thank you. You're a gentleman, sir."

"Okay, Abe," Andy said. "We're out."

22

THE PACKING HOUSE where Kareen and her mother worked was a rusted sheet-metal box about seventy yards long and thirty yards wide with a slat-board floor covered in patches with sawdust. At seven thirty in the morning, the big wooden doors would swing open and groups of women and men—wives and husbands, daughter and mothers—would troop in just before the first fruit arrived from the fields. For nearly a month now, Valentine and Kareen had arrived about fifteen minutes late every day because Valentine could not persuade her daughter that her hair need not be bunned as neatly as Kareen insisted it be. While Valentine prepared their lunch of sliced cucumbers, tomatoes, bread and cheese, she chided Kareen, "You are going to pack fruit, not to some ball!" Still, Kareen always entered that place with a maximum amount of respectability—no matter the baseness of the work.

The women, clad in aprons, climbed steps stationed on either side of the conveyor, up to a long platform roughly four feet above the ground. Three such conveyors were operating in this packing plant, average in size. Slowly, the peaches would come toward them, rolling as though in slow motion—a swarm of living things, jostling for position before being plucked up and packed in boxes according to their size—twenty-four, thirty-six and forty-eight count. The women filled the boxes the way bees cell by cell fill a hive. After a month Kareen noticed that her arms were firming up and that she could spot a split-pit, bruised or scarred peach almost without looking at it, as if her hands had developed their own intelligence. Into bins below and in front of them the women tossed the culls where they would slowly turn into a sort of disgusting jam twitching with ants, flies that sparked off of the fruit like pellets of rain, and fruit flies that made the air above the bins shimmy. These bins were forklifted away by drivers who stole looks up under the women's skirts, whistling and winking at the prettier ones, some of whom, at the risk of losing their jobs, cursed and slung rotten peaches at their heads, while some simply suffered the men's eyes. Kareen and Valentine would start to talk and then their talk would eddy and idle and sink beneath the swell of fruit and the roar of the fans and clatter of the conveyor.

They would have already been fired for their tardiness if not for the fact that the foreman—son of the owner, Sorenson—had an eye for Kareen. He had been out of college for three years and was still waffling about what to do next, so his father decided that in the meantime he should learn the ins and outs of the packing business. Right away he had noticed that Kareen was uncommonly beautiful, but besides that, while at the end of the day all the other girls' aprons were smudged and stained, Kareen's apron, except for a streak here and there, was miraculously spotless. How did that happen? For two weeks he had watched her as though he were doing detective work. He also noticed this short stocky guy in overalls, with thinning hair and a limp, coming to pick up Kareen and this other woman, probably her mother or aunt. Surely she couldn't be serious about this guy who was nowhere near as handsome as she was beautiful.

He watched her even more closely now, he watched the way she lifted her skirt when she stepped onto the platform, the way she carefully rescued a stray strand of hair with a finger, the way her hands moved fluently over the fruit as though in a former life she had been a pianist. And especially he watched the heavy, breasty, almost tragic sighs she took from time to time. He concluded that in spite of her satisfactory performance on the job, she was, nonetheless, above it. Finally, after he heard her say something to her mom in flawless French (he'd had two years of it in school), he could no longer contain himself.

With her mother, Kareen was sitting beneath a tree waiting for Andy to pick them up after a long day of work. Sorenson's son was tall, handsome and blond, and he wore a polo shirt and chinos, and he was, after all, the owner's son and the foreman. Still, when he asked her name, she could see his hands tremble.

She told him.

"My name is Dennis," he said.

She tucked her dress underneath her legs and said, "Like the Menace," the only other Dennis she knew.

"Yes," he said. "Anyway, you pack really good. I was thinking about having you be a floor lady."

Her mother, from the few words she could understand in such rapid English, tried to make out what they were saying.

Kareen didn't want any job that would take her away from her mother, so the offer didn't much interest her.

"Oh?" she said, and sunk her teeth into a section of apple.

"Yeah," he said, "I'm the foreman. My father owns this place."

"Your father," Kareen asked, "is Mr. Sorenson?"

She looked up at the big sign bearing that name that dominated the door of the packing house.

"Actually, we own it together."

"Very nice." With each breath, her breasts seemed to rise beneath her dress.

Valentine asked Kareen in Armenian what he had said. She told her. "In that case, then tell him," Valentine told her, "that there need to be more fans. There aren't enough, and even the ones they have howl like wolves."

Kareen passed the message on.

Dennis froze as though he'd just learned his fly was open. It had never occurred to him that workers might have complaints. He figured they were all just happy to have jobs.

"That's something we got planned to do," he said.

"They're going to do it," Kareen told her mom in Armenian.

Valentine dismissed the answer with an upward wag of her hand and lay back in the grass. Kareen returned to her apple.

Dennis smiled and asked her where she was from.

She answered him, "Egypt."

His mind got swamped with exotica—camels, pyramids, date trees. What was he supposed to say now, that he'd graduated from USC? He decided he shouldn't waste any more time. He glanced over his shoulder, then asked if she liked jazz.

"Yes."

"I've got two tickets to see Dave Brubeck down at the Rainbow. I thought you might like to go with me."

Kareen thought she might not have heard right. She knit her eyebrows together, shook her head. Dennis repeated the offer.

She wondered if she would go out with him if Andy weren't around, what it might be like to date an *odar*. She thought of fast cars and surfboards and two-story homes and weekends at the beach.

Beads of sweat had gathered on his tanned brow, and he looked, at that moment, no older than fifteen. "Well?" Dennis asked.

Valentine waved. Dennis turned around and saw a truck negotiating a U-turn across the road. Kareen began to fold up her brown paper bag. Andy rolled up to the dirt lot and stopped. The two women stood, gathering their dresses out from under them. Dennis looked at Kareen like a dog waiting for a bone. She blew a blade of hair away from her moist face and thanked him for offering her a floor lady job. Kareen and Valentine got into Andy's truck without a second look.

The truck barreled down the long boulevard, lined on either side with tall palms that led into town. The women sat with their knees pinched together, hands folded politely in their laps. Kareen felt confused and remote because she was now worried that her job depended upon her saying yes to Sorenson's son.

"Who was that guy?" Andy asked. "Good lookin' kid."

Left on her own, she might have lied. But she suspected that her mother had figured it all out and would sooner rather than later correct her if she did.

"He's the owner's son."

Valentine rolled her eyes as though she should be impressed.

"He wants me to be a floor lady."

That was true.

"Did he ask you out on a date?"

It was as though he'd been hiding in the tree above them.

"Something like that."

Andy smiled kindly and asked her what was her response, jealousy barely rasping inside of him.

"What?" she said, pretending to be mesmerized by the hum of the tires on the road.

Valentine tilted her head back and closed her eyes, more than happy, now that the matter was plainly on the table, to stay out of it.

Andy lit a cigarette and waited for her reply, feeling more like her father now than her husband-to-be.

"What am I going to say?" she finally said. The tone of her voice was dismissive. But of what, or rather, whom?

"Well, I know what I hoped you'd say."

She lifted one of his hands from off the wheel. They were short, stocky, callused and the color of old varnish.

"You are my only *pasha*," she said.

He nodded his head just like a *pasha,* proudly. She'd answered well. He'd better ask her to marry him soon.

At work the next Monday, one of the floor ladies, Lucia, tapped Kareen on the shoulder and told her that Mr. Sorenson's son wanted to see her in his office. Valentine looked at Kareen. She told her mother, "He wants to see me."

Sorenson's son sat behind a big brown desk in the office, clean-shaven and wearing some musky cologne and a fancy suede cowboy hat. He looked up from paperwork when she walked in, told her to have a seat and scribbled on a sheet of paper. When he was done with that, he slid the pencil behind his ear, grabbed the steaming mug of coffee by its neck and looked her in the eyes with a trace of self control that had in no way been evident the week before. The air was silky and cool in his office, and the whir of the air conditioner was like a song that made her sleepy. Kareen began to realize how the other half lived.

"I thought," Dennis said, "that we might have an opportunity to finish our conversation in private."

"But I have to work," Kareen said.

Dennis sniggered and told her that he decided who would and who wouldn't work. And just now, she wouldn't.

Since Kareen had no choice in the matter, she also felt no obligation to respond.

"Yesterday," he said, "you left kind of quick. Maybe you didn't get a chance to answer my question?"

"All the floor ladies are good; why do you want to replace one of them with me? I don't think I have the experience to be a floor lady, anyway."

"I wasn't really thinking about the floor lady part," he said.

Kareen shook her head as though she wasn't sure what he was asking.

"I asked you on a date!"

Kareen turned her head and cast her eyes down, as though he had just slapped her.

"A date," he said more calmly. "Last night I couldn't get you out of my head. I've got feelings for you."

"But you don't know me."

"I know you better than you think. I've been watching you for weeks."

Kareen felt violated.

"You're playing with my mind, aren't you?" he said.

Kareen didn't know what he was talking about.

"What, don't you think I'm good-looking enough?"

"No," she said, "You are a very nice-looking man."

"Lots of girls think I'm better than that."

Kareen crunched her shoulders, then quickly nodded her head. Who was she to disagree?

"How would you like to go to Frisco this weekend?"

"Frisco?"

"San Francisco. One of the most romantic cities in the world. You been?"

"No."

"We can go there, have dinner and go dancing."

"But I must work this weekend."

"Don't worry about all of that right now. We'll take care of that later."

Kareen stood up.

"Where you going?" he asked.

"Back to work."

"Why don't you answer me, girl? What's wrong with you?"

"I cannot go with you anywhere, because I have a man."

"That guy?" Dennis exclaimed. "That guy who comes to pick you up?"

"Yes."

Dennis guffawed.

Kareen wondered whether such transformations occurred in all men when they sat behind desks.

"How long you been together?"

"For three, four months?"

"Then you're just dating. You're not serious or anything. Sit down."

Kareen remained standing.

"Where's he from?"

"Fresno."

"I mean, what's his race?"

"Armenian."

"Armenian? You're going out with an Armenian?"

"I am Armenian, yes."

"Thought you said you was from Egypt?"

She trembled with fear, anger.

"Okay," he said. "You can go."

Kareen nodded and walked toward the door. She put a hand on the knob, turned around and said, "I thought you were a nice man yesterday, Dennis Sorenson, but today maybe I'm not so sure."

"I don't pay you to think I'm a nice man, lady."

Kareen went back to the packing line in a daze. When her mother asked her what had happened, she told her everything. They stared at the fruit moving on the conveyor as though they'd forgotten what to do with it. From the corner of her eye, Kareen saw Dennis come out of the office, looking taller and more formidable than he ever had before. She felt her stomach tie up in knots as he passed below, between the conveyors, surveying the situation as though nothing between them had occurred.

"What am I going to do?" she asked her mother.

Her mother said nothing, but Kareen could see her hands come to a halt over the peaches.

As Dennis swung himself onto the platform, his boots thudded the wood slats. Over the machines, the hands, the fruit, he ran his eyes. He had a few harsh words for some of the other girls, appearing to use them as warm-up for what he intended to do to Kareen. She could sense him closing in. When he stopped in back of them, her heart panicked. His long tanned arm appeared, and with his hand he plucked a peach out of a box. In the periphery of her vision, Kareen could see him scrutinizing it. She heard him bite into its flesh, she heard him slurp up its juice, the distance between them full of ugly significance. He brushed against her, the muscles of his chest like a board against her head. A small cry came out of Kareen. Valentine turned around with a peach in her hand and asked him, in Armenian, "What do you want?"

He looked at her with all the arrogance of a boy who'd just trapped a rabbit.

"Take it," she said, and shoved the peach at his chest.

For a second he stood there, stunned. Then he wrenched the peach out of her hand.

A few girls stopped working.

Dennis flipped the peach in the air and caught it.

Kareen's heart boomed and she wondered what her mother would do next.

"You're fucking fired," he said.

Valentine searched Kareen's eyes for an answer. She told her and reached down to grab her purse.

"Let's go," she told her mother.

Valentine's whole face went crazy. In Armenian she screamed, "Spit in your face!"

Dennis flinched.

She turned and flipped over a box of fruit onto the conveyor belt.

"Hey!" he yelled.

She picked up a peach and flung it across the shed.

"Hey!!"

Valentine started pitching peaches. Packers ducked. Dennis had never encountered anything like this from a woman in his life.

He caught one of her arms and twisted it around. Valentine screamed. The packers froze. Even, it seemed, fruit on the conveyor froze. "Listen bitch," he said. "Who the fuck do you think you're fucking with?"

Instinctively, Kareen reached for an empty crate. Dennis turned his head....*Bam!*...into the oncoming force of a crate. He felt his nose get fat with pain, and blood flooded out of it. When he finally caught his breath, the two women were scampering down the steps. It was over, just like that. Everyone turned their eyes back to the peaches.

Half a block down the dirt road, Valentine was still cursing. Kareen had to plead with her to stay away from the packing house. But not before Valentine had spit at the fans, the doors, the big Sorenson sign way up there. Every five steps she'd spit at the ground, repeating, "I spit in your face."

"I saw something like this coming," Andy said later, back at Valentine's house. "I guess I'll have to go back down to that shack tomorrow and beat the motherfucker to shit."

Valentine paced back and forth. A cigarette bobbed between her fingers. "Please, Andy."

Andy lit a cigarette of his own, took a big long toke and shook his head at the awful mess he was going to make of that blondie.

"I beg you, no. He's just a college boy who thinks he's more."

"I'll handle it," he said. "Don't worry."

"If you love me, you won't do it."

Andy calmed down. "You got some wages coming, don't you?"

Kareen nodded her head yes.

"At least I'll go down and pick that up."

"Just our money, what we've earned."

"I promise."

Dennis Sorenson had never taken close account of Andy before, but as he walked, or rather limped, toward the office that next afternoon, he did. He's short, sure, but he's built like a gorilla, a bear, he thought. His arms were the size of Sorenson's thighs. Sorenson had this fear of short, dark people built that way. Something so muscular and low to the ground was hard to stop once it got going. He'd rather fight a buck than, say, a boar.

He lit a cigarette and put an ear to the door.

Andy walked into the air-conditioned office, removed his hat, and stepped up to receptionist's desk. Real polite, he asked to see the boss' son to settle the account of Kareen and Valentine, who'd been fired the day before. The woman called another woman, Patty, and told Andy that this Patty was the one who kept track of such matters. Patty sat behind her desk, a cold fish. She barely lifted her eyes from her nails, which were going tippy-tap on a typewriter.

After a couple of minutes, and at just about the point where Andy was going to have a word with her himself, she looked up, kind of exasperated, and asked, "Can I help you?"

Andy told her what he needed.

"Well, are these the two girls who assaulted Mr. Sorenson yesterday?" she asked, as though it were an issue that the courts were preparing to handle.

"Don't give me trouble, ma'am. Just draw me the money owed them and we won't have another word about it."

She let out a puff of disgust and said, "I think they owe *him* something, not the other way around."

Andy shook his head like he hadn't heard her right. "I'll ask kindly one more time," he said, "and then we'll try another option. Now…"

But before he could finish, she had picked up the phone and dialed a number.

"Mr. Sorenson, a man is here demanding money for those two girls yesterday." She nodded her head. "Yes, sir. He's beginning to make threats. Yes, sir." She hung up and went back to typing whatever it was.

"Well?" Andy asked.

"He will be with you shortly."

Andy could see that her hands were rattling a tad. Dennis strode out of his office, his confidence obviously fake. Andy followed him with his eyes over to Patty's desk and watched them exchange a few words. Patty handed him a couple of timesheets.

Andy heard, "Write him a check for eighty-five dollars. Minus three dollars for a box of peaches."

"Cut the check right," Andy said, "or I'll break your fucking neck."

He said it matter-of-factly, as though he were tired of saying it. Sorenson realized that either he didn't mean it, or he meant it so much that any show of emotion was superfluous.

To buy himself time, Sorenson said, "Now, wait a minute."

"In that case, make it cash, no check."

Patty lifted the phone off the receiver and held it, ready to dial. Who? The cops? This layer of society likely has its connections with the cops, Andy thought, and decided he didn't give a damn, that if spending a few days in jail was what it took to see this weasel squirm, so be it.

There was a half-door at the end of the counter that led to the other side where Dennis was standing. Andy started for it.

"All right," Sorenson said. "Okay." Andy stopped with a hand on the door. Sorenson reached into his pants pocket and took out a wad of dough. He flipped a few bills out on the desk, then, shaking, handed them to Patty. Patty handed the money to another woman and told her to give it to Andy. At this point things were getting pathetic, so Andy made sure to give the woman who eventually did hand the money over a calming smile. Andy licked a finger and slowly counted the cash, then folded it up and stuffed it in his shirt pocket. Satisfied, he fixed his hat back on his head, told Sorenson that he should watch his back for a while and left.

The money mother and daughter made packing fruit wasn't much, but it bought them groceries and rent and now and then some fabric for a dress. They could easily pick up work at another packing plant, so losing the job wasn't a disaster. What was a disaster, though, was that Kareen should have to work at all. Andy felt responsible for what had gone down at the packing house. But he couldn't very well say he'd take care of her without making her into a kept woman.

Kareen rushed into the kitchen and poured two glasses of chilled mint tea when she heard Andy's car pull into the drive. Through the window she saw him sitting in the car. His head was tossed back, as if he was applying eyedrops. She opened the screen door quietly with her hip and stepped onto the patio with the tea. And waited. He jerked to attention when he saw her. He rubbed his face and stepped out of the car.

"What came of it?" she asked, offering him a glass of tea.

With one hand he took it and with the other he lifted the money from his shirt pocket.

"Everything's fine," he said. "Here's your wages. I guess what they gave me is about right."

She took the money and searched his eyes for something more.

"All is all right, then?"

"Let's sit." Andy felt kind of sick, sullied. He perched the glass on the armrest of the wooden chair and took her hand.

She let her fingers skim over the soft brown hair of his arm. She noticed that her pale skin stood out more against the charred color of his own.

"I don't like the thought of you working in these places," he said.

"Maybe I can get work cleaning houses."

Andy shook his head.

"What then?"

"Frankly, I don't like the thought of you working at all."

She cocked her head and narrowed her eyes. She tried to get a fix on where he was going.

He took a long draft of the tea, let out a deep breath and said, "I had a dream about you that I didn't tell you about. *Before* we met."

Kareen gave him a sweet go-ahead-with-it smile.

"I was at Willa's house in Frisco and all my sisters were sitting in the living room talking in a circle, the way they do. Somehow, I was sitting there too, with all them women. Then, from out of the kitchen this girl comes with a tray full of Turkish coffees. She starts passing them out, one by one. Finally, she comes to me. She hands me a cup of coffee. That girl, her face was yours. It was you I saw in my dream. Your face."

"You're crazy, Andy."

"I swear by God, I had such a dream."

"Before you met me?"

"God be my witness."

"Maybe it was from the picture of me that you saw." Kareen lowered her eyes, flattered and embarrassed at the same time.

"Maybe."

With a hand, she skimmed the cold water that had beaded on the glass and rubbed it across the back of her neck. "But what," Kareen looked up, "does this have to do with me working?"

"Well, what I'm trying to say, sweetheart, is I figure we should get married."

"Are you asking me to marry you?"

"Yeah. Would you marry me?"

Kareen had dreamt of the day when a man would ask her to marry him.

He would sneak into her room...window...moonlight...on his knees, catch his breath. He would from his tuxedo pocket lift a small felt box...candles...roses...the diamond sprinkling a thousand hues of light. He would take her by the hand...party...a balcony...foggy...night...cologne...whisper in her ear...I love...

She was twenty-three, it was a sizzling summer day in a place called Fresno. Her dress, soaked with sweat, stuck to the chair. Across from her sat an overweight farmer she had barely kissed and who had a limp to boot. She batted away a fly darting around her head. Barring any disrespect, the proposal was so incongruous with the image she'd held in her mind for so many years, it took her a full minute to reply: "Yes."

Abe terraced the rows while Andy broke up the block of trays—dusty and cobwebbed and sooty with dry mildew—that had been stacked behind the barn. He sorted through them and piled those trays that had survived the brutal winter rains on the back of the vineyard wagons. He swore he could feel his blood pressure jump, just thinking about the chance they'd missed. Especially with the way raisin prices were tumbling. He should've fought Abe on it. Instead, he had just rolled over and played dead. On the other hand, say Gallo was delaying with an eye toward pulling out altogether. Then they would really be fucked; then they'd be looking at pig slop.

From off the back of the trailer, he lifted a stack of trays in his arms, and one by one he spread them two feet apart on the terrace. Actually, what bothered him most was that he had to dicker with Abe at all. He wanted to decide his own fate—for better or worse. His sister Betty was right; they needed to split the land up, someway. How? I need my own earth, Andy said to himself. And the second he said it, he felt it, its rock-hard inevitability. Maybe it came down to this: money was starting to matter more than it ever had before, and he didn't want what mattered most to be decided by someone other than himself. That was fair enough, wasn't it? As long as he was a bachelor, being broke, or nearly broke, was hardly an issue. But he wanted something more for his wife, his kids, more than he had ever given to himself.

They started picking the next day. By eight o'clock the hoppers had warmed up and were jumping around in the rows, thick as a shower of rice, so thick you had to spit and blow your nose, clear your ears and wipe the bugs, still alive, from your eyes every fifth, sixth vine. A few Mexicans couldn't take it and came bolting out of the rows, flinging their arms around as though they had been driven insane.

This is not a good sign, Andy thought.

Sure enough, come lunch the Mexicans were jumpy. Then he heard someone say *ándale*. Andy had hoped they could get through the crop in a couple of days, but now it looked like there might be a general strike, at least among the Mexicans. And if the Mexicans moved, the Filipinos just might follow suit.

Andy called Gabriel over and asked him what the hell was going on.

"Boys no wanna work, boss. *Mucho* hopper." With his pinkie, Gabriel flipped one out of his ear.

"The Filipinos aren't complaining, Gabriel. What do you got, a bunch of cinderellas out there?"

"My boys no Filipino. Sinnerela, I dunno."

"Anyway, what are you telling me, Gabriel?"

"I dunno."

"Are they going back in there or not?"

Gabriel shrugged his shoulders and said, "We see."

"What the fuck do they want, Gabriel?"

Gabriel puckered his lips and shook his head, as though it was equally mysterious to him.

"Are you the crew boss here or what? If you don't know, who does know?"

"I try to talk dem."

"Now, how many years have you been working for me, Gabriel?"

"Too many."

"I pay you right and timely, don't I, Gabriel?"

"We got no problem."

"Well, you're going to have a problem, a big problem if your boys pull out at this point."

Gabriel tossed his hands up. It was out of his control.

From the corner of his eye, Andy could see half of the crew had now gathered in a group and were sizing up the conversation from a distance.

Abe walked up with a bundle of bandannas.

"What's going on?" Abe said.

"I'll handle it, Abe."

Gabriel dropped to his haunches and began scribbling something in the dirt with his finger. This meant he was calculating a raise.

"I'll be a son of a bitch, Gabriel, if I'm going to pay a fucking half-cent more a tray."

"Dat's up to you, boss."

"I'll tell you what, Gabriel. How many boys you got out there?"

"Tirdy, tirdy one?"

"You tell them, for their efforts, at the end of the day we'll give them a six-pack to every two men."

Gabriel stood up, nodded his head. That was a pretty good deal.

"Plus," Andy said, "these bandannas."

Gabriel took the bandannas and headed toward the group.

"Now let's see who's going to stay and who's going to leave," Andy told Abe.

"Fucking spics."

"They saw the situation before they even went in. This was all figured up front. That's what pisses me off. Once they're in, they've got you over the barrel."

"The Filipinos are going to ask for the same," Abe said.

"If they bitch, we'll tell them not to come back tomorrow. Problem is, it's Sunday. They're all hungover. Tomorrow there'll be plenty of crews willing to work without any complaints."

Abe nodded his head.

Andy looked at a few clouds high up in the sky. The air was getting a little touchy. Or maybe it was Andy who was touchy.

Fall was getting closer by the day and fall meant rain, and rain meant disaster to raisins drying on the ground.

Gabriel trundled back and told them it was a deal.

"How many of 'em are staying, Gabe?"

"All of dem."

"That's what I figured."

"And tell 'em," Abe said, "I want those damn bandannas back when they're finished."

Gabe nodded his head politely.

"And another thing, Gabe, this depends on them picking at a regular rate. I leave it up to you to see nobody falls asleep out there."

"You don't say nuttin' 'bout dat."

"It's obvious, Gabe. I only brought it to your attention because altogether you're a little slow today."

Gabe crunched his shoulders.

"Too many *cervezas* last night, huh?"

Gabe smiled lazily, stuck two fingers in his mouth and whistled. The crews filtered into the rows, half of them tying back their bandannas like bandits and the other half stuffing them in their pockets.

"Go get those beers, Abe. I'll watch the crews."

"How many did you say?"

"Three cases. Make that four. We'll need one ourselves by the time this shift is over."

The crews stayed on the next day too. Gabe apologized for the day before. Sundays. Everyone agreed, shook hands and let it go.

The crop now lay on the ground. On the east side of the terraced rows the grapes, amber-green clusters, sparkled in spots where the blush had been rubbed off. Studying the grapes, Andy would sometimes think they were pretty enough to frame. No sight more beautiful, Andy thought, and at the same time, more vulnerable.

Andy and Abe inspected the rows for unpicked vines or grapes hastily thrown down on the trays. They admitted the job was done well. Clean. With the harvest over, the juice deal that had fallen through was a little easier to swallow. Andy reminded himself of how dangerous it was to think one season at a time—in farming you had to think long term or you'd drive yourself nuts. Even if the price wasn't something to celebrate, it would still put a few dollars in their pockets. Money, after all, is money.

For the last few weeks, the pressure of the harvest had put Andy's emotions for Kareen on hold. If Kareen intended to be a farmer's wife, she'd have to get used to the fact that at certain times of year a farmer would brook no distraction from his work. But when he examined it more closely still, he found that a part of him wanted to show Abe and Zabel that his allegiance was first and foremost to the farm, so they couldn't blame his loss of focus if any disaster came their way, God forbid.

When Andy went to pick up Kareen that afternoon, he wondered whether he wasn't juggling too many loyalties at once. It seemed the average man didn't charge himself with such responsibilities as did Andy. Maybe having grown up for a large part of his life without parents had made him able to care for others as well as himself. Andy also felt he'd inherited from his mother a certain nurturing spirit. Calipse, that beautiful woman, would never turn away a soul in need. She took in any strays, anything that ambled into their house or yard, be it dog or man. When he had polio, everybody was shut out from his room, on the doctor's orders. But his mother barely left his side. He remembered her putting cool towels on his forehead when he had fevers, he remembered the coolness of her hand when she held his own. She prayed on his body. She truly believed that her love for him was stronger than any disease. And how about that indelible image of Abe peeking at him through a slit between the door and the jamb? His face showed fear, not for Andy, but for his mother, the only source of love left him after his real father died.

He carried these thoughts with him into Kareen's house and shared them with her in part. His eyes, Kareen thought, looked older than she'd ever seen them before.

Three nights later, Abe jerked up in bed with what felt like electrical shocks in his chest. He shuffled to the bathroom half-blind, flipped the light on. From an invisible crack in the corner, a line of ants were constructing a trail across the floor. At the last trickle of piss he heard something on the roof and looked up. At first he thought it was a squirrel on the roof or rats in the attic. His imagination.

Out on the patio he could smell a mulchy breath of ash and wood and sulphur and earth. The air, it was wrinkled, nervous. Finally, he took a few steps onto the dirt. A drop. It hit him on the nose, like the clouds had been aiming for it. He put his palms out. In his pajamas and slippers he looked like some ancient prophet petitioning God. Then, lightning vascularized the sky in the east—a white flash stunned the yard. He waited for thunder like a man pending a judge's sentence. It came caving in—the air was sustaining an avalanche. His neighbor's porch light went on. Andy came limping out in his underwear, muttering, "Shit." They listened to the rain, trying to judge its intensity from the sound, from its pecking at their heads. Zabel was in the doorway, her hands out in front of her, shaking, as though she were struggling to hold something up with them.

"Nayenk," (Let's wait and see), Andy said.

Abe said, *"Pachtes, eh,"* (It's my fate).

They were both up before the rooster, working in the sagging gray light. No rain fell, but the earth seemed to be wetly breathing, the atmosphere thick and sticky. They agreed to push the trays beneath the vines so that the canopy would shield them from further rain. They were well into an acre when the sun shot its rays over the Sierras, a crown of light. Beams colored the bottom of the scoria clouds pink, so that they looked like the underbellies of black sows. Within minutes, the sun broke the craggy horizon, a trembling blood-red wafer, before it disappeared behind the clouds.

The clouds hung overhead, a kind of phlegm. Within a couple of hours, Zabel had joined them, her skirt tied up around her knees and her hair under her hat in a tousled bun. The children watched from the window in wide-eyed bewilderment. Abe flagged down a few Filipinos. They reluctantly agreed to help. By noon it had begun again, the drops delivered in quiet, almost lulling pulses. They shoved trays speedily underneath the vines, like criminals ridding themselves of evidence. Abe dragged Teddy into it. The boy would push two, three trays beneath the canopy and put his hand out to catch the rain in a beggar's pose. Soon the mud covered their shoes, the water drenched their wide-brimmed hats and their clothes stuck sickly to their bodies, as though they had each broken into a fever. Just before noon, the Filipinos gathered in a small circle, deliberated in that quick tongue, nodded their heads in concert and quit. "We pinish, boz," they said, and crunched their shoulders, putting out their hands for the few dollars due them. Abe told them he'd pay them by the hour. "Too much rain, boz."

Andy and Abe came out of the vineyards as if from a swamp. They could feel nothing of their bodies. They ate flatbread on the porch, folding in it cheese and meat, munching like idiots. Two or three times the sun broke through the clouds in great and shifting tunnels of light, as though probing for something below. When they walked back into the vineyards, Andy all at once stopped.

"Looks like shit," he said.

Zabel went hysterical.

"Slow down, Zabel," Andy said. "Listen Abe, this is no use. Let's leave the rest of the trays be. The leaves are sopped by now," he said. "It won't matter one way or another. Leave them be and let's just pray we don't see any more rain."

Zabel sunk her eyes to the bottom of Abe's eyes.

Andy knew then that all this had been wasted motion. What they were involved in was a sort of martyrdom to a dead cause.

"Don't worry, Abe. I think things are breaking up," Andy said, measuring the puddles of blue in the sky. Two days had passed and the rain went and came and went and came. Abe sighed and leaned against the shovel as though he might have reason to put it to some use. Even if they had given the vineyard over to nature, at least they could keep a human eye on it, at least they could exert worry over it. Andy dropped to his haunches and made curlicues in the dirt with a finger.

"I wonder how other people got it?"

"Can't say, but my guess is in the ass, the same."

"Except for them that laid 'em down early. Lucky fucks."

"We've had our luck too, Abe. I suppose everybody gets their turn in this life."

"Remind me when," Abe sniggered.

"This farm, for beginners."

"Is that right?"

"Handed to us on a silver platter. A livelihood dropped into our hands just like that."

"What kind of livelihood is this? Some kind of livelihood."

Andy didn't know whether to give Abe hope or give in to the fact that Abe was hopeless.

The next day the sky cleared completely. The air was clean and things sparkled brilliantly in the sunlight. They pulled out what trays they'd pushed under the vines. On the fourth day they did their best to flip the wettest grapes over to get the bottom side dry. No doubt, the mold was there. How bad it would get, they didn't know. A few berries on every bunch had turned a pasty gray color, wrinkled on the tray like miniature brains.

Farmers who'd laid them down early sympathized in public with those that hadn't, and licked their chops in private. Everybody figured a quarter of the crop was wiped out, which would raise the price per ton proportionately.

They picked them up ten days later. Andy took charge of the hand crew. Tray by tray, acre by acre, they worked the avenues, tossing the raisins into the gondolas until they brimmed over with them. Abe handled the sifter with two Filipinos. The raisins shook on the mesh, the stems piled below, and the dirt hovered constantly in the air like a cloud of gnats. Abe raked the stems down to the big wooden bins, paused now and then to scoop them up in his hands and let them fall through his fingers.

Instead of the traditional *raki* and lamb to celebrate the end of the harvest, they ate three-day-old *moussaka* and moved around like old folks.

Abe knew it was just a matter of time before Zabel started in on him. But she said nothing about it, instead telling him that she wanted to see her mother and for him to keep an eye on the kids. He nodded his head mutely, working his teeth with a pick. He and Andy waited for the car to pull out of the drive, then broke open a fresh bottle of *raki*. Andy poured the clear liquid into two small cylindrical glasses. They sat on the patio. It was quiet, except for a faint breeze rustling the trees. Andy held the glass up to his nose and inhaled its old-world licorice scent. It burned on his tongue, and slid warmly down his throat, and in his stomach it glowed, consoled.

The vines were barren of grapes and, from where the trays had lain on the terrace, there were a series of rectangular smudges in the sand. One by one farmers filed into the coffee shops, pulled up chairs around long tables and sat bent over their coffee cups mutely, like vagabonds just come in from out of the rain. They asked what they had done right, what they had done wrong. Now and then someone would proffer an answer, which they would all thoughtfully consider, slurping their coffee and nodding their heads like a gathering of delegates at a convention of dubious purpose. Others would use the forum to confess their lack of foresight or timing. "Should've given 'em another shot of sulphur mid-August," and "Should've picked 'em up a week earlier" were remarks commonly heard. Others claimed they saw the weather coming. "Every fifth year there's rain in September. It's like clockwork," or "When there's still snow in Sierras in July, watch out."

The Armenians, especially the old-timers, had another explanation still: *pacht*. Fate. Some of the younger Armenians thought it foolish to link one's personal misfortune to such a large and impersonal source as *pacht*, and not a few arguments broke out around dinner tables about the value of such an attitude. The general feeling among the younger farmers was that once you gave into fate, you already had half a foot in the grave.

"You start thinking like that and there's no hope for tomorrow."

Andy explained it to himself this way: God, fate or whatever you called it didn't have anything to do with anyone's hardship. All you had to do was observe the lives of other creatures—birds, flies, mice—to understand that everything was in some struggle for survival against a set of events set up by chance. Of course, this made Andy sound atheist. Others figured that either God determined things or he gave you brains enough to figure out how to avoid it next time around. Claiming events were fated was one thing, but claiming they were a matter of chance, hell, that was a kind of blasphemy.

At least to Zabel it was. "What are you saying?"

"God's around, but he's around to help us get over our setbacks—he's a kind of comforter." Andy explained.

"What a small thing you've made of God. Comforter?"

"Better God be a comforter than the cause of my suffering. What kind of God is that?"

"Who are you to question God's will? You only suffer when you don't see that it was all God's will. This is the root of man's suffering."

"I don't know what Bible you've been reading, but if it's the same one I've got beside my bed, nowhere does it make God out to be the cause of anybody's suffering."

"Yes, because that's the devil's doing." Zabel said.

"Now you're giving me a headache."

"Look at Job. Our people are like Job. The devil brings suffering on the head of Job, and when Job questions God, God asks him who is he to question him."

"Well, it would take God to figure out that one. Not me."

"There's nothing to figure out, it's right there in his word."

"I suppose."

"What happened to you? I think all that schooling has confused you."

"Ya think?"

Actually, the conversation shouldn't have been about God at all. But there was no way to talk about *pacht* outright. *Pacht* was some zone that opened up between God and humanity. If you pushed it, you might even say that *pacht* ruled over God himself, at least as old as, maybe older than Genesis. And though Andy wasn't quick to admit it, the word was so deeply embedded in the Armenian brain, his Armenian brain, that a part of him couldn't help thinking it himself. Getting rid of *pacht* wasn't so easy as coming up with a few logical objections. Not thinking *pacht* was like speaking without using the word "the" or like trying to leave your Armenian heritage behind by dying your hair from black to blond or changing your name from Paboojian to Smith.

More than all that, when folks talked *pacht,* they brought the force of a culture twenty-five centuries old along with them. Getting rid of *pacht* was like trying to fend off an enemy army with a six-shooter. No matter how good your aim, no matter how many dropped in their tracks, they just kept coming and coming. All the lost lands, the lost bodies, the lost churches and *khatchkars* were somehow recovered by that word. Even the sound of the word—*pacht*—like a tiny explosion in your mouth, made it seem like there was no fucking with it.

Pacht or no *pacht,* everyone was anxious to know what the packing houses would say about grade. It was possible that they could reject the whole of your crop, or some portion of it. It was all in the packing houses' hands. Which was the other problem. Make no mistake, the packers were going to reject raisins that didn't make grade, but all the farmers knew that on such years they might reject more than deserved to be rejected and pocket a few bins here and there behind their backs. Grading was no science. If you protested their judgment, it was your pre-rogative to haul those rejects away. But if you did that, you might find that what they'd passed no longer sufficed. So, every farmer prepared to have a couple of bins, as a kind of surcharge, stolen from him. It was already in his calculations, it was a given. Misfortune breeds misfortune. Big-time farmers, like Chamichian, now that's a different story. No packer would ever mess with him, might even let a few bins slip in his favor. It wasn't worth losing the business of a big farmer for a few bucks. Not only that, they let Chamichian and his like know grade right away. It was the small guy who had to sweat it out. Packers took their own sweet time with the small guy. So much so that when the farmer finally got his answer, he felt he'd been done a favor, whatever the results.

Damn shame, Andy thought, but that's the way it is. Robbers don't go after the gold in Fort Knox, like in the movies. No, they go after the jar of money saved up by a widow tucked in the back of a cupboard; if she's lucky, they won't beat her silly on the way out. The story of the good Samaritan, it was just that—a story. The strong don't need *pacht,* Andy thought. The rich don't neither. They make *pacht.* They are *pacht.*

23

IT WAS GETTING SO THAT ZABEL WAS INSULTED by anything that had touched Andy's skin, anything his body had left a trace on. This phase of her hatred toward him started when she found a magazine folded in half and stuffed underneath his mattress while she was changing the sheets.

What's this? she wondered as she flipped it open.

Half-naked girls sitting on pillows or reclining on couches, their full breasts dangling in front of them like objects. Blood rushed to her face. Who were these sluts with their seductive grins? Were these the tramps he dated at that college, is this what he'd gotten into? The word "filthy" boomed in her head. She noticed the pages were sticky and there were smudges on it too. Her heart went into alarm. Could it be? Shaking, she shoved it back where she had found it, rushed into the bathroom, lathered her hands with soap and washed them over and over until the images of those naked girls that flashed in her head began to fade.

After that, she could no longer scrub his underwear free of skidmarks. When she handled his bedsheets, she was filled with revulsion. Soon his overalls, his towels, his socks—especially those that fit the ugly foot—were untouchable. After a week she imagined that all of the dirt and grime and even dust in the house was his, as though the man molted the way snakes do. She was sickened to think that he might have farted on a chair seat, or that she might find a single toenail clipping of his in a crook of the couch, a booger glued to a chair.

What's going on here? Andy wondered. His clothes had been piling up in a hamper in his room. Zabel had hardly spoken to him in two weeks. Not that this alone didn't disturb him, but now he suspected that behind her silence was yet another species of resentment.

"What's going on, Zabel?" he asked.

"What?"

"I guess you're not doing the clothes anymore."

"What do you want from me?" she asked.

Abe looked up from his dinner. "What do you mean?" he asked.

"Nothing of mine has been washed in over a week," Andy told him and showed his pants, caked with dirt, as an example. "These things are starting to itch, they're so dirty."

Abe looked at Zabel for an explanation.

"You can do everybody else's wash but not mine, is that it, Zabel?"

"I've done your wash long enough," she said.

"And you'll do it a little longer."

"Have your wife do it," she said.

"My wife?"

"That Egyptian girl. Whatever her name is."

Andy said, "Fuck you."

Zabel let out a kind of yelp. Then, in Armenian, "Foul!" she spat back.

Andy was actually kind of surprised that he'd said it. But now that he had, he might as well go the whole way.

"Fuck you and fuck your bullshit. Don't do my fucking wash, then. I'll do it myself."

Andy lurched out of his chair.

Abe put out a hand to stop him.

"Hold on now."

"You better get a handle on your fucking wife, Abe. Beat some sense into her."

Zabel's face was jumping with rage.

"What is it?" Abe asked Zabel.

"I'm not his slave," Zabel sneered.

Andy limped out of the room.

Abe just shook his head. He didn't know what to say; he didn't know what to do.

Andy came out with a bulging sack slung over his shoulder.

"I guess I've done my own wash before, and I guess I'll start doing it again," he said.

"Where are you going?" Abe said.

"Let him go where he wants," Zabel exclaimed.

"But I'll be back, Zabel. Don't worry about that."

Zabel's hands were out in front of her and shaking as though she were choking something with them.

Andy opened the door.

"I've got news for you, sister-in-law, I'll be back to sleep in my bed, in my house."

"Go! Street dog!"

He shot out down the street at a breathtaking speed. Hate was awesome inside of him. Witch. The puffs of disgust, the comments, the bitchy grins, the loopy logic of her every move, her extravagant selfishness and most of all his own schoolboy excuses for her over the years no longer had purchase. His stomach roiled, his head buzzed, his fist spontaneously clenched on the steering wheel. He could feel his father's blood boiling inside of him. I'll be a son of a bitch if that whore is going to dictate my moves, he thought. His anger was so hot it seemed to evaporate his body and fog the windshield, and he steered down the road less by sight than by a kind of reckless faith. He was inches away from suicide just to relieve himself of the pressure.

Abe was still at the table, waiting for some course of action to gel. Every half-minute he'd go to make a move and then, with nothing hooked, sink back stupidly, like a novice at fishing. Not doing Andy's wash was one step away from not cooking for him, and not cooking for him was as good as saying he might as well disappear. Well, how was the man supposed to disappear from his own home? In the old days, of course, he would have taken a belt to Zabel, right then and there, like he once had when he first came home from the war. He dragged her around the house by her hair, spat on her and told her he'd kill her if she ever fucked with his mind again. She said it was over, that the war had turned him into an animal, and left. For two days afterward he drunk himself sick on whiskey. When he sobered up, he felt more alone and desperate than he'd ever felt before, more alone and desperate even than during the war. He pleaded for her to return. If the war had made him a killer, in another way it had depleted him. He needed her. Whatever it was, it had gotten to the point where he was afraid she might beat *him* to shit if he pushed it.

Abe needed an explanation, any explanation, just to bust loose of the confusion that now paralyzed him. The dishes were piled to the side of the sink and the faucet plipped in a pool of soapy water. The clock showed it was a little after eight. He scratched the back of his head, got out of the chair and walked around the house looking for her.

She'd taken off already. This time with the kids.

Andy was too riled to go to Kareen's, too riled to go anywhere short of Sammy's bar. A drink was either the last thing he needed or the first. It was anybody's guess.

Sammy could tell that Andy was in a rage by the way he asked for a double without so much as saying hello. Sammy poured him a triple, left the bottle there in front of his glass and let him gear down with that drink on his own. When he saw Andy was done, he strolled the length of the bar, picked up the bottle and poured him another and asked him what was going on.

Andy said, "I don't want to fill your ear with it, Sammy."

Sammy looked the near-empty bar once over and showed his palms were empty, nothing better at the moment to do.

"I'm going to kill the bitch, I swear."

Sammy hoped he wasn't talking about his new girlfriend from Egypt. He buffed a glass with a towel until he found out what bitch Andy was referring to.

Andy slurped the vodka and snarled, "Fucking bitch can eat my shit."

"Who's this?" Sammy had to know.

"Damn wife of my brother."

Sammy nodded his head. He'd been there before himself.

"She's the kind of woman that will lead a man into confusion, then chop his dick off when he's not lookin'."

"There's them type."

"You can't tell at first, that's the thing. Man's got to be on guard from the gitty-up. Hell, before this woman came into my brother's life, he was a good guy."

"Abe?"

"Yeah. Abe." He let a puff of disgust issue from his nose.

"Damn shame."

"It is a damn shame. Here, we're given a gift, fifty acres of grapes for free. You'd think we'd be counting our blessings from there on out. But no, she wants more, more!"

"I've seen it myself. Especially with the *Hyes*."

"I hate to say it."

"It's the truth."

"You'd think a people that went through such hell would stick together at any price. You'd think the last thing they'd do is start hacking at each other. But once they've got some earth beneath them, that's the first thing they do."

"You see, the Jews, they stick together."

"You're right. Armenians are bad Jews is what they are."

The liquor was elevating the conversation into greater and greater levels of abstractions, which suited Andy just fine. He'd rather have that then sit in the quicksand of particulars from which a man couldn't move this way or that without sinking deeper still. He was glad to be there with that drink, and he was glad to have Sammy's company. Good ol' Sammy. He wished he'd had Sammy for a brother. He slurped the vodka up and felt his mind sharpen, its edges now dazzling.

"The thing with the Jews, though, is they got their recompense," Andy said. "The Armenians never got such a thing. So it's like the Armenians are looking for the devil among themselves. I've seen animals behave this way. Master beats up on his dog, the dog sits there and takes it the way dogs do. As soon as the master leaves, some other dog strolls along. Guess who gets bit? Not the master, not the one that beat him, but one of the dog's own, maybe even his littermate that happens to pass by."

For a moment, both men let the analogy sink in.

"Point is," Andy clarified, "everybody needs a demon. As long as there's human injury in the world, someone's got to be the cause of it. Got to lay the blame somewhere. If the real demon keeps denying that he did it, pretty soon a man will think, Could be that demon's right, and he'll go searching for the cause of his injury in his own backyard, whoever is closest to him."

"Could be," Sammy said.

"I don't know what else explains it."

Zabel drove, oblivious of the road, of everything but her own ire, which had multiplied and acquired depth like a hall of mirrors inside of her. Why she had brought the kids along was a question that even Teddy was forced to ask himself. His brother and sister were fast asleep in the back, and he felt very alone at that moment—the way eldest sons sometimes do—his insides gnarled with fear and confusion. He held onto the door handle, certain that at any moment the door would wildly fly open, consistent with the temperament of the adults that night. All Zabel knew for sure was that she couldn't be near "the beast." It stopped her heart to think that her child might have stumbled upon that magazine.

Any single tongue could not contain her hysteria, so Zabel fulminated in three languages, English, Turkish and Armenian, a hurl of words splattering over everything. Once she got to Angel's house, her mother listened to her greedily, repeating, "Vakhh," nodding now and then and sucking on her pipe. At a certain pause, Angel told her that she'd heard enough and that Teddy should be cleansed with incense and prayer immediately. But first, Angel wanted to know if she'd found a substance—resembling bone marrow—bespotting Teddy's sheets. No, thank God. Had she, then, noticed whether his eyes rolled up into his head when he touched the mossy bark of any tree, or perhaps crabgrass? No. Her mother told her this was good, and estimated that at present the spirits were but a thin film on her son's soul.

Teddy was sleeping on a thick bed of homemade quilts in the spare room when Zabel came to fetch him. His mother led him by the hand into the den. The air was already oppressed by the smell of church incense, and all around him the flames of candles jerked ruthlessly at their wicks. Even in the dim light, he could see his mother's eyes were glassy with tears. His grandmother told him to kneel in prayer against the couch and began working an embrocation of rose water and olive oil through his hair. The hands of his grandmother were cool and smooth on his face and neck. Their prayers, startling and deep, frightened and aroused the boy at the same time. He grew emotional (from what he could not say) and all at once he understood that they were protecting him from some evil—some evil that ran in the blood of men. His mother was bent over him, caressing his arms. He was ashamed of his body, he was ashamed of his ways. He felt something open, like an orchid, inside of him. A kind of gasp of joy issued from Zabel when her little boy began to cry.

Meanwhile, there was work to be done on the farm. There was always work to be done on the farm. It was like a baby who never grew up. They carried on with it, the entire household at an emotional stalemate.

They hooked up the ripper to the big Massey. Andy could feel the earth tug on the tractor, like it was holding its own against a very strong fish. He turned back, saw the long blades plunge deep into the dark earth, and watched the earth open and crinkle and in spots collapse in flakes and chunks, the smell handsome and bittersweet.

As *pacht* had it, they heard from the packing house that week. Half the crop was pig slop, the other passed grade. Barely. Nothing to write home about, but a little better than either brother expected. They'd have enough dough to cover the loan payment and cultivation costs for the coming year.

All along Andy was wrestling with another problem: how he was going to finance the wedding. He barely had enough cash to throw a cake-and-punch reception. Kareen had no idea of the financial bind he was in, and he wanted to keep it that way. He reasoned it was hard for folks to understand how farmers were sometimes cash poor but could still be land and equipment rich.

He was less nervous asking Kareen if she'd marry him than he was now, announcing it to Abe and Zabel. Even though before the harvest he'd talked to Abe about marrying Kareen, not another word was spoken about it since. He recalled Abe's agreeing not to mention a thing to Zabel, and now he wondered if Abe had kept his promise.

No matter how mature a man is, there is always at least one door that he fears opening, one door that will make him look and act like a child. For a full week, Andy poked around just outside that door; a full week he took to rehearse what he'd say, until finally he flung it open.

"Abe, Zabel," he said. "I'm getting married." The words came out of him as a kind of apology.

Abe nodded his head. "That's good," Abe said. And said it again.

Zabel studied the ceiling lamp and echoed Abe's words.

"She's a good girl. Maybe she's not perfect in everybody's eyes, but in my eyes she's just right," Andy said.

Zabel crunched her shoulders, as though she could take it either way.

"If Dad were around, I'd ask him. You're the next closest thing to him I've got."

Andy got down on a knee and bowed his head.

"I ask for your blessing, Abe."

Zabel swung her eyes away from the lamp, as though Andy were the lamp.

"You've got my blessing, brother."

Zabel calculated the kind of money it would take to throw the wedding, where they were going to get it.

Abe, with the palm of his hand, touched Andy's head.

"Thank you," Andy said and got back up to his feet. His eyes were moist with tears.

"Let's pour a drink and toast," Abe said.

From the dining room table, Andy watched Abe shuffle into the kitchen, fling open a cupboard door and reach for a bottle of homemade *raki* and shot glasses. He came out with the drinks extended in front of him.

"Here," he said. "To you and Kareen."

They clinked, lifted the glasses and slammed the liquor down. Abe went back into the kitchen.

"I'd like him to be my best man," Andy said.

"Who else was it going to be?" Zabel asked.

"Nobody else."

Abe came back with the bottle. "What's that?" He poured them some more.

"I was just telling Zab that you're the only one that I'd even consider being my best man."

"That's right." Abe slurped the *raki* up. "One more," he announced.

"That's enough." Zabel said with a tone of exasperation.

Abe slapped Andy's face affectionately and yodeled, "My baby brother's getting married."

Andy laughed, as happy for Abe as he was for himself.

For once, Zabel seemed to have no say in what came next, how many they were going to drink. Could be the whole bottle if they liked.

"It's enough!" Zabel raised her voice.

"Quiet!" Abe came back.

Andy looked at Zabel. Her face was frozen in disbelief, her lips in the shape of an O.

"I like Kareen," Abe said. "She not bad lookin' either."

Andy smiled.

Zabel jumped out of her seat in a huff, paced out of the room and down the hallway.

Abe winked and with a finger directed them to the patio.

Abe kicked his feet up on the railing. Andy did the same. The bottle of *raki* stood at attention on the pedestal to the left of them. The light drained down slowly through the ashes of flies and mosquitoes and moths in a lantern above.

"Got to get to that lamp."

"We got to get to plenty of things," Andy added.

They were both kind of mesmerized by the ecstatic dance of the moths around the light.

"It was one helluva year," Abe said.

"I'll say. I just hope we can start building up from here on out. I feel rain comin'," Andy said.

"Fuck the rain. Let it come down all it wants now. So you're gettin' married?"

"I figure it's about time, Abe."

Abe drew snot up through his nose, let it ball in the back of his throat, volleyed it over the railing and nodded his head.

"That's good. I say it's good."

"I think so."

"We all think so, don't you worry about it."

"'Preciate it."

"I'll make fucking sure we all think so." Abe gulped some more *raki*. "No," Abe said, "you've run around enough. Time to settle down. It's good, though, you've gotten your fair share of ass."

"I've done my duty."

Abe chortled, "To God and Country," and slapped Andy on the back. Then he grew serious and admitted, "I should've waited a little longer myself."

"Think?"

"But that damn war changed everything. Everything changed after that."

"I guess it did."

"It did, in ways you could never guess. You know, I told myself during the war, 'Abe, if you can survive this thing, there's nothin' to be afraid of from here on out. Nothin'. But I was only accounting for myself at the time."

"You're talkin' kids, a wife."

"That. That and more. A man starts living his whole life for things other than himself. Pretty soon you can't be sure why you're living at all."

"Like a cog in a wheel."

"What's that?"

"A cog in a wheel. You know."

Abe nodded his head. "You see, the other thing is, you got to go to college. Truth is, I wish I had that education myself."

"I wonder what good it really does me out here. Sometimes I wonder. I really do."

"It does you plenty of good, don't question it."

Andy wasn't about to question anything. It had been so long since Abe had opened up to him he was chary of speaking at all.

"Remember that old coon, Otis?" Abe asked. "I was remembering him the other day."

"Dad's Otis. Black as the ace of spades."

"Had himself his own patch of dirt—coupla acres off Mountain View just this side of Hanford. I ended up at his house that time I ran away on the horse."

"When Dad came after you with that gun."

Abe chuckled darkly and said, "When *your* dad came after me. Yeah. So, when I told Otis I'd run away from home, he says his grandpa had run away too, from white folks who used to treat him worse than a mule. And then Otis looked over at the fireplace. 'See them,' he said. 'Them ah dah chains they used to lock 'im up wit. Those what he done wiggled his way outta.' Like one of those coats of arms, they were hanging over the mantel. These loops and chains."

"Those Negroes back then were something else. Brave."

Abe said, "Anyways, I got to thinking about how a man can be chained to something without even knowing it, which amounts to something worse than being a slave. At least when you know you're chained, there is some hope of getting free, the chance of escape."

Andy wondered how much of this had to do with Abe's marriage, with married life in general.

"I figure," Andy said, "married or not, one way or another, a man is chained to something."

"Hmmm." Abe leaned over to grab the bottle and took his chair with him. "Whoa," Abe said, a man pulling in reins. "Guess I'm a little drunk."

"Guess we're both."

Abe's mind sloshed around. Just when it was settling down, Andy said, "Hand me your glass."

Abe threw the glass forward.

"We'll drink one more and then we'll hit the sack." Andy made to pour, but stopped. "We haven't talked in so long, I was beginning to think we'd forgotten how, Abe."

First he had to make that point, as though that point was what he was purchasing the next drink with.

"It's that damn wife of mine, is what it is."

Andy poured liberally. "I'm not saying nothin'," he said.

"You don't have to. You don't think I see the way things are around here? What do you figure me? Blind?"

Andy was kind of sorry they were getting down to business half-drunk. He was sorry that probably the next day none of this would be recollectable. Still, he asked, "How are things around here, Abe? You tell me."

"There's nothing to say. Things is the way they is. What is is what it is."

"Then I guess there's no use talkin' about it."

Abe tapped the ashes off his cigarette into the cuff of his pants.

"I attribute a lot of this crap to that mother-in-law of mine. Watch your mother-in-law is all I can say. You marry her first, then your wife."

"She's nuts."

"If she was just nuts, that'd be one thing. But she's operating at a different level than you and me. She's connected to the spiritual world."

"I hear she's got voodoo dolls. She conjures up ghosts and shit. You don't believe that crap, do you?"

"I don't know what to believe in anymore. There's all sorts of things that happen at levels that the average man can't see down into. *Your* dad was a believer in such things. Remember, the Bible say to fear God."

Andy said, "When I think about it, there's all sorts of shit that is sitting right in front of us we can't see. I don't see the point in worrying about seeing what I can't see if I can't see what's in front of me. That shriveled old thing doesn't scare me in the least."

Abe shook his head. "You don't get the nature of women," Abe said. "They write between the lines. In some fucking invisible ink. They trade messages this way, between them." Abe looked through the glass to Andy. "Anyways, the way it goes is, you wake up one day and you don't know if you're coming or going. When you have kids, the scenario gets worse. Up until then, you stood some chance. Come the kids, you amount to a second-class citizen in your own home."

Abe heard these dangerous words flow out of his own mouth and was surprised at how good they sounded. He knew that tomorrow he'd have to pay hell for the way he'd jumped at Zabel, and that he would accept that punishment, but the liquor put a temporary buffer between him and that eventuality.

"Your job?" he concluded. "Put the bread and butter on the table and shut up."

Among Armenian men, such a lament was constant as a chant. A part of Andy thought, No way that's going to happen to me. But a larger part of him was hard put to dismiss a complaint that was so widespread as to be a kind of law.

"I guess we'll see."

"You'll see is right."

"You make it sound like a threat, Abe."

"It is the way it is."

Andy hated those words; they made it sound like nothing was going to change, could change.

"Look." Abe thrust his glass in the air. "I wish you, you and your wife-to-be, a good life together."

Andy kissed Abe's glass with his own.

"Whatever happens," Abe said, "you'll have each other. Like I've got Zab."

24

LIMP AND ALL, ANDY WAS STILL A CATCH. All around town, those mothers who'd been working behind the scenes to set Andy up with their daughters inquired if they'd heard correctly, if Andy was serious about this newcomer, and if he was serious, whether there was any chance he would change his mind. As the wedding date neared, rumors spread of dowries offered, last minute, under the table. Privately, Andy's sisters agreed that Kareen was marrying their brother for his land. They heard that the priest had sized Andy's finances up, and only after that had Kareen shown interest in their brother. Only the spirit behind that allegation would have offended Andy, not the allegation itself. For him, a woman who claimed she wasn't concerned with a man's holdings wasn't worth having, because she was either a liar or desperate.

As far as Andy was concerned, a small wedding would have sufficed, but for Kareen's sake he wanted a first class affair—Armenian music, shish kebob, open bar, the works—never mind that he was near broke. The centerpiece of the ring, guaranteed to settle any doubt of the magnitude of Andy's love, was a gasp-inducing carat and a half that ruled over eight quarter-carat stones. Where did he get the money? He could've dipped into the kitty, taken himself an advance from the account they'd set aside for the upcoming year's cultivation costs, but he didn't want to hear about it from Zabel. So he borrowed three thousand dollars from an old-time friend, Ralph Bagdassarian, against some farm equipment. That would cover the wedding and the ring. It was all done hush-hush in the form of a promissory note that was due in full after a year.

Although there were two orthodox churchs in town, there was no question St. Paul's was where they were going to get married. That's where Andy had been baptized, that's where he had laid both his parents' souls to rest, and that's where he'd lay his own. Plus, that's where Reverend Jambajian, the very priest who'd set them up, officiated.

They went around and around about whom to invite, and in the end, to avoid insulting even their most distant acquaintances, invited just about everyone. Every family within a square mile of the ranch was sent an invitation—and they accepted. They had three hundred people, give or take. Little Nancy was appointed flower girl, Greggy ring bearer.

He moved out of the house into a tidy two-bedroom apartment in town a week before the wedding. Zabel helped him put the place together with some furniture and kitchenware and towels and bedding, once again proving that among Armenian families, the connection between devotion and animosity was as complicated as events are in a dream.

There was a lot of preparation for the wedding. Three days before, it was so hectic that Andy barely had a chance to get a handle on what he was about to do. He was feeling claustrophobic. Should've gone to Vegas, he thought. "I need to get away for a couple of days," he told Kareen. "But I'll be back for your hand." He drove up to the mountains two days before the wedding and checked into a musty lodge by the Fresno side of Bass Lake.

He hiked to a cove and, all bundled up with his butt on a log, he pitched stones—*bloop*—into the emerald water and watched circles echo creamily on the surface. He thought about what was coming, how his life was going to change. Andy was struck by the paradox that at just the point in his life when he was coming to terms with the fact that he was a loner, even tinkering with the notion of giving into this loner in him totally, he decided to get married. When he looked deeper into himself, he concluded that what gave him the courage to marry was precisely this belief that he could, if he chose, live alone. He wondered whether his old man ever should've married his mother. One thing for sure, Yervant wasn't prepared for five kids who weren't his own—the responsibility overwhelmed him until anger became his only outlet.

After all that thinking by day, Andy dumbed down in a booth in the lodge's bar at night. He sipped Jim Beam and studied the stuffed, intransigent heads of deer, especially one ol' boy with a fantastic rack, big enough to rake gravel with. Measuring the life of taxidermists against his own, he decided he felt closer to those deer than to the

locals—would-be miners, has-been whores, toothless drunks who'd
lost track of time, who time had also lost track of—who filtered in and
out of the bar like ghosts. The day before the wedding, he put together
a laundry list of all the women he'd dated, all those that he'd had crushes
on, from as far back as the seventh grade. He was surprised at the depth
of his heart, the spaces inside where such memories were holed up.
Then he packed all those memories on a kind of emotional canoe and
set it loose. For a long time he watched it float away, and he wondered
if at some point it would wend its way back.

Andy chain-smoked up until just before the ceremony, struggling with
the damn bowtie that had a half nelson on his neck. Arsen handed him
a whiskey flask ten minutes before the ceremony, slapped him on the
back and said, "Your last drink as a single man."

The ceremony—which Andy had seen many times—was
Orthodox. That meant a lot of standing and some kneeling, and prayer
compounded upon prayer in classical Armenian. Substitute a scythe
for a scepter and the priests might have been mistaken for reapers.
Andy thought that for a wedding they might have decked out in something more colorful, but no, they donned the same black gowns, black
hoods and, more than that, the same grim demeanor. At one point,
crowns symbolizing Andy's and Kareen's likeness to the first king and
queen of Armenia were slapped on them, and they were made to stand
with their foreheads fused together for fifteen minutes while Abe, as the
best man, held a cross over them and the priest with the Bible in his old
hands chanted and thumped them three times each with another cross.
Three seemed to be an important number. Three times the priest asked
him if he would be faithful in body and mind to Kareen, and three
times he answered, "I will, Reverend Father, by the grace of God."
Three passages from the Bible were read. All the gestures—passing,
lifting, nodding, signing by hand—gave Andy the distinct impression
that something invisible was methodically being assembled in their
presence, and that the real issue wasn't them, but rather their being correctly joined to that thing. "Heavy" was a word that came to Andy over
and over again. They drank from a chalice symbolizing the water that
Christ turned to wine at a wedding way back when. The whole time,

the only part of Kareen that was real, his and his alone, was her hands. He held onto them as though he were blind. Later people would tell him that she was beautiful, he handsome, both of them beaming, and that it made them cry. In the periphery of his vision, he could see folks, abstract as shadows in the pews, and the only moment, years later, that would continue to shimmer for him was when the organ bellowed "Here Comes the Bride" and the doors swung open and he watched Kareen float down the aisle toward him. He felt like an anchorage and he knew that he would forever take care of this woman, no matter what.

The foyer was a sea of smiles. Everyone was kissing and hugging them. It was like he'd survived a gauntlet—that all these folks were congratulating him on making it out alive. They ran through a rain of rice down the steps where a limousine was waiting for them. He was holding Kareen's hand but it wasn't until they stepped into the limousine that he was able to feel close to her—all he had ever wanted to begin with.

"You look beautiful," he told her. "I love you."

"I love you," she answered.

He kissed her.

"I love you, my wife." Hearing himself utter those words, he got choked up with tears. She could feel his flushed, clean-shaven face against her own and thought to herself, This is my friend, my husband, my child, for life.

A four-piece Armenian band—*oud*, clarinet, *dumbag* and fiddle— ushered the bride and groom into the reception hall. Andy strutted forward first. He was waving a blue dish in one hand and a handkerchief in the other. He slid the dish on the ground, did a figure eight, and stomped on it—*smash!*—snapping the handkerchief. "Opah, Opah!" the men cheered as they watched Kareen—her wedding dress trailing behind her elegantly like the long tail of some tropical bird—step up and with her husband dance around the shards of porcelain. Valentine, who was a notorious dancer, slipped in and for a few minutes mother and daughter wove around one another, darning the air with their hands. Over the roar of the crowd, Andy hissed like a cat, acknowledging the voluptuousness of the women, until the energy mounted and men started to make the peacock's rusty call and the perimeter began to collapse onto the dance floor and witnesses became participants, drunk with joy and the pleasure of the body, unbridled by the music and champagne that poured freely and without regard to the next day, the next minute, the next breath.

There was so much food on the table—plump shish kebob the size and color of hot coals, and buttery rice topped with slivers of toasted almonds, and green salad and *peda* bread baked fresh, and *borag* bubbling with cheese inside, and *kufte,* along with the regular spread of *maza*—some people began calculating, before the food even hit their bellies, how much of it they might tote home, purportedly for their pets. After the food had been passed around a second time, a few old women start packaging chunks of meat and *kufte* in their napkins and stuffing it into their purses, their husbands' coat pockets.

At some point during the meal, toasts were made at a microphone off to the side of the head table. Roxie Shishmanian made the observation that this marriage was particularly blessed, as the couple's ancestors hailed from two great cities, Van and Dikranagerd, noted for great intellectuals and great cooks, respectively. Arsen recalled the afternoon that Andy had dropped by the gas station where he was working. "One day I showed Andy a picture of my own beautiful wife, and he asked if she had any sisters. The next day I brought by a picture of Kareen. From there on he was hooked."

Then Benjamin, husband of Andy's sister, stepped up to the microphone and said he had a few words for the newlyweds. Andy had already emptied four flutes of champagne and was getting cozy with all the attention. He was actually in the mood for advice, and anybody who knew Benjamin knew that was exactly what Andy was going to get.

Benjamin put up a hand and waited for the crowd to quiet down.

"Now, brother Andy, I speak on behalf of our family. You have been bound to your wife in the presence of all these witnesses, but more importantly, in the presence of almighty God. If anybody hasn't told you yet, life doesn't get any easier once you're married. That doesn't mean that there won't be any good times. There will be. Plenty of them. But only a marriage that has the Lord Jesus as the foundation can survive the hard times."

The couple looked at each other earnestly.

"Now, there have to be two essentials to a sound marriage, and those are prayer and forgiveness. Every day you and your wife sit down together and pray. Bring your concerns to the Lord. Lay it all out on the table together. Hide nothing from each other. Second, as the good book said, don't let the sun go down on your anger. Every couple has their fair share of disagreements, disputes. It's only natural. But it becomes unnatural if the wound festers. Forgive each other as God forgave you both. You show the mark of God on your own life by the degree to which you can forgive your mate. In the end, that's all that counts."

So many heads were nodding, you could hear them.

"And one other thing, brother Andy. God has ordained that the man is the head of the home. When a woman takes over the decisions in a family, the household is full of confusion. You must treat your wife fairly and with sincere love and devotion, yes. But in the end, the judgment will be yours. And remember, you won't be making this judgment based on yourself anymore—no, you'll be making it with your marriage in mind. That's all. Keep these words close to your heart and you'll have a God-fearing family and you'll be blessed all of your days together."

"Amen" ping-ponged around the hall.

"Now, I think it's right your brother say something to you."

What?! In front of Abe were hundreds of persons, all eyes. He stood, what was his option? Walking to the microphone he felt a little like a fugitive fabricating a story on his way to court. He found his way to the microphone at the far end of the platform. Andy got emotional. This was as close as he could get to having his own father speaking at his wedding. Kareen touched her husband's hand. Abe tapped the microphone. It squealed. He recoiled, like next it might bite, then gingerly leaned into the mouthpiece and cleared his throat.

"Thank you, Benjamin. Thank you for those words. I can't add much to what you said. So, congratulations Andy, Kareen. We wish you the very best."

Seeing this was Andy's only brother, and that it was a brother's obligation—not to mention the best man's, any man's!—to cobble together a speech, no matter that he was saddled with the charge at the last minute, everyone hoped that Abe was just warming up. In a way, even

Abe did. Only Zabel understood that that was it. A spattering of guests
rushed in and raised their glasses to prop up the scene—which was all
the more pathetic because Abe had nothing in his glass to toast with.
Beneath the general embarrassment, some grumbling was detectable.

Andy wasn't disappointed. He felt a stab of pity for Abe, like one
feels toward a spastic relative.

"Thanks, brother," he said, and leaned over to hug him. Abe half-
turned in his chair. They embraced, awkwardly.

"Thanks," Andy said again.

Abe shook his head as though he hadn't heard Andy.

"I said thanks, Abe."

"It's time," Kareen whispered in her husband's ear, "to cut the cake."

25

WINTER PASSED QUIETLY. Andy visited the vineyard a couple of times a week, even when there was no work, as though to keep an eye on it, as if earth could be stolen or evaporate like fog, or as though he had only imagined it was there from the start. Since Andy moved out, Abe had taken on a kind of diplomatic air with him. He wanted to work up a pruning schedule. He asked Andy to call when he planned on coming by. At first, Andy thought he must be joshing. Then he asked himself, What if Abe just suddenly dropped by on me and Kareen? Occasionally, that would be fine, but not once every three, four days. Maybe, Andy thought, a little formality, the way the *odars* did it, was just what the doctor ordered. On the whole, Armenians were too mixed up with each other; in such homes something as simple as locking the bathroom door was taken as a kind of rebellion. Maybe the tension around the farm had to do with the fact that there was one too many bodies, too many wills barging in on one another. He now wondered to himself why he'd stayed out on the farm as long as he had.

Andy figured he'd make a few dollars on the side—help pay down his debt—by hauling produce to Los Angeles. They had a truck and set of double-axle trailers sitting in the yard. He worked on getting that truck cleaned up, and then negotiated hauls with the packing houses downtown. It didn't sit well with Kareen that he'd be gone all night two or three times a week.

"Don't we have enough money?" she asked.

"We got plenty of money, honey, but a little extra change wouldn't hurt. I'm thinking of getting a whole new angle of this farming business going."

She nodded her head, but she was full of worry.

"Look, you have to work with me on this one."

"I'll ask Mama to come and stay with me when you're gone."

"I think that's a good idea."

His first haul was broccoli. They loaded him up at a cold storage plant next to the downtown tracks a little after midnight. He watched them forklift the boxes six high on a pallet onto the truck-bed in silence. It was cold out as he pulled onto the near-empty highway, but Andy never could tolerate driving in a closed cab, so he rolled down his window before he even threw the vents open to let hot air blow from beneath. As the truck opened up, he felt in command behind the wheel, but he was also cognizant that the truck could, at any second, turn against him, that in the last analysis he was at its ten-ton mercy. By the time he hit Visalia, he'd settled into the lonely spirit of the haul, and volumes of thoughts began to open up to him.

The first two months of marriage had been sweeter than he ever could have imagined. Life with Kareen was a joy. That's the only word he had for it. Joy. Different than happiness or fun or even pleasure, all of which Andy had had plenty of as a bachelor. Sometimes it seemed that Kareen cared for him more than he cared for himself, so much so that she could anticipate his need before he even knew it existed. One day he came home from weeding the fields and, lo and behold, she greeted him with a hot tub full of water. How she knew he'd be home before the water turned lukewarm boggled his mind. She was so good at marriage he more than once had the sneaking suspicion that she'd done it before. Fact was, the gal was a natural at being married. Maybe for this reason, Andy was reluctant to let her in on what was happening with Abe. He didn't want to break the spell. This is the only thing in my life, he thought, where there's no questions asked. Just the opposite, like all he got was answers. In bed, as they were nestled together like rose petals, he sometimes felt it was himself he was holding close, as if the fluent exchange of their hearts had blurred the boundaries of their bodies. Loving her was like loving a part of himself that he'd only just discovered, or as though she'd been there, next to him, his entire life and had only recently materialized. A single word, a broken sentence, moans and sighs and giggles were coded with volumes of feeling, so much so that he felt a kind of formality, artificiality when they sat down and had a "real" conversation. It's good to be married, he thought. What the hell was I waiting for all these years? He caught himself from time to time actually looking forward to their growing old together.

Marriage had its share of complications, too. No big problems, no deal breakers, but still…The issue of cleanliness was one thing. He'd never seen anyone clean like his new wife could. She cleaned places he'd never imagined dirt had the genius to worm into. It was like she'd been to cleaning school, more, like she'd conducted clinics in cleaning. Lining cabinets was nothing Andy had ever even considered before, and if you did, why scour the bare wood first? Then there was the matter of going at the windows with vinegar, and taking a toothpick to the grease that had built up in the grooves of the stove. She got down on her hands and knees and went at the carpet with soap and water round and round with her arms, like he'd once seen some old Mexican ladies once pray. At one point he told Kareen she was taking that line, saintliness is next to godliness, a little too seriously. Sometimes he'd walk into his home and wonder whether he was allowed. She buffed up the porcelain toilet so well, he was almost ashamed to use it. He was afraid that he was next. One night he dreamed she'd made him take a bath in Clorox, went at his feet with Brillo.

He joked with himself that if he didn't get her pregnant soon, she'd scour clear down to the foundation.

"This girl cleans day and night," he told his brother-in-law Arsen. "How about Alice? The same?"

Arsen nodded. "She won't let me come in the house with my shoes on."

"No shit."

"If she's anything like my wife, this is just round one." Arsen chuckled, amazed at how long he'd put up with it.

"We're sitting here in the dead of winter, and already spring cleaning," Andy said.

"When it comes to cleaning, the Egyptian girls respect no season."

"It's the damnedest thing. I kinda get the feeling the house is more important than me."

"Get used to it."

"No kidding."

"Welcome to married life."

"She's a good girl, don't get me wrong."
"And she'll make a great mother."

With Andy out of the house, Zabel figured to do some cleaning of her own. She cleaned for a week straight. She didn't gripe and groan either, she went about it the way a lumberjack stoically and methodically fells a gigantic tree. It was less about cleaning than it was a ritual to prevent dirt ever returning. The kids had never seen anything like it. When their mother lugged Andy's mattress up the hall all by herself, down the steps and out to the yard, Teddy made a move to help her but she put a hand out to say no. She poured gas on the mattress and set it aflame. "It's old and it has mites and fleas," she explained, in which case Teddy wondered how she could've let Andy lie in it, ever. In the cold morning fog they watched smoke build on smoke and were mesmerized by how beautiful and awful the rumbling flames that cleared the air of fog were.

Andy hauled a few days a week. He gave no thought to his mind or body, only to how each load was chipping away at his debt. He had never been a lazy man, but as of late he acted like he was out to prove that he wasn't. He wondered how hard he could push the ox in him before it would collapse. Maybe his strength came from the fact that, for the first time since he'd come back to Fresno, he was making money that Abe would have no cut of; maybe it was because he had a wife. He was proud of himself and miserable at the same time.

Andy tried to spread out the hauls so he wouldn't be away from Kareen two nights in a row. He'd usually get home around noon, hit the sack for a couple of hours and then get up in time to run a few errands for her before dinner. Valentine came over to cook with Kareen on the days Andy would haul, and she'd stay the night on the couch. Sometimes Lucy, Alice and the kids would join them, and they would bake or sew or play games with the kids in front of the TV that was always on—their window on America. Even when they were not watching the television, it was going, as if to protect them the way in old times a watch fire might have when the menfolk were gone.

At eleven o'clock at night, Andy would slip out the door with about as much fuss as a man going out to get a pack of smokes. She watched him go from the window. Under the yellow light of the street lamp, he hobbled across the road, stepped into the shadow of the truck, swung open the big door and tugged himself with his strong arms up into the cab. The engine coughed over and over again, and she wondered if all trucks were this obstinate or just Andy's. In any case, Andy struck her as a kind of healer when the engine finally turned over. She prayed God be with him, her heart at once aquiver and full of courage as the truck rolled away. Lying in bed, Kareen would focus on the truck's roar until she lost it, until it vanished into silence. When she was a girl, her mother had told her that during infancy all the sounds on the earth are available to us, but as we get older these sounds are slowly drowned by the voices of people close to us. Still, there are some men in the old country (she knew one of them) who could hear the call of a bird on the other side of the world, so uncluttered are their minds. Kareen wondered how far she could track Andy's truck if she emptied her head of voices. She thought that maybe someday she could follow the truck as far as Los Angeles, follow it on its way back home, so that even when he was gone, she would be near him, and know that he was well.

Andy pulled off the highway just before he hit Ridge Route, to catch his breath and fill up with diesel. The truck jerked and grunted and finally came to a stop, hissing. He stepped out of the cab and tried to make out the mountains in front of him. It was going on three o'clock and it was black as a coma up there. The cold wind barreled off the mountains, swatting at his jacket and the jacket of the joe who pumped the gas. He exchanged a few words with this joe about the wind, its strength, its severity. They agreed that the wind on the Ridge Route would be even worse.

Andy's father, a believer only when there was no other resort, had once conceded he'd rest a crucifix on the dashboard when he'd now and again travel the Ridge Route in the twenties. Back then it was a two-lane, thirty-mile road—suited more to cows than cars—that from a certain elevation resembled a creek winding through the confluence of those three great mountain chains—the Tehachapis, the San Gabriels and the Sierras. It was so full of loops and turns and curves that it took, his father claimed, an entire morning to cross. It reminded Andy of the passage an escapee might cut trying to lose a pack of bloodhounds. Up near the summit, he'd observed sightseers, a peculiar type of American he failed to fathom, come to read the flotsam of cars that scabbed the earth below, like some more civilized men study old maps or rare diseases. The road that Andy now drove was four lanes and straight and well paved by comparison, but still not without its tricks, including a few shoulders near the summit that took a kind of instinct to negotiate, especially on nights as starless and windy as this one, when the dark was palpable, and even with the trucks' headlights brooming it away, it kept coming at you, in waves.

Regarding that truck, Zabel began to think that Andy should be paying Abe for using it.

"Shit, Zabel," he said, "we hardly use the truck."

"And that's why it is in such good shape. By the time he's through running it up and down that mountain, akhh, it will be a piece of garbage. See, Abe," she said, shaking her head in disgust. "This is why you can't think for yourself. It never entered your head," her voice was like a dagger now, "that the wear and tear is going to come out of our pocket!"

"It wasn't in that good a shape, to be honest with ya, Ma."

"It was like new."

After a pause and what appeared to be a kind of reconsideration of her position, Zabel said, "Okay, maybe he can have the truck then."

This was the first mention of a deal, a kind of test to see if Abe would bite; or rather, how deep.

Abe tapped the spoon on his plate.

"Zabel," Abe said, "I think we've come to a point where Andy's gonna have to find himself a place of his own to work."

"If he wants to, let him."

"We've got a family of our own to think about, we got the future of our kids. I just think the time has come. In terms of business, it's time to go our separate ways."

"It's between you and your brother."

"He's got one truck and, like you said, maybe we can set him up with another. Let him get a trucking outfit going. I don't know what, but for the first time in his life, he's going to have to think about what he wants to do with his life."

Truth was, Abe was kind of getting used to having the place all to themselves again. It was the Armenian way to keep your kinfolk close—but maybe this proximity was also the source of the problem. The *odars,* they don't live together. They do their own thing, now and then they have a picnic, a party where they can enjoy each other's company; they play golf or tennis or whatever, and when they go home, it's not a divided home; a man's home—modest as it may be—is his own. Same with work. In fact, the *odars* thought it was a bad idea to get into business with their own blood. He began to see no reason his brother and he shouldn't relate to each other after this fashion. In other words, Andy with his place, Abe with his, a certain distance between them, and good luck to them both. If Andy considered himself a kind of gambler, well, that's fine, just so long as Abe wasn't on the losing end of those crapshoots anymore. Could have doubled their acreage by now if they'd played it a little safe, followed Abe's gut instincts. But, hell, what's done is done. Truth was, it gave Abe some pleasure picturing Andy out there all alone in the cold, trying to make it on his own. He didn't really want Andy to be eating off the streets or nothin', just to struggle as Abe had struggled, just to taste how bitter life could be. Abe chuckled. But there was no mirth in his chuckle. Not that he'd leave him out there all alone in the cold. No, Abe wasn't that kind of man. Still, say, just for the sake of it, Abe was that kind of person. Well, then, he'd have nobody to answer to, since for years he'd supported Andy, put him through school and basically set him up for life. Yeah, Andy had lived the life of a pasha compared to Abe.

There was a part of Abe, now that Andy was out of the house, that felt things were as they always should have been. Zabel had settled down, there was a semblance of peace and quiet in the house for the first time in a long time. Abe couldn't recall just when he'd started to feel this way, but somewhere along the line he'd lost all feeling for his brother, and he realized that he wouldn't care one way or another if he never saw Andy again, which made him wonder if he'd *ever* really liked his brother, or if what had kept them together wasn't a kind of obligation that had worn skinny over time. Worse, he was certain Andy didn't feel the same way, that Andy kept hoping things would be like they were in the old days—which made Andy look, at least in Abe's eyes, like a sucker, the type of person Abe never had much sympathy for in the first place.

There were a whole lot of things Abe couldn't really stand anymore. For instance, Jews. Niggers. Spics. Wops. But especially the Jews, especially them. Abe heard they owned half of L.A. That's how they got in trouble the first time around, bringing attention upon themselves by picking up dirt for cheap, anything for cheap—then turning around and selling it for an ungodly profit. During the war, Abe—and he'd tell anybody who asked, what did he care?—was fighting for America, for America's freedom and interests. What was supposedly going on with the Jews at the time, though he didn't condone it, wasn't what the Americans were aiming to stop. Hey, who stepped in to stop the Turks when they were butchering the Armenians? Nobody. That's who. Did the Jews ever step in to stop anybody from getting slaughtered? Abe wanted to know. Huh? Did they? Abe wanted to know, he really did, would them Jews, push come to shove, show any charity to the Armenians the way they expected the whole wide world to show them? No chance. Just the opposite. Wait and see. Soon enough, they'll be claiming, just to make themselves special, that what happened to the Armenians was zilch by comparison. Just wait. Jews got back Israel, their supposed homeland. What did the Armenians get? Another spanking, that's what. All them Armenians who claim Jews are brothers, and that the Armenians were the supposed lost tribe of Israel or whatever, were just kissing the Jews' asses.

In fact, to be truthful, even the Armenians were starting to get under Abe's skin. Always out there pushing deals this way and that, and then hollering "broke!" Stashing money away like someone was gonna come around and steal it. Kind of made his stomach turn. Never lifting a finger for each other, never reachin' into their own pockets to help their own kind. Penny-pinching race, the Armenians—if you want to know the truth, not much different than the Jews. Abe was American. Fact was, he was—pure and simple. He fought under the American flag, about all that needed to be said. About all there was to it. He wasn't protecting no Armenia, he was protecting the land he was born unto. America. Not that he was inclined to line himself up with these white people, these pancakes, these meatless doughboys; they made him sick, just thinking about 'em did. Fact was, short of Zab and the kids, just about everybody made him sick one way or 'nother. Anyways, as regarded Andy, anybody else in Abe's situation wouldn't have kicked his butt out of town a long time ago, wouldn'tve put up with his drinking, his back talk, especially the way he talked to Zabel—the very woman who scrubbed the shit from his underwear and ladled soup into his bowl. Sometimes Abe would get so caught up in this kind of conversation with himself regarding Andy, the Jews, whatever, an hour, an hour and a half would pass before he'd cut it off. And after a while it got to the point that his conversations regarding Andy, the Jews, the Armenians became a kind of obsession and he'd find himself—all of a sudden—pop in the middle of it, where seconds before it was nowhere in sight. Just walking along doing nothing much and then boom, like a man steps deep into a hole, he'd step into it. It got to be that that's all he could think about. It'd start eating away at him, like when a man is really horny, so that he could almost feel it pressing in against his temples, excavating beneath his ribs, like, uh, say, uh—a rat, say a rat if it crabbed up your ass and all the way up to your chest and starting feeding on your heart would—but not really— only as a way of speaking. Sometimes, it got to making Abe feel a little weird, like he was going off the deep end, like all of his feelings had caught up with him at once. Like it wouldn't be a bad idea to just leave it all behind for a while, just to get some air. A breath of it.

26

ANDY WAS SO BUSY, by the time he stopped long enough to notice, it had been three, going on four weeks since he'd been out to the farm. He was pulling down three hundred bucks a week from the hauls, enough to tide them over for a few months. With the winter vegetables turning to seed, his only other option—which wasn't an option—was to haul freight across state. Andy got to thinking about the second truck sitting in the yard. With some work he might get it up and running so that come February they could either lease it or get someone to haul for them, working toward a small-time trucking outfit that might eventually grow into something.

It rained all day. The sky was so smoky with clouds that it was dark as dusk at noon. The way the clouds were setting up this time, high and packed tight as sandbags, Andy suspected he might get rain all the way to Los Angeles. A more intelligent man would have stayed home, tuned into a ballgame that night, Andy said to himself as he tossed the tarps over the load. But I'm not an intelligent man, Andy thought, I'm a fucking ox. With the forklift driver on one end and Andy on the other, they squared the tarp over the top, crossed the ends, dropped corner irons and a couple of v-boards—to play it safe—and tied it all down, neat and snug. They walked back up to the loading dock.

"Pretty enough to put beneath the Christmas tree," Andy said. "Ain't it?"

"Not goin' nowhere, that's fer sure."

From a distance, through the rain, a howl.

"Sounds like some wolf," the forklift driver said.

It ebbed, then came again.

"Don't it though?"

Except they were in the middle of the city, where no wolf was allowed. The men narrowed their eyes and searched the dark anyway.

"Damnedest thing," the forklift driver said.

"Yeah, well, I'll see ya."

"I'd keep my eyes open tonight."

"Just hope it don't hail."

"Road'll get slick as green onion then."

"There's when you just pull over and let it pass."

"Cold enough though."

"Just about." They judged from the steam that dribbled out of their mouths. The forklift driver went for a cigarette.

"I'll have one of those, if you please," Andy requested.

The driver tapped one out for Andy, then one for himself. They stood there, edging forward, their hands cupping the flame. They looked like two men about to bless one another. On the asphalt, the rain seemed to swarm. Andy took a fat suck on the cigarette. The driver took a suck on his own. For over a minute, they quietly smoked. Andy was touched by the gentlemanliness of the moment, touched by how two men who hardly knew each other could observe a measure of silence, as though out there was something bigger than either of them alone, both of them put together.

"Well, I'll be getting on," Andy said.

"Good luck to ya," the driver said.

"'Preciate it. Somehow, tonight, I think I'll need a little luck."

All the way to the Grapevine summit the road sizzled with rain. From all the racket in the cab, Andy plugged his ears with toilet paper. At spots the rain came down in buckets on the windshield, blurring the road. Just outside of Pixley, Andy was forced to come to a near stop. The runoff was so heavy the shoulder had given. Mud had flooded the road. Berms had already formed. In the headlights he could see tumbleweeds, branches. Give it a beaver, a deer, and you'd have yourself a bona fide creek. The site looked staged. He crossed the spill slowly, almost carefully, queerly respectful of this scene that had set itself up so innocently, spontaneously, this scene where nature was pathetically reclaiming a portion of what civilization had stolen from her.

Just before the Grapevine, the rain stopped and the temperature plunged. Andy pulled into the truck stop, cut the engine and waited for the gas guy, who was standing inside the station, to come out. After a minute or so, it became apparent that neither man was going to commit before the other. When the gasman saw it was Andy, he came to his senses and rushed outside. Andy climbed out of the cab to give the guy moral support. Cash in hand, he watched the numbers spin like a slot machine into which he'd dropped some serious money. "Cold" was the only word exchanged between them.

When Andy jumped back into the cab, he felt his bones holler from the cold. The stick was so freezing it hurt, and he gasped from the trauma when he grabbed it. He pulled out and headed up the mountain, nudging the truck slowly forward, maybe ten, then fifteen miles per hour, in low gear. The transmission rasped and the engine growled and the whole truck shook as it climbed. A few miles upgrade the cab started to warm, and he could feel himself come back to life. It occurred to him that he'd nearly forgotten about the load back there. He recalled a story one of his ballplayers, Big Freddie the Injun, had told him about how his ancestors initiated their boys into the tribe by charging them with the delivery of a sealed sack to a distant place. In this sack was something precious that was the boy's to keep when he'd reached his destination. A scout trailed the boy to make sure he didn't die, or cheat. The sack, nearly as heavy as the boy, took three days and everything the boy had, and more, to deliver. The scout met him at the designated place and told him he'd done well and that now the contents of the sack were his. The boy took his knife out, cut the rope and reached into a sack of stones. His reward was the perseverance he'd learned. Nothing else. As Andy passed Gorman, he asked himself, Is the broccoli back there my sack of stones?

The road was getting icy now, and Andy could feel the tires scrabble for the asphalt, the truck now and again lurch, and he began to see veins of snow, and as he climbed up higher, clumps of it on the side of the mountain like napping lambs. He took the road slowly, aware all the while of the danger and the oily blackness and slickness of the road and the ravine on one side of him that was as merciless as it was deep. The truck churned on, and a little past the summit there was a clearing in the sky and clouds drifted across the swollen moon, and the light was so velvet and heady that Andy rolled the window down for a few minutes to feel the luminescence, to take a gulp of it.

He felt the road slope down, and he shifted gears and let the truck descend at its own momentum. Gradually, stars appeared and boulders shone and he could tell, by the way the tires hugged it and hummed, that the road was dry. It was a little past five o'clock in the morning and in the valley below there was a spattering of lights. He was going to be late. Andy fumbled for a pack of smokes in his shirt, fished one out with his lips, exchanged the pack for the lighter, and flicked the metal hood back. The flame was jumping in front of his nose when he touched the brakes and noticed that the truck didn't respond. He waited a couple of seconds, took a suck on his cigarette and pushed a little harder.

The truck was going fifty, picking up speed. Andy started to pray and pump the motherfucking brakes. The awesome magnitude of the truck heading headlong and blind like some avalanche down the hill struck him as beyond the scope of any initiation, Indian or no. He pulled on the hand brake. White smoke blew up from the wheels, the back end skidded, and Andy thought, This is it. He released the brake. The back end squared but at the cost, it seemed, of the truck's speed doubling. His heart hammered in his chest. There was no runaway ramp and if he downgeared he'd dump his transmission on the asphalt. His only hope was to pull right and work his high beams to warn the cars in front of him. He was full of hysterical fear, like in a nightmare. He asked God to take care of his wife and then he heard a siren blast. When he leveled his eyes in the rearview mirror, red and white lights streamed all over the road. He rolled down the window and waved his arm in big circles and honked for the cop to pass him, but the bastard just kept nipping at his ass. He could see he was closing in on a couple of cars at the bottom—two, three miles away—and the truck was starting to jump at spots, and he knew, if he was forced to swerve to avoid a car, he'd flip over. All at once the cop punched into the right lane and roared across and pulled out in front of Andy. Andy thought he saw the cop signal "okay" with a hand. In the darkness he couldn't tell for sure. He knew the degree to which they remained connected in that dark would determine if he came out of this thing dead or alive. Fuck the broccoli. Andy saw the red taillights of a car veer to the right, and both he and the cop zoomed past it like it was parked. He allowed that the truck was driving him, not the other way around. The cop was pulling away gradually, and Andy wondered whether this meant that the cop had given up and was making to get the hell out of the way himself. And then, in a split second, he stopped wondering. It's yours, Andy, he told himself, your life lies with you. Forget the cop, forget God, luck, nature or machine.

The way he told it, it was just at that moment that the truck started to fall in line. Of course, they were on level ground—that fact couldn't be overlooked. But still, Andy could feel himself connect with the road right through the guts of the motherfucking truck. The load that was jumping around back there settled down. Even his fear, it seemed, settled down, no longer caroming around inside of him. He watched the road, he watched the speedometer, he wasn't even thinking about the cop.

When the truck had slowed down to thirty, Andy shifted to fourth, then third, pulled off onto the shoulder and rolled the truck to a near standstill. He came to a stop fifty feet from an off-ramp and shut the engine down.

The cop was backing up toward him, lights still streaming in a thousand different directions.

Andy sat in the cab for a few minutes, confused. He had no idea where he was. Only the fact that he was alive was obvious. Light started leaking from behind the mountains. A few cars swooshed by. The whole world seemed unbearably at ease.

He saw the cop start out of the car and run toward him.

"You all right, pal?" The cop was shaking.

Andy nodded his head.

"Must've lost your brakes. I never seen nothin' like that."

Andy shook his head. "Me neither," he spoke, but in fact thought that language couldn't reach what he was feeling. He lit a cigarette. He could feel his heart pump, he could see his hands tremble. He puffed on his cigarette, stared at it, dimly aware of the smoke that caressed his chest. He felt he should be crying, screaming, something. The cop waited, one foot on the step, a hand ready at the door. Andy took inventory of his body: his hands hurt, so did the back of his head. And neck. The muscles in his legs, his lower back were stiff.

When he finally stepped out of the cab, he looked back up at the grade first thing to get an indication of what he'd just gone through, which seemed at once to be still happening and utterly remote.

"Steep," he said.

"As hell."

He marched around the truck, dragged his eyes up and down and across the load. Not a bin had shifted, not a knot had come undone.

In the periphery of his vision, Andy saw the cop reach for something in his coat pocket. On what grounds, Andy wondered, might he arrest me?

"Here." The cop pushed a whiskey flask at Andy, with all the seriousness of a man paying back a debt long overdue.

He took a swig and handed the flask back politely, with a nod of gratitude.

The cop took a swig too, another, and with a finger, twirled the cap back on, an expert.

Whiskey burned like a fire inside of Andy. He wanted it to burn brighter still.

"If you don't mind." Andy pointed to the bottle.

"Keep it. What do you got back there?" the cop asked.

"Broccoli."

"Broccoli?"

"Son of a bitch, isn't it?"

"Really is."

"Have yourself some. Much as you want. Take a bin. Whole damn load, if it's your pleasure. Merry Christmas."

Now and again Abe would take the deed of trust out from the ammunition canister hidden beneath his bed and study the pages, run his hand over it, hold it in the air, thump the table with it, stand near it, then far, as if he were debating with that scrap of paper. While holding the deed of trust he'd sometimes start up an imaginary conversation with his sisters, explaining to them his decision and countering their every objection, although he was certain that at some level they would agree one and all with what he was planning to do. Though they might not admit it, their hatred for their so-called father had been as fierce as his own, and again, though they might not admit it, they had never considered Andy their true brother. When Abe was in a generous mood, he'd even entertain giving them each a few hundred dollars of the inheritance to show them that what he was doing was righting a wrong that had affected them all. Abe was the eldest male, by God. He had been the rightful head of their household after their dad died. Abe got all choked up thinking about how he was going to reclaim his rightful place after so many years, make whole what that Yervant had turned to ruins.

"This boy."

"The one who limps?"

"That one. Soon we are going to clean our hands of him, Mama."

"It will be good, it will be as it should."

"My home will be my home."

"Thank God."

The next afternoon, while soaking his sore body in a tub of hot water, Andy told Kareen that his hauling days were over for a spell.

Kareen stepped over a bundle of dirty sheets she'd just stripped off the bed and entered the bathroom. The windows were steamed up, the tile dewy, and her husband's body blurred beneath the water. Since he'd returned from his last haul, he wasn't the same. She sat on the toilet, a pile of neatly-folded towels on her lap. His heart tuned more to the *blip blip blip* of the leaking faucet, it seemed, than to her.

"The truck?" she asked.

"Naw. I'm just tired, that's all."

"Okay."

"The season, it's just about finished anyways."

He asked himself, Should I tell her what happened up at the summit yesterday? Should I tell her that on top of the truck breaking down I just about lost my life? He wanted her comfort. He didn't want to worry her. He didn't want to worry about her worry.

Andy cupped some water in his hands, let it drain and then regarded the wrinkles in his fingers.

"This is how they'll look when I'm old," he said. "Like," he said, "sometimes I already feel."

She asked, "And the *tuhram?*"

Money again. Fucking *tuhram*. He wondered if ever there was a woman for whom it didn't mean everything, he wondered if ever there was a couple who could live in harmony without it. Maybe she suspected they were in debt. He felt a sort of panic.

"Anyway," he said, "we've been through this a hundred times. I told you, this was just about pocket change to begin with. Why do you question me? Don't you trust me? Come spring, we'll start up again. Don't worry."

"If it was just me and you, I don't worry." After a pause she said, "Andy, soon we are going to be a family."

Did she think he wouldn't be able to provide for one when the time came? When was it going to end?

She stepped up to the bathtub, dropped to her knees and put her hands on the lip of the tub, a woman giving alms. What did she want now?

"No, Andy. I mean I'm pregnant."

The Demerjians and the Voskijians went separate ways during the holidays. Andy and Kareen spent Christmas and New Year's with Valentine and Alice and Arsen and the kids, and the only time Andy saw Abe except at the farm was at church on Christmas Sunday, when everyone was polite and full of fake holiday cheer.

When it wasn't raining, Andy was out on the farm rebuilding the engine of the Peterbilt. He took the engine apart and on a drop cloth he laid out the parts like pieces to a puzzle. Abe would come by and look at Andy's project, pick his teeth, grunt, whatever, like Andy was some hired hand. Which should have bothered Andy but didn't, since he allowed that anybody who waits around for another man, brother not excepted, to help him finish a project might never get anything done.

Zabel stayed locked away in the house. Every once in a while she'd scuttle down the steps with the kids, shove them in the car and drive off, probably to her mother's. The air around her was so thick, it got to be that Andy would avoid going into the house, even to take a shit. Seemed even Teddy was keeping his distance from his uncle Andy. Poor kid. Didn't matter, though. Andy's love for Teddy, for all the kids, was selfless. But enough about the Voskijians. Andy had his own family—the Demerjians—to worry about now. They weren't about to go hungry or without a roof over their heads, but still, they were in the hole, three thousand dollars deep to be exact. He knew he would support his family and, by the way he cared for his nieces and nephews, knew he'd be a good father.

After three months, Kareen's stomach, tight as a drum, showed the most fine-spun roundness, the subtlest voluptuousness. When he held his wife, Andy would sometimes feel the baby too; not literally, of course, but in the same way a man sometimes feels the presence of a will to grow in plants and trees in spring. He would lie with an ear to Kareen's belly and listen to the gentle churning inside. When Kareen would step out of the shower, plump-breasted and all steaming and wet, her skin seemed radiant from the life that was budding inside of her. Even her breath was sweet, milk and cloves, he thought. "I barely touched my wife, after she got pregnant," Abe had once told him. Now that his own wife was pregnant, these words came back to him, full of significance, a window opening onto Abe's unlucky life. Andy couldn't keep his hands off of Kareen, she was like a magnet, a moon, and he could feel his heart wax and wane for her, like the tides, all day.

Abe and Zabel received the news like a brother and sister-in-law should, congratulating him and Kareen both and digging up baby clothes and offering them a crib and old-fashioned stroller made of wood.

"Do I have to use these clothes?" Kareen asked. They were so raggedy, they reminded Kareen of what the poor Arab children wore in Alexandria.

"I don't see why not."

"Anyway, Mama and me are making baby clothes on our own."

"I thought it was nice of Abe and Zabel."

But after that initial gesture, neither Abe nor Zabel asked about Kareen, how she was doing, was she sick in the morning, could they do anything? Where Kareen was concerned, Andy tolerated no slight. Forget about Andy himself, hell, they could pile shit on his head. Already had.

Andy was kind of surprised at how matter-of-factly his whole family, sisters included, took the news. Maybe because it was such a big deal to him, he felt it should be a big deal to everyone else. Maybe the fireworks would start after the kid was born. But from the first day Kareen told *her* family, *they* doted over her like she was a princess. Being around Kareen's family, Andy couldn't help but notice how cold his own family was by comparison. Where Kareen's family smothered their children with hugs and kisses and welcomed others to do the same, his family's affection was a kind of hedge that grew around the child to keep others from coming in, to keep the kids from going out. Even though his family seethed with competition and jealousy, Andy had always been mostly oblivious to it. Being the baby brother, he had felt immune to, and frankly above, the petty quarrels that had come between the sisters. Now he wasn't so sure if he was immune. Over the months, he'd picked up clues that a few of his sisters didn't much like Kareen, that they considered her an outsider. The way she cooked—delicious *chorag,* Betty said, like the peasants make—or talked—a kind of Armenian that's half-Turkish—or when she rushed around to serve them ("Don't worry yourself, nobody is looking over your shoulder anymore"). Come to think of it, Andy had never felt comfortable telling his family about what was going on in his life. Could have been he was afraid that at some point down the line it would be used against him, even the good news. It started to dawn on him why he'd come to love his crazy mother-in-law. And Arsen, who lately was more like a brother to him than his real brother. He felt more at home with them than he ever felt with his own family. He felt welcome.

27

THE SIERRAS WORE A LONG SHAWL of gray clouds. To the west, the sun lowered. Ball bearings, flywheels, pistons, gears, pipes, lay in a puddle of gray light. Everything was petering out, including Andy, who was ready to call it a day, when Abe appeared out of nowhere and asked if he wanted to take a walk around the vineyard. Andy figured it had to do with the pruning, how many spurs to leave and so forth. But in the near dark?

"Okay. Sure. If you want."

"I want," Abe said and took a deep breath.

They walked into the vineyards. Something's on Abe's mind, Andy thought. Abe dragged his fingers through his hair, the way a man with a full head of hair might, and his lips, they moved like someone trying to memorize a Bible verse. A few vines in, Abe turned around and grabbed Andy's wrist to stop him, as though Andy's next step was aimed at the tail of a rattler. He thought, What the hell, and took his arm back. There was a trace of violence in the mark Abe's fingers left on Andy's arm. Abe's eyes were locked on the ground and his face was full of teenage confusion, like he was going to cry or holler or run away.

"It ain't gonna work anymore." Abe's voice trembled. He couldn't wait for the pruning. He had to be done with it. The pressure, it was gonna kill him.

Andy's hands went up, Peace, I'm not the problem here. "Your marriage?" Andy guessed from the way Abe's head was lowered in shame.

"Me and you."

What the...? Andy fumbled for a cigarette in his shirt pocket.

"How can we come to an end, Abe? We're brothers."

"Brothers is one thing, this land's another."

Andy shook his head like he didn't understand. Then, slowly, he plugged the cigarette in his mouth, one eye, through the match flame, leveled at Abe. With all the calm of a card shark, Andy upped the ante, only half-certain what was at stake, or rather half-believing. "Wrong, Abe. The way this land goes is the way we go."

Abe went quiet.

"I've got work to do, Abe," Andy said. "We've both got work to do," he reminded him. He shook his head again, like this was all kid stuff.

"What's done is done." Abe's voice was full of a kind of uncharacteristic resolve, as though neither he nor his brother had a choice in the matter, as though what was at work was *pacht*.

"Whatever you say, Abe."

Andy turned away and started up the row absently. He could hear the icy earth crunch beneath his boots. It was just past dusk and the truck parts had all but lowered into a bog. He found the tarp up against the barn and dragged it over the parts to protect them from dew, a man going about his business as usual. He could see, barely, Abe come from out of the row and cut toward the house, into the penumbra of the porch light. He watched him bend over and loosen his shoelaces, step out of his shoes, pick them up and drop them next to the door, the end of a day like any other day.

Andy had two philosophies of life. One, you go straight to the heart of a problem. If you find yourself hemming and hawing, making excuses because you're afraid, you just have to put all that aside: the only way around, someone once told him, is through. Two, you let things go, you get up and walk away from the source of your confusion or pain. You ask yourself if it is worth it, and if your answer is no, you honor that answer. Neither of these philosophies of life applied to the present situation, as it stood.

So, after two days of turning in circles, Andy decided to go back out to work on the truck. Even Abe had to allow a man to finish up a job that he'd started. As he pulled into the yard under the cover of dense fog, he felt like—imagine this—a visitor, or worse, a trespasser, a trespasser on his own land. The tarp was still draped over the parts, which he took as a sign that Abe expected him to come back. He rolled up right next to the gutted truck, lit a cigarette and stepped out of the car. The fog had turned the day into a kind of white night, and from where Andy stood, the house was an abstraction of pale yellow squares, the windows from which light blearily bled. Although he'd laid out the parts according to a precise order, this order was no longer at hand. It had withdrawn like the order of a dream withdraws when one wakens. He studied the parts as though he were piecing together a mess someone else had left behind.

Footsteps. He picked up a part. The piston was so cold he nearly dropped it. Abe appeared from out of the fog.

They locked eyes.

"You got something normal to say this time, Abe, or are you just out here to cause more confusion?"

Abe shuffled his feet.

Andy said, "What, you didn't expect to see me?"

"We need to talk."

"We're talking."

"What I said the other day, I meant."

"What are you telling me, Abe? That this farm is yours, not ours anymore?" Andy chuckled at the impossibility.

"If that's the way you want to put it."

"How else should I put it, Abe?"

"You put it any way you want, but it adds the same."

"Look, Abe. You want out, or me out? I'll tell you what, if you're serious about this, let's go about it simple and decent. We divide the land in two. Right down the middle. Equipment the same. We put a value on the house, and you pay me half of that."

Andy paused for a cigarette.

"Give me one."

Andy slid two out of the pack. Handed Abe his and lit them both.

They breathed in the smoke, exhaled.

Andy said, "That's one way. The other way: we put the whole she-bang up for sale, pay off our loans, divide up what's left, and start over, each of us to his own. There's two options, then. Everything else is wasted motion."

Abe nodded his head. He was either softening up or humoring his brother.

"You think about it, Abe."

Abe tossed the cigarette on the ground and crushed it out with a boot.

"When you gonna be done with this truck?"

"Figure a week."

When Andy got home, he called his brother-in-law, Benjamin, and explained to him what was going on with his brother. Benjamin couldn't believe it either and told Andy that, whatever the outcome, Abe was his brother, always, and they must keep the peace. Andy told Benjamin that Abe was pushing him awful hard, and that, up until that afternoon, it had looked to him that Abe was just plain going to kick Andy out on his ass, or try anyway. Benjamin told him that was unbelievable and that he'd talk to Abe, see if he could get some clarification. "You need to convince my brother that splitting the land up is a bad idea for both of us," he told Benjamin. Andy thanked him, and the next day Benjamin called back and told him that Abe and Zabel were coming to Pasadena in the next week and that they were going to make a proposal. A proposal? Apparently they wanted to split the land up. "Okay. Well, let's see what they have to say, Benjamin. Something has gotten under Abe's skin. See what Zabel has to say. There's where the buck stops."

By the end of the week he'd put the truck back together: engine, clutch, transmission, every part well greased and clamped and bolted and screwed. It took him five minutes to get the engine to turn over. It groaned and coughed and finally, bingo, it bellowed handsomely, like a big fat baritone. Andy took the truck for a spin, spitting some gravel up beneath the wheel as he pulled out onto the road. All the parts slipped into place smoothly, and Andy felt satisfied with the work that he'd gone about so methodically, especially in the midst of all that confusion.

Even with the truck episode on the Ridge Route still haunting him. Out of nowhere, the episode would jump into his heart and he'd find himself reliving that moment with terrifying vividness, more terrifying than the actual episode, because now he'd be outside looking in, and he'd see the truck lose control, flip over, and he'd see his body toss and turn like a pillow in a laundry machine, and he'd hear crashing and feel his bones snap, head crush. He'd play out the fate of his wife, he'd see her mourn, fall in love, in time, with another man, he'd see relatives and friends mourn, and he'd see them, as he'd seen them when he was alive, get on with life the way the living do. He'd see the memory of himself fade over time, until it vanished altogether.

His drinking picked up, smoking too. After work he'd sit on the porch and have a one-man picnic, parsed down to a six-pack of Coors and a few Winston cigarettes. For every bottle of beer, he'd have himself two cigarettes (Kareen counted), and he'd drink one after another until the carton that had cradled the full bottles cradled them empty. He'd fashioned his pant cuffs into an ashtray. Kareen didn't know which to worry about more, his drinking or his catching pneumonia or his catching fire from those ashes. She'd put down the dinner earlier and earlier. "Andy," she'd call, "we're going to eat!" With a hand he'd bat ashes off his lap and move unsteadily inside, greeting her with a smile that saddened her deeply—in no way did it match his listless eyes. She'd watch him attack the food, bumble with his utensils as though he was more accustomed to eating with his hands. When his plate was clear, he would look up, all at once, catch his breath, burp, grab the napkin and take a swipe at his mouth. She'd sit quietly beside him, moving her own utensils slowly, extra-fluidly, conducting an adagio with them.

"Andy," she'd ask, "what is happening?"

"Huh?" He'd look up from his food dumbly.

"You're drinking a lot these days."

"Can't a man have a few beers before dinner?"

Either her husband was going through a hard time or his true nature was finally coming out. Which, she did not know. And neither did he.

Andy finished up his work on the truck on Saturday. The next Tuesday, he got this letter:

> Dear brother Andy,
>   Friday, Abe and Zabel came by the house to talk about the situation. It now appears that they are not willing to split up the land, but instead they want to buy you out. What happened between the time I talked to them and the time they arrived here, I can't say. Zabel explained that the family relations were so strained that there was no straightening them out at this point. From Zabel's perspective, it was something she claimed that you did that made this situation

unmanageable. Without your side of the story, I am no one to judge. But where we stand is where we stand. I don't know if the figures are correct, but according to Abe you two owe $30,000 on the land, and a few thousand dollars more in outstanding bills. Their offer to you is $25,000, minus all debts, equaling half the equity on the land. I've drawn up an agreement. If it meets with your approval, sign it. I've sent a copy to Abe as well.

Sincerely,
Benjamin

The document, titled PROPERTY SETTLEMENT OF FIFTY ACRES OF FARM LAND, RECEIVED BY INHERITANCE, stated all the facts, their debts ($30,000) and the fair market price of the land, including house and tools and equipment ($80,000). The document also spelled out how the deal was to be structured. Andy would give Abe a loan of $25,000, what amounted to a second mortgage. At the end of each harvest, Abe would pay Andy $1,800, including four percent interest, until the loan was paid off in full. If Andy wanted the trucks, he would have to subtract their value ($6,000) from the loan amount of $25,000. The last point articulated in the document, just above the date and the blank spaces left for their signatures, was this: "This instrument does hereby cancel and close all grievances or outstanding matters between both parties."

He read it over a couple of times, folded it up and put it in his pocket. What does Abe take me for? A fool? A lousy eighteen hundred bucks a year. Not even that if you subtract the trucks! I'll be a son of a bitch, Andy thought. Abe gets the land, a loan for cheap, keeps the equipment and trucks, and what do I get? Chicken feed, that's what! He was angry that Benjamin would deign to write it up! Might as well just ask Andy to hand over the land for nothing. Pretend like it had never been his to begin with. Andy fired up a cigarette as a kind of protest.

Fuck Abe.

Piss on Zabel.

Andy could see the fat accruing on his wife's body. She seemed at once vulnerable and wise. There was no way he could hide what was going on anymore. As though he too had a baby that was ready to pop out.

He told her how he'd signed his half of the land over to Abe a year ago. He told her what Abe had done. He went over it again, in detail the second time, hoping the particulars might unlock the shock on her face.

"Then the land isn't yours?"

"It's mine," he told her and explained it to her once again.

She nodded her head, but she did not understand. He read to her the portion of the agreement which stated, "Whereas, both parties of this agreement are brothers and that said property was left to both of them by their mother, the late Mrs. C. Demerjian, to have and to own equally." She stretched her neck to get a look at it, her hands folded on her lap. Andy was surprised to find himself relying upon the agreement Benjamin had drafted to certify his claim, especially as he'd just about flushed it down the toilet, as though his word was no good without it, as though the written word was superior to any man's.

"Then the land isn't yours anymore?"

It was like she was clubbing him in the head. He threw up his hands. "Okay," he said, "then the land *isn't* mine."

She nodded, though she was more confused now than ever, not about the facts but about the trustworthiness of her husband, whom she loved. Why hadn't he told her earlier? Sadness seeped into her confusion.

"They offered me chicken feed, Kareen. Chicken feed."

Some money was better than no money, she supposed, and told him so. Obviously, she couldn't see how unfair the proposal was.

"What happens now?" she asked.

Andy hadn't decided for himself. He said, "Nothing. Nothin' happens. All I know is that the vines need pruning starting this week."

Several times a day he'd lift the proposal out of his back pocket, carefully unfold it and read through the sections that, all taken together, recapitulated in language winnowed to an excruciating minimum of emotion the history of that land from the time his mother had died to the present. *Whereas,* each section began, his mother had given the land to them both; *Whereas,* in the course of events, the original small farm house was destroyed by fire and a new house was built where it once stood; *Whereas,* it read, Andy (second party) signed over his share of the land in order to secure a GI loan; *Whereas,* it read, they had both lived on the land, up until very recently, when (second party) Andy, having married, moved out.

He wondered if such rubber-stamped expressions as "*Now, Therefore, both parties do hereby agree to the following terms and conditions*" were achievable in the Armenian tongue, and he wondered what terms and conditions could heal the damage that was already done, could ever cancel and close all grievances. No, even if Abe and Andy came out of this thing flush, in other ways their relationship would never be the same. Andy wondered, Had Abe even fucking thought about that? The answer, tough as it was to swallow, was obviously "no." Andy had seen it before: a man sets up a family, and over time others, even his nearest kin, seem superfluous and get left by the wayside. That was one thing, but painting your kin as the enemy was another. If not Andy, who was Abe going to turn to in times of need?

Andy allowed that a *ken* (feud) was in the making, a lifetime of bad blood was being planted. Armenians were famous for their *kens,* his own father on his deathbed nurtured five of them still. The old man barely had enough strength to chew food, but when he was told that Aram Arax or the twins, Manoog and Esahag, had come to visit, he whipped up curses so hearty and venomous that some thought his illness exaggerated, if not a monumental hoax. They underestimated the deep resources of hatred, more powerful, resilient and contagious than any emotion, not excluding love. No, Andy thought, hatred is a kind of foxfire that continues to spread even when the body is damn near eaten through with death.

Andy called Benjamin and told him that he couldn't accept Abe's offer. He'd rather, he told Benjamin, have nothing at all. The offer wouldn't leave Andy with any way to make a normal living. Frankly, it was worse than an insult. Andy told Benjamin that as long as the land was there, he'd work it, Abe or no Abe. No way his brother was going to kick him off his own dirt. Andy asked him if he'd heard from Abe. Benjamin said, "He called yesterday, asking whether I'd received your copy of the agreement. I told him I hadn't heard from you. This doesn't look good. I'm sorry to see things working out this way, but I've done my best," Benjamin added.

"If you wouldn't mind, Benjamin," Andy said, "do me one more thing. Call Abe and put his mind at ease. Tell him I won't sign any agreement that takes me for a punk. Tell him those are my words, not yours."

"Something terrible is happening," Valentine spoke.

Lucy, who'd become one of Valentine's regular friends, placed her demitasse on the coffee table and folded her hands on her lap.

"Abe wants to split up the land that their mother gave them together."

"The farm?"

"Yes."

"Akkh." The sound was of a blade piercing her.

"My daughter fears her husband will lose his share of the land. She is very troubled."

"This is impossible. My heart breaks," Lucy said.

"As does mine."

"I fear," Lucy said, "Zabel has her hands mixed up in this."

"I didn't want to say it myself. But often a woman is behind such things."

"I ask myself, Were you blind, Lucy, for so many years? Could you not see the bitter seed in Zabel's soul? How many years," she said, shaking her hands, "we were friends. How many times I stood beside her when no one else would. I believe my love for the children, who were like my own, made me hide my eyes from the truth."

"To have cut you off so suddenly from them."

"I will always have here," she said and patted her heart, "an empty place." Lucy's eyes grew moist with tears.

Valentine understood her suffering, she could feel the hollow of a womb that no child had ever filled, but maybe the spirit of a man once had.

"Have a piece of *baklava*, Lucy."

Lucy smiled and took a piece.

Dikran, Lucy's poet. Valentine pictured Lucy in her youth, walking arm in arm with Dikran down country roads. She pictured them feeding each other words, like honey. She recalled the words of Lucy's favorite Armenian song, "I will lay you beneath the apple tree," she heard, "and I will pick an apple, and I will cut the apple into a thousand pieces and sliver by sliver I will feed you beneath the apple tree, until all the apples are gone." And then Valentine thought of her Turk, father of the child who had died, wondered where his life had led. Was he somewhere dead, had he married another woman, Turk, Armenian, Kurd, and did he ever dream of her the way she dreamed of him? She wondered if Dikran the poet and the young Turk from Istanbul would have grown to be friends.

28

EARLY IN THE MORNING, Andy Demerjian rose and sharpened two pairs of pruning shears, using a stone and his spittle, until their sharpness tested his thumb. With a finger he swabbed grease on the joints, working the shears until the two blades moved together smoothly. He told his wife he would be back by early evening, and she handed him a sack lunch and told him to be careful driving in the fog, God be with him. He laid the pruning shears, a pair of gloves and the sack lunch in the trunk, and took Clinton Avenue West. He wore a long-sleeved shirt under overalls. Over that a wool-lined coat. Only his hands and his face were cold. His visibility was cut, because of the fog, to fifteen feet, and he drove with one eye ahead and one eye on the white stripe in the middle of the street. He crossed over Highway 99 and passed Ararat Cemetery. He reached Dover, a county road, where dividing lines and most signs of any sort, except for an occasional school crossing, disappeared from the roads. The fog was all around him, and though he moved, there was no sense of distance covered, as though he were churning in place, like the toy car rides at the circus. The whiteness of the fog made him vaguely dizzy, and gnats of light swarmed in the periphery of his vision, and he could only guess how far he'd come, which caused him to wonder how well he knew those roads after all.

He'd just inched his window down (did he mean to sniff his way there?) when he saw a crucifix trimmed with red ribbons and a bunch of plastic flowers stuck up against a telephone pole. Two months before, a Mexican kid barely old enough to handle a bike, much less a car, had slammed into the pole. A woman who claimed to be his aunt had asked permission to put the crucifix on their property. He recalled her brown eyes, sad and Catholic, and asked himself, Compared to her suffering, what do you have to worry about, Andy? He made the sign of the cross and pulled off the road onto the dirt avenue, idled past the cement standpipe and then made a right turn into the yard and stopped the car. The house was set back fifty yards or so, and from where he stood he couldn't see any lights on.

From the window of the living room, where he was worrying some beads, Abe saw a pair of headlights bob into his yard. He wondered, Who the hell? and then the headlights went out.

Andy walked to the back of the car, popped open the trunk, grabbed for his gloves and a pair of pruning shears. He tried to clear his mind of all but the work in front of him, clear it of whereases and therefores. He lit a cigarette and studied the vines, the thick trunks, shaggy and knobby, that rose to a head from which sturdy cordons grew and wrapped snakewise along the wires on which they were trained. He took in the tangle of long canes that sprung from the cordons and draped immoderately to the ground, seeming to invite the kind of violation that they would in short order know. He planned to leave as many canes and buds as he could, to maximize the yield and get a decent enough berry size, but he wouldn't know what it would take to get the vineyard there until he stepped into the vineyard itself, until he got up close to the vines, each of which had come up according to its own particular nature, over the past year, over the past thirty. He spat his cigarette out and put on his gloves and stepped into the vineyard aggressively, pumped up. He snapped at a cane, registered its resistance, and continued to snap and select, making sure not to let the canes crowd. He cut and selected and tossed the cut canes aside in a single motion, cognizant of his own skill, thinking an artistic group— coiffeurs, sculptors—ought to make a study of his artistry. That's how good he was at pruning. The way he thrust the head of the shears forward, quickly, moving in and out and around the vine with economy and intelligence. Seven vines down he stopped and looked back, not to check his progress, not to catch his breath, but because he'd heard the crunching of footsteps. Like the fog, the sound seemed to come from no single direction, but from all directions at once.

By this time, seeing it's Andy's car, Abe relaxes his grip on his shotgun. Kind of.

"Who is it?" Abe asks.

It's Abe's voice, but where's Abe?

Abe's at the top of the row, surmising all on his own: the negotiations, they're over; one of us has to go.

Now Andy can see Abe through the fog, scumbled. What does he mean, Who is it? He's practically sitting on my car.

"Who do you think it is?" Andy notices the gun, that is, he notices something that looks like a gun, then—it is a gun!

He can hear it moving up and down, like Abe's measuring its weight in his hand. He isn't exactly pointing it at Andy, but it's no walking stick either.

"What are you doing here?" Abe says.

These aren't questions, Andy thinks. This is a game. He answers by swinging his pruning shears back and forth in one hand, the way a priest does a censer.

As if the gesture were a threat, Abe raises the shotgun perpendicular to his hip, swiftly, like they do in some westerns. Andy stands stunned. If not right on it, Abe's finger is very near the trigger. Andy's the trespasser Abe meant to confront with that gun.

"You've got nothing left here," Abe says. "It's over." There is a certain hysteria in his voice, a kind of panic.

There's Andy, looking down the barrel of a shotgun. He fears for his life, he's shaking in his boots, sure. But not to the degree that you might think. In fact a part of him says, "What the fuck, shoot me. Just shoot me." Not because he feels brave, not because he hopes to be a martyr, but because he wants the extent of the injury already done to be fully exposed—to Abe, to Zabel, to all, clear-cut as a corpse. For a second.

"All right, Abe," Andy says.

Abe drops the gun to his side, slowly, like he might lift it up again. Andy doesn't know if he's shivering from the cold or the uncanniness of it all or both. Already he knows, even before he's out of harm's way, that nothing will ever match this moment.

Andy stoops and crabs his way beneath the vine over to the dirt avenue adjacent the road. When he gets upright again, he's gulping down fear, his fear redoubles. He'd almost forgotten the pruning shear in his hand. He tightens his grip on it, the purpose blunt. He can't see Abe, he can't tell if he's dropped back into the fog or retreated to the house. He can't know whether Abe is going to change his mind at the last second and gun him down anyhow, or whether, the way madmen do, Abe is going to shoot Andy and then himself too. When a man is in the clutch of such unknowns, time thickens, time turns into a beehive, palpable and agonizingly porous. That's why such a moment never leaves a man, because of what it does to time. Andy takes quick, rapt steps back to the car, his body buzzing with adrenaline. *My wife* flies through his mind, *my child*. He swings open the car door and jumps in, his heart clamoring in his ears. The car doesn't want to start, like it's in on it. The engine turns over. Andy punches the stick in reverse, lunges out onto the road and peels away from the farm.

It isn't until he's a mile away that he feels the barrel of the gun swing away from the back of his head. Still shaking, he pulls off to the side of the road and turns off the engine. Clips of Abe and that shotgun, Abe's words, full of resolve and insanity—"You've got nothing left here"—flash inside of him. *It's over.* Not the shotgun, not his fear, but these words, these words pound against him, a wrecking ball. They pound at him from every angle, until—until his heart is mincemeat. It's along the lines of losing someone you're deeply in love with, along the lines of discovering your wife has been cheating on you. Maybe worse. Your life has changed, Andy. In a matter of minutes, thirty years of brotherhood is pulverized. Over what? Over a piece of dirt. That's what, what the fucking world has been shedding blood over since the beginning of time.

Numb, Andy stares at ten big-chested pigeons that line the telephone wire across the road, like they're waiting for a quorum to form, like when enough of them convened, something meaningful will happen: court will begin, justice will be done.

"It's over, Ma," Abe tells Zabel.

"What's over?" Zabel asks.

"Andy and me."

"What happened?"

"It's just over, that's all."

"It was Andy out there?"

"Yeah. It was Andy."

Abe sets the shotgun back on its rack neatly, as though he'd just finished polishing it.

"God be with us," Zabel says.

"God be," Abe says.

For the next three days, with nowhere to go, Andy ended up in church. He wasn't even sure why. Maybe because it was the only place that was warm and guaranteed to be quiet, where he wouldn't have to explain anything to anybody, not even God, who knew it all to begin with. Andy would have guessed that, under the circumstances, he'd have gone to the phone and made what had happened plain to the world. But he didn't. He discovered that when a man is deeply wronged, an unexpected thing happens: he wants to be left alone, from shame. Abe hadn't brought shame on himself only, he'd brought shame on Andy too. The only thing Andy had told Kareen was that Abe had been acting funny, and the day when they were no longer capable of working the earth together was near. He passed off his chills and gasps for air on being tired. A surefire way to keep Kareen from asking too many questions.

"I don't know why, honey, but I'm wearing thin. One thing is piling up on top of another. That's all."

She knew that something more was going on. He'd sit on the sofa, his eyes wide open, his brow pleated, a man holding in pain. So he told her about the trucking incident. He told her that even though it wouldn't keep him from driving the truck again, it affected him still. That sometimes he would have dreams about falling off the edge of a cliff. Andy was surprised at how emotional he got; he'd meant it as a decoy but he was genuinely relieved once he'd talked about it.

He began to wonder if talking things through was such a bad idea after all. On the fourth day he looked for the priest. Even though Andy didn't think much of him as a man, he still allowed he was a man of God.

"Father," he said. "I'd like a word, in private."

"Of course, my son."

They shuffled off together to a corner of the church.

"What brings you here so early in the morning?" The priest folded the flaps of his frock onto his lap.

"I suppose what brings these old ladies here."

They were kneeling, maybe seven of them, randomly in the pews around the church, perpetually sorrowful, their heads uniformly wrapped up in black.

"Nothing as terrible as the genocide of our people, I hope."

"Not quite that bad, Father."

"Um. What do you think about our plans for the new church, my son?"

"It's a good idea, I suppose."

"It will be the biggest Armenian church in the entire valley when we are done."

"That's what I hear."

"You know," he said, "the life of the church depends on the tithes and offerings of its congregation."

"Father, I've been betrayed by my brother."

The priest narrowed his eyes with concern.

"Abraham? In what way, my son? Has there been a dispute?"

"Him with me, for sure. Him and Zabel with me. But, God be my witness, never a thing came between Abe and me that I didn't think we could resolve peacefully."

"What is the matter of the betrayal?"

"He claims that the land our mother willed us is no longer mine."

"This sounds like something a child would say."

"There's circumstances that make his claim serious."

"You two boys have farmed that land together for years."

"Yes, we have."

"Sometimes we are tempted to take more than what is our share. After a period we see better."

"I'm afraid it's too late for that."

"It will pass, my son. Let time help him see straight again. It's never too late for God to work on a man's heart. Listen to my words."

"He threatened to kill me."

The priest clicked his tongue against his teeth.

"There is nothing that tears at the Body of Christ more than brothers at war. These are merely words. Let us pray that God melts the stone in his heart."

"He took a gun to me, Father."

The priest touched the cross on his chest.

Andy said, "A few days ago this happened."

The priest wagged his hand in amazement and said, "This is a vast sin."

"That land is my livelihood."

"God will provide for you, my son."

"My wife, as you know, is in a family way."

"She is a God-fearing girl. You must take this problem to our Lord together, as one flesh."

"I ask myself, Father, is this a punishment that God has given me for some wrong I've committed?"

"Is there something you wish to confess?"

After a pause, Andy said, "I suppose my sins are many. But none that deserve such a punishment."

"It is not only your sins, my son. The Word says that a man can reap the bitter fruit of sins seeded for generations past."

"On the other hand, I think about Job."

"Job?"

"An upright man. Done nobody wrong. And what hell, pardon me, was heaped on his head?"

"But in the end, God reproaches him for lacking faith in his providence, and then restores his means."

"At some point, doesn't God require man take his providence into his own hands?"

The priest was silent.

"I swear, Father, I don't know what my next move will be." Andy could hear his voice shake.

"You must take this matter to God."

"God be my witness."

Andy didn't expect to say it, but now that he'd thought it…

"I am this close to the worst kind of revenge."

"Revenge is the Lord's, my son."

Two days before, a different priest, this one from the San Francisco diocese, had received a phone call from Zabel, requesting that he come to exorcise the farm. She had explained to him the tragedy that had befallen her family in all their undertakings on that dirt.

The priest had listened patiently. He was used to honoring the spirit and not the particulars of a request.

Zabel explained that these tragedies were linked to her husband's half-brother, who carried a cursed and murderous bloodline.

"This half-brother's grandfather betrayed his own people, our people," she said.

"Yes."

"He was an *Agha,* Father. A Turkish puppet. And then everything this half-brother's father touched turned to dust." And sadly, the half-brother's efforts, every one of them, were equally disastrous. Now that the brothers had parted company, she wanted the land to be cleansed of this curse.

"Mrs. Voskijian," he assured her, "your distress of course is of our utmost concern. I will be traveling with our bishop through Fresno next week. We will pay you a visit. But please, spare the bishop these details, madam. To attempt to locate the source of a curse is an undertaking even the most spiritual of men approach with great trepidation. Though your explanation may suit your needs, the spiritual world is woven of a different material. The eyes of God see from all points at once, we humans occupy only one point in an immense field. We can only pray for his goodness and mercy on us. Until then, madam."

29

MORNING'S FROST SPARKLED ON THE DARK DIRT, and as the cold sun came out, the dirt steamed up, as though breathing. Patches of black clouds lay in the green foothills while above them, white clouds, soft and fleshy, folded themselves into pockets. Still higher in the sky, the clouds traveled slowly in great caravans heavy with their charges, towing their bulky shadows along with them. From up there, the rows and rows of vines were a vast series of meticulous stitches on the skin of the earth, which had withdrawn all evidence of its fecundity from sight.

Neither Andy nor Abe had mentioned what had happened to any of the sisters. It was as if they had conspired to keep it quiet. Andy was two men. To Lucy, his in-laws, his sisters, his wife, even to the postman, the bank teller, the guy who pumped his gas, he was the Andy each had come to expect—generous, gentle, nearly always a smile on his face. He didn't want to alarm anyone, even if the other man, the man inside of him, was crushed and still flying in every direction from the impact of the betrayal, even if he already reckoned the betrayal had lopped ten years off his life and made havoc of his heart, literally and symbolically. He found himself charged with a painful rearrangement of facts every waking moment, and even sometimes when he slept. He revisited the past in detail and tried to reconcile Abe's threat to kill him with Abe's every act of kindness. Had Andy been blind, duped from the beginning? Had he seen the betrayal coming? Did he ignore it, from desperation, from lack of faith in himself? What is the value of a man's labor if in the end some evil over which he has no control turns the object of his labor into rubble? What god would give evil such privilege? Who are you to trust if not your brother?

Andy would now and again lie inside the cab of his truck to get used to the fact that the truck was all that he owned, and even then only part of that since he'd taken out two loans against it. As he lay there, the formula of life seemed out of his reach, held by a few and kept totally from others, as if there was only so much of it to go around, and if one person was rich by this formula, then by necessity his neighbor must be poor. Only the anger that gripped him like a sudden loss of air delivered him, however briefly, from despair. For hours on end he'd calculate means of revenge. Should I kill him with my own hands, to let him know all the better the rage of my body? Or with a shotgun, should I do as he meant to do to me? Or should I, without any respect for his humanity, exterminate him swiftly, the way hit men do? But in the end, these plots that burned bright as flares only manifested more profoundly the darkness of his situation. No man who had other options—legal or otherwise—would resort to such schemes. Nothing he could do would ever again restore his rights to that land. Short of killing him, what else might he do when he next saw Abe? Say he bumped into him at the supermarket, church or coffee shop. Would they pass like strangers, would they say hello and leave it at that, or would Andy spit on him and curse his name? And the kids! The kids! The loss of Teddy, Teddy's loss of Andy. It crushed him to think about it. And again, hadn't Abe asked himself these questions?

Maybe at another level, less conscious, Abe had done just that. It started with his sleep. A couple of hours after he nodded off, he'd wake with all the urgency of a man late for an appointment with his attorney, his priest. For who knows how long, he'd lie awake and listen to the clock tick, his mind and body agonizingly alert. The rest of the night he'd churn beneath the sheets, roused without purpose, restless without visible cause. Against this tide of sleeplessness, he found it harder and harder to get out of bed come morning. His body was a sponge soaked with water, his mind barely able to lug a thought forward. First he had to remember that he needed shoes, then he had to recall that he had shoes, then he had to ascertain where they were and then how to put them on. It was like he was starting all over again from scratch. Like he'd woken into a world where all things—shoes, the tick-tock of the clock, razors, cups, chairs, even people—were excruciatingly new. The horizon, for instance. One windless twilight, he saw it peeling. Strips of pink sky had been violently ripped off. He stood in front of the horizon like a man does a museum painting, studying it. A good fifteen minutes passed before he realized the jagged black forms were the tall cypress trees. The way the shadow from the window crawled slug-like up the bedroom wall was another thing. He watched it crawl for an hour, maybe two, more. Who knows? When your mind slows, time slows. Time needs motion to run. Zabel's voice seemed to travel from a great distance, through sieves of space. Her words reached him, pebble-like, filtered of sense, like a dog's bark, an owl's hoot. Even when he got what Zabel said, it took effort to drum up an answer, more even than if he had to write it out—which is saying something, considering he'd given up writing like some men give up sports in their youth.

"What's the matter with you?" Zabel asked. "What are you thinking about?" She told him, "Clean that back porch off before it makes me sick." She screamed, "Akhh!" She said, "I've given up on you. You're worthless."

Maybe one word of what she said—"worthless" or "sick"—would stick. Other words that stuck were *esh* (jackass), *shoon* (dog), *cockeress* (shit-face), good-for-nothing, and *peroushan* (wanderer, lost, direction-less). Especially *peroushan* sounded like he felt: empty-throated, vaporous. It got to the point where he couldn't get out of bed at all.

"What, do you have a cold?"

"No."

"What then?"

"I don't know. I'm not sleeping. I have no energy. I have no appetite for food. For nothing."

"Go to the doctor, then."

"I think I will go."

"To Sivas. Here, take him some walnuts, maybe he'll give you a discount."

It took him an hour to get there, half an hour just to drive ten miles into town. Buildings, trees, billboards seemed to roll past him, not the other way around. There's how slow he was going. Downtown, where Sivas' office was located, was a maze. Cars honked at his car. The fellow in his brain that usually helped direct him this way or that kept nodding off. He circled the block three times before he realized he had. All the stalls were taken, and before he had a chance to drive up into an empty one, another car would beat him to it. As compared to himself, everything and everyone else seemed blessed with superior intelligence, dexterity—if not cunning. Walking was no better. It took him who knows how long to walk two blocks to the doctor's office. He'd stop, sit on a bench. He looked like a hobo. When he finally stood up, he'd lost his direction again. *Peroushan.* If Andy was two men, Abe was struggling to stay one.

"You are suffering from depression," Dr. Sivas told him.

It sounded like something that might happen to valves, irrigation pipes, water hoses and the like. He was vaguely relieved to know that it had a name.

"A nervous breakdown, other people call it."

"Am I crazy?"

"We don't call it that. Let's say your mind is sick."

Abe's eyes drooped and he breathed deeply. He lay down now, his arms folded on his chest, politely.

"Would you like to rest here?" Dr. Sivas said.

"Someplace."

"I think that would be good."

The next morning, Zabel called Abe's sisters, each and every one of them, in a panic.

Andy was reading the paper, looking up now and again to see Kareen patiently walking through the steps of making yogurt. His wife had boiled the milk, poured it into a bowl, let it cool some and stirred in the starter. She was bundling the bowl up in thick towels when the phone rang. Andy answered. It was his sister Betty.

"What do you know about what happened to Abe?" Betty asked.

"Say what?"

"Our brother."

"What about him?"

"He's in the mental hospital."

"The mental…?"

"Zabel called to tell me this morning. She was going crazy herself. You don't know? Why don't you know? How don't you know?"

"Nobody told me," Andy said.

"Why haven't they told you?"

"I'll be damned."

"The mental hospital. I can't believe it. Our brother. What happened? Did you have a fight with Abe?"

"Kind of."

"I knew it. Well, are you going to go see him?"

"I don't know."

"You don't know?!"

"I got to think about it, Betty."

"Think about it? What happened?"

"Where is he?"

"Zabel says the Veteran's Hospital. It's like everybody is going crazy these days. I heard Johnny Topazian—Abe was in the war with him—ended up in the mental hospital too. Abe was never the same after he got back from the war."

"Abe being in the hospital's got nothing to do with the war. Least not the one you're thinking of."

They agreed to talk again in a few days, and Andy hung up the phone.

Was madness the price Abe had paid for his betrayal? Or was his betrayal a sign of madness that had now come to full bloom? Or had he brought it upon himself as a variety of penance? Or could it be, Andy wondered, that Abe is trying to tell me something, that his going mad is a message, sent in a kind of code he means me to read? Could it be Abe's going crazy was the sanest thing he'd done in months? Knowing Abe was mad had the queer effect of alleviating to a degree Andy's own madness, as though there was only so much of it to go around.

"What is it? Who was that?" Kareen asked.

"Betty. Sweetheart, Abe's in the nut house, the mental hospital."

Kareen's eyes widened.

"What happened?"

It became suddenly obvious to Andy that the right time to tell her might never come.

"I think it might be because of something that happened between us that I haven't told you about."

Andy could see Kareen's body brace for bad news. It took all his might to go on with it.

*

"I didn't want to worry you, honey. That's why I haven't told you so far. Abe and I split up. The land is no longer mine. Abe kicked me off."

Kareen put a hand on her stomach, as though the child inside her was startled too.

"What are you saying? He kicked you off? How about your half?"

"I'm on my own."

"He's not going to give you your half?"

"No."

"What do you get, then?"

"Nothing. I've got nothing anymore. Just that old truck and you."

She sank into a kitchen chair, fixed her eyes on the linoleum and folded her hands, powdered with flour, on her lap.

Andy walked up and took her hands in his own, as though he meant to help her up.

"Maybe something can be done. I don't know. Part of me thinks Abe is there for a reason."

"We have no money? How are we to pay our bills?"

"We're not desperate yet. We're not at that point."

"How much money do we have?"

"Enough."

Kareen covered her face and began to sob.

"You lie to me, Andy, but more than that, you lie to yourself. This is what hurts me even more," she cried.

"I was just trying to protect you."

"Protect me?! Is this how a man protects his wife?"

The wind got sucked out of him.

"I shouldn't have told you."

"So that each time a bill collector came around, I would have to tell him I don't know where you are?"

"What bill collector?"

"Some man says you owe him money."

"What son of a bitch says I owe him money? Why didn't you tell me."

"I don't know who he is. An Armenian, Bagdassarian. Did you borrow money from him?"

"That son of a bitch."

"Did you?"

"I'll tear his fucking heart out."

"How much?"

"A couple of hundred bucks, the prick."

"You lie! Get away from me!" She jumped out of the chair. Her face flared up in pain. "I don't know why I married you!"

"Don't worry," he said.

"Don't worry?! We're going to have a baby and you have nothing but that ugly truck!"

Andy could feel his jaw stiffen. She'd never talked to him this way before.

"Goddammit!" he yelled. "I told you not to worry!"

Anger rose up like a geyser inside of him. He turned around and went for the door.

"Liar!"

The word smashed against the back of his head. He slammed the door behind him and stepped outside, dazed. He could hear her cry, gulping down pain. But he pitied himself more—forget about her, what did she know about what *he* had suffered these last few months, and for whom? For her and their child! That's who! He deserved her compassion and all he got was a beating. You're beaten on all fronts, Andy, he thought. Don't look anymore for sympathy from your wife; look only for blame.

Routed off his own land, routed out of his own house, he got in the car and started down the road. It was as though his entire life had become a series of thresholds, with no room to stretch or breathe in between. Wow, he thought, you're finally alone, ol' boy. Really alone, not just when it suits you, not for a spell, but in the widest, deepest way a man can be alone. Your wife was your last hope. Now that hope is wiped out, just like the others. Forget that you've tried your whole life to do things the right way, figuring that in the end there would be some reward. Nobody was keeping track anyway.

He wanted to cry, but then again, what use was crying? Who would hear him? He slowed to let a dog amble across the road and thought, I'm worse off than you, you mutt. Worse off than even the measliest fucking mutt! Only when an animal is on his last leg is he finally left on his own. Like elephants. When their time is up, they drop back from the pack, without any hoopla, and find themselves a private place to die. Humans are worse off than elephants. Elephants face the humility of death but once, humans face it a thousand times before they finally expire. No wonder men commit suicide. It's a way to spare themselves the humiliation of so many deaths. Andy was so swarmed over by these thoughts that he was surprised to find he'd driven straight onto Jensen Avenue, toward Highway 41, the route he used to take to college. What the hell, Andy thought, this road is as good as the next.

No, the suicidal type has got it right, Andy thought. All this time I've wrongly pegged them as cowards. Suicide is an act that requires courage. The kind of courage Rocky had. Rocky. All these years I'd gotten you wrong, pal. He spoke out loud, he heard his own voice as though it were someone else's. You had it right: you must have seen life, that war for what it was. I called you a coward, he said. I was wrong. I'm sorry. He could feel tears gather in his eyes. I betrayed you, you never betrayed me, I betrayed you. Forgive me, Rock. His tears were warm, and they comforted him. The old Armenians had it right. The refrain from one of their most famous songs said it all: *"Soodeh, soodeh, soodeh, amen pan soodeh"*—"Lies, lies, lies, all the world is lies." The question that Andy now faced was did he have the courage to commit suicide? And if he didn't, what kind of life was there left if it was all a lie? It came down to those two choices. The world wasn't going to change just because Andy thought it should. No, Andy was going to have to change. If life is turning left and you turn right, don't blame life if you fall off.

By the time Andy reached Elkhorn Avenue, his breathing had steadied and his body and mind had reached a kind of exhausted equilibrium. He turned his eyes out onto the eminence that unfolded in front of him. The frost had thawed and in the morning sun the grass was a sea aglitter. The dark oaks were silvery, the road in front of him glistened like a snail's trail. Crows, like specks of ash, wheeled aimlessly over a distant barn. If not for the sad circumstances, the contentment that settled upon him just then could have easily been mistaken for a kind of joy, as if the moment possessed intelligence, clarity greater than that possessed by any single man. He had the peculiar sense that if he should stop driving it would be a toss-up whether he'd burst out in laughter or kill himself.

"Yes, ma'am," Andy said. "I'm here to see my brother, Abraham Voskijian."

The nurse picked up a clipboard, flipped a page and nodded.

"He's in room 208. Visiting hours end at five."

Andy looked at the clock. It was twenty till.

"I understand."

"Then follow me."

"If you don't mind, ma'am, I'd like to see him alone. Does he have any visitors at the moment?"

"Not that I know of."

"Would you mind checking for me?"

The nurse, clipboard in hand, turned around, cut a path through a row of desks and disappeared down a corridor.

"Thank you," Andy said quietly to himself.

The place was serene, the way a mortuary is serene. The wall heater's cough was audible, and there was the tick of heels on the square tile floor, but there were no banshee-like screams, cursing or eruptions of nonsensical speech like he'd expected.

The nurse came around the corner and with a finger motioned for him to come. He followed her with lowered head, hands folded against his belly as though he were ashamed, or of a supplicant spirit. The corridor was white and long and Andy noticed that some of the doors, closely set, had chicken-wired windows.

"Did you tell him I was coming?" he whispered.

"I told him he had a visitor, yes," she said and extended a hand toward the room.

Would he be in a straightjacket, strapped down to his bed? Exactly what kind of madness was he looking at? Would Abe spit at him and scream, break down crying, glare, dumbly stare? He expected half of him would pity Abe, while the other half would gloat with satisfaction at the way he had turned out—a menace turned to mush.

The room was narrow and deep. Instantly, Andy realized that something deeper in him than hate or revenge didn't want to see Abe any way but whole. Abe, he sat at the far end, smoking, half his body in shadows, the other half glowing from the warm afternoon light that flooded in from the window.

"Abe," Andy said.

Like a picture of Christ beseeching sinners to come forward, Abe put out a hand and said, "Come." It seemed like Abe had been waiting for him, not just for a few minutes, but for days, weeks.

Andy walked to him, as though through a tunnel, a long tunnel with nothing in view but Abe.

"Sit," Abe said.

Andy did, in a chair opposite Abe, an arm's length away, a rifle barrel's.

There were bars behind the windows. Abe's hair was cut to stubble. The chairs were metal, there were straps rolled up beside the bed. All the physical evidence of a madhouse was there, except for the madman. Abe was so pellucid that Andy felt self-conscious in comparison. Indeed, an observer might've been hard pressed to say, of the two men, who was mad and who was sane. Abe's left arm crossed his stomach. The elbow of the right arm rested on the back of his left hand. He cocked his arm and drew the cigarette slowly to his lips, exhaled and said, "You've come."

A long pause.

Andy didn't know what to say. His anger was there for sure, but for the moment, anyway, there was no person, no surface for his anger to get any purchase on. In his madness, Abe had grown somehow sage.

Abe said, "I was hopin' someone would tell you I was in here."

"Betty. So how you doin', Abe?"

"Better. They've got me on some medicine. It's good medicine. It makes me feel better. Like for a long time I was someone else without knowing it. I like it in here. Got me a good doctor. You know Petropolis? Dr. Petropolis."

"Never heard of him."

"Good man. Helped me out. You should take some of his medicine."

"I just might, Abe, way things been goin'."

Abe nodded, as though he understood what Andy was getting at.

They sat there for a spell, as though together they were waiting for someone else.

"We've known each other for a long time, Andy."

"What are you talking about, a long time? Forever."

"Forever. That's a long time."

"Sure is."

"I was mulling over a memory just this morning," Abe said. "When you was a kid, this was a long time ago, I gifted you a bike. But one leg, your bad leg, was too short to reach the pedal. I remember watching you kind of swing at the pedal with that leg when it was goin' around, like you was pedaling normal while all along you was only pedaling air."

Andy felt a pang of compassion for that kid. "That was a Schwinn. A cherry red Schwinn."

"It was plain that lowering the seat a couple of inches, you could have pedaled with both feet. But I never told you. Of course, after a while you figured it out for yourself. So I ask myself this morning, why didn't I tell you? The easy answer is to let you figure it out for yourself. But if I got to be honest with myself, there's other reasons could be at work. I guess these are the kind of thoughts a man has when he's got nothing else but time on his hands to think."

"I've been doing a lot of thinkin' myself," Andy said.

"Could be I didn't tell you 'cause I felt guilty that you was lame and I wasn't. I didn't want to hurt your feelings by bringing it up. Maybe making a case about that seat would put you out, like I was makin' a case about that leg. But here's the thing, the one that stuck more than the rest. Could be that even when you was that young—ten, it had to have been—I reckoned your only handicap was that foot, and that mine were many. Maybe I liked to see you struggle with the only thing I knew you had a struggle with. You were cute as a bug, had a big personality, a father: the whole shebang. You was cut out for some kind of glory. In my mind, you was."

"Glory," Andy said. "Some glory."

"Like without that foot you'd fly. Fly and leave me behind."

"Who's left who behind here, Abe?"

"Folks is cruel, Andy, but not always for the reasons we give ourselves. I'm saying it like it was, just the way it was, without makin' any excuses. It's like this medicine has let me slow down to get a good look at things."

Andy drew a smoke out of his pocket. He noticed his hands were calm, the flame steady beneath his cigarette. He wondered if he'd forgiven Abe. What kind of idiot would forgive him so soon, so easily? Was there such a medicine that could transform a man in a matter of days, as this medicine had supposedly transformed Abe? Andy watched Abe inhale smoothly, a philosopher, perhaps a con man?

"What else you been thinkin', Abe?"

"Lots."

"Like what?"

"I'm not stupid, Andy."

"So you've told me before."

Abe turned his head toward the window. He shook his head sadly. The light was getting milky, thin, returning whence it came.

"I can't take any battle right now, Andy. I'll tell you, I can't."

Things got delicate, all of a sudden.

"Every now and then I feel it. Like a dark cloud lowers on me. When I first got here I lied in bed for three days. There were lugs piled on my chest. I couldn't get to the toilet. I can't believe I'm telling you this. I shit on myself in that bed. I don't know what happened, Andy. Things went out of control. Kept piling up. One disaster, then another. I lost sight of things, important things."

Andy said, "We'll see, Abe."

"Yeah, we'll see."

Streamers of smoke hung between them. Just then, they were like two enemies thrown into a cell by a third.

"When are you getting out of here, Abe?"

Abe thought. "What day is today?"

"Sunday."

"Sunday. I'm getting out in two days. What is that? Tuesday?"

"Tuesday. You're getting out Tuesday?"

"That's what my good doctor says."

Andy nodded his head.

"I'm fine Andy. Don't worry about me."

"We need to settle things, Abe. "

"We will."

"First thing when you get out of here, we need to."

"Whatever you want."

"Just what I got coming to me. That's all. I don't want anything more."

"That's fair."

Andy was crossing a shaky bridge. On the one hand, he didn't want to push his luck for fear the bridge might collapse, but on the other hand, he'd be no worse off if it did.

"I don't want to get into it, Abe. I came down here to see you; that's all. But I need you to hear me: what's right is right, we need to settle things. There's a lot of water come between us. Don't know how we're going to deal with all of that, but I got faith, once we get the major issues back on track."

Abe mumbled something.

"What's that, Abe?"

"No," he said. "You're right, Andy. What you say is right."

"I haven't told anybody what happened. We can call what's done done, and try to get on to building a future together."

"I see where you're coming from. You got no quarrel from me. Bring that paper, whatever it takes, we'll sign it."

The nurse marched into the room and told Andy that visiting hours were over.

Andy hesitated, like he was afraid of breaking a magic spell.

"I'm sorry, sir."

"Okay."

Andy stood.

Abe looked up at him.

"We'll see you Abe. When you feel better, when you're out of here, we'll work things out."

And without shaking his hand, he left.

30

THAT WAS IN APRIL. July the tree fruit season began. Andy picked up a steady line of local hauls of plums and peaches and nectarines to the packing houses or canneries. He'd also picked up three more loans, two to pay off his previous loans and one to finance some cantaloupes he started to cultivate on a ten-acre parcel right off of Highway 99 in Selma. He cut a deal with the Italian, Sconzi, who owned the land; Andy would finance and farm, the Italian would put up the land, and they'd split the profit in half.

The verbal agreement the brothers had made in that hospital room, to settle things up once Abe was out, never happened. One month passed, then two, and then a third, without so much as a call from Abe. Twice Andy tried to contact Abe himself, and twice Zabel answered, telling him that Abe wasn't well enough to talk. Andy held out hope for the better part of six months before he finally admitted what he had feared all along: that once Abe had gotten home, Zabel would resume her voodoo on him.

He conferred with two attorneys in town about the possibility of legal action. Both told him what he'd expected to hear. No court would take up a case founded on fraud, especially fraud against the federal government.

As far as Kareen was concerned, Andy couldn't decide whether she had forgiven him or whether her focus had turned away from him and onto the child that was about to be born. All Kareen saw was that her husband, by hook or crook, managed to bring home the bacon. Eventually Andy would declare bankruptcy, but that was three years off. For the time being, they had a roof over their heads and food in the refrigerator, a windfall of fruits and vegetables from the haul. Kareen converted the spare bedroom in their apartment into a nest for the baby.

Polaroids and home movies show her handsome, fat with baby, and in her polka-dot dress, super-American. She poses on the steps of the colonnade at Roeding Park, a rug of rusty leaves spreading from her feet. Against a massive tree in their yard, relaxing. And so on. Andy is conspicuously absent from most of the movies. It takes a moment to realize he's behind the camera and not entirely gone. When he is in the film, he's usually alone: he rests on his haunches, brushing the lens away with a hand, over toward someone else; he eases a stack of lawn chairs into the trunk of the car for a picnic; later, Coors can in hand, he turns hot dogs on a grill.

Only rarely do he and Kareen show up together in a picture. They are in the Sierras in front of a small cabin, patches of dirty snow in back of them. He sneaks an arm around her waist, and in response she recoils an inch, as a sea urchin would when you'd poke it. Suddenly, realizing the film is rolling, she strikes a pose, as though the camera were competing for her affections. Maybe he understands this is for his kids, or maybe he understands how this will look in twenty years, or maybe he loves Kareen more than she loves him. He draws her closer, as though this is all about her being coy, and kisses her cheek.

With the birth of their first son, Yervant, the relationship between husband and wife improved. Perhaps because now, with a child, she saw no way out, or perhaps because their immense love for that child brought them closer together, giving them enough in common to keep others matters distant. At times, Andy's whole world would revolve around that baby, and he'd be amazed at its extraordinary presence for something so small and helpless. At other times he would feel that boy as but a burden he'd been charged with, which magnified his sense of loss to the point of physical pain.

In one Polaroid, milky from time, it's November 15, 1959. Kareen always jotted down the dates on the back. Andy wears a suit, Kareen a pretty red dress and a wide-brimmed hat. Looks like they've come back from church. Or better, from the way the morning shadows stretch from their feet, just getting ready to go. With the baby cradled in his arms, Andy gives the camera his best. In the soft light his face is slim and pearly and happy. Kareen is caught looking down, a hand flat on her stomach. Is she smoothing her dress, did she spot a stain? Or did she feel a flutter? I wonder. Was she regarding me?

EPILOGUE

DURING MY CHILDHOOD, for all I knew, the Voskijians didn't exist. These were the 1960s and Fresno was still a small town, with an Armenian community that was especially close-knit. It's not hard to imagine Andy bumping into Abe somewhere, but if and when he did, he never mentioned it to my brother or me. For what Abe did to my dad, all five sisters ostracized their brother. The Voskijians, as a result, were absent from any extended family functions—weddings, baptisms, and the like.

I had but one window into the relationship in my childhood. We were living in a tidy little two-bedroom house in Armenian Town that we rented for seventy dollars a month, and to make ends meet, my dad hauled fruit, farmed small plots of vegetables here and there, peddled shoes or life insurance door-to-door. Back then it seemed to me that he had a different job every other week. Once a month or so, at the most unwelcome hour, the phone would ring. On the other end, there was this lady, a bona fide loony tune, who didn't say, "Hello" or "How are you," nor did she identify herself, but instead said only, *"Incheh genes eenzee,"* or "What are you doing to me?"

"Dad, it's *Incheh Genes.*" That's what we'd named her.

"Give it over."

"What do you want this time?" he'd ask her in Armenian. "Uh huh, ummm, really...is that right?" For whatever reason (respect for the elderly?), he'd actually let her spew for a minute or two before he hung up.

"Crazy bitch," he'd mutter.

"What, Dad?"

"Incheh Genes thinks I'm pestering her in her sleep, that I've got some kind of mental telepathy going on her." He lit a cigarette. "You guys go to bed."

We could see that the call, the interruption of sleep, bothered him all out of proportion. It got to the point where I hated this weird woman, what she was doing to him, to our sleep. So my brother and I put together a plan. The next time she called, we charged out of our bedroom, brandishing toy Tommy guns.

"Let us do it, Dad," we told him.

He handed us the phone. We shot a few merciless rounds, *ta ta ta ta ta ta,* into the receiver, then slammed the sucker down.

"I'm going to let you guys handle it from here on out," he told us. "I really am."

And he did. A few more episodes with the Tommy guns and *Incheh Genes* stopped calling. Dad had found a solution.

"We killed *Incheh Genes,*" I told him.

"Maybe you did, Baba. You just might have."

It was when I was in high school that I started to piece things together. *Incheh Genes* was Angel, Abe's mother-in-law. Other facts fell into place, too: the identity of the guy standing next to my dad in my parents' wedding photos; why my dad never responded to our requests to see the home he grew up in, though we knew Biola was just a few miles away; and also the reason my dad constantly told my brother and me, even when we were *weren't* fighting, "If nothing else, you two boys have to always love one another, never let anything get between you."

Abe died about nine years before my father. I was living at home and going to Fresno State. This would be 1980. We were in the middle of dinner when my dad's office phone rang. After years of floundering from one job to another, he'd established himself as a wine grape broker, and we were used to farmers badgering him about this or that, irrespective of the hour.

"Can't they let me rest?" He put his utensils down, excused himself and rose from his chair with a heavy sigh.

When he came back out of his office, he was dazed.

"That was Betty. Abe, my brother, he died."

"Mer Christos," my mom cried. "How, Andy?"

"Some farming accident. That's all I know."

Speechless, he sat down and poked at his food.

What does a man do with his bitterness, I asked myself, when the target of his bitterness dies? Does the bitterness die too, or does it graft onto something else and flourish? Or does a man turn that bitterness on himself? For the next couple of days, from the side of my eye, I watched him, watched to see if he would break down, cry. The degree to which that betrayal had warped his life had become apparent to me by then. I hoped that Abe's death would release him of the hate, or more accurately, the *negative love* that had possessed him for so many years. He went to the funeral by himself.

When he got back, it was closing in on dusk. I went to hug him. His eyes were reddish. Tears? There was bar smoke on his shirt, sour whiskey on his breath. On the stove, dinner was cooking, but none of us had the appetite. We plodded out to the back porch where all the important conversations occurred. I remember the light was gaunt, the air mulchy, heavy, pressing in on us. He leaned back in the chaise longue, lifted a pack of smokes from his shirt pocket and said, "Get me a beer, Baba." I fetched ones for my mom and me too.

He took a couple of swigs, shook his head. Then came out with it.

"Word is, he was on the tractor and somehow fell off. He was..." with a finger, he made little circles, "discing."

My heart froze. I looked over at my mom, who was confused, she hadn't gotten it yet.

"Ground up like hamburger meat into the very earth itself."

"Akhh, Andy." I felt her soul fold.

"Some reason, after the funeral, I decide to go by the old house. First time I been by there in I don't know how many years." He let out a little grunt of remembrance. "Driving up, you could see the tractor, where he lost control. The end post is knocked down. The discs scared the asphalt where the tractor crossed the road."

"Lucky nobody else got killed," I said.

"Huh? Oh. Lucky is right."

"Akhh," my mother had her hands over her mouth.

He took a hit off the cigarette.

"So. I pull off onto the dirt avenue, get out and walk around. As I approach the end post, it occurs to me: this is the same place he met me with that shotgun. There's blood on the vine. I'll be damned if he didn't fall off at exactly where, shotgun in hand, he told me he'd kill me if I ever came back. God be my witness. Same corner of the vineyard. On just that spot."